RECOLLECTION OF A JOURNEY

A road emerging from woodland drew towards us in reluctant curves and at last ran close beside the line. Here carts and wagonettes were moving in the same direction as ourselves; the strange outlines of their loads, figures huddled among sacks and baskets, furniture piled high, appeared at the level of the windows and fell behind. The road swung off to round a hill; when it joined us again the concourse had thickened, handcarts and heavy wains, cyclists with calves in tow, an ancient gig which bore two children and a sewing-machine. The trian had slowed again, our pace was only a little greater than theirs. Drowsily watching them, the horses plodding in their sleep, children with bundles tied to their backs, I fancied myself a part of the ghostly carnival.

D1341108

*Also by R.C. Hutchinson
in Hamlyn Paperbacks*

**A CHILD POSSESSED
JOHANNA AT DAYBREAK**

RECOLLECTION OF A JOURNEY

R.C. Hutchinson

RECOLLECTION OF A JOURNEY
ISBN 0 600 20655 6

First published in Great Britain 1952
by Cassell & Co. Ltd
Reissued 1981 by Michael Joseph Ltd
Hamlyn Paperbacks edition 1983
Copyright ©1952 by R.C. Hutchinson

Hamlyn Paperbacks are published by
The Hamlyn Publishing Group Ltd.,
Astronaut House,
Feltham, Middlesex, England

Made and printed in Great Britain by
Hazell Watson & Viney Ltd
Aylesbury, Bucks

For Margaret

The names given to people and to many of the places in this book are fictitious

I

i

HERE it is, my darling. You asked me to put together an account of those uneasy days, and I have done it as well as I can.

It has taken a long time. My eyes give trouble now, I do not sleep very well and the task of recalling even recent happenings tires me quickly. The rumble of the trains passing all day long continually provokes fresh memories and then confuses them.

There have been so many journeys, since the one that took a scared and lonely eight-year-old girl across half Europe from Poland to Lausanne; so many days of narrow confinement and relentless jolting, merging in recollection into one prolonged experience; so many nights of shallow and broken sleep, the closeness of strangers, the grey impersonality of lamp-lit stations, sterile dawns with the same trees dragging past. Sitting here in darkness, close to my small window, I see quite sharply the faces in a train drawing out of the town, faces of people weary from the day's work, old men's and children's faces. Often there is one I seem to recognize. And then, drowsing, I think that I am in the train myself, the long journey still not over; that all existence is confined within the slender breadth of a train, the pulse of the heart itself locked to the grinding of wheels.

For Paul, you said; you said it would be good for him, when he grows up, to know these things. It may be so. But you may have heard the theory that certain illnesses, serving as sparring partners do to a boxer, are nature's means to increase the body's strength. Sometimes I think the human mind must undergo an assault of the same kind before it reaches its fullest power of understanding; and if so, one cannot have such exercise at second-hand. In the earliest days of my first marriage, wanting a small income of my own, I used to send descriptions of scenes and incidents, sometimes in

[7]

verse, to the Geneva papers. That was easy, since I wrote for people who shared the climate I was living in. For Paul, breathing the air of another continent and epoch, these memoirs may be incomprehensible; the causes of the sickness which afflicted me will be so remote from his experience that he may find the malady itself unreal, as if he were reading about some disease which occurred among the Sumerians and has not been heard of since their time.

No, I doubt if we can penetrate deeply the minds of those who have come before us, however much we may know about their affairs. Perhaps, through certain preconceptions, the ones who are near us in time and relationship are still harder to understand than those farther away. And surely it is vain to think that we can save our successors from getting lost in their country by telling them where we missed the way in ours. The voice of reason may be clear, but it is not so powerful as other voices.

Those thoughts have discouraged me. And yet I believe that if I had known from my childhood something more of what preceded it, I should have been less subject to my own impulses, more tolerant of other people's. No such knowledge could have parted me from the Kolbecks, since my ties with them were made from something more powerful than circumstance, more tenacious than wilful emotions—a force as constant as the gravity which binds us to the earth. But had I been taught enough about their earlier life to look out from their point of vantage, I should at least have been less handicapped in matching my course with theirs. When Paul reaches manhood I shall be nothing but a figure from the past, with just the value one attaches to old playthings found in a garden shed; and perhaps it is only a residue of vanity that makes me want him to think of that figure with sympathy, which is understanding brought to a greater heat. But the past is woven into us, however far we travel in time or space: the lives which you and I have lived have conditioned his life, some part of what I have been must reappear in him. Whatever the nature of his journey, there will be times when he finds himself possessed by griefs, by animosities and fears, which immediate knowledge will not explain; and I think he may deal more bravely with such disorders of the spirit if these memoirs of mine, glimpses of the season which saw his birth, can help him to trace their source.

I do not want him—neither will you—to be one who broods too much upon his own sensations. But as our understanding of other people can only come through knowledge of ourselves, our feelings towards them—I believe—will cease to be shallow emotions only when we discover their depths through depths of our own. I could leave a sermon for him, entreating him to search in other men for what I have found unique in value. But I think it is better to give him only these leaves from my experience, to let him watch our flutterings as a naturalist would and draw such meaning from them as he can. He will surely have intelligence, for no one of Kolbeck stock entirely lacks it: he will see us with detachment, possibly with some contempt, but perhaps with pity as well, realizing that we have been overburdened in these years. Then, if he sets his own perplexities against those which I and my generation had to deal with, he may discover that we belong to the same pilgrimage. The rest he must learn in another way. These scraps of reminiscence may suggest an approach to life; but only life itself will teach him whether the minimum that remains when the flame has passed is enough to justify the toil of living, its valiance and its pain.

ii

I am sorry that I have written almost nothing of your father. You will believe me—we have come to know each other so well—when I tell you that this failure is not due to any kind of diffidence; for the passing of more than twenty years, not empty of events or feelings, has placed the period I spent with him where I observe it almost as dispassionately as a professional historian. At this distance I can picture more nearly the creature I must have been then: absurdly young, vain about my looks and the generous praise a few Swiss professors had bestowed upon my essays, inflated with the specious self-assurance of those perpetually conscious of inferior birth. I see myself, in short, as Casimir knew me. But if time has brought that piece of life into truer perspective, it has also blurred the outlines. My mind has kept a dozen snapshots of Casimir; no solid image at all.

One's memories of childhood are seldom clear visually; and in the earliest of the three periods when I belonged to Setory, Casimir was little more than a background figure. I suppose we played by ourselves at times, and I do remember his gentleness—it was he who would always comfort me when the others had hurt me in a rough-and-tumble. Ungratefully, I paid him no attention when Victor was about, and in my recollection of all our games, our expeditions to the lake, the Christmas parties, it is the godlike Victor who not only holds the centre of the scene but appears to fill it;

Victor wooing us all with his effortless charm, Victor raging at the frightened Henryk, Victor, black-haired, white-faced, sitting on his own bough in the Kingdom Tree, perfectly still, commanding our absolute obedience with nothing but the brilliance of his Kolbeck eyes. So my earliest picture of Casimir as a complete and independent being belongs to the *pension* at Montreux, to the balconied drawing-room next Mme Baudry's own, fussy and genteel, the smell of furniture cream and of jasmine, reflected sunlight dimmed by lemon blinds. There, eager and alight, crying absurdly "You don't know who I am!" he remains as clear to me as the pastel sketch you used to keep; his fair, artist's head against the dark mahogany door, his delicately sinewed hands holding my own. 'A grown man,' I remember thinking as I felt his schoolboy moustache against my cheek, 'after only nine years!' And I recall exactly the tone of his voice, saying "Goodness, Teffy, what are you crying about!" But from the moments and the weeks which followed no steady picture returns.

Was it a kind of foreknowledge which focused that meeting so sharply in my memory, or is it only romantic retrospection which makes me think so? I have come to believe that the tears I shed sprang less from the joy of seeing Casimir himself than from a buried nostalgia which he discovered, a panorama of lost associations, the very odour of Setory which he seemed to bring into that foreign room. You, in the calm years we spent there, came to have some fondness for that countryside; but for me, in early life, Setory held more than natural charm. If it did not belong to me, as it belonged to Victor and his brothers, it was still the only place I could think of as home; and since the modest wits of dear, brave 'Aunt Betka' had become so enfeebled that she could no longer be a mother to me, Setory was all I had to fulfil a child's demand for background and security. It was, I think, this hunger for the safe familiarities of childhood, kept darkly through my schooldays at Ste Thérèse d'Aubonne, which Casimir brought to the surface. From the moment of his coming I wanted to possess him, not only for his smile and graceful body, his glowing kindness, but for Setory's woods, the slow, unchanging life of its pasturelands, lamplight on nursery walls. Perhaps what I really needed, then, was to have him as an adopted brother; but nature does not allow us adopted brothers.

I see him for an instant, taut with anger, protesting publicly to the lecturer who has made a slighting remark about our Country. There are glimpses of him struggling with a dress collar, playing the piano, smiling with an enchanting shyness upon the people who crowd to greet us in the ballroom of some pompous hotel. I catch faintly his serious profile as we sit side by side, lying about our ages to the blind old priest at Aigle. And again I hear his voice—his face is turned away—saying "We can't be kind enough to Ilse, she's had no happiness at all, and we're so happy." Then there's the feel of his hands; one would not forget those.

Ilse Wachholz: I have a picture of her as well, in a yellow frock run up by some village dressmaker, standing all alone against the rail of the Chillon steamer; with her straight black hair at shoulder length making a perfect frame for her narrow and hungry face; the over-large eyes which sometimes go with a weak chest, and which lit superbly when we spoke to her. That picture is the only one. All that happened afterwards has become as lifeless as a text-book of history, and when I think of that beautiful creature now, it is once more with a pity I can scarcely distinguish from love.

Yes, my mind is like an old woman's, and the old do not remember much of the middle span. The broken net retains some bric-à-brac of vanity: a cloak with a silver collar-chain which Casimir got me for our visit to Paris; painters and diplomats we came to know; a few absurdities, as when we mistook an English nobleman for a porter and made him carry our bags for half a mile to a Nice hotel; while so much that one would call important has fallen out of sight. I do not remember whether I took my degree, or which of the Montreux hotels we lived in when we returned from our honeymoon. I cannot even recall whether it was Casimir or I who suggested that Ilse should have the top room, which we did not need for ourselves, in our house at Neuchâtel.

Much that I have written in these pages will be lost in the same way; and if I were to be alive and reading them ten years hence, events now vivid in my mind would come as if from outside experience, divested of their actual sensations. Once more some of the details that matter least, casual follies or discomforts, will perhaps be the last to fade. And yet I have come to think that memory does more for us at last by what it loses than by what it retains, that our private journey towards truth is a process of forgetting the things which should not count. The masks by which our fellow-beings are hidden have such an air of reality that reality itself, when we chance upon it, may seem to be only another disguise; but in the struggle of time and memory it is the counterfeit, I think, which perishes, leaving the man himself to stand out clear. What I remember most of Casimir, now that his face has grown so dim, is devotion and gentleness. That, I believe, is the man he was; the rest was accident. And so, surely, the last remaining memory of those others whose lives have been joined with mine will be the truest of all. The pictures all recede, each slide blurs a little the one behind, some salient lines are merged while the slighter features disappear. The trenchant sculpture of the Countess's tiny mouth and chin, the great rings on her arthritic fingers, are no longer visually clear; that girlish laugh of Henryk's which sometimes enraged me sounds too feebly to stir up any emotion now, the screened light in Julius's eyes is already too far off to haunt my waking hours, and even the tones of Victor's voice will soon be beyond my reach. But while oblivion closes on those externals, it falls as well upon my own prejudgments, on the feverous intuitions, self-distrust and self-esteem, which distorted the nearer view. The fretful day is almost finished, the glare subsides, and in the settled evening light one's vision works more patiently. Strangely, as the faces that I knew draw farther away the presences they enshrined seem closer at my side. Is it irrational to think that when darkness finally shuts down on our delusions we shall see with some lens of a less faulty kind, and that disseverance in time or space will cease to be valid in that illumination?

2

HERE the street was almost empty and we could move at our own pace. The uproar had dwindled to silence, the sound I heard now was the shuffling march of the crowd that streamed along the parallel road below. From farther off came the repeated whistle of a locomotive, and a crackle like dry twigs breaking.

"But Mummy, I don't see how we're ever going to find Grandfather when we do get to the station!"

I did not answer, because I was tired. I was wondering if I had remembered all the things which Victor, in our hurried talk on the telephone, had told me to collect; whether Setory would look the same after six years, and whether I should find the Swedish cot I had once used for Annette. For no reason, I was thinking about the time I had been in disgrace at Ste Thérèse, and I was also wondering if Victor's batman would sniff at the hasty darn I had made in one of his winter vests. A loose wheel on the pram we were pushing with the luggage made it travel in crazy curves, and this presently sent Annette into giggles. She was tired as well.

Where a building had collapsed we could see down to the main road, with the people moving all in one direction, steadily, but slowly, as if in their sleep. The carts, piled high, had to go at the same speed, and no one gave way to the motor which was hooting impatiently in their midst.

In a lull in the firing, not many minutes before, the clocks had been striking twelve; but now it felt as if dawn were already near: small winds like those of early morning were playing freshly along the narrow streets and a dull semblance of daylight, hardening the shape of roofs and pinnacles, gave to this least beautiful of Polish cities a sullen, transient grace. That light was constant. Intermittently a whiter, pulsing light, which must have come from fires on the south side of the town, threw all the scene into sharp relief, and in those moments the shadows moving along the road solidified into human shape: a man on crutches with a bowler hat, another supporting his wife, a little, hobbling woman who carried a suitcase and a child. They were quiet, these people moving in shapeless procession, their voices reached us only like the distant mumble of a congregation at prayer; their pace never changed, the figures which the flaring light revealed seemed to be repeated as if the same company of actors came round and round across a half-lit stage with the same fantastic shadows wavering on the grey wall behind. In-mostly, I was absorbed by the secret of which I had been certain these two days past. The knowledge of the separate life I carried in my body—progenitor, perhaps, of as many lives as these which flowed along the street—had brought to me once more the peculiar sense of consecration; and it seemed as if the mystery of this continuous twilight, the diorama of roofs and gables ranging on livid smoke, smoke drifting like a veil against the reddened cloud, were only a reflection of the dark rapture which possessed me from within. Our street descended, turned; we were carried now in the grey current ourselves, warm bodies pressing in, our senses wrapped in the crowd's thick breath and murmurous voice. This quietness and this constancy of motion soothed me. With these tired people I shared the liberating sense of mild activity, of relief from immediate danger, accepted despair.

"Mummy, my foot's hurting rather. I think there's something in my shoe."

The patience in her voice, conveying to me a hint of martyrdom, vexed me. With just that sweetness her father had once made his small complaints. It was my fault, however, that in our scrambling departure from the flat she had come in her indoor shoes. We steered the pram across the stream and went up a turning to the right.

Close to where we stopped a party was working methodically at the wreckage of some small house, shifting fallen joists and shovelling quantities of débris into the road. As I sat on a pile of rubble dealing with Annette's shoe, I saw them drag out what looked like a bolster torn almost in half, and then a smaller bundle. I watched with only a casual curiosity; we had passed scenes of that kind all the way along.

The breeze playing about my legs was wintry, it carried a smell of fire I did not like. I heard from not far off what sounded like a rifle-shot—it may have been a slate falling in the street behind—

and then, from the man who was holding the smaller bundle, a sentence of five words. In recollection, it seems that I was expecting it: a peasant's voice, husky from fatigue, almost nonchalant:

"Here, look—the child's alive."

ii

Alone, so small an incident, set in the confusion of that night's thoughts and sensations, would scarcely have found a place in memory, much less have become a callus on the mind, an ovule of perplexity. It would not have been here recorded.

There are explanations of how it comes about, the sensation, familiar to almost everyone, of living through a moment for a second time. I have had that experience often, and I had it then. There was, however, a difference: I knew immediately the nearer source of recognition. From early childhood—I did not know how far back—I had been troubled by an alarming dream which came at intervals of perhaps two or three years, perhaps much longer than that: such a dream as one does not remember when awake, but recognizes upon each recurrence. It was, then, as if this dream, belonging to the greatest depth of sleep, had risen suddenly to confront me in waking life: a dream of being cold and dimly frightened, the smell of burning, a sharp report which makes me cry out with terror, then the rough voice of a labourer, somewhere close by, 'Look—the child's alive.'

"What are you looking at, Mummy?" Annette asked me.

"We must hurry," I said. "Grandfather will be waiting."

We went on through the old vegetable market and joined the crowd again where it was tightening to squeeze across the bridge.

iii

'I don't wish to discuss that.' I had kept this phrase ready from the time when Victor had telephoned, as one keeps a coin handy for a cab-fare. 'I'm sorry, Beau-père, but Victor told me strictly I was not to talk about that.' These were the outworks of my hastily improvised defence.

They had cordoned the approaches to the station; but people had worked their way in by other routes, and the cordon, made from raw troops, was now totally ineffective: the crowd beyond it had become as dense as that on the open side. A raucous, amplified voice announced repeatedly that all the trains had been taken for military use: no civilian trains, it said, before Monday night. In response, family groups all over the carriageway were getting out food from their many bundles. Policemen rode about, shouting that the raiders would be back. "You won't have a chance if you stay here, packed together like this!" With their heads on suitcases or on the kerb, exhausted women settled themselves for sleep.

I stopped an officer who was pushing past us. "You don't happen to know General Kolbeck—General Kolbeck of the War Department? . . . In the station somewhere—I can't get through—I think he may have given someone a message."

He was sorry. He knew General Kolbeck by name, of course—only by name.

I don't wish to discuss that. . . . Should I recognize Julius Kolbeck if I saw him in the crowd—here, where the standard lamps had been partly obscured? Would he recognize me? Slack from want of sleep, my brain groped feebly for a picture of my father-in-law's face as I had last known it. I saw a slight figure, oddly young, hair blond like a Norwegian's, and that was all. In my seven adult years at Setory I had scarcely spoken to him except in the way of routine: from my position between poor relation and superior servant I had looked on him more as a figurehead than as a human being, a creature whose pale eyes, when he patiently surveyed you, were clouded with political affairs in Warsaw, with labour troubles on his own estate, the dignity and burdens of his father's House. I had feared but scarcely disliked him: he was too remote to be disliked; and if he had seemed hostile to me, the hostility was like that which climbers see in a towering face of rock. Would he still be remote when he met me for the first time as Victor's wife? 'You must get to the station somehow—I've arranged for Father to meet you there.' These words of Victor's, too peremptory to be questioned, had thrown me into a fever of apprehension; but the dread had been submerged by weariness, and I scarcely troubled now about how Julius would receive me; enough, in this dark extension of an endless day, if I could find him.

"Mummy, do you think we'd better go home again?"

"Darling, how could we, through all this crowd!"

The panting of a locomotive roused the people who had fallen asleep. Bearing a plume of sparks, a long train dragged into the station and stopped: it was headed to the west, and probably crammed with troops; but it stirred the optimism latent in crowds, and everyone started pressing again towards the station building as if a gale had risen behind an inflowing tide. Leaning on the handles of the pram I clutched Annette close to me, afraid of our being torn apart, and still more frightened lest someone barging against me might do some harm, even as early as this, to Victor's child.

She was patient, Annette. I had often thought her far too babyish for her fourteen years, but now she never whined or grumbled, as children round about us were doing. Resting her head against my side, she was presently dozing, and my own eyes closed.

'Look, the child's alive.' I was far less certain now that I had dreamed that scene the first time it enclosed me: the cold wind, the smell of burning, these seemed to have called up previous sensations too real to derive from dreams alone. But if the source was actuality, it was too far back for me to find: memory would reach no farther than 'Aunt Betka's' little house at Setory, Aunt Betka's voice calling me as I played on the wooden verandah; and in those placid years of my earliest childhood, when the fall of a cedar-tree was something to be remembered for always, there had been no violence or fear. Perhaps Aunt Betka had known, perhaps there was something she had meant to tell me when I was old enough to understand. I fancied I was back at Setory now, not with Aunt Betka but in the Countess's little workroom, surrounded by ledgers and potted seedlings, Annette in my arms, with the Countess saying in her level voice, "I know that Casimir is much to blame—but you have both been extremely foolish," so that the louder voices about my ears—'It's only a dodge, of course there'll be a train!' 'It's something holding things up along the line'—arrived without any meaning, like the noise of radio in a restaurant. I said aloud, "No, Grandmother, I don't intend to be under obligations to your family. I can give Wanda her lessons—I won't accept anything I can't pay for in service." Then someone clutching my arm said, "Careful, lady!"—the pram was moving under my weight—and Setory had given place to a siege of confusing shapes, faces seen grey in the near darkness, the crowd's conglomerate voice.

'There's bound to be a train!'

'I couldn't find her little coat—the lights had all gone out.'

'Here in less than a week.'

'The Government will fix it up. Those bastards haven't anything against us, once it's settled over Danzig.'

'She just said nothing would make her leave her home.'

You saw little flashes everywhere as men lit cigarettes; a tiny hunchbacked creature twisting through the crowd was selling fruit and the newspapers of the day before. Just behind me a woman hummed softly as she rocked her fretful child to sleep. It was a dark burlesque of holiday.

The light increased, not that of morning, but from a timber-stack a short way up the line which had suddenly burst into flame, throwing the station buildings into gaunt relief. When a second and a third train rumbled past we had a glimpse of soldiers, grey shapes immense in their accoutrements, packed tightly into open trucks. Just once, as the last of those trucks was passing, I caught through the rattle of bogies the sound of singing—a snatch from one of Slowacki's songs, which our men will always sing on journeys like that. Behind me someone in the crowd caught and echoed it, I saw a few men waving, women in tears. All of us watched those trucks, but most with something resembling apathy, as inveterate gamblers read the news that they have lost; we had learnt in the last few hundred years not to think of security or freedom as a permanent possession for us. For myself, just then, I was content that this disturbance had occurred while my son was safe inside me. Annette was still asleep.

The bloodless voice of the loudspeaker, with its warnings and exhortations, went on unheeded. How could any of us get loose from the crowd, and where were we to go? I was drowsing again when I heard the name 'Kolbeck'—"Attention, please, message for Kolbeck: will the wife of Colonel Victor Kolbeck go to the Military Transit office in Plac Mickiewicż. General Kolbeck is waiting for her there."

A mounted policeman was only a few yards away. I called to him, "That was for me—can you help me?" and he began at once to force a passage for us through the crowd.

iv

"You'll have to wait a few minutes," Julius said. "I've got things to see to."

Annette went to sleep again, lying on the bench with her head on my lap. A soldier brought me tea. The doors at either end of the long, garishly-lighted room never ceased to swing and slam as a stream of officers and civilian clerks went through.

"You are travelling—out to the country?" a soldier asked me kindly, over his typewriter. "It will be nice in the country now. The trains of course are very full. You have lost your home?"

"No, it's still there, up to now. Part of the roof and the windows have gone."

"Ah! But it will be nicer in the country. And the young lady is going as well!"

The voices from the other side of the plywood partition were tired and passionless.

'. . . and add fourteen hours to the route?'

'. . . case of adopting the minor risk.'

'. . . care what the Corps Commander says! You can't put an infantry brigade in four coaches.'

'The British may do something.'

'The British will go on sending protests. They send more stylish protests than anyone in the world.'

Occasionally I caught my father-in-law's patrician voice: "Yes, I've put some of my valuables in the bank, but I shall be very much surprised if I find them again after the Germans have gone. . . . No, not unless they send for me. I think that's unlikely. It appears that a soldier of fifty-four can't be of any service to his fatherland. My son may be of some use—my son Victor. He has never been friendly with politicians of any party—that's a great advantage to any man who has the modest ambition to die for his country."

He returned presently, in his greatcoat, with some vague person to whom he casually introduced me ("My daughter-in-law, Stefanie") and a pair of orderlies.

"Are those all your things? That perambulator will have to stop where it is. It may help the Colonel here with his transport problems. Or the Germans with theirs. Walery, you'd better lead the way."

We left the building by a back door, crossed a yard and one of the crowded side streets leading towards the station. A sentry, on a word from Julius, admitted us to a walled passage which became an open cinder-path beside the railway. Perhaps a kilometre from the station a train of half a dozen coaches stood on the track, unlighted and engineless. A man in uniform, whose face looked cadaverous in the unnatural light from the burning stack, came up to tell us that no one was allowed to approach the train.

"You're in charge of this train?" Julius said, surveying him distantly. "Very well, I want three places. I have military travel-vouchers."

The official was extremely sorry: the train was full from end to end, there were people all along the corridors.

Julius said, "I want three places."

[19]

"But—with the highest respect, General—there isn't one place in the whole train."

"Three places—you must clear them—and I shall want a lamp in the compartment until the electricity comes on. If you haven't got one, you must send to the station. Walery—here's my torch—find a decent compartment and clear three seats. Yes, you can take this case with you—come back for the rest."

While the men were bustling this way and that he smoked a cigarette with slow appreciation, as they do in advertisements. He never wasted nervous energy, as both Victor and Casimir did. I said:

"I didn't realize you were travelling as well. Victor didn't tell me."

He ignored that, upholding men's right to silence with their womenfolk. But presently he did speak to Annette.

"I suppose you feel as if you're quite grown-up now! Thirteen, is it? Fourteen, yes, of course! You'll like being at Setory again?"

"Yes, Grandfather."

"Better than being here?"

"Mother says there won't be any bombs there."

"You can't be sure of that," he said, as if he were talking to an adult. "You may get bombs and you may get tanks as well. You see, it's not like the last war, when we were all in the same trenches for weeks. The Germans have thought of something better than that: they've learnt how to move their armies at an incredible pace. They're clever, the Germans. They study things thoroughly."

"Oh."

"So you may find that you're living in a country which has been conquered. Conquered, I mean, in the physical sense—German soldiers all over it."

I said: "Annette's very tired."

"But if you're only fourteen," he continued, "that doesn't matter. You've got another sixty or seventy years to live—at least, I hope so—and you may have sons who will be living nearly a hundred years from now. All you've got to do is to remember that you're a Pole. You've got to teach your sons that they're Poles—Poles and Catholics, for us it means almost the same thing. They've got to learn from you to make the freedom of Poland the one object of their lives."

I thought that such grandiloquence would be meaningless to an exhausted child. I was surprised when she said, with that apparent simplicity of children which one can never quite evaluate:

"Granny's a German, isn't she?"

I intervened: "Annette, I've told you, Granny comes from Lithuania."

"Your grandmother is a Pole," Julius said calmly, "because she's my wife."

"The same way as Mummy's a Pole?"

"I suppose so."

Walery, reporting, said, "Three seats ready, sir. And we've got the lamp."

v

I remember that the carriage was foul with cigarette-smoke, orange-peel all over the floor; that the people who had been turned out, a Galician couple and their son, were arguing violently until a single word from Julius silenced them. Chiefly I recall the ineffable experience of safety and repose. The anxieties had not drawn far away. With the shadow-show repeating and repeating, figures that passed before a blazing house, faces which rose and sank in the tumbled sea of the station yard, I found the day's problems creeping back as if I had not already given them solutions: what clothes to take for Annette for autumn and winter, where to leave the keys of the flat. But beneath this surface fidgeting, my mind was possessed with a feeling of security, mainly engendered, I suppose, by Julius's presence. The parting with Victor was now far behind, accepted as one comes to accept the loss of an amputated limb. The major decisions had all been taken, I had nothing to do but sit in this stifling box and let myself be carried into the next stage of existence; to wait quietly for the coming of Victor's child. The violent jolt when the engine was attached hardly disturbed me. Luxuriating in repose, I felt with deepened satisfaction the lame dog-trot of the train starting to move.

Annette, between us, with her legs drawn up and her head on Julius's lap, had long been asleep. Except for Julius, upright and incessantly smoking, everyone slept. The train fell into a lumbering gait, slightly faster, perhaps, than that of a cantering horse.

Now inquietude returned. I thought it was Victor who sat beside me, that the train was taking us to Holland for our marriage there; but the zest of that impetuous flight was gone, leaving only a bitter sense of my ingratitude to the Kolbecks for the years when they had sheltered me. I wanted to explain that misery to Victor, but his eyes were always turned away; and now I saw, as if incorporate in this wedding journey, the bleak consulting-room at Wilno

[21]

where our first hopes of a child had ended, now the cream-washed walls and useless flowers of a private ward in the Komarow hospital where they told me that my son had been stillborn. That scene was more than I could endure a second time, I cried out "Stop! Somebody stop the train!" and although my voice issued silently the train immediately came to a halt. My eyes opened. The oil lamp which the orderly had tied to the rack was still feebly burning. Some distance off a single gun had started firing, with the gruff bark of an old farmyard dog.

As the train became inanimate, its teeming population woke to life. Someone was shouting, "They're back, the raiders are back!" and all the doors were opening. The tangle of legs and coats on the other seat broke up into separate figures which jostled out to join the scurry in the corridor. Through the rising uproar I heard a woman crying hysterically, "Let me out, I must get out!" and a child screaming.

"There's no point in moving," Julius said. He had not stirred, and Annette still slept as if she were in her own bed. "The child may as well sleep as long as she can. A train's an awkward target in the dark. Are you warm enough, or do you want something over you?"

I said I was warm, but feeling slightly sick; at which he turned his head to look at me for the first time since we had met.

"Does that mean you're pregnant?"

"Yes. At least, I'm almost certain."

He nodded, as if some junior officer had brought him a satisfactory routine report.

"The third time, isn't it? I mean, since your alliance with Victor."

The word 'alliance' started a mechanism which brought almost to my lips the phrase I had kept in readiness, 'I don't wish to discuss that.' But I altered it.

"Oh—Victor wrote to you?"

"He sent a message to his mother. On both occasions. . . . You must be very careful, you must avoid any sort of excitement. Poland can't afford to be wasteful of children."

"Neither can I."

"Not even the children of irregular alliances."

I said, "We were married in the Stadhuis at Amsterdam. I can show you the certificate, if you'd like to see it."

"There is just one kind of marriage for Catholics," he answered, "and it cannot be celebrated when a previous partner is still alive."

That did not hurt me, for his voice was without hostility; he was stating facts, as he knew them, with scarcely greater emotion than a lawyer reading out some regulation to his client; and I was too tired to be upset by expected opinions. I could hear the approaching planes now, and with the experience of the last few days I judged that there were four or five of them. I said:

"Perhaps Annette would be safer under the seat."

"I doubt it." He leaned forward, so that his body made some sort of shield for Annette's head. "Tell me, are you bringing her up properly? Does she attend Mass on all Days of Obligation?"

"Nearly all."

"Remember," he said, "there are two things which count in our existence as a nation: our own power of resistance to assimilation—and our religion."

His voice just then was Victor's, Victor in one of his dogmatic, schoolboy moods. And now, as I watched his profile with the concentration derived from physical fear—the intellective eyes fortressed by heavy brow and high, flat cheek, a young man's face except for the dryness of skin and the thin mouth's finality—I found the forgotten Julius returning as if we had been separated for days instead of years. He had grown no older: he would never be old, for he had never been really young. In appearance he showed much less of Victor, this spare-bodied man with his colouring almost golden in the lamplight, than of his other sons. Yet this, I thought, is a Victor with all the outgrowths of emotion so austerely pruned that the ordinary relations between one human and another are impossible with him. His passions belong to the mind, not to the heart. Even his antipathy to me is less a sentiment than a logical process, the commander's rational distaste for a soldier whose ignorance of discipline distracts his officers from their duty.

I should have said no more: there is little use in questioning men's dogmata. But the sound of the planes, now much closer, was fluttering my nerves, and I had to speak aloud to ease them.

"Only it seems to me that religion and tribal aspirations ought to be kept apart. I suppose I'd feel differently if I was Polish-born."

The noise of engines, diminishing, gave place to the sigh and whistle of cloven air. The explosion, perhaps two or three hundred metres away, reached the train as if a shovelful of snow were hurled against the windows, and from one of them a shower of fragments splashed on the seats and floor. Annette, opening her eyes and sitting up, remained quite still, only her mouth moving like that of a boy who has set himself to endure a whipping. The backwash of silence was followed by isolated sounds from those who had stayed in the train, cries of fright and hysterical prayers.

Julius, with the mechanical efficiency of a servant making a bed, put his arm round Annette and pulled her head down to its former position on his lap. "I don't think I understand you," he said to me abruptly. "You were brought up at Setory—or have you forgotten that? Were you ever treated as different from us?"

"Yes, I've been well treated."

My ears were straining for the return of the planes, which might have been dissatisfied with their first attempt; and that distraction, added to my weariness, gave me a sense of irresponsibility. I found myself addressing him as I had never dared in all the years when I had belonged to his household.

"You were very generous. There was some reason, I suppose. I've wondered all my life what it was."

For a few moments he scrutinized Annette's face as a doctor would. A splinter of glass had made a cut in his cheek from which the blood flowed profusely, and he was dabbing it impatiently with his handkerchief.

"Reason?"

"Why you took me on in the first place. It wasn't Aunt Betka's idea, to begin with."

"No, it was mine."

"There were always plenty of orphans in the village, if you felt inclined for that sort of charity. There was no need to go out into the highways and by-ways. And you needn't have chosen a child of Ruthenes, since you've always hated them."

He asked, casually, "Who told you your parents were Ruthenes?"

"Belle-mère did, once. That's all she ever seemed to know about me."

"Indeed?" He bent to listen to Annette's breathing, and nodded approvingly, finding that she was already sleeping again. "And you were always hoping she'd tell you something romantic? You thought you might be the child of a Russian Archduke or someone? I suppose all girls have their heads filled with that sort of balderdash. You're wrong about the Ruthenes," he continued, with the thin smile which people use when a child exhibits some naïveté, "I don't hate them all. Well, you know how many I employ at Setory. We get on very well. I merely don't take it for granted that they've got the same ideas of honesty as I have."

It was not difficult, even with so little of my mind at work, to see what that remark implied.

I had crossed the boundary of a region where I had never ventured before, and that achievement tempted me farther. I said, as if we were merely gossiping about someone we had both known in the past, "No, I don't think my head was ever filled with Archdukes. I did occasionally wonder if I was the result of someone from your own family going astray. That isn't such a very romantic notion. It would explain a great deal."

"Oh—I'm sorry to disappoint you." Putting his handkerchief away, he got out another cigarette. "If that had been the case I should hardly have let you spend your childhood playing with my sons. It's a pity old Zygmunt is dead—he would have told you all there is to know. He was following a boar-track when he found you. It's not an unheard-of thing, you know, children being abandoned. Not in the district we were hunting then."

"You found a great many?"

He did not answer, and now I was thankful to be saved the effort of continuing so sterile an exchange. Perhaps he had spoken the truth, and it was only a girl's idle imagination which had made my adoption by the Kolbecks an affair of mystery. It was commonplace for men like him, devoid of sentiment, to perform an occasional act of sentimentality and then grow hostile towards the object of their benevolence; that might well have been the reason for his early coldness. What did it matter! He had firmer cause for hostility now. We have known each other, I thought, for more than thirty years, yet here we sit, side by side, as if we were strangers brought together by chance alone; and if we were to stay here for the rest of our lives we should still have nothing to share in conversation, since nothing can stay alive in the disparate temperatures of his mind and mine.

For the time I was content with that. The framework of my life had once again been pulled apart, and in the weariness which such upheaval brings I found it luxury to regard myself as a creature steered by chance, without responsibility. My eyes fell shut, I heard as part of a dream men's voices shouting that the raiders had gone, the rising hubbub of people crowding back into the train.

vi

At some time in the night Annette slipped down and found herself a new position, curled on the floor with her head between my feet. It was her voice which at last roused me.

[25]

"Mummy, are you awake? . . . Mummy! . . . Mummy, I think Grandfather's died."

The lamp was almost out, but the darkness outside had thinned. Morning, but where? The fields passing, the ricks and barns, told me nothing. The power of sleep still held me, I looked through half-closed eyes at the shapes in the corridor of people sleeping on their legs, at the huddled figures on the other seat, faces, yellow before, now turned to masks of grey.

Died? Julius dead? That would mean complications, things to be arranged. My head had fallen on his shoulder, and I would not turn it to look at his face, nor would I make any response to Annette, whose eyes, anxious and docile like Casimir's, I could just discern in the semi-darkness. This lethargy was a comfortable bondage from which I did not want to escape.

I could see his hands folded on his knees, exactly as they had been before. He must have shifted during the night, for his coat was round me and tucked behind my back; but I neither saw nor felt the slightest movement now. When at last I turned enough to see them his eyes were open and quite expressionless. They did not scare me, as the eyes of the dead have done; perhaps I was too somnolent to be scared; and I saw just then the beauty that belongs to Greek sculpture in this face which had only so much life as a sculptor's genius can bestow. Even the dried blood on his chin appeared to me, in this faint light, an added dignity rather than an object of revulsion. I thought, dreamily, how the face of Victor dead on a battlefield would have just such nobility as this.

I fancied they had passed before, the roofless houses which I saw in blurred silhouette against the dark sky, this church with its belfry torn away. And now beside the old woman's head nodding at the window the featureless pastureland began again, the same squat trees. Dawn seemed to be in arrest. In the corridor no one moved: the line of heads, the shape of bundles on the rack, familiar now like the view from home, only jerked and swung in the laborious rhythm of the dragging train.

Then Julius spoke aloud. "I didn't know—I tell you I didn't know about the woman—I thought there was no one in the house but him!"

I moved to sit up straight, to see his face more easily. His eyes were still unlit, no muscle stirred. I thought presently that the solitary utterance, in a voice so unlike his normal one, must have come from my own imagination; and my eyes returned to the ragged gap in the window.

[26]

The trees crowding together brought us back almost to total darkness. When they thinned I saw that a light rain was falling. Except at the horizon, where a single stroke of green was drawn above the line of hills, the sky was held by cloud; and the light it gave, grey like that of a cave in snow, was still too meagre to bring the outward scene to actuality. The carriage itself, drearily repeating the tattoo which had accompanied my dreaming, still felt like the shell of a dream. Drowsy, a little faint from morning sickness, I watched the turbid countryside as young children see moving pictures, a semblance of reality remote from themselves.

In that passive state I was not disturbed at feeling Julius's fingers exploring along my arm, at finding my hand enclosed in his; nor surprised to hear him say, "Where are we—tell me—where are we now? The snow's all gone!"

His voice stirred the woman by the window. "The snow?" she asked curiously. "The snow?"

He did not answer. His hand was shaking. I turned to look at his face again and saw that the eyes were clouded, damp from the tears of an old man struggling with some once-simple problem; and though I did not realize then where the night's troubled wandering would have taken him, I could feel a momentary pity for such weakness in a man like him. I said, "We're going to Setory—you remember?" And he answered vaguely, "To Setory? I suppose so, yes."

Annette presently got up and sat on his knees. She was too old, I thought, to behave like that, but he did not seem to mind.

A road emerging from woodland drew towards us in reluctant curves and at last ran close beside the line. Here carts and wagonettes were moving in the same direction as ourselves; the strange outlines of their loads, figures huddled among sacks and baskets, furniture piled high, appeared at the level of the windows and fell behind. The road swung off to round a hill; when it joined us again the concourse had thickened, handcarts and heavy wains, cyclists with calves in tow, an ancient gig which bore two children and a sewing-machine. The train had slowed again, our pace was only a little greater than theirs. Drowsily watching them, the horses plodding in their sleep, children with bundles tied to their backs, I fancied myself a part of the ghostly carnival; and seeing that Julius's eyes were fastened on this spectacle, I remained untroubled by his presence and by the stiff grasp of his hand.

"Poor Sandra!" The words, husky with weariness, were not

meant for me. "Poor Sandra! Yes, we've been unlucky with our sons. God wished it, I suppose."

The little station we went through looked as if a giant hoof had kicked it. There people lay in rows asleep; a few stood up to stare at us, as if they had only just received their sight. I caught a glimpse of bandaged arms and heads, of bundles covered with blankets which did not move. The rain had stopped, the green streak in the sky was broadening to a crimson band.

"I never thought that Victor would deceive us like that. His brother's wife—I never thought of such a possibility! A man like him, a Catholic and a soldier!"

I said in a whisper, "I didn't think of such a possibility either. Not when Casimir left me."

And then, slowly, he turned his puzzled eyes towards me. "Stefanie? Tell me, Stefanie, do you think God punishes our sins, or does he leave us to punish ourselves?"

The voice he used, so burdened with fatigue that it could carry no hostility, was hard to recall in the weeks that were to come. When I am tired now, and enclosed in some slight sickness, I see the mysterious fall of earliest September sunlight on a misted countryside, where the road has drawn away and the carts creeping along it are like toys on the nursery floor. This sublimation of light gives to the drowsy faces on the other seat, the sprawl of baggage and crumpled clothes, a peculiar unreality, as when sunshine falls through tinted glass on a museum's faded curiosities. I smell the morning freshness, dispelling by degrees the odour of bodies packed together too long. I see Annette's fair, tousled head on Julius's shoulder, the face of Julius himself, unshaved, too freshly stirred from sleep to show its normal frigidity. And then, stitched closely in this tenuous fabric of sensation, that voice of his which I had never heard or imagined before sounds in my ears again.

"Yes, Stefanie, we are both in God's hands. It's in His justice that He uses you as punishment for me."

My mind, in that hour's inertia, would not stir far enough to wonder what he meant. Only the grief in his voice stirred me; and while the small flame of that emotion was burning it showed me how I must appear to him: a creature to whom he had given all life's needs, and who had repaid him by deliberately seducing his sons. I believe that in those moments when the old relationships were lost in our exhaustion, we came close to a kind of sympathy; and if we could have stayed for a time in the seclusion of that experience, our senses numbed by the rock of the train, weariness turned to tranquillity by the early morning radiance, we might have discovered a plot of ground on which we could meet again.

"You've had some sleep?" he asked rather distractedly, staring at my hands. "You were tired, yes—these have been troublesome days. For me as well. And having Victor away, of course that's an anxiety for you."

I asked if he meant to go back to Warsaw, but he did not answer that question. He said pensively, gazing at the gentle fall of pasture-land, "Yes, 'living-space' is what they call it. They use such words for things like this."

His eyes narrowed, like those of a teacher trying to make things plain to a very stupid pupil; and now the husk of sleepiness was falling away from his voice.

"It isn't our space they really envy. They know that Poland's something more than so much forest, so many hectares of arable land. We possess a spiritual heritage—in some dim way they realize that—and it's something they can't get hold of, because they haven't the minds to comprehend our faith in freedom and make it their own. That's why they want to destroy it, once and for all." He was no longer speaking to me. He had pulled his hand away, and I doubted if he remembered, just then, who was beside him. "They've tried for centuries—they never succeed. These Prussians, and those barbarians on the other side, they suppose they can make an end of Poland by seizing our people and crushing their bodies; they think they can bury the whole history of our nationhood, make us forget our own tongue. . . ."

vii

We were attacked again, twice I think, but the train did not stop. The two bombs which were dropped both fell some distance behind, and did us no harm. We did stop, for some two hours, at a station farther on, where a line of boys in uniform kept the crowd away from the train.

There were rumours of all kinds passing up and down the corridor: the Government had opened negotiations for a truce, a British flotilla was in the Baltic, the Germans had got Turun; but no one was sufficiently alive to pay more than a cursory attention. We in the train were more concerned with the possibility of getting something to eat or drink, those outside were chiefly occupied in scanning the sky. For the rest, the two assemblies stared at each

[29]

other dumbly, with something less than curiosity. It was like a party at which every topic of common interest has been exhausted but the guests are too shy to depart.

From that shyness Annette was exempt. She stood with her head at the broken window, passing the time of day with the soldiers, even making them laugh.

"Turun!" Julius said, when that rumour came to our carriage. "Yes, that's possible."

Sitting rigidly now, smoking, he showed no impatience at all; he did not seem to notice the lack of anything to eat or to read. When he spoke again it was as if someone had arrived rather inopportunely to take his orders for the day.

"You're going to be in that cottage Betka used to have, the one you lived in first of all. I've wired them to get it ready for you. You'd rather be there than in the house, I suppose."

Answering "It makes no difference to me", I was surprised to find my voice tremulous. "You realize," I said, "that I'm only coming to Setory because it's Victor's wish. We had no chance to talk it over."

"You mean, you were hoping to avoid seeing any of us again?"

"I mean that I don't want to incur any obligations. When Casimir left me, I had a certain claim on you—at least, that's how I felt. It seems to be rather the other way now. Of course I shall pay you rent for the cottage as soon as Victor gets some money through to me."

I spoke in a way that amounted to rudeness. He was quite unmoved.

"Rent?" he said. "Well, yes, if you want to. The question seems to me rather academic."

"Not to me."

"The essence of the business," he continued prosaically, "is that you are going to bear my son's child—his son, I hope—and the event has got to be looked after properly. The child himself will be no more guilty than any other baby, I shall regard him as a member of my family, and as far as conditions allow I shall see that he's brought up accordingly. The question of what you call 'obligations' doesn't really arise."

I said, as calmly as I could, "It's a matter for Victor and me, how he's to be brought up. We'll be making our own arrangements— I'll be taking the baby away from Setory as soon as possible after he's born."

"As soon as possible—how soon do you think that will be?"

"Well, a few months, perhaps. Victor will have to decide."

"I see. You think we shall have held the Germans, driven them right back, and imposed terms of peace in the course of a few months?" He held his cigarette in front of him, and watched the twisting ash as if there were some message to be studied there. "I think it's better to face realities. In such a war as we're fighting now there are going to be very heavy casualties. On our side, I mean. In every battle the incidence of loss is highest among the best units, because they automatically get the stiffest tasks. Within those units the bravest men are the ones most likely to be lost, whether they're rank-and-file or quite senior officers. Simply because they *are* brave. Victor's the kind of man who will always find opportunities for taking personal risks—risks that are unnecessary and even unjustifiable. It's in his nature. Personally, I'm glad he's like that."

I was trying to show no impatience. It was, after all, accepted by men of his kind and generation that one must talk to women as if they were children. I said with as much forbearance as I could find, "But do you think I've never realized that? Do you think I've never worked out the chance of Victor being killed in the next two or three weeks?"

He nodded. "Very well, then!"

"And if that happens I shall simply have to make my own plans. I expect I shall go to Switzerland. I still have friends there."

"To Switzerland? You think the Germans will give you a permit to travel through Czechoslovakia? Or do you suppose the Baltic's going to be open to ordinary passenger traffic?"

"Possibly through Russia," I said. "I know it won't be an easy journey, but I shall manage it one way or another. A child has a right to the most peaceful and happy life his mother can give him, whatever it costs her. If I have to bring up my children alone, I shall get them away from Poland somehow. I've made up my mind about that."

I felt glad to have had the chance of telling him my intentions so plainly; and my statement seemed to have ended the discussion, for he received it in silence. But some time afterwards, when the train was moving again, he said quietly,

"No, Stefanie, it's not the business of the mother to decide these things. If it was, we should breed no men at all, only lap-dogs. If Victor comes through—well, he must do what he likes. Otherwise it will be my business as head of the family to act for him."

I remember that this fabulous announcement did not come as a shock to me. I had spent a great part of my life at Setory; I knew the world, the age, to which my father-in-law belonged. Only a great weariness came over me, as I thought how many times I should have to fight this battle again, armed with words which could not wound because they would never penetrate an understanding so archaic as his.

"Then I have no rights at all?"

"Your position would be different," he answered soberly, "if you were Victor's wife according to the laws of God." And then, indeed, I was startled, even scared, by a sudden anger which stiffened the muscles of his face and made his voice tremble. "Rights! How can you talk about 'rights' when you've never thought about your obligations—to God or to other people? You've stolen seeds of life which were never sanctified for you. Rights? No, certainly you have no rights!" Edged by passion, his voice was no longer private; but he did not seem to realize, as I did, that our fellow-travellers were listening with dumbfounded curiosity. "The child you're carrying is a Kolbeck. He's going to be brought up by people who understand what that means. We—we Poles—we have a mission in history. There won't be too many left to go on with the struggle. I'm not going to see one lost."

Annette, still at the window, had turned round. She looked more than ever like her father as she gazed at Julius's face with the innocent interest of animals and children, with what looked to me like a faint smile of admiration. I did not speak to her or to him. I knew that the child to be born must be wholly mine, and for the magnitude of that resolve there was no vehicle large enough but silence. I turned to look the other way, where between the patient travellers in the corridor I could see men harvesting who never stopped to look at the sky. In the gloss of the September sun, now at its greatest strength, that scene had the quality of a Canaletto, reality so firmly drawn that it seemed to be immutable. I could not picture armies here. Our neighbours were starting to talk again in their monotonous homely voices: of troubles with shopkeepers, a daughter's Name Day that was coming. The sense of being severed from the past might even now be illusion.

viii

Somewhere we must have stopped again for a long time. I know that when we reached our destination the daylight was weakening, so that outlines were softened and the faint glow of street lamps gave a certain mystery to the dull, small town.

When I got down from the train my legs felt like artificial ones. Hunger and fatigue had partly numbed my senses; the ground seemed to be unsteady and objects came to me in a false perspective, as if seen in a distorting glass. 'No, no more trains, that one was the last.' 'But you did bring the little bowl which used to be in Auntie's room?' '. . . a new line on the Vistula and the San.' Voices greeting and inquiring, shreds of news which blew from mouth to mouth, meant nothing to me at all.

A face here and there was vaguely familiar, that of a bank clerk I had known, a young woodman's, now framed alike in clumsily-fitted uniform. These improvised soldiers had been there perhaps since morning; they had broken from line into groups of two or three, surrounded by a litter of equipment and by civilian friends, who watched them dumbly, having exhausted the means to show emotion. One or two who were alone smiled in hazy recognition as I jostled past them, and I should have answered with some word of sympathy, but my mouth was dry and nothing would come. Julius was a few yards in front of me, with Annette holding his arm.

The square was full of gigs and wagons, the evening smell of the place was the same as of old. There were notices printed in huge type on boards that leaned against the Sobieski statue, and people were stopping to gaze at them with the empty eyes of children in an art museum. A row of army lorries stood beside the cattle-pens. Beyond them I saw the Kolbecks' ancient German car.

It must have been Szwarce's hotel where we had some kind of meal: I have a recollection of a gigantic sideboard and of curtains with a Magyar design in green. I remember the look of almost fatuous contentment on the face of Annette, as she sat eating prodigiously and sunning herself in her grandparents' tender admiration. I have, too, a clear picture of the hat which my mother-in-law had chosen for meeting her husband, a triumphal arch of violet foliage mounted on blue velour; and I see the tears forming in her dull and honest German eyes while she talks to Annette in the heavy voice which never lost its Kovno intonation: "So tired! So good! Such a journey for a little one!" In a way I was thankful for the presence of Henryk, whom Sandra had brought with her to the station, and who was babbling all the time, as a child would, about my looks and the prettiness of my clothes; although his nonsense embarrassed me, I was glad on this occasion to have a more obvious excuse for shyness than the real one. To Sandra herself I was grateful for the ponderous fuss she made over getting us settled in the car, the fastening of side-screens, tucking-in of rugs; when one is tired and empty of virtue, one values the very limitations of those whose mental life is enclosed by practical needs.

Julius drove, with Sandra beside him. Through Henryk's giggles and chatter I heard snatches of their conversation: ". . . Yes, my public life seems to be finished. As things are, I suppose it's of no consequence. . . ." " . . . I wanted to turn it into a drying-room, but your mother said she had to have it for her young turkeys. . . ." Once and again Sandra turned her head. "You are all right, Stefanie? You are quite warm?"

The sky, pale green in the west, still held the last of the sun's light; where the street lamps stopped, it showed like faded snap-shots the forgotten corners which in earlier years had been gently familiar: a turning by the convent wall, the gateway where Victor had once mended my bicycle. Here summer was lasting in the smell of the cooling air, dusty and dry. The days of harvest parties had worn into evenings like this, and in those distant, peaceful summers the shortening of daylight had only brought fresh promise: of a life more circumscribed but not less rich in small contentments, bonfires in the orchards, skating on Sofia's Pond. Could none of that return? Already, with the sky so calm, free from the rever-beration of engines, the alarms of war seemed far behind—as if I had passed from a troubled dream to the safety of morning. Here were people whose ways I knew, whose looks and voices could give me the comfort of old association, whose beliefs, however far from mine, were never cheaply held. These, in return for my rational humility, would give me the security I needed for the birth of my son, and in our present case Victor himself would surely wish me to accept their complete authority. Had I any tenable ground for opposing my will to his? Was the voice forbidding me to be subservient only the voice of self-esteem?

". . . prefer the Germans, if I had to make my choice between the two. The Germans have the single merit of not being Asiatics."

"But, Julius, they'll never get here? Not to Setory? . . ."

When we turned by the saw-mill the woods were drawn like a curtain across the last daylight, narrowing our scene to the strip which the headlamps carved from darkness; as if their beam shone back into memory, it disclosed in turn the features which the years had overlaid, a marble Calvary, the snow-plough lying beside a fallen beech. Here the road was rough, its margins indistinct; the smell which came was of exhausted fires. It brought to me, this flavour of the past besieging all my senses, a hunger for Victor more painful than any I had felt before: I shut my eyes, but the

[34]

voice of Julius uttering terse, flat truths about the War had a note of Victor's, there was something like Victor's laughter in the babbling of Henryk at my side. Annette was caressing my hand, whispering "Are you tired, Mummy? Do you feel sick?" but that was not the comfort I needed. I wanted quietness and safety, not this phantasm of a life from which the genius of life had gone.

In this fresh, bitter loneliness I longed for sleep to give me release. It would not come: the lethargy which returned with the car's comfort was only a counterfeit of sleep. But now, as smaller lights are visible only when the sun has gone, the very darkness of my state seemed to disclose in brightening illumination the fragment left me from the dissolution of my world. It was wrong, I thought, to seek an escape from being alone; loneliness should be accepted as the rampart of a citadel where one could live in the safety of independence. Here, knowing that Victor would not return, I should learn to be satisfied by his imagined presence; and in time the place I jealously kept for him would be occupied by the child he had begotten, another Victor, hard in lips and skin, contemptuous of physical pain, whose life would yet escape the constricting loyalties by which his father's had been shaped. That was enough. Lacking every source from which it has drawn breath, the inmost being can survive on nothing but the purpose it fights for; and as one voice will rally a crumpled squadron, this flash of hopefulness rekindled the fire which had burnt too low to give me any warmth. The tired voice of Julius, flowing now as evenly as the handwriting of clerks, filled all the gaps in the car's squeak and rattle with a procession of plans: to organize patriot groups, establish secret communications—who else had needed in the past to learn those methods as thoroughly as they!—so that even under occupation the nation's independent life could be maintained; designs to refute in advance the statement of history, plans begotten from passionate courage by prodigious sanity. And how small, how nugatory, they seemed beside the work to which I was dedicated now—to give first breath to a body made from mine, alone to exercise upon that life the most potent influence it would ever bend to, so to order the passion and genius of its heritage that this man, born into the narrow destinies of his race and time, would override them to establish a destiny of his own. Was any ambition of Julius comparable with mine! Was the fretful energy of the Kolbecks, the cumulate force and passion of struggling generations, so powerful as the single purpose held in one woman's body, her mind and will!

Annette's small hand, delicate as Casimir's, still lay on my wrist. I moved it away. Breaths of woodland from the driver's window had given place to the fresher smells of pasture; a pattern of lights far over to the left was one I recognized, and the shapes appearing now, dark against rising fields, a stilted water-tank, silos like the redoubts of a fortress, were shreds of the returning past. Setory gathered about me: timber cabins crouching against the roadway where the long file of limes came to an end, blind windows passing to each other the light of the car's lamps, a door which opened at the scrape of our tyres to release with a narrow oblong of light the smells of saddle-soap and dairy, the clamour of an old dog barking. From the scurry of half-lit figures, tangling voices, in which we were absorbed, I heard the voice of Anusia exclaiming upon Annette's tallness and maturity. I slipped back into the car's shadow, afraid lest she or the very breathing of the house might offer a welcome, hardly to be resisted, to me as well.

3

BUT it was foolish in reality to suppose that I could live contentedly within myself. Such living may be possible for special people, geniuses or saints: not for a woman used to cities and to some admiration; not, at Setory, for me. Here, as a child, I had never felt myself much different from the Kolbeck children, and the place I had later occupied as daughter-in-law, if not a high one, had at least been dignified by a recognition of the wrong I had suffered in Casimir's desertion. That place had satisfied my need—the need of every human—for a patterned frame, and seldom, in either of those periods, had I felt as a disablement my lack of a known birthplace and parentage. I felt it now. The proposal to put me in Betka's cottage had been rejected by Sandra, who thought it unwise for one in my condition to live alone; so I found myself in the very midst of the Kolbecks, and every consideration they showed me now was a reminder that I had forfeited all claim to a place in their community. In this new state of life, where something was needed to replace the former sense of privilege, the old, sporadic curiosity about my origin was reawakened. In youth I had indulged in dreams not much less romantic than the one of which Julius had accused me. These started to return with the force of an obsession. I did faintly imagine (with a childishness I am now ashamed to record) that I might discover a birthright equal in dignity to that of the Kolbecks themselves.

The excuse I can make is that I was sleeping poorly. During the last nights at home there had been little opportunity for sleep: I had always been waiting for the ring of the telephone, which might bring some news of Victor, and whenever the guns started I had had to decide whether I should take Annette downstairs. In the quiet nights at Setory the feeling persisted that to sleep would be to neglect my duty. From the long hours of wakefulness I passed only into a vivid counterfeit of conscious life where, while the noise of planes drew close, I hunted for trinkets which Victor might some day ask for, set out again upon the feverish journey through smoking streets, watched fearfully the men who were dragging bundles from under débris, waited for the voice which would call out 'Look, the child's alive!' That voice always roused me; and then, dreading to fall back into the haunted shadows, I would lie with my eyes open until the earliest daylight shaping stable roofs and the trees behind brought me the assurance of reality. In those hours my mind ranged and hovered like a kestrel in flight, so slenderly attached to actual sensation that I often expected to see the outside world move past the window, to find Julius seated at my side. Sometimes, indeed, odd sentences he had spoken in the train—". . . old Zygmunt's dead. He was following a boar-track . . ."—were repeated in my mind so clearly that I thought they came in his live voice; and once I answered him aloud, "That's not the truth, not all of it—you're hiding things!" so that Annette, wakening, came over to my bed to ask if anything was wrong.

The mist which covered the ground those mornings dissolved quickly. For three or four days no cloud showed; at noon the sun was so strong that the fields were hazed. With such fullness and constancy of sunlight it was hard to realize that the year had come to September; away from the house you had that sense of permanence which colours the life of southern lands, with each day lit to copy faithfully the pattern of the one before.

I must rest, Sandra told me, standing in the doorway of my room with her arms full of bed linen, looking vaguely towards the window: I had been through a trying time, I must guard my health carefully for the sake of the little one to come. Under her orders Jendrėk carried a wicker chair to the top of the orchard, and there I sat for a part of every day, sometimes too lazy to return to the house at meal-times, letting Annette wait on my needs and also do my share of the household duties. Seldom had I been so idle; and the somnolence of the countryside, drugged by the sun, seemed to extenuate that idleness. The noises which came to me, a fitful chatter of poultry, the rhythmic whine of a mason's saw, were drowsy, timeless noises.

That somnolence was an illusion. With more than half the men already called up, everyone left on the estate had twice the usual work to get through. Only the tempo had not altered, since the pace at which country people go about their business never alters. The wagons, journeying all day long to the Dowry fields and back, went no faster than a hearse; in response to the drivers' litany the percherons seemed only to stamp like idle soldiers, and as I watched the plume of dust which they spread along the lower ridge they appeared scarcely to be moving at all. About midday, just as in years gone by, Adam, the oldest of the herdsmen, would come across the yard, doff his sheepskin cap to the place where there had once been a crucifix on the wall, relight his pipe and lumber off along the track which his own feet had worn across the meadow. Occasionally Jendrek emerged from the stable he used as farm office and shouted for someone who never seemed to hear. Two or three times in the day the Countess appeared at the farther door, wearing what remained of the fashionable coat which Julius had once bought for her in Berlin, with a bowl of scraps lodged in her arm. Clamped by arthritis, even her movements were slow now; slow, but not less determined than in earlier years; and as she mounted the steps of the portico and picked her way through the ruins of the earlier house (the one the Russians had burnt after the '63 Rebellion), I could fancy I was watching a mechanical toy, rusty from long neglect, which would still perform infallibly whenever the motor was wound. Farther off, there was constant busy-ness among the village houses, women at their washing, handcarts moving through the passageway which led towards the shop. But none of this activity had the look of purpose that one recognizes in cities, where houses are swept away for greater ones to rise, and the surge of motored wheels has the shape of a continuous assault. Here all the traffic I saw, like that of the thousand insects at my feet, was only an unreasoning obedience to natural law: the unending labour to maintain a life which meant no more than staying alive.

This, after seven years' absence, was a mechanism I no longer understood: the tune was familiar, the words were lost. But remotely I had some share in it, for as I sat there idle, not even turning the pages of a French novel Annette had brought me, I was always conscious of the process which continued in my own body. Even now the microscopic cells were forming, parting, coalescing; the primal essences of heart and skull, machineries for seeing, reflecting, uttering thought, had already started to evolve; and though one's part in this work of creation is passive, I never felt it so. I felt, rather, that in keeping my body at ease, my mind as nearly at rest as could be, I was making active preparation for the struggle to which both fœtus and matrix were set.

It was close to here that I had first seen Victor when he returned from his attachment to the French Colonial Army; our earliest walk together as adults had started along the path where Adam was walking now. I had accepted what happened then as a course to which I was destined; and I was content to find that course continuing, as if all that had intervened during our life in cities and in military stations—our disagreements, our failure to achieve parenthood—had been an irrelevance scarcely touching upon reality. . . . Presently I should go and walk in the woods. I might find my way to the cottage where Zygmunt had lived, and if any of his family were there they might recall some detail about his finding me which would ease my curiosity. But for a little longer I should stay here resting, enjoying the sun.

Once, on the third or fourth day, a single aeroplane passed overhead, very high. Once I thought I heard a noise like distant thunder from the west, and I saw Jendrek come out to look that way. But nothing, of course, was to be seen, and after a few moments he went in again.

ii

The flagged hall where we had meals in summer-time, always cool, with a moist smell, turned at the far end into a passage which led to the yard. There, opposite the door of the Countess's workroom, the telephone was fastened to the wall. For years something had been wrong with its bell, which instead of ringing made a clucking noise, as if thousands of crickets had been brusquely disturbed. One realized soon that the whole household was continually waiting for that sound.

I tried to guard myself against this nervous infection; for if the hope of getting a letter from Victor was small—and few letters from any distant place were arriving—the chance of hearing his voice on the telephone was virtually nonexistent. When, like the sudden bark of an order on a parade ground, the chirrup brought everyone to attention, and you heard the scrape of chairs, and the Countess's door opening, I went on with whatever I was doing in the pretence that the current of expectancy did not reach me. But it did.

The sound came rarely—twice in some days, in others not at all—since this link with the rest of the world was only functioning faint-heartedly. Occasionally the Countess was able to speak to friends a few miles away, but more often the answer to her call was a surge of entangled voices from which, at last, that of a tired operator emerged to say crossly "Indefinite delay!" Once Julius, who had gone off to Grodno on political business, managed to get through to us. But however often Sandra tried to get a connection with Lublin, where Wanda had been working, she was told that all the trunk-lines were in military use. Our isolation, then, was almost complete. There was a rumour round the village that General Sosnkowski had won a great victory and was driving the Germans back towards Lvov, but we had no newspapers to confirm it. Henryk, fussing and giggling all day long over the radio-set, got nothing clearly except bursts of martial music from Berlin, or at best a Galician voice which offered us mellifluous encouragement from the Radio Company in London.

"I suppose Julius knows best," Sandra said, pausing in her work to stare out of the window. "I should have thought—if he had to go away again—well, I thought really he might have gone to see if he could be any help to Wanda. Wanda, she's always so bad about catching trains."

The Countess, carrying a boxful of estate papers towards the stairs, stopped to look at her daughter-in-law with the tenuous patience that busy women spare for children.

"Wanda? What is she now—twenty-two? A child of that age can look after herself. She's not like Henryk."

Henryk was standing just behind her, fiddling with his beard. He laughed in his nose; he was used to his grandmother's observations.

Sandra said, "But everything must be so difficult. With all these soldiers everywhere. The Germans may be in Lublin, for all we know—judging by what Julius told me."

"Well, Wanda was always saying she wanted some new experience. In any case you can't expect Julius to spend all his time on rescue expeditions. These days there's more important work for men like him."

"I've got her bed made up," Sandra said vaguely. "I think after dinner I'll try the telephone again."

She must have tried it more often than any one of us knew. Several times I myself saw her slipping off to the passage in a furtive way that was entirely foreign to her ordinary behaviour. But the look of faint, perplexed anxiety which she wore all day was nothing new—I cannot remember that I had ever seen her without it. She was not, I think, deeply depressed. She had nursed her three sons and her daughter through the illnesses of childhood, she was accustomed to seeing her family go away, to knowing they were exposed to various kinds of danger, waiting patiently for their return. The important thing, with her, was that they should find things as they expected. And now, if she did waste some of her time with these fruitless attacks upon the telephone, she neglected none of her duties. You heard her calling after old Anusia as regularly as the cock crowed—had Anusia remembered the mat outside the Count's room, the place on the wall behind Miss Wanda's bed? The morning-room, where Julius worked when at home, was her special-care, and no one else was allowed to share in its ordering. Every day she was there for an hour, perhaps two hours, sweeping and scouring; dusting the framed plans of Khotin, burnishing the swords and the cigarette-box with Pilsudski's inscription, care-fully replacing the baize cover on Julius's desk.

"Stefanie! Stefanie, was that the telephone?"

"No, Belle-mère, I don't think so."

"Oh. Oh, I thought there might be a letter from Julius this morning. Perhaps he's written to his mother, she doesn't always tell me. You don't mind having Annette with you in your room? She's grown, hasn't she?—sometimes she looks quite grown-up. Of course if Victor comes on leave—well, I suppose Annette could go in Wanda's room. Victor, of course—well, Victor was never very good about writing home. It was Casimir. . . . I was going to say, you don't mind doing your own room? You see, we've only got Anusia in the house now. I'm afraid the dust does collect rather in that cupboard. Of course I meant to have the room redone, only you can't get men for anything now. The mobilization, it's upset everything. I think the best way is to use a small brush and pan. You're sure that wasn't the telephone?"

As usual she was on her way to the kitchen, with her yellow duster in her hand, a bundle of linen under her arm; irresolute, like a shy man approaching a room full of strangers. She kept glancing towards where I stood on the stairs, but avoiding my eyes, as if it were she who had done me some injury.

"This afternoon, perhaps Annette could help me. I've got to do the house accounts. I've got rather behind—you see, Anusia is so slow now, she's thinking about the war all the time, though none of her menfolk are in the army. Annette could copy the figures out of the day-book and add them up in pencil."

I promised that she would. "Belle-mère, there's something I wanted to ask you. Zygmunt the huntsman—you remember him—are any of his family still living in the cottage he used to have?"

"Zygmunt? Zygmunt's family? Why, Stefanie?"

"I only wondered."

"Zygmunt's been dead a long time. He was a terrible drinker, you know. But clever at his work, Julius always said."

I reminded her, "It was Zygmunt who found me."

"Zygmunt? Yes. Yes, of course. Only I wasn't there, you know —Julius was all by himself on that trip, just he and Zygmunt. He never took me to that district. There were very rough people in those Ruthenian villages, it wasn't a place for a gentlewoman. . . . You don't think it will tire Annette, doing the figures?"

"No, of course not. Belle-mère, did Zygmunt ever tell you what I looked like when he found me? I mean, was I wrapped in a blanket or anything?"

She searched the floor for an answer, as schoolchildren do. "It was all so long ago. You could have asked Betka when she was alive; Zygmunt must have told her about it." And then she smiled, as if the tedious lesson was over. "It was wonderful for Betka, she'd always wanted a child she could call her own. . . . I must go and help Anusia. You'll call me if you hear the telephone?"

Just afterwards I heard her saying in the kitchen, "It's very foolish, Anusia, listening to all these rumours. Yes, I know the Germans have made big advances—Jendrek has given me all the news. That's a thing for the menfolk to look after. I think I shall take the clothes off the General's bed, and hang them in the open, in the sun."

We owed our comfort to her plodding industry; and in almost all our exchanges she showed me a kindness which I had ill-deserved. Yet I could not help feeling that what she wanted, in return, was not so much my friendship as my support against her own mother-in-law. For her fear of the Countess, which I had perceived even as a child, had not diminished in the years. Even the sound of the workroom door opening brought tension to Sandra's movements, a fresh anxiety to her pale, Prussian eyes. At meals the small, contemptuous hiss which the Countess made as a comment on Sandra's fussing would reduce her to total silence. And in her own room she said to me more than once, glancing about as if the Countess might steal upon us inaudibly:

"Yes, I suppose it's very feeble of me to worry about my sons. My mother-in-law never thinks about hers!"

You could not tell if that taunt had any substance; the Countess had so long kept her emotions in concealment that no one knew if they still functioned. In her eyes, which were always moving, you saw a continuous irony: had they been still they might have revealed a less inclement depth, but then it would have needed a peculiar audacity to look at them at all.

[43]

The burden which her presence seemed to lay on her daughter-in-law could not be assigned to interference. She kept to her own province, which would have been sufficient occupation for a woman far younger than she. Every tray which went to the Count's bedroom—tea or coffee four or five times a day, soup in the morning and at night—was carried by her, for at this time no one but she was allowed to see him. The poultry were under her personal management, so were the estate accounts; and I doubt if Jendrek took any major decision about the work of the farm without her authority. At any time in the day you were likely to find him in the passage waiting for her, morose and statuesque, with his cap under his arm; or else there would be a sheepish queue of labourers who had some request to make, and from inside the workroom you would hear the old woman's bleak voice, half-broken like a schoolboy's.

"Yes, go there by all means if you think it's safer than here! Nobody's forced to work for me. I merely hope you'll find somewhere for your family to live."

She must have existed with very little sleep. However late I went to bed she was still about, generally in her dressing-gown, carrying something downstairs; a curious figure, so small that she gave me the impression of a child made-up to act an old woman's part; and when I woke in the morning I could often hear her dot-and-carry step along the corridor outside. These extra hours, by which she greatly lengthened her working day, were devoted to a labour which I only understood by degrees. She was taking all kinds of treasures from various parts of the house and carrying them downstairs: family silver, relics of the period which she and her husband had spent in Siberian exile, documents and articles of virtu saved from the former house: she was wrapping these possessions in many sheets of newspaper and in hessian sewn with cobbler's thread, packing them in wooden boxes and nailing on the lids. Outside, at the farther end of the ruins, one of the labourers was digging out the earth and rubbish which had long filled an old wine cellar; and from my window, one early morning, I saw him carrying a tea-chest in that direction, with the Countess, still in her dressing-gown and in high rubber boots, limping officiously at his side. In these activities she wore the air of dispassionate calculation which belonged to her normal routine: busy, aloof, never in haste. Whenever I caught sight of her stumping across the hall with one more armful of household gods I thought of a squirrel methodically burying its winter hoard.

Superficially she appeared to be as much absorbed in her own occupations as Sandra in hers. When Henry came to her babbling excitedly that Warsaw was now surrounded, she behaved as if she did not even hear him (though, as I knew, there was little wrong with her hearing). The little attentions which Annette seemed determined to show her met with no greater response. She would listen to anything Jendrek had to tell her, sometimes to the workpeople. To the rest of us, when we spoke, she paid much the same attention as if one of her chickens had started talking: she appeared to find our utterance of some small naturalistic interest, but boring when it happened the second time.

"Anusia says a lot of people have come to the village," Sandra told her.

No reply.

"She says that most of them come from Siechin. She says there was bombing there, two nights ago."

"Well, what did you think it was, all that noise? Did you think someone was beating drums to scare away the nightingales?"

"No, I didn't think that. I didn't know what it was. I was thinking, if it goes on like this there's going to be trouble about food. They say there's a shortage in the town already."

"I should think that is quite a possibility. Unless the people in the town have stopped eating. You're not suggesting there's anything I can do?"

"No, of course not! Only it's about these people from Siechin. They say there's no more room in the village. I suppose they might want to find space for them here."

"Yes, I suppose they might."

"I wish Julius was back. Julius always knows what's best."

"I suppose," said the Countess, "that's why he isn't back."

It was just then that the telephone, after some two days' silence, chirruped again. Each of us strained to run and answer it, but while Sandra and I stayed motionless it was the Countess who went, as if by right. We heard her saying "Yes. . . . A disaster, I agree. . . . Yes, it looks as if everything's practically over", and then she came back to us.

"Sandra," she said, "I wish you'd tell Anusia not to put hard cabbage stalks in the stuff she gives me for the poultry. They can't bear them."

She picked up some medallions she had left on the table and returned to her own room.

[45]

The children—I never thought of Henryk as anything but a child—seemed to be unconscious of any strangeness in this season of narrow tranquillity. Annette, enjoying old familiarities, blithely helpful even when I was least patient with her, might never have heard bombs fall; while Henryk, with his two or three schoolboy jokes and his erratic radio, had all he evidently needed for his range of enjoyment. Did their elders not suffer a feeling of insubstantiality? Is it only in retrospect that I see the house, in those days, as one which ghosts were ready to possess?

They did not crouch, these ghosts, in the ruins outside. Those, a little altered in apparent size, were still the Magic Island and the Kazak Encampment that Casimir and I had once made them, still the open-air schoolroom where I had often given Wanda her lessons. There was nothing spectral about the townsfolk who, appearing like creatures emerged from their winter hiding-place, stood in listless groups along the village road; and the faint disturbance of the western sky, a noise from far away like wagons crossing a boarded bridge, at night a pale flickering, was not more fearful than the approach of a summer storm. It was the house itself, its stillnesses, from which the sense of evanescence came.

You seldom study the things you grow up with, and in earlier years it had not occurred to me how differently it was equipped from others of the same dignity; how little there was of gracious furniture, how much that was stamped with voyage—tin boxes used as cabinets, such chests as soldiers take about the world. Of the portraits which must have lined the former house only two or three had been saved for this; and where the rest should have hung there were only drawings in ink or crayon, mostly Count Kolbeck's youthful work or Julius's. I found, studying them for the first time, that some of the Count's sketches—the two-roomed house he had lived in for six years in the Yakutsk province, the faces of tribesmen who had been his neighbours there—revealed a certain skill and power. His son's pictures of life in the Kadorka prison, the cell he had occupied, the morning exercise, were bolder in conception, more crudely drawn. Yet their work showed me a certain affinity in feeling, and a water-colour hanging nearby, an artless landscape which suggested a female hand, was touched with the same melancholy, a sadness at once of intimacy and estrangement. It was not remarkable that people who were young and in exile should have made these pictures. But I found it strange (and faintly risible) that they should want the rest of their lives to be surrounded by such souvenirs: by faded Warrants of Expatriation, the scorched remains of Polish school-books, a rusty ankle-chain; as if the past gave them a sense of certainty which they could not hope to find elsewhere.

Coming upon me in the dining-room, the Countess might have been listening to my thoughts.

"What are you looking at those for? They mean nothing to you!"

I answered, "Well, I grew up among them."

"They mean nothing to you," she repeated. "You only feel at home where there are shops and theatres, things like that."

I was not afraid of her, as in former days; and yet, as I looked at the brown skull which showed between tight grey coils of hair at the level of my shoulder, I still felt rather like a schoolgirl in the Principal's room.

"It was you," I reminded her, "who made Aunt Betka send me to Switzerland first of all."

"Yes, yes. The trouble is, we have so many people here to whom our country means nothing. You know what's been happening? These Germans"—she pointed carelessly with her chin—"they're finding someone to show them the way at every corner, someone who tells them all about our men's positions. I wanted to give fire-arms to the men on the farm here; I thought they could make some use of them. Julius wouldn't have it. And he was right, of course. They'd be just as likely to turn and fire at the house."

"But surely not if they've been treated properly!"

"My grandfather treated his people very well," she said, with the warmth which every opposition provokes in old people, "even his Ruthenes. He built houses and even schools for them. And they still looked on him as an enemy because he found them work—which they couldn't have found for themselves—and because he punished them when they were too lazy to do it. Nowadays nobody's punished—we're all brothers and sisters. So now they think they don't owe us anything, and they'll sell us to the first bidder. Of course Sandra doesn't believe me."

"What you mean," I said astringently, "is that you think it's dangerous to have me in the house!"

It was perhaps the slight distemper from pregnancy which made me speak so brusquely. I was surprised by my own vehemence; and she, who can seldom have suffered such a frontal assault, was momentarily shocked into silence. I continued the attack:

"You talk as if people like the Kolbecks were a separate creation.

[47]

You think the people I come from have just the same sort of rights as the livestock on the farm. You treat them like wilful children, and then you complain that you can't trust them."

For the first time in my life I saw her passionately angry; and I was surprised to find how much smaller, more commonplace, her fury made her. I remember thinking, 'This, after all, is nothing but the tyrant of a hen-run, a sibyl of the provinces.' And when she spoke again her voice, ragged with emotion, might have belonged to any village woman in a market brawl.

"Trust them! Trust the Ruthenes! The people who've betrayed us again and again!"

I said, "If they'd been treated as human beings——"

"Human beings! Do you know what my husband did for that creature Nilniewicz? Sent him to the finest sanatorium in Poland, then paid for his course at the university——"

"Nilniewicz? I've never heard of him——"

"I'm telling you, Nilniewicz was the sort of man we trusted; we thought we had reason; Julius thought so. There was nothing Julius didn't let him see——"

"But——"

"And how did that creature show his gratitude? Do you think he didn't know those papers were incriminating! Do you think he couldn't have warned Julius, taken the police agent to another room!"

I had no idea what she meant: I discovered only later that she had been talking of Julius's complicity in the 1905 rising. But I did not try to interrupt her again: an old woman sailing before the wind of wrath must go on till it blows itself out. Her voice fell into a relentless monotone.

"That man, he owed everything to us; he admitted it. He was supposed to be the most loyal servant Julius had; devoted to him and Sandra, always sentimentalizing over their child. Don't tell me he didn't know what he was doing! He knew what the Russians were after—they'd been paying him for years, most likely. He must have known what the sentence would be if they got what they wanted. You talk to me about trusting Ruthenes!"

For a moment her breath was exhausted; vigorous as she was, her physique was not equal to such an expenditure of emotion, and there was something pitiable as well as ugly in the spectacle of her small, ancient body vibrating with a passion she had not the strength to use. But she was not a woman I had learnt ever to pity. I said, with the frigid cruelty of the young towards the old:

"I was merely asking you if you think it's dangerous to have me in the house—if you think I might signal to the Germans or something."

She gasped, "That's just what I——"

"And apart from that, I was talking about your general attitude to Ruthenes and other people who spend their lives working for you—not about special cases. This Nilniewicz, he may have behaved as badly as you say; I don't know or care—he's nothing to do with me."

Then, for an instant, she was terrifying. I had spoken with only a casual impertinence; but my words affected her as a puff of wind draws fresh, bright flame from a smouldering fire. The anger in her voice, when she answered, was no longer the dark anger of resentment; it was lit with sarcasm and triumph.

"Nothing to do with you!"

That was all.

Henryk, in his aimless wanderings about the house, was often in his socks. I had not noticed him arriving, and neither I think had she. We only realized that he was in the room because he started to laugh. The Countess turned on him.

"What's the matter with you, Henryk?"

He went on laughing. "Oh, I say, Teffy! Putting Grandma in a bate! Oh, I say!"

I thought it would make the old lady angrier still, this ill-timed buffoonery; but it had the opposite effect. In truth, she always treated Henryk with remarkable forbearance, and the habit of allowing for his feebleness evidently recalled her now to her normal temper. She said, with her voice only slightly tremulous, "The trouble with people who have nothing to do is that they waste other people's time!" And then, still more calmly, while she seemed to be gazing through a hole in my body, "Yes, it's foolish to talk to people about someone they never knew." She limped off down the corridor, and presently I heard her calling for Jendrek again.

Later that day she told me that Count Kolbeck had expressed a wish to see me; she would arrange a time when he was well. And although she made this announcement in a most casual fashion, I guessed that the sequence was not quite accidental. She had evidently said something about our altercation to Sandra as well, for Sandra's manner to me that evening was sodden with embarrassed benevolence—the manner of a virtuous child towards a young brother who has been whipped for mischief. But the Countess's own behaviour returned so quickly, so entirely, to its normal pattern that I found myself almost doubting if the incident had occurred; I came to think of it as children think of the one occasion when, incredulously, they saw a stolid parent in tears.

Yes, it seems to me strange that we should have chosen that time for an infantile quarrel about differences that belonged to the past. I suppose our nerves were a little overstrained. However self-sufficient she appeared, I believe that the Countess was restless for news of her son; while I, for my part, had abandoned self-deception, and the itching hope of some word from Victor—a sheet torn from a message-pad, his voice on the telephone—was infecting every hour of my day. Perhaps these kindred hungers, not to be shared, helped to bring us into open conflict. Perhaps the precariousness in which we lived made me, as well as her, attach new value to the past, seeking there some kind of substantiality.

The phone had gone dead again; there was still no mail. Among the rumours which arrived with every batch of refugees, to sprout luxuriantly among our labourers, there was always a small crop of victories. Once more we heard that the German motorized divisions, outrunning their fuel supplies, were practically at Sosnkowski's mercy, once more the French and British were about to draw the weight of the Wehrmacht across to the west. But a cyclostyled bulletin which one of the newest arrivals brought us, only two days old, spoke of 'local penetrations' and 'blunted spearheads', and those were phrases we could already translate. Beside the drone from the sky, seldom empty now, we were conscious one early morning of a new undertone, which continued through the day. It came from where the trunk road, a mile or two to the south, broke through the Dunik hills, and from a knoll close to the house we could see, like tiny models, a group of lorries creeping beneath a pall of dust; ten or more in a string, with motor cyclists hiving about them, now the outlandish shapes of mobile kitchens, now the minute antennæ of guns; the vanguard, someone told us, of one of our reserve divisions moving to new positions farther east. At dusk I climbed the hill again—it had been a custom of Victor's and mine to take that evening walk—and the column was still passing: a necklace loosely strung with the beads of light which emerged in slow succession from the woods. Some villagers who had also come to watch stood near me, curiously still; and on my way back I passed the Countess herself standing outside the house, a graven image enlarged by the failing light, listening with a critic's sardonic patience to a music she had too long understood.

It went on through the night, that engrossing undercurrent of noise. I found it strange in a house so self-absorbed, where no creak of a hinge, no echo came unfamiliarly, to have the silences possessed by alien sound: as if a ship I lived in had put to sea while I slept, and I had woken to find her absorbed in the tremor of her engines.

iv

I do not know exactly when Cousin Rosalia came. Despite the imposing terraces into which she dressed her steel-coloured hair, her gigantic cameo-brooches, the ruchings and the pleatings which diversified her rather serviceable clothes, the change her presence made in the feeling of the house was a small one. In my earlier life at Setory she had often been with us—looking very much as she looked now—for weeks at a time; and a few days after such a visit we younger members of the household had vaguely realized that she was no longer there. She had once been married to a sailor of some kind—an Admiral, I believe, in the Swedish Navy. He had taken part in an Atlantic exercise and had failed to return to her; from forgetfulness, some said.

Wanda's arrival was a different affair. A corn merchant's van brought her out from the town. Annette found her in the hall, sitting on one of her bursting valises and fiddling at the buckles of her high-heeled shoes: dishevelled, villainously dirty, crumpled with fatigue. When Annette said, "Shall I take your things upstairs?" she answered bitterly, "Take them where you like!" and then burst into unnatural laughter. Even when her mother found and tried to hug her, she only said, "I wish you'd all just leave me alone!" Yet only a few hours later, after a bath and a short sleep, she had so recovered her ordinary temper that it seemed as if she and I had scarcely been parted since the time when she had been my pupil; and I felt then as you do when a vase of daffodils, freshly picked, is brought into your room. She had hugs for all of us now. "Annette, you sweet thing, how dare you grow up without my seeing! . . . Teffy, darling, I've remembered every single thing you ever taught me. I went to Paris—did Mother tell you?—I talked all the French I knew the very first day. They told me they'd never known a foreigner who spoke Portuguese so well."

I see her as she sat at dinner that evening, still tired in the eyes but glowing with the animation which follows weariness: the brilliance of the black hair that I had so often braided, dressed now in a Gallic version of the Polish coiffure; the pliancy of her pen-stroke mouth, which seemed to show me more of her thoughts when idle than when in use. In her ramshackle baggage from Lublin she had contrived to carry uncrushed a dress of olive velveteen with the oblique, low neckline which had been in fashion a year or two before. No lighter stuff would have framed so consonantly the ivory flesh of her neck and breast; and if the light reflected from the tablecloth showed her skin too perfect for a living creature's, her pearls by the contrast of their cold perfection gave it back the warmth of life. To me she was still partly a child (although, coming just twelve years after Victor, she must have been twenty-two at that time), and as she sat there tilting back her chair, letting Sandra fuss over her, winning Annette's idolatry and even Rosalia's crippled smiles, she was like a schoolgirl home for the holidays. But her Kolbeck forehead, the austerely sculptured cheeks, were no longer a child's; the unconscious art with which she moved her graceful arms did not come from the schoolroom, and the smile which I had known as a gloss on her idleness seemed now to draw its light from a subtler self-understanding.

Her family talk was what it had always been—odd sentences allowed to float away as they chanced to reach the surface of her mind.

"But, Mama, I wrote lots of telegrams. I kept giving them to the little porter man; he thought he could send them on some train. Teffy darling, you'd have loved him, he had a little face exactly like a gargoyle. He was a pet, really; he always gave us back the things he'd stolen if he thought we really needed them. Only in the end some Germans came and shot him. No, you see, Mama, he couldn't send the telegrams in the ordinary way because the office wasn't there; it was all in bits across the road."

Hardly listening, Sandra smiled sentimentally, as if her child had only just learnt to talk.

"It doesn't matter, darling—now that you're home." And plainly nothing mattered that night. The troubles of the world were at least half over—one of her brood was safe. "You're sure that's exactly how you like it? I could get Anusia to brown the top a little more. If only I'd known, I'd have tried to get some fish—you were always so fond of fish."

"And where," the Countess inquired, "would you send to for fish?"

"Everything is so difficult nowadays," Cousin Rosalia said.

It amused though it faintly annoyed me to watch Annette, who was leaning over the table and feasting on Wanda's charms. The

Kolbecks could never stop admiring each other. It did not matter that Annette had always been the victim of her young aunt's teasing and superiority: she had eyes for no one but Wanda now.

"Did you get that dress when you went to France? Do you go to dances in it? Do they have dances at the hospital you work in?"

Even Henryk, sitting rather apart as usual and fidgeting idly with his food, showed a flickering interest in his sister's return. He kept glancing at her with screwed eyes, and then at his mother.

"Why is she back? Didn't she like it? Did they turn her out?"

"I showed the Matron Daddy's letter," Wanda was saying; "only she didn't really read it, she was too busy not giving way to excitement. She kept coming and shouting at us to keep perfectly calm. And at night she dashed into all the wards and woke people up to soothe them." She turned to me again. "Teffy, what sort of journey did you have coming here? Was it terribly tiresome?"

"It was slow," I said, "and we were rather cramped."

I went and fetched a winter dress of Annette's which had to be let down; and when the others moved to the verandah, to enjoy the sunset and the softness of the cooling air, I stayed a little way inside the room: I would not be tempted into that circle, where Annette as Casimir's child had her rights but I had none. Wanda herself may have understood my feelings, for she ceased trying to draw me into the conversation; but she kept on throwing me small, sympathetic smiles, and at some of her mother's interjections— "It's a pity you couldn't bring your trunk with you. But I suppose the railway people will send it through"—I caught from her eyes an appeal where humour was shaded with despair. I had seen such a look in the eyes of lecturers worn out by stupid pupils, of grownups jesting to hide their troubles from children. Yes, she had reached maturity.

But was Sandra entirely blind to her daughter's weariness? Was she, like simple people in a theatre, too much bemused by the performance to see an actor beneath the disguise? Or was she just content, with childlike wisdom, to let herself be enclosed in this hour's tranquillity? The light from the window reached her sparsely, and now that the smaller flexions were invisible, her heavy, square-cast face showed something of the dignity which belongs to primitive man. Except to deal with her knitting—she was turning a heel—she hardly took her eyes from her daughter's face. I doubt if she even tried to understand what Wanda was saying: she listened—to the rippling account of hospital life, of the twelve hours' journey in a lorry full of soldiers—as mothers listen to schoolboys boasting of their sports. And yet it seemed to me, just then, that the intensity of her devotion raised it above mere sentiment. If the gifts she brought to maternity were not remarkable, she exercised them with something near to an artist's singleness of mind.

"But, childie, surely the officer who was sitting by the driver would have given you his place if you'd asked him! . . . But it's dreadful, dreadful to think of people losing their homes like that! . . . Listen, darling, you'll have to go through your winter things with me. I moved some of them into my own big cupboard, it's best to let the air get at them. There's probably enough to keep you going till the trunk comes. Only nothing you could wear for a party."

"Well, perhaps that doesn't matter——"

"Such a beautiful dress," said Rosalia, "my little sewing-woman made for me. The one in Franciszkanska. With twin swans worked in passementerie. I couldn't bring it with me—my little sewing-woman said it couldn't possibly be folded. I suppose I shan't ever see it again now."

"Poor Rosalia!"

"And I suppose, in any case, the fashions will all be quite different after the War."

"It's possible!" the Countess said.

Incapable of idleness, she was plucking a cockerel she had killed that afternoon, with a piece of sacking over her knees. Seated a little apart from the rest, engrossed like a small grey spider in her work, she appeared to be an invigilator rather than a member of the party. But her head was turned so that her better ear would catch what Wanda was saying ; once or twice I saw her glancing towards her granddaughter's face, and her swift fingers momentarily resting, as if even she were charmed by the phosphorescence of this creature's tired vitality. She herself was showing signs, rare with her, of weariness: and I think she was glad to let herself float, with us, in this pool of time which the current seemed to have left behind. The moon, screened by cloud, must have been near the full that night: the evening haze peculiar to Setory in this season showed as a blue-white curtain, almost opaque between the trees, a boundary wall to the tract of darkness in which our small island of light was set. Within this boundary the freshened air, still warm, smelling of stone, lay against our faces like the water of a clear pool. The murmur from the trunk road had petered out, and in the succeeding quietness the sounds which came to us from the village as if through an instrument of extreme fidelity—a burst of laughter, a woman's voice scolding—were the sounds of every day, comfortably familiar, remote from our concern.

"You're sure you don't feel cold, Grand'mère? Perhaps we ought to go inside now. Perhaps Wanda will sing for us?"

"Oh, Wanda, do—please!"

"I'm sorry, Annette. No, Mama, I don't think so, not tonight." Henryk had started tittering. ". . . Like a corncrake!"

"She sings so beautifully!" Cousin Rosalia said. "How I remember—ever since she was a little girl! Aren't you pleased, dear, to be safe at home? Oh, I think it's so wonderful to be safe!"

"Perhaps it is getting rather chilly now. That dress of Annette's, it's rather thin——"

"She has a jersey if she needs it," I said.

But no one moved. And although, with Victor missing, there was nothing to join me to those people, the force which kept them in their places held me as well. Was it only the force of inertia? Or were we like children who, screwing their knuckles into their eyes, imagine themselves transported to some magic country, and almost believe that it will still be there when their eyes open? It is easy in retrospect to imagine that certain moments came with a feeling of significance, when in truth they have derived their meaning from events that followed. All I know is that the image of that session remains upon a separate page of my memory, like a photograph in a family album; blurred at the edges now, and with the peculiar unreality which such photographs reveal, a posed and dated look. There is Sandra in the little nursing chair which she always preferred, with a high muslin collar that her own mother might have worn and a taffeta dress which pours like a drift of sand from her shoulders to the floor: a Veronese madonna copied by some German amateur, a figure of tradition, immutable as the earth itself. At the other side of the bamboo table Rosalia, holding herself as girls were taught in the upper-class gymnasiums of the nineties and mincing at her needlework, belongs to the same costume-piece; and beside their period bloom there is something faintly exotic in the appearance of Wanda—with the light from an upper window falling lavishly on her urban toilette, on the conscious sensibility of her mouth and eyes—as if an epoch instead of a mere generation divided her from them. I see Annette in her demure Sunday dress, chin on folded hands, as a child of their time rather than Wanda's; while the Countess alone, watching from the farther shadow, so far aged as to be ageless, seems to be contemporary with them all. Even the sounds from the village have subsided now, and the stillness which comes upon us like the stillness of expectancy lays hold on Henryk as well. The grimaces he is always making, the nervous working of lips and jaw, have ceased, so that in those few moments the child-like eyes, resting curiously on Wanda's face, have almost the innocent beauty which Casimir's once held for me. Rosalia has put down her work, the Countess's hands have fallen to her side, there is only the fluttering of moths where the shafts of light intersect.

When Annette had gone to sleep, that night, Wanda came to my room and sat on my bed. She said:

"Teffy, darling, why are you such an old sulk? Why do you keep backing away from us, as if you'd got some infectious disease?"

I told her, as well as I could.

"But, Teffy," she said, "that's all past history—now that Casimir's right the other side of the world. And since he'd got a new wife of his own before you ran away with Victor——"

"You can argue that out with your father," I said (gently, I hope). "I can't."

"But in any case you don't think that I come into the quarrel?"

"You belong to them," I told her.

"But don't you, too? Don't you want to?"

"Only to Victor."

She nodded then, in the serious way of her childhood, accepting my correction of a faulty exercise. "It's all so stupid, now." Just as in childhood, she let her body fall back till her head rested against my side; and it was partly a child who presently spoke again, with her eyes shut, in the flaccid voice of one whose reserves are long overdrawn:

"The way Mother talks, it frightens me—it's like someone talking in her sleep. They don't realize in the least what's happening—none of them understand."

v

If that was so, they were a little enlightened next day, when Julius returned. He arrived in what looked like a military car, and went straight to his mother's workroom, where she and Sandra were having one of their uneasy conferences about the finances of house and farm. Presently Sandra, looking about for someone to confide in, came and found me in my room.

"The General's come back," she said, keeping her eyes away from mine.

I said something like 'I'm so glad!' but she did not respond to this show of sympathy.

"He's talking to his mother," she told me, as if to sustain a flagging conversation. "He says the news is very bad."

"The Germans are still advancing?"

"It's something to do with the Russians. It's not very clear; I don't think even Julius knows exactly what's happened. . . . I'm worried about Annette. Perhaps you'd better not say anything to her—we must try to find something to keep her occupied; there must be some old books of Wanda's, or perhaps she'd like to do something on the farm. . . ."

Julius himself had not much more to tell me when we met in the hall a little afterwards. He first walked past me as if I were some farm-hand who had come for an advance of wages, but then he returned to ask, with an unexpected and rather embarrassed kindness, whether Annette and I were in good case.

"You've heard," he said sombrely, "the Russians have crossed our border?"

"Does that mean we've got to fight them as well?"

He shrugged his shoulders. "If we can find any sort of force to fight them with!" and went on to his own room.

Oddly, it was Cousin Rosalia who seemed to grasp the significance of the news more firmly than anyone else. She got me into a corner that evening and whispered, with a schoolma'am's disconcerting gravity, that she had been studying a medical book all afternoon.

"And now," she said, in a voice of fluttering complacency, "I know exactly how to obtain my Release when the time comes. I am quite certain that is the right thing to do. My husband was not all that he might have been to me, but he would not have wished me to be violated by the Bolsheviki. You do agree with me, dear? And you won't say anything to Sandra? I should not like her to have any kind of anxiety, she has always been so generous, I do not wish her to be troubled by any plans of mine which may interfere with her own."

vi

For myself, I still felt only an outsider's interest in what was happening. Plainly the Kolbeck women could no longer regard the War as something which affected them only indirectly. But since

I was detached from the Kolbecks, I had the illusion of detachment from events they were involved in as well: the War was a Polish concern, and I had preserved till then a latent pride in not being a Pole. That, at least, is how I remember my impression of those days. But most of that tract in memory has become relatively featureless because of a single peak which dominates it all. In the night that followed Julius's return, there was one half-hour which had the distorted reality of a vivid dream; and as the effluvium of such dreams persists in wakefulness, so the colour of that experience tinges all my recollections of the season which followed.

In the first, shallow sleep I was just aware that the sound of movement from the trunk road had started again. This did not disturb me, and I was only partly wakened when a car, approaching noisily, halted with a violent scraping of gravel outside the house. I think I fell asleep again, but was freshly roused by voices from the stairs; and then, feeling intuitively that I was somehow concerned, I opened my door and stood there in my dressing-gown to listen. The voice I heard was Julius's—his deadly quiet, military voice.

"*Only* half an hour? You've surely served long enough to know that battles can be lost by smaller margins than that! . . . Brigade Commander? I don't care if you had permission from the Commander-in-Chief, that's not what I'm talking about. You're not fighting for the favour of Generals, you're fighting for Polish soil."

The voice which answered that tirade came so faintly that I could not hear the words. In one instant I thought it was Victor's, in the next that this was hallucination; for rational people do not expect the hopes they live by to be fulfilled. But when the visitor spoke again I caught the words ". . . make the slightest difference! . . . my wife, whatever you say, and I've got the right to see her." Then I was no longer in doubt.

The instinct which urged me to run to him headlong was checked by another, derived perhaps from a sort of cowardice, perhaps from the knowledge that Victor could never bear me to be demonstrative in public. I found myself walking quite slowly, and as if casually, towards the head of the stairs, and though my whole body was trembling I do not think the tremor showed.

Julius was standing near the bottom of the staircase. He saw me starting to come down and made a movement as if he would have barred my passage; but he was, of course, too sane a man to do anything like that. He merely watched me intently as I passed him, and said undramatically:

[58]

"You'll be very foolish if you keep him away from his duty. He has absolutely no right to be here."

The light in the hall was poor, intermittently fading as it always did when the batteries had run low. Victor was leaning against the dining-table with one bootless foot on a chair, while Sandra, on her knees beside him, unwound a bandage from his ankle. When he caught sight of me he said, "Oh, there you are, Stefanie!" and immediately turned to Sandra again: "Mother, it really isn't worth the bother—the orderly did it a few hours ago—it's only a graze, anyway." I went to him and kissed him soberly, as one would a brother: in this house, where our known relationship had been that of brother and sister, it would not have seemed natural to do anything but that; and his response was almost as casual as a brother's would have been. While Sandra said patiently, "Still, Victor, do keep still!"

When I tried to speak to him I found myself wordless, as if the nervous system connecting brain and vocal chords had been taken away. Yet I could speak to Sandra, and though my voice sounded more brusque than I intended, it was not an abnormal voice. "I'll do that!" I said, and I took the bandage away from her. She did not resist.

The wound, as Victor had said, was a shallow one, but it had been clumsily dressed and there was dirt in it that even I could see. I said, "Wait, I'll have to get some water," and then found that Sandra had a warm solution of disinfectant ready. She had everything ready. She handed me as I needed them a fresh dressing, a bandage, a clip-fastener; silently, as a professional nurse would. The operation must have given Victor some pain, but being a Kolbeck he showed no sign of it. He only said rather irritably, as I worked, "Don't get it too tight. . . . There are one or two things I wanted to get fixed up. I can't stay more than ten minutes; I've got to get back in the column at Nunokie." That was obviously meant for Julius, though addressed to me.

The outside door was still open, and on the rim of vision I saw a soldier standing 'at ease' there, an orderly or driver stolidly awaiting his next instructions. But he and Julius were not the only spectators. A sound above made me look towards the balustrade which fenced the upper landing, and there the Countess in her poultry-farming coat was gazing down at us with a contemptuous impartiality, as if to supervise some chastisement which she herself had ordered; while Rosalia, decked in a laborious modesty of cap and shawls, stood just behind her, uttering little gasps of fatuous concern. No one said a word; and beneath this cloud of silent witnesses Sandra and I continued kneeling side by side, with the object of our embarrassed devotion observing it in glum detachment, the light continually fading. This situation I accepted then as one accepts the incongruities of dreams. In time, I thought, in time this crust of sensation will break, and the heart's spring will start to flow once more.

I made the bandage as neat as I could and pulled his sock over it; helped him to put on the boot again. "We'll go upstairs," I said, taking his arm. He hesitated, looking about him in an incredulous way which I understand now that I see how the house must have looked and felt to him. Then he said in the voice of his angry moods, "Yes, we'd better," and marched stiffly across the hall.

If Julius had interfered with us, I should have had an excuse for the outburst which I needed to relieve my feelings. But he denied me that catharsis. In total silence, like children in disgrace, we went past him up the stairs; and only as I was shutting the door of my room did I hear the Countess's frigid voice:

"I should have thought she might have found him something to eat!"

'My room'? There were clothes and other things of mine about it, my child asleep in the smaller bed, but the room was never mine, much less mine and Victor's; it belonged to the house, and this house, where our love had been so trammelled by the need for vigilance, still held us in its constraint. Almost a stranger, he sat on my bed, fingering my hand as if it were just a part of his equipment; a man imprisoned by uniform, smelling of river slime and of all exhausted soldiers, staring with bloodshot eyes at some scene from the hours behind.

"The fuss!" he said bitterly. "He talks to me as if I was a deserter —and as like as not I'll be at Nunokie before the first squadron— I'm saving ten kilometres, whatever the road's like. Does he really think I'd give away a chance like this—what does he think I am, a —— machine! Does he realize I was fighting those swine less than eight hours ago! And now it's those devils of Russians; we're going to be right in among those bastards before tomorrow's out, if the programme works. Does he realize that! Or does he think I'm being just bloody idle because I stop to spend five minutes in my own home!"

Five minutes—and one more was flowing to waste. But I knew that this mood of his could no more be charmed away than sickness, it could only work itself out. And now his vehemence had wakened

Annette, and she was sitting up to stare at him with sleepy curiosity.

"It's Uncle Vic! Mummy, how did he come?"

Her voice reached his understanding as mine had failed to do. He said, "How's life, Annette?" with the smile he had not yet found for me. I was desperate now.

"Annette," I said, "you must go away—I can't have you in here!"

"Away? Where to, Mummy?"

I answered ruthlessly, "I don't mind where you go, you've got to get out of here. Quickly—go on!"

I watched her, bare-legged in her skimpy night-dress, moving towards the door with a languor which at the time I thought mere wilfulness. I waited, teeth in lip, while the door shut slowly behind her. Then I went swiftly and turned the key. Victor sat with his chin on his breast, his eyes nearly shut, gulping spastically as labourers do in summer heat; and I knew it was my business then—not his—to remain collected, finding courage for us both. But the torrent of thoughts dammed up in weeks of loneliness, now rushing to escape into one small pool of time, was no longer subject to my control. I found myself talking frenziedly, as a homesick child would—"Victor, I can't stay here—they treat me like an adulteress—your father . . . "—with the words floundering in a race of tears; I clung to him like a frightened swimmer and felt his tired body shaking with the convulsion that tore my own. So clasped we fell like a single trunk across the bed; it was he who found a residue of strength, to bring his mouth to mine; and for one unmeasured interval of time the huge simplicity of passion supplanted every misgiving, all complexities, all grief: until his crushing embrace relaxed and I realized—after a little while—that he was dead asleep.

The temptation to let him sleep on would have been too great; but the sound of cautious steps and whispering outside the door reminded me that we were not really alone. At first he would not wake: I had to wipe his face with a damp towel, and then to pull up his head with my hands clasped behind it. Once roused, however, he came immediately, in the way of seasoned soliders, to an exaggerated wakefulness. He was on his feet in a moment, shaking himself out, glancing about for his helmet. "What's the time? You shouldn't have let me sleep!" His hands were attending automatically to straps and buttons. "Nunokie, thirty kilometres—thirty-five. I'll have to be quick."

[61]

For me the phase of hysteria had given place to a deadening weariness, as if a fever of the heart had passed its crisis and steeply abated. The occasion began to look as commonplace as a hundred others—the impersonality of bedrooms in hotels or married quarters, Victor scrambling to get to some duty on time—and my speech had recovered its ordinary calm. "Does the bandage feel all right? You'll send me news when you can?" It was a small voice only, from within, which said persistently, 'This is the time you've longed for all these days. . . . This is the last time.'

"Victor!" That was Julius calling.

He answered, "I'm coming now."

The small voice at that moment took command. I heard myself saying in the tone of every day, fluttering only a very little:

"You do realize I'm going to get away from here if there's a chance? I don't belong here—I only belong to you."

He said abstractedly, "Away from here?"

"I've got an idea about getting to Lemberg. The Germans will want people to work in the hospitals. I can do that, I can nurse after a fashion. If I got there, I could live with the Sosnkowskis."

"The Sosnkowskis?" With a map spread on the bed he was tracing his route to Nunokie, still hardly listening to me. "Lemberg? The Germans don't let people move about as they like. . . . Thirty-two, thirty-three—yes, thirty-four kilometres. . . . No, even if you could move (which you can't), you've got to stop here."

"Victor darling, why?"

"Because I say so. Because you've got to be looked after—there's the child coming."

"That's why I want to get away. He won't be my child if he's born here. He'll just be another Kolbeck."

"That's what I want him to be."

Someone was banging on the door now, and this time we heard Sandra's tearful voice, "Victor! Victor, the time's going on!"

"All right, Mother! I'm just ready."

His eyes had clouded with a look I had sometimes seen in his childhood, when we others had got him trapped in the game of Cossack Patrol: the incredulous anger of one so confident in his own powers that he cannot understand frustration. On a calmer occasion I should have known how to lead him away from that bewilderment, and often, in weeks to come, I was to blame myself for having clutched at those precious moments so greedily that they were broken and lost; yet I see, from this distance, that the squeeze of time did not allow me to act or speak as a sensible woman would. I started trying to explain my feelings, and he overrode me with a weary petulance:

"Stefanie, listen, you've got to be reasonable—it's not fair to me, this talk of running away from Setory. I've got to know that you're being looked after——"

"By your father——?"

"I know you don't like him—you've never really known him ——"

"Is there anything to know! Anything but chauvinism and callow piety! Victor, can't you understand—do you suppose he can care for me when he thinks I'm not really your wife at all?"

"It's not a question of what he thinks!" He spoke with his lips hardly moving, his eyes were almost shut. "We aren't entitled to have a child—if you don't realize that, I do. We can't undo what's been done already. But the child can be dedicated. He can be brought up as a Catholic, he can be taught to give the whole of himself to God and to Poland."

"Is that all you want for him?" I asked. "Nothing but that?"

And now he caught hold of me by the arms.

"Listen, Stefanie, listen, you've got to promise me that! You've got to swear you'll let him be brought up here in the way Father wants—the way I want. You've got to promise me that!"

In an uprush of bitterness which made me almost speechless I whispered, "Why? Why should I promise you things if our marriage had no meaning——?"

"Promise me!" he repeated, as a spoilt child would. "Promise me!"

His hands, fastened on my arms like the teeth of a vice, were hurting me severely; and had this cruelty continued I might have resisted, for I had never submitted to that part of the Kolbeck nature either in Casimir (where it showed very rarely) or in him. But when he saw that I was actually crying he relaxed his grip, sliding his hands into my armpits and holding them there in a way of his own, kissing me damply on the temples and on the eyes. He began to plead, in the little-language we had made for ourselves, and I think that he himself was weeping. He was a child still, but a different child, against whom I had no defences. I whispered, "Yes, picci' diletto . . . yes, beloved, yes!"

If we embraced again it left no impression, for the power of human creatures to feel emotion is mercifully confined, and the stupor which overcame all but my physical senses prevented me in those moments from imagining what morning would bring to this forspent soldier, or the coming weeks to me. I had watched so often the little, instinctive actions he was performing now—the adjustment of the brace, the finger-check of pouches—that I failed to remind myself 'This is the last time. . . .' And when I heard his light, familiar phrase, "Au pas, camarades!" and my own "Adieu!" the words had no importance because I could not accept the finality they contained. I still had sense enough to know that we could not part in the family's presence, so it was in that room that he left me, almost as casually as a business-man going off for his morning train. And even as I listened to the voluble farewells in the hall, and afterwards to the dwindling whine of the car, I had the feeling only that a tiring incident was over, not that the dark of loneliness had finally closed down. I remember that when Annette returned, and told me she had been frightened by the noise of the guns, I said, "What guns?"—thinking she must have been dreaming about our earlier experience. When she asked me in a childish way what Uncle Victor had come for, I said truthfully that I could not remember—it must have been for something he had left behind.

"You must get to bed," I told her; "you know you shouldn't have been running about the house as late as this."

vii

The stupor seemed to wear off, as a dentist's narcotic does; only the grief did not immediately return. What came, as I lay awake, was merely physical pain, of an odd, small kind: the play of thoughts, like fish crossing and darting, produced a species of heat which hurt me behind the eyes as strong sunlight does.

Silence and darkness magnify such trivial afflictions. For some time I sat on the edge of my bed, fearing that if I put on the light I should waken Annette, who had already suffered too much from my unkindness; and at last, unable to bear the incandescence of my thoughts, I gathered my clothes, dressed, and went down into the yard.

Here the coldness of the air soothed me, and the solitude which had been intolerable indoors grew swiftly into a sense of tranquillity. The darkness was beginning to weaken, letting the outlines of the farm buildings show as in a misty photograph; there were faint, friendly sounds from the movement of the wind and the stirring of beasts. I should have stayed there, leaning against the water-trough, in something like contentment; but presently the sound of schoolboy tittering from the direction of the house told me that I was no longer alone. That sound, at such an hour, was wildly alarming; but when the shock of it had passed I remembered that Henryk had always made a habit of wandering about at night, and I was not surprised when the figure that emerged from shadow gathered shape as his, dressed in the peasant blouse and linen trousers which were his everyday wear. He came to me confidently, as one used to moving in the dark, held my hand in the simple and affectionate way he sometimes had, and began to talk as if there were nothing extraordinary in such a meeting as this.

"The old brother," he said, "—old Victor, he's been here. Saw him myself. They didn't think I was looking. I saw him, all the same."

I answered that I had seen him too.

He laughed. "All got up for the War—blood on him, too; I saw it!"

"Yes, he's had a flesh wound on the ankle. It's very slight."

He became more serious. "He'll get killed, I suppose. That's what happens—I know that." This reflection seemed to occupy him not unpleasantly for a few moments, in which he repeated, "Get killed—yes—it always happens, it comes on the radio." And then, abruptly, he asked, "What are you doing? It's too early, there's no one up yet."

"I thought of going for a walk," I told him.

"A walk? Yes, a walk, a walk! With me? A walk with me?"

There was a note of childish pleading in that question. I had spoken impulsively, merely wishing to get away from him; but now I felt that I could do with companionship, and that a creature too simple to be curious about my thoughts would serve me better than any other. I said, again upon impulse:

"Do you remember old Zygmunt? Zygmunt the huntsman? I was going to try to find his cottage. I went there once before."

"Zygmunt? The old man? Zygmunt's not there, he's dead, ever so long."

"I know, but I'd like to see his cottage. Could you find it, Henryk?"

"Cottage?" he repeated.

I had learnt to be patient with the loitering of his mind. I waited, and after a little while he set off along the track which the herdsman used, leading me rather as one leads a foal. In that fashion we reached the lower ridge, and then in single file we took the first of the paths which climbed through the demesne woods. He was, indeed, almost a perfect companion for that excursion; for he knew

[65]

the paths so well that the darkness scarcely seemed to hinder him, his pace was easy and he did not talk at all.

How far was it, by this route? A dozen kilometres? I have only earlier memories to guide me, since I spent part of this expedition as nearly asleep as one may be when one's legs are moving. Even where we started to go downhill and the thinning of the woods encouraged the small increase of light, I felt as if I walked in sleep; for my bodily fatigue was overreached by the deadness of my senses. The path, made in parts by watercourses, was very rough, here paved with ragged boulders, here rutted by the timber sleds, ridged by the roots of trees; yet my feet took it so surely and—as it felt—so lightly that I was hardly aware of its awkwardness. The sight of Henryk's shoulders, as he plodded a few yards ahead, gave me continuous confidence. Even the knot of pain which the night's distress had lodged in my forehead was easy to bear now, and in this liberation from the body's harness I could surrender myself to the morning, its freshness and calm. Few birds were awake. The twigs I trod on were dry from the long summer, and the stir of leaves in the early wind came with a dry, brittle sound; but where the trees stood thickly the hillside had kept some moisture from the spring rains, and at this first hour the earth's breath was moist, smelling of wood-moss and rotted leaves. Such sweetness of odour and sound, and the coldness of the wind on my face, gave to this ethereal world a reality against which the night's deformities appeared to have been illusion; a completeness, which the protraction of dusk seemed to make permanent. What light there was, from a heavy sky, filtered by the tracery of branch and leaf, resembled the light in city churches, mysteriously opaque; and a gap carved by the fellers was like the great east window of a church, through which I looked across an archipelago of tree-clumps floating in mist to the grey, succeeding contours of the wooded country beyond the Selm.

This new creation of shadow and mist, of pungent earth and licking wind, was all my own; until a bush I saw, darker than the foliage round it, detached itself and assumed the shape of a child, who called on us to halt and demanded our business. He was dressed up as a soldier, and since he had a rifle pointed at us we halted. I said—it was the first thing that came to my mind—that we were on our way home after a tour of rabbit-snares; and after some colloquy with a second soldier who appeared he let us go on, advising us to hurry. Farther on we were challenged again.

And now all the country seemed to be planted with soldiers, who lay in clumps beside the path, wrapped like chrysalids in their field-coats, or with a blanket to cover two or three together. A few, leaning against the trees, turned their heads to stare at us with the dull curiosity of cattle, but most of them slept like corpses, and one against whom I stumbled—he was lying with his legs right across the path—only murmured a protest, not moving at all: it did not alarm me, this population which had grown out of the ground, for most of them, as I saw, were only boys, resting so still that they disturbed the new day's quietness no more than the surrounding stumps and scrub. We crossed a metalled road—it must have been the shorter and rougher road which eventually reaches Nunokie—where a wagon train was halted, with its horses grazing on the verge. Here men were cooking at the roadside, others attending sleepily to the wagons, making rough screens of branches to hide them; and one who rode up and down the line on horseback was calling on all and sundry to look alive, but without much effect. A young officer, with the irises almost submerged in his drenched and bloodshot eyes, told us that we should do better to get home and stay there. When Henryk began to ask him questions, he turned to lean against a horse's flank and there fell asleep as he stood.

I could see that Henryk was anxious now, in the way that dogs are when you take them on some new kind of journey. He kept close to my side, constantly glancing at my face in childish inquiry. "The noise," he asked, "does it matter, is it all right?" My own ears caught no sound, but I knew what he meant, for the wind had dropped and the air, still and tight, seemed to vibrate a little; the horses were showing signs of disturbance, and the motley groups of soldiers, sprawling all over the short turf like holiday excursionists, seemed to catch their restlessness, so that here and there one struggled to his feet, turned his head all ways to listen and then sank into sleep again. I took hold of Henryk by the arm, afraid lest the concerns of these strangers should intrude on our spell of peacefulness. I said, "Go on, go on, it's quite all right!"

For some distance the voice of a man in a tilted truck followed us, saying over and over again, "Reception weak, reception weak, repeat your signal!" but when we had passed through another tongue of woodland it faded from my ears and my gliding thoughts. The causeway that we followed now, built up with turves and fortified with brushwood, skirted a mere which went dry in summer, leaving a tract of hardened slime with a fringe of grey rank weed; it was a place I remembered well, for in childhood we had often come here in the pony-carriage, and once Victor and I had

[67]

skated on the mere by moonlight. At this point I might have turned back, since the stated object of our walk hung only loosely in my mind; but the wildness and mournful colouring, the petulant cries of wildfowl flying low across the mud as if they had lost their homes, were in harmony with my present mood. Here, with Setory well behind me, my mind was at least in freedom. Henryk, whistling contentedly, had got some way ahead, and I hurried to catch him up.

viii

Although my recollection of Zygmunt's cottage had been so hazy, it seemed familiar as soon as I caught sight of it: one of three or four, pitched down between a sluggish brook and a wind-brake of limes, dwellings so crudely made of larch and mud, patched up with strips of iron, that in the settled early light they looked like a child's modelling. They showed no sign of human life, not even a chimney-pipe smoking; and but for the presence of a mangy she-goat tied to one of the trees, a profusion of draggled hens scratching in the dirt or squabbling for perches on the roofs, I should have thought the place had long since been deserted, in the way of such primitive habitations. Nearly all the windows that I saw had boards or branches nailed across them. I shouted and got no reply.

The cabin nearest the stream was the one Zygmunt had lived in; I think the others had all been occupied by relations of his, without much distinction of ownership. When I knocked on the front wall of this one I thought I heard a faint noise from within, and that encouraged me to go round to the other side, where I tried the door without success. Henryk came to my help then. "You want to go in?" he asked; and before I could interfere he threw his weight against the door, which, with a sound of matchwood splintering, yielded. Inside, in the half darkness, I found an elderly peasant woman crouching back against the farther wall, clutching a great gilt crucifix against her breast, almost paralysed with fright.

How earnestly, now, I wished I had never started on this impulsive and senseless errand; but to leave the petrified creature to find her own senses was a cruelty of which—light-headed as I was—I was not quite capable. With a smile that must have looked artificial and foolish I greeted her, and found a place to sit on a bench which stood there. I said:

"You mustn't be frightened, there's nothing to be afraid of—please, please, I come as a friend."

It must have taken me a quarter of an hour to calm her; and though I can smile a little at the recollection, I did not find the experience amusing. For a long time she would not listen to a word I said. She knelt on the floor, holding the crucifix in one hand, with the other stretched out as if to ward off a blow. She begged for mercy, addressing me and the Blessed Virgin by turns, sometimes whimpering like a beaten puppy, sometimes gabbling incoherently about the Germans and how she had never wished them any harm. (She may have been drinking; I did not know, for among the foul odours of that hovel her breath gave me no clue.) And all the time that I was imploring her to trust me, and she grovelling and pleading, the insufferable Henryk continued to watch us from the door, the charmed spectator of a fashionable comedy, occasionally giggling as if we had reached a specially witty line; while the hens walked past him in and out of the room and fought each other for the crumbs they snatched from the folds of the woman's dress. But at least, as my eyes got used to the gloom, I discovered who she was. I remembered a woman of rather distinctive appearance I had seen about this place in earlier years, who was understood to be a casual daughter of Zygmunt's by a French girl the Kolbecks had once employed, and the straight nose and high cheek-bones told me that this dilapidated creature was the same. I was able, then, to address her by name—"Don't you remember me, Tilka? I used to come and see you!" and, using it constantly, to talk about her father.

"He was so kind to me, Tilka, he made a little whip for me. Don't you remember? I was grieved when I heard that he was dead. It must have been a great sorrow to you, Tilka."

She was calm enough, at last, to answer a few questions about Zygmunt, much in the way of a poacher who is being cross-examined, with sidelong glances at my face which were by no means those of a senseless woman: probably she had been hiding food and such poor treasures as she possessed, and still imagined that the Germans had sent us to trick her into revealing them. But she had the peasant appetite for talking of her kin, and by degrees this weakness overcame her caution. Her father had been a good man, she told me, and had never ill-treated her except at times of 'weakness'. In his last days he had suffered from his 'heart' (by which I understood that she meant some kind of mental disorder); afraid to sleep, because of the evil dreams which troubled him, he had often talked to her throughout the night about his life and the sins he had committed against the Holy One; but he had

[69]

died with the Father and the Blessed Oil, so she supposed his soul might be at rest. This recital came in gobbets, out of all order, interspersed with the crudest piety, naïve self-justification, fumbling irrelevance. And all the time she was watching me with a sly curiosity and with something more than the shrewdness of her kind. I said, at length:

"You do know who I am?"

"Of course, Ladyship, of course, everyone knows."

That was nothing but conventional politeness.

"I come from the Great House——"

"Of course, Ladyship. The whole country knows you."

"And I owe a great deal to your father, whom God rest."

"No, no, Ladyship; the other way, the other way! Zygmunt was giving thanks to God all day for your Ladyship's goodness."

These civilities might have continued till nightfall, but I was not in the mood to relish them as she did. The pain in my head had increased, I longed to get back to the freshness of the morning.

"You know," I said, "that it was Zygmunt who found me when I was a baby—I should have died if he hadn't."

This statement, made quite casually, had a curious effect, as if I had remarked to a servant that some small article was missing from my room. The set of Tilka's face hardly altered: only her eyes became quite blank, as if a screen had been drawn over them, and from many dealings with such people I knew that behind this screen her mind was working like a horse-thief's, at frantic speed. There was just a moment's silence, and then words poured from her in a cataract.

It was nothing to do with her, she said, and she didn't know what the Ladyship meant—Zygmunt had never talked about what happened on hunting trips. A good servant, Zygmunt had been, an obedient servant, who had never done aught but what the young master (she meant my father-in-law) had told him. The little house might have caught alight by itself—Zygmunt had never known. The young master had said there was a thief in the house; he had told Zygmunt to fire a shot to frighten him. A gun might easily fire wrong, you could never be certain, especially in the dark, and no one had told him about a woman being in the house—the young master had said there was no one there but Nilniewicz himself, who was nothing but a Russian spy, so the young master had told him. . . . Without experience of country people, I should have made nothing of this rigmarole; but having grown up among them I had an idea how the pattern of truth could sometimes be traced

[70]

within the mosaic of their falsehoods and evasions. I asked, rather abruptly:

"It was at night, then?"

"At night, Ladyship?"

"This shooting you've mentioned. It was at night, so Zygmunt couldn't really see what he was doing?"

"But of course—it was the darkest night of all the year, he couldn't see his own hand in front of him."

"Of course, your father was not much of a shot," I remarked. "He was not as good as some of the other huntsmen."

"With gracious pardon," she answered, "there was never a better hand with a gun, not the young master himself—not in all Poland!"

"But he couldn't shoot well at night, your father?"

"With gracious pardon, he killed her with his first shot. The young master himself——"

"Killed her—killed whom?" I asked.

Confused, she became cautious again.

"How should I know, Ladyship? No one knew if Nilniewicz had a wife or not. There were some that said—after he'd run away from the Great House——"

But I would not let her wander any more, I meant her to go at my own pace now. "You tell me," I said, "that your father didn't know there was a woman inside when he set fire to the house?"

"But it wasn't Zygmunt!" she said with vehemence. "I've told your Ladyship—I tell her again, with gracious pardon—it was the young master put fire to it."

"And Zygmunt was to wait outside and shoot at Nilniewicz if he tried to escape?"

"How can I tell? An old man such as Zygmunt was when he died, an old man isn't clear what he remembers. It may have been only one of the bad dreams he had."

"But the child he found, that wasn't a dream?"

"I tell you," she said fiercely, "he did no harm to the child, there was not a mark on it, not a scratch. How was he to know it was a child she had—it might have been a bundle of clothes, anything. Not a scratch—the young master will tell you that, he carried the child himself, all the way back."

"That old thing," Henryk said suddenly from the doorway, "she'll talk to you all day long."

In my preoccupation with Tilka's meanderings I had forgotten Henryk's presence—which it was often easy to forget. Indeed, at

[71]

that moment I had almost lost sight of Tilka herself, as when listening to certain kinds of music one forgets the artist playing it. Beyond the closer scene—the old woman's resentful eyes, the dreadful poverty of her mottled skin—the vision I saw was of a panic-stricken creature who ran from a blazing hut, of Zygmunt himself watching from the darkness, raising his boar-gun, taking expert aim. Yet had this picture been given me in a Warsaw drawing-room it would scarcely have affected me as it did, for in that safe light I should have seen it as a page from the barbarous past, remote from existing reality. In this fetid hovel, where Zygmunt's traps and guns still hung among the litter of utensils on the wall, I was not so protected. Here the past was not divided from the present, not painted over with a layer of historians' varnish; it had not ceased to exist.

"Yes," I said to Henryk, "we must go now."

Having brought no money, the best I could do for Tilka was to bid her adieu in the affectionate form one uses for old servants, promising to visit her again. Mistrustfully she came after us, still pouring out a jumble of explanations, continually grasping and kissing my hand; and this pitiful, degrading spectacle might have continued until she dropped from exhaustion if a chance, happy for me, had not intervened.

For some time I had been faintly conscious that the sound of distant artillery, which had become almost a part of the fabric of every day, had increased a little in volume. And now a series of four or five explosions, near enough to make us feel a tremor in the air, was followed by the sweep of a squadron of aircraft overhead, so low that their markings were easy to read. It did not occur to me that there was anything dangerous to ourselves in this, for there were no high buildings nearby to fall on us, and my thoughts, in any case, were engaged elsewhere. But the effect on Tilka of such a demonstration was to supplant her new fears by the old. She uttered a piteous scream, pitched down as if dead, scrambled up again and ran as I should have thought impossible for so decrepit a being. Almost before I had realized what was happening, she was back in her hovel with the door slammed behind her.

Henryk gazed after her, fish-mouthed. "They shot her?" he asked, with a small, foolish excitement. "Someone shot her?"

I answered, with my thoughts already far away, "Yes, they shot her." Then as if a curtain had fallen, as if my visit to Tilka had meant no more than a landlord's routine call on one of his tenants, we continued our walk, turned now towards home.

At this stage he was boyishly talkative: " ... Silly, silly! Like old Zygmunt—he went on like that! You know him, Zygmunt? He's dead. Drink, he was always drinking, he thought a witch was after him. . . ." But he did not seem to require any response from me.

The screen of cloud had thinned, letting a pale sunlight come upon the countryside, so that this appeared to be another day, as different from that of our outward journey as a boy in adolescence from the child he was before; and in my recollection the outward scene of our slow walk home is detached from neighbouring experience, belonging only to the mind's peculiar journey. To this new country the heightened colour gave solidity. Leftward, the monochrome horizon had broken into moulded hills, where the elbow of forest pointing down at us was changed from one dark mass to a tessellation of broken lights, dull blue and umber splintered with silver and green. A cluster of peat-stacks, black and uniform before as barrack buildings, had become an arresting pattern of browns and greys; the path itself was vivid with chequered light, woven by countless surfaces into fillets of smoke-white and tarnished gold. Yet all that spectacle, lying immutable in the steady sunshine, has stayed in my possession only because it is married with images more deeply incised upon my mind. With my thoughts moving in retard, I was back in the fevered half-hour I had spent with Victor: imposed on the placid vista of bole and yellowing leaf I see the faded curtain in my bedroom, Victor's map-case lying on top of my clothes, the mud on his tunic, the obduracy of his tired eyes.

Grief, like physical pain, when it comes in overwhelming force will sometimes bring its own alleviation: the instrument of feeling, suddenly overcharged, almost ceases to respond. That relief had been granted me, but it was at last exhausted. I think that what I suffered, now that the period of amnesia was over, was not the ordinary sorrow of parting, nor even the bitter sense which partings bring of wasted opportunity: it was rather the feeling that the nucleus of my life had been revealed as illusion. It did not matter that such a man as Julius, or even that Victor himself, should regard our marriage as counterfeit; that was a question merely of terms and sanctions such as women, in the end, are too much realists to have any use for. Only, I doubted now whether our union had possessed any kind of validity save that of immediate passion and its response. In those few minutes, the last (I could only believe) that we were to spend together, had any unalloyed kindness passed between us? Had we added anything to our common fund of understanding? Was there any such fund to be increased? I had thought the child I was to bear would be enough for the fulfilment of our love, that in the creation of this new life my own would be justified. And now I saw, although with shadowed understanding, that love cannot suffer imperfection; that it finds completion only in itself, and when it does not achieve finality can only be counted as total loss. If I could see him once more, I thought, if I could talk to him for an hour, for a few moments only, I might find some missing piece which would restore to our wasted partnership the wholeness of life; and with that I should be content, not grieving that our time was over, only living in thankfulness that what was finished had finished perfectly. But such a grace was not even to be hoped for now. And while my eyes rested on sunshot woods, on the gentleness of turf and scrub in the candid morning light, I was searching the places Victor and I had shared, our fitful conversations on tired evenings, our meetings and journeys, for some sentence or some look of his to convince me that we had known the totality of love.

So, in my memory of that morning, the painful, useless search fills all the foreground. Behind, there is the tranquillity of country that men have not much interfered with, of sunlight which autumn is already refining. The disturbances we encountered take only a minor place, for they seemed to be irrelevant, as if they belonged to some other occasion.

I was faintly vexed when Henryk, walking contentedly beside me, stopped suddenly to call out, "Look, Teffy, look!" And at first I took no notice, for any little thing, a squirrel running or a dead bird lying on the path, would often excite him; but I saw a moment later that the object of his interest was something less usual than these. There emerged from a clearing in the woods, two or three hundred metres ahead, a machine which—at first glance—I took to be some new instrument of forestry, and which I watched for two or three seconds before I realized that it was a vehicle of war— a German tank of which I had seen photographs in the newspapers. It progressed rather as one pictures elephants moving through jungle, meditative, sure-footed, with ridiculous majesty; while at even intervals four more from the same litter appeared behind it, and these, as they reached the open country, fanned out to make an arrow-head, drawn with a drill-sergeant's precision. In that shape

[74]

the whole parade went forward across the dried marshland, where, if one of them faltered for a moment, lurching and twisting on a soft patch, the rest would instantly ease up, so that their formation was never seriously broken. From all their engines the din must have been gigantic, but of that I have no recollection: I remember it as though occurring in silence, the spectacle of these monsters ranging the landscape so calmly, under such faultless control; appearing, for all their metallic crudity, to be creatures of intuition responding to some natural law. There was but one break in the peacefulness of their behaviour; when, from some point in the farther woods which I did not identify, a machine-gun set up a querulous barking. As if this were a signal, long prearranged, the leftmost tank immediately answered the rebuke with a spit of flame, and a moment afterwards two more were firing with a fury that rocked them on their haunches, so that for half a minute the ground quivered with their violence, while a scarf of smoke spread twisting across the combe. Before this had cleared, the machine-gun was silent. The tank flotilla, with its pattern unaltered, rolled on sedately till the diminishing shapes were lost against the darkness of the trees.

We came to the road we had crossed before. Of the convoy we had seen resting there, the greater part had moved away and the rest was unfit for further service. One wagon, almost complete, lay half across the roadway with its wheels in the air, while the others, crumpled beyond identification, were piled together on the verge, with fragments scattered for a hundred metres along the road. Above the limbs and viscera of horses, widely spread, the flies were swarming in great multitude.

Beside the path we had used a few soldiers had remained, some lying almost exactly as we had seen them before. But these were dead now. It was strange, in the dappled sunlight which fell between the trees, to see them there, like figures from a waxwork museum, so lifelike and yet so still. One, I remember, sat upright, supported by the trunk of a beech, with a cooking-pot between his knees; only his forehead was gone.

"The War!" Henryk said, grinning as some children do when the unfamiliar scares them. "The War's come—hn?"

"Perhaps," I answered.

Until he spoke I had not thought of 'war' as the label for such untidiness, these casual and anonymous items of destruction. I had imagined war to be more imposing, a sustained and compact spectacle in which the cardinal design could be discerned. In later reflection I saw that this had been a naïve conception: war is a masculine concern, and it is foolish for us, who do not understand its logic or subtleties, to be disappointed by examples of the art which come our way.

At the time I had little opportunity for such academic thoughts. I had stopped to brush the flies away from the face of a fair-haired boy who lay beside a small crater, and to assure myself that I could do him no other service, when the silence was invaded by a fresh uproar of engines. At headlong speed a convoy of ten or a dozen half-tracked lorries came down the road, crammed with soldiers, who, with their rifles held at the alert, had the look of performers in some patriotic carnival. I did not think that people so intent upon their business would have any interest in outsiders like ourselves; but a cough which broke through the rattle of bogies could only come from a light machine-gun, and when a plaintive whistle—familiar to me from the Lipno ranges—sounded close above my head, I saw that nothing should be taken for granted in the region of these activities. I caught hold of Henryk and dragged him between the trees; under whose cover we went on for a kilometre or so before we ventured back to the path.

For some way I could still hear the noise of spasmodic rifle-fire and of distant guns. But these sounds were largely stifled by the trees, and once again they became irrelevant, like the filtered sounds of traffic heard in a room where friends are talking. At the level of the pines—as far as I remember—they ceased altogether, and the picture of men lying so unreally in the sunshine had already joined the flotsam of incongruous memories which the stream of experience leaves behind. I was now, I think, a little faint from hunger, perhaps from physical shock; for the rest, my senses were occupied by what was nearest at hand, the resilience of the needle-carpet under my feet, the shredded light, the dry and resinous air which splashed against my sweating skin. Henryk had started weeping, overtaken by the grief of what he had seen. "They were hurt," he said, "those people—I think they had died!" But I could only comfort him distractedly, since my thoughts were again on a path of their own; wondering whether Victor had known—always—the facts I had gleaned from Tilka's maunderings, whether a quixotic sense of justice, only disguised as love, had been the essence of his care for me. He and I had walked along this path, often in silence, my thoughts upon him, his far away. What was he doing now, on a morning which these woods held so gently? I had had a dream of his standing in my room, soiled with battle and too much preoccupied for tenderness: of his tired voice, 'We'll be in among those bastards before tomorrow's out.' A dream?

When the path began to go downwards the quietness was intensified; except for our own footsteps, the only sounds were those which insects made among the fallen leaves. In all the country which the trees gradually disclosed I saw no movement, no vehicle upon the roads, no men in the fields; and in the soft afterglow of summer Setory, with its water-towers and granaries modelled to scale, reposed in the hills' lap with the placid beauty of a child asleep. All that was foreign was a stem of livid smoke which, springing from where the little houses were hidden by the belt of limes, rose straight and slender to a surprising height before it spread against the still, opal sky. Henryk was once more silent. With the curious feeling of having landed in a new country, I led the way slowly down to the house; where young soldiers, standing in the yard, cross-examined us in nursery Polish before they would let us go inside.

x

The hall was empty of people but littered with soldiers' impedimenta: coats, mess-tins, portable cooking-stoves. I noticed on a table by the wall an unused bandage and a bottle of disinfectant; things which Sandra had brought—when? ... in the dream? ... in some earlier life?—for the dressing of Victor's leg. The air was close and fusty, as if the house had just been opened after long disuse.

At the top of the stairs I encountered Julius, dressed in clothes he must have got from one of his own labourers, dirty and unshaved, but alert and calm. He asked me whether I had been watching the fire in the village. I told him no, I had been to see Tilka. He showed no surprise.

"Old Zygmunt's child? I didn't know she was still alive; she always drank like her father. Is she well?"

"As far as I can tell."

"A great romancer," he said reflectively, "but otherwise a harmless person." I thought there was something he would add, but he appeared to change his mind. "Well," he said, smiling rather remotely, "we have the Germans with us now."

[77]

4

DURING the short time they were with us we found these Germans to be straightforward, if in some ways a little undercooked. They were generally honest and incorruptible; they took what they needed but very little more. It happened that some of the pieces in my bedroom were chosen to furnish the room which had been assigned to the Sub-Area Commandant; the removal took place on an afternoon when I was out of the house and had left my door locked. By the time I returned, the forced lock had been quite skilfully repaired. I found a pendant of sapphires and diamonds, once Casimir's gift to me and a thing of obvious value, placed tidily on top of the clothes which had been taken out of the drawers.

The earnestness of these people, their conscious martial attitudes, made it difficult at first to take them seriously. There was a characteristic scene on the evening of their arrival, when the whole household was ordered to assemble in what had been the morning-room for 'moral instruction'. Here, under the supervision of a very young corporal, we women were allowed to sit down, while the men stood in a row behind us. Absolute silence was ordered. Presently the Commandant arrived, escorted by one of his junior officers, and took up his position behind Julius's desk. He was a man in the late forties who had obviously been a professor of some kind: his military bearing sat on him about as congruously as his uniform, his pale eyes were scholarly, and the sternness overlaid upon his normal expression of rather timid benevolence produced a synthetic countenance as unconvincing as any I have seen. The speech he read to us, holding the paper close to his unspectacled eyes, was evidently of his own composition, in almost faultless Polish of a stiff-jointed, literary kind. Parts of it have stayed in my memory, because Wanda afterwards took pleasure in quoting them again and again.

'. . . Every species created by all-wise nature has some purpose of its own. The cattle give us milk and meat, carrion crows devour the corpses of animals which would otherwise become putrescent, millions of minute insects perform their special functions in soil-refertilization. So it is with the various human species. Some are appointed to the highest, some to the lowest, tasks, and none must think that his race has no purpose in the nature-system. But neither should any aspire to a place different from that which nature has appointed. Many races are appointed for labour, they are the humble material, dignified by obedience to nature's law, from which the foundations of higher life are formed. Negroes, Polynesians, Chinese are all races of this order. So is the Polish race. Those Poles who perform their functions in loyal conformity with their racial status will be granted civilized justice and humane considera-tion. . . . Every German soldier is to be treated with supreme deference at all times. No Polish person is permitted to be outside his certificated dwelling after six o'clock *post meridiem* or before seven o'clock *ante meridiem* without special permit signed by the house-group-commanding Non-commissioned Officer. Penalty for first offence—service in military labour establishment. . . . Ques-tions?'

The 'Questions?' was uttered with a click which implied that none was required; and the older members of the audience accepted that guidance. I was startled when the stiff silence was broken by Wanda's gentlest, patrician voice.

"If you please, Mr Commandant! There is a Polish wolf-hound in this household named Jason. He is accustomed to leave the house every evening at ten o'clock in accordance with natural law. Will a permit be required, please?"

I glanced sidelong at her face, which was grave and ingenuous as that of the corporal beside her; then at the Commandant's, and I could see that even that short-sighted creature was stirred by her beauty. He coughed and fumbled.

"A wolf-hound? A large dog?"

"Please, Mr Commandant, about fifteen kilograms."

Recovering his severity, the Commandant said brusquely, "Passes unnecessary for dogs. The Adjutant will deal with any further questions."

They were all a little like that. They had the faces of busy, anxious fathers, errand-boys who have risen to possess their own small shops. If no one was looking, they would occasionally do some trifling service for Wanda or for me; there were smiles of fleeting

[79]

gallantry, the look of hunger for kisses. Annette could even make them laugh.

But they meant what they said.

A prisoner cage had been established about a mile from the village, and there were notices everywhere that anyone found within five hundred metres of it would be punished by execution. Two of our people, an elderly labourer and his fifteen-year-old grandson, decided to circumvent this prohibition, in the hope of getting some news of the man who was son to the one and father to the other. They were caught of course. From my bedroom window next morning I saw them being led past the house by some of the callow creatures who surreptitiously sought our favours every day, and presently we heard a burst of rifle-fire from the nearest woods.

We entered a life of great inconvenience. The ground-floor of the house was wholly occupied by the soldiers. Since our beasts and produce had been commandeered, we had to go to a Civilian Issue Depot at the other side of the village for all our food, which was poor in quality and meagrely supplied. Summer and our freedom had gone out together; the sky was sealed off by a layer of low cloud, a light rain seemed to be always falling.

ii

It was decided by the vain and rather viperish little N.C.O. who had charge of such matters that there were more women in the house than its work justified. Accordingly I was detailed to spend a great part of every day in an old granary half a mile away which had been turned into a billet for supply troops. There I scrubbed the floor and tables, washed out blankets, helped in the cookhouse. My partner in these fatigues was Julius, who, to avoid being drafted to a labour camp elsewhere, had persuaded authority that he was an elderly workman, abnormally stupid and very lame. I thought the fictitious lameness was risky, but he played the whole part with a skill that surprised me.

The boredom, the niggling discomforts of which such a period is made, escape through the mesh of memory. Just once, in a late New England autumn, a chilly wind catches my face as I turn a street corner, a wind with rain in it and a kitchen smell: then I am back for a moment in that draughty shed, I see long ranks of tables and the neatly dressed equipment behind them, buckets, swill bins, the rain blowing across the va-et-vient of muddy transport lines.

For the rest, I can recover only feebly the sensations of that time. It appeared, in the literal sense, to be infinite; for as winter settled upon the narrow scene one could not imagine another summer coming, or any outlet from that state of life, any conclusion. Even the peculiar sense of progress which pregnancy gives deserted me in those days. I looked forward to nothing, not even news.

A mind so deprived of ordinary nourishment feeds greedily on what it can find. Had I been living a normal life, with thoughts and emotions occupied, I should probably have dwelt on what I had learnt from Tilka no more than any woman of intelligence dwells on some family scandal of the previous generation. For what, after all, were the facts? A young, hot-blooded man had suffered gravely through a servant's treason; belonging to a country whose history is seamed with savage cruelties, he had planned a capital revenge, and to this design chance had given a twist of peculiar brutality— for which he had done his best to make amends. In such terms as those a rational person, who had once studied history under Le Parquier and attended Gustav Ellrich's lectures on moral philosophy, should have reviewed an event of more than thirty years before. Could I, in a different season, have considered it as impersonally as that? I only know that in an existence which contains no future you do not think so coolly about the past.

I had never known the woman who had given me birth. I could make no picture of her now, nor even a guess about her age, her personality, her manner of life. But I did not need to. More and more, as I came to identify myself with the woman running from Nilniewicz's house, I seemed to see her from within.

The house itself I saw as one like Tilka's, little more than a divided shed such as hunters use to sleep in, remote from other habitation. In the inner compartment of this cabin I pictured the woman lying with her child beside her, listening to the eerie voice that winter draws from forests; thinking again and again that she hears Nilniewicz coming, when the sound is only the creak of boughs in the wind, the cabin's timbers straining. At last she is certain there are footsteps outside. She calls: there is no reply. A light suddenly shows through the cracks in the partition wall, and as she watches it, too frightened to move or speak, it grows in intensity; a crackle starts, as when a stove is freshly lit; the first whiff of fire reaches her, and all at once there is smoke pouring into the room. Instinct works for her where reason has failed. She gathers up the baby girl, with the hand left free she tears away a board beside the narrow aperture that serves as window, forces her body through, not caring that she falls outside on shoulder and head so long as her arms protect the child. Perhaps for a moment or two she lies on the ground, with her powers spent. But as the fire takes the whole of the cabin in its grasp the heat is great enough to drive her farther away, and she knows, even in those moments of bewilderment, that as the fire did not start itself a conscious enemy must be close at hand. She looks about her wildly, as cornered animals do, and then starts to run towards the shelter of the trees. How vividly I saw, how closely I could feel that dash for safety: the solitary shape of the running woman against the light of the flames, the rasping pain which every short, dry breath brings to her lungs. Swayed by the weight of the whimpering child, she stumbles and falls. Now she is up and running again. And now the darkness of the trees to which she looks for refuge, only a little way ahead, is split into a flash of light, something springs like a beast from the shadow and she feels her body torn by a spit of fire. From lungs already filling with blood there is one small, broken cry, and the body which has been alive, feeling and understanding, becomes like one of those which Henryk and I have seen by the Nunokie road. She hears, as the darkness closes on her agony, or perhaps she does not hear, the voice which calls out 'Look—the child's alive!'

In this picture (which I now believe was close enough to fact) many details must have been wrongly imagined. I realized that; but where the mind requires a scene to be complete it will create such details for itself and then cherish them. At first I dwelt on my mother's death rather as timorous people force themselves to the parapets of high buildings; I believed that if I looked at the facts clear-sightedly the horror of them would be weakened. That was ingenuous: the horror remained. And soon, in the way of sufferers who resort to laudanum, I came to need the supposed remedy for its own sake. It scared and sickened me, this flight of the hunted which I made again and again; yet the very terror of it grew into a necessity, like that of daring horsemen for fresh dangers; and the anger it inspired, grief's counterpart, became a fire to which my spirit turned increasingly for warmth in those cold days.

Working again and again over the monotonous length of that barn, the little wave of dirty water retreating slowly before my brush, my lungs filled with the smells of a place where soldiers have been sleeping, I required some other country for my thoughts to wander in. They turned often to hours I had spent with Victor, times when he had been full of gentleness; but on all those memories the dark uncertainty of our last meeting had thrown its shadow, so that their colour had grown too faint to refresh me. It was easier, when love had proved to be only illusion, to let myself slip back to the cruel certainty; to start the dreadful passage once again, feeling the heat of flame at my back and the child's weight on my arm; to run breathless and stumbling towards the spot where Zygmunt coolly waited. Absorbed in the climax, I scarcely thought of what had gone before; I never tried to look into the mind which had planned it, or to picture the scene where master and servant, running to inspect their handiwork, had found two objects in the human shape, one which had been a woman and the other alive. I would not let emotion be enfeebled by speculations: my mind needed only the central fact, my heart would accept no other relief than anger, its stature and its simplicity.

iii

"You're very quiet, Stefanie."

"Is there anything to talk about?"

"Are you thinking about Victor?"

"I wasn't."

"I'll try to get some news of him—later on. One has to be careful."

"News? How could anyone get any news?"

"There's more than a thousand of our people in the cage—over there, you know. Some of them may have been with him."

"The cage? You can't get anywhere near it; no one can."

"Not easily," Julius said. "But some people have been."

The Corporal who supervised our discipline, having a smattering of Polish, was coming across the area. Julius picked up the buckets and limped away to refill them. He called back over his shoulder, "You might get started on the vegetables. I'll finish that floor."

It was his habit to do a share of my work as well as his own; he was, unexpectedly, as good a fellow-labourer as one could have wished, patient, hard-working, imaginatively helpful in a way I perceive more clearly now than I did at the time. If I could not be grateful for his support, at least I valued it even then.

Being so close to him every day, I found in my father-in-law a new personality: it was almost as if we had never met before. I am not speaking of the character he had assumed for his protection. That, of course—the unkempt appearance and slovenly behaviour, the bovine stupidity he wore on mouth and eyes whenever our Corporal came within range—was something altogether new. No,

I mean that even when we were alone, and no masquerade was needed, he showed me a different man from any I had known in him: one younger, less embalmed in the lineaments of privilege. I believe this greater suppleness came chiefly from the fact that the gifts he valued most, those of the born soldier, were fully occupied. Questions he frequently asked me—"Did you see the markings on that fellow's shoulder?" "Anyone come to the house last night— any strange officers? What rank, did you notice?"—were enough to show how his mind was mainly engaged, collecting every scrap of information which came our way, interpreting, recording it in the tidy files of a military brain. Moreover, I fancy—from the bulk of certain envelopes I carried secretly from him to his mother— that he was even then in touch with others doing the same kind of intelligence work elsewhere. Such industry, this boyish delight in the exercise of an old professional skill, brought him nearer to my range of understanding, for I was not unfamiliar with the mental shape of soldiers. But beyond that, I think he became more accessible because utter defeat had brought him to a curious tranquillity: the tranquillity of acceptance—not of submission.

"Are they any use," I once asked him rather sourly, "all these facts you keep collecting—how many buttons each man has on his shirt? I thought the Germans had won their war, as far as we're concerned."

We were cleaning the cooking-pans, and he said inattentively, "Leave that one, I'll get at it with soap and gravel, it's the only way. . . . Won their war? Yes, of course they have. We knew they would. When you think in purely military terms, there was no answer to Krupp von Böhlen—no answer that we had handy. We didn't admit it. It's the business of Generals to know the facts and not to admit them—that's why people think all soldiers are fools."

"Well, if the war's over——"

"History's not over. We've come to a low point in our graph, that's all that's happened. We know where we are now. Look at these creatures all round us—the conquerors. What do you think of them? They know their job. But apart from that, what are they? The petite-bourgeoisie of Europe masquerading as Titans. What chance do you think they've got in the end, these tradesmen, these squalid Lutherans, against Catholic Poland!"

"You, what are you talking about?" the Corporal shouted, hurrying towards us in one of his fevers of suspicion.

With a smirk of bucolic deference, Julius raised his hand to his forehead.

"Gracious pardon, Mr Corporal, it was about these pans."

"Well, what about them?"

"I was saying the German soldiers have much better pans than the Polish soldiers."

"Everything in Germany is better than anything in Poland," the Corporal said.

"There!" said Julius to me. "I told you so!"

"And you can mind your own business, anyway," the Corporal added. "Discussions about German produce are disallowed by Regulation."

"And is it true, Mr Corporal, that babies are born bigger in Germany than anywhere in the world?"

"Disallowed!" the Corporal repeated sternly.

Again my father-in-law's earnest, imbecile eyes were turned to me.

"Mr Corporal says that in Germany babies are disallowed. It is a country of great marvels."

The Corporal turned on his heel. "Get on with your work, dunderhead!"

Julius waited till he had turned the corner of the cookhouse, and then allowed himself the faintest smile.

"You see!"

I smiled in return: that much of understanding had grown between me and Masziewski, as he now called himself. Understanding? Working close to someone else, for hours, for days together, you fall into the easiest code of behaviour that offers. I said, "You go too far, even with a fool like that. You'll make him suspicious."

"One's life becomes a little tedious," he said, in the very voice that Victor would have used, "unless one risks it now and then."

Yes, there was satisfaction of a kind in having this man as work-fellow, whenever I could forget who he really was; in seeing his resilient energy, his indifference to every humiliation. The life about me was all of the same colour, that grey-brown monotone which armies give to every place they inhabit, and the dullness of the sodden view imposed itself in turn on the soldiers themselves; for all their drill-book behaviour, the rasping orders, the wasp-like cruelties they practised on each other and on us, these men who scuttled through the rain from their comfortless billet to the wind-swept store-tents were a crew of homesick children bored into flabbiness by the tasteless fruits of victory. On this lifeless stage the scrubby figure of my father-in-law was alone in its vitality. He could leave himself unshaved, but he could never disguise, from

[85]

me, the austere vigour of his cheeks and brow; he could slouch along with the buckets like any farm-hand, but in the structure of his shoulders and his thin, hairy wrists you still saw the body which the Kadorka had first hardened, and every movement of his hands —hands shaped like Casimir's—showed me at once a nervous force and a self-control which every hardship left unimpaired. In earlier days I had thought of his eyes as colourless from insensibility, but they did not seem so now: within their limited range they were perceptive eyes—like those of Frenchmen, they appeared to regard an object simultaneously from without and from within.

When I was tired and had to snatch a rest, sitting on the floor in a corner, he would find some job to do beside me. There he would stand so as to conceal my idleness if anyone came, and would entertain me with a flow of low-voiced sarcasms about our conquerors; glad, I think, to have even so dull a listener as I. He offered me no consolations of the sentimental kind; but he would often speak of my condition in a dry fashion that was not devoid of understanding.

"You get a lot of pain in the back? Yes—yes, I remember what Sandra was like before Victor came. Of course the Russians were keeping us short of everything then. By the way, there's a tin of milk I found—it's hidden behind the water-tank. Don't go till it's dark. . . . Yes, you ought to be getting extra food, it's a great strain on the physique. On the mind as well. . . ."

The comfort I got from this rough sympathy lay a good deal in the fact that I did not need to respond. Other men who had been kind to me had expected a return of smiles and gentleness. He wanted nothing. Self-contained, impersonal, he made it clear that his interest in me was confined to my usefulness as matrix for the coming child; and this gave me a sense of safety, for which a woman much plagued by men's admiration is often grateful. My gratitude was of the impersonal kind one feels for a fine day—or I thought so then; and I do not remember being troubled at that time by the discordance of my emotions. In all my inward life I was engrossed by the vision of my mother's death, by the sense of unfulfilled duty into which anger is resolved. It did not seem unnatural to find relief from that black loneliness in the presence of the undemanding creature who worked beside me; to value such minor virtues as were plainly attached to him—his integrity and patience; even to find a kind of pleasure in the virile structure of his hands, in the stoic humour which would bend a little the hardness of his mouth, the mordant voice sheathed in calm assurance.

". . . I'll get you taken off this work if I possibly can. The lieutenant's a very stupid youth, I think he may be open to flattery. You mustn't ever lose heart—I've known strong and healthy children born in worse conditions than these."

"From Ruthenian mothers, you mean?"

Preparing to answer, he looked at me directly. I remember that, because our eyes did not often meet in seriousness—neither of us was inclined for that sort of communication—and because he wore an expression I had seen only once before, during our train journey: a look of complete simplicity, as if his mind were bare.

"You've forgotten that you're Polish now?"

"By marriage, yes."

"No," he said reflectively," no, Stefanie, being Polish isn't really a thing that comes to you with marriage. It belongs to the spirit, it comes from innate possessions of one's own—endurance, the power to suffer without crumpling."

"Whether one wants to be Polish or not?"

He took the other handle of the washing-pail we had between us and carried it himself.

"It doesn't arise, that question. Not when you've once understood what it means to be a Pole. In time I think you may come to understand."

iv

I had paid no special attention to Julius's remark about the prisoner cage, and I might have forgotten it altogether. But on a late afternoon, when I was drawing the next day's vegetables from the military ration tent, I came upon old Tytus, one of our farm-hands, loading a tilted cart there, and when I asked him where the cart was going:

"To the cage," he said.

"Do you go there often?"

"Tuesdays and Fridays."

"Always at the same time?"

"About this time."

There was no chance of a long conversation, since our Corporal made a habit of timing me on these errands, and imposed severe extra fatigues if I took too long. But a minute or so was enough to get me some useful information.

"You drive the cart right inside?"

"Yes, I go to the ration store they've got there."

"And who unloads it—do you?"

"Well, there's generally one or two of the prisoners to help me."

"Do you speak to them at all?"

"Speak to them? Holy Mother, the sergeant there would put a bullet in me if he just saw my lips moving."

"How long does the unloading take?"

He shrugged his shoulders.

"Ten—twenty minutes."

"And then you drive straight back?"

"Yes, Ladyship."

"You'd know a cavalry soldier if you saw one—by his uniform, I mean? Well, you know what Colonel Victor's uniform was like?"

"Oh yes, Ladyship."

"Have you seen any uniform like that in the cage?"

"You will graciously understand," he answered with dignity, "I have missed the scholarship."

He meant, in short, that he was not accustomed to the intelligent use of his eyes; and since he had become very nervous—the Ration Orderly a dozen paces away was already glancing at us—I did not press the old man any further. In truth, the chance that someone with news of Victor might be in the cage was pitifully small—it was far more likely that any of his men who had survived were now in Russian hands—and when I considered the question soberly I saw that this line of search was not worth pursuing.

But the suppressed craving for news, for some shred of certainty, was inevitably made fiercer by that brief exchange; and among the draggled lumber which my mind carried at that time a new fact found its place—that before long the regular trips which Tytus made to the cage would take place when darkness had fallen.

v

I doubt if even the elderly take pleasure, as a rule, in being mothered by their daughters. To a younger woman it is still less tolerable. I offer that as excuse (of the poorest kind) for having received so coldly the devotion which Annette never failed to show me. Or perhaps I instinctively resented the change I saw in her. Before, she had seemed so slow in emerging from childhood; now the experiences which war had brought were hastening that process abnormally, and because she was so much more with her other relations than with me I imagined that she was growing—as though wilfully—into their pattern, forsaking mine.

All day I was living mostly with my own thoughts. Solitude, experienced in too great measure, came to possess me as habits do, and in the evenings, when I was dismissed from work, I returned to the house with less and less eagerness for others' society. I did not want to be fussed over, or even talked to.

Annette would hear me being challenged by the sentry and would come running downstairs. At the foot of the stairs she would wait while the quarter guard commander (who knew my face as well as his own) examined my papers to assure himself that I had the right of entry; then, as if on a gust of air, she would fly to me, and with her lithe body, taller every day, would hold me tightly, pressing her face into my cheek. I tried, I tried to respond to such a welcome. But my own body was flaccid from the day's labour, my mind estranged. Some part of me refused to believe in her sincerity.

"Mother, was it awful today? You look so dreadfully tired."

"No, no, it wasn't a bad day. I had a talk with Tytus."

"Tytus? The old carter? How is he? What did he say?"

"Oh, nothing really."

"Oh . . ." She had her arm round my waist as we went slowly upstairs. She was old and young, eager and constrained. "Mother, I've applied for another interview with the Commandant. I'm going to get us changed round if I can, I'm going to tell him once and for all an expectant mother can't do the sort of work they've given you. Wanda's promised to work him into a good mood first——"

I said, "Darling, I'd rather—I'm sorry, but I'd be so much happier if you wouldn't interfere. I like having something to keep me occupied, and I can't do anything with your grandmother and people all round me."

"But Mother, darling, you do want to make sure everything's all right for the baby——"

"Darling, really, I'd rather not talk about that."

"Oh . . . Mummy, what are we going to call him?"

"I don't know."

The last of the downstairs rooms had been commandeered as ante-room for the officers' mess, and the old night-nursery now served as living-room for us all. The Kolbecks had fitted it for its purpose as well as they could, with a table rescued from the Countess's room, two or three easy chairs from Julius's; but with china stacked on a wash-stand, books on the sewing-machine, it had a makeshift look which suggested travelling rather than living. It was a room full of draughts, and people sitting there seemed to be only waiting as they do in the lobbies of hotels.

[89]

"Oh—Stefanie—you look so tired!" They were for ever saying that, all of them. And now it was Sandra, looking up from her ironing with the patience of one inured to troublesome surprises. ". . . so tired. I didn't know it was so late. I wonder—do you want your supper at once, dear? There are just these shirts of Henryk's. Is there anything from the General? Is he all right?"

"He's very cheerful."

That was my answer nearly every time, but she always accepted the news with grateful wonder. She took the note I had brought for her and turned away to read it.

"I expect there's something for his mother as well?"

They were a source of gentle grievance to her, these letters which passed between mother and son.

"Just a business letter," I told her.

"Yes, of course. She's in the bedroom—she's not very well to-day, but I expect she'll come in for supper. You don't mind if I just finish these things?"

Annette said, "I could do those, Grandmother."

"Oh—but I think I'd rather do them myself, thank you, dear. You have to get the cuffs exactly right or else they look dreadful. And you see, everything's got to last till we get back to normal times. You don't think, Stefanie, I could send Julius some clean shirts?"

"No, Belle-mère." I had explained all this a dozen times. "No, he wouldn't have a chance of wearing his usual ones."

"I think it's so stupid of these Germans," Cousin Rosalia said pettishly from behind the old newspaper she was reading, "imagining we can go on for ever without any more clothes."

"Hush, Rosalia, please! Annette, shut the door!"

"I could get the tray up now, Grandmother," Annette said. "Wanda said she'd have it ready as soon as she'd done the Commandant's dinner."

"Well, if your mother's very hungry——"

"*I'm* quite ready to wait," said Rosalia.

"I could set the things on that other table," Annette persisted.

Sandra looked grieved. "Well, that's not really a dining-table."

"There's no hurry at all," I said. "I'm not hungry. Annette, what you'd better do is get your hair tidy."

"You do see how it is?" Sandra said to me appealingly. "These shirts of Henryk's——"

"Of course, Belle-mère!"

I did see how it was—and I resented it. The Kolbecks had

reduced their life, meagre as it was, to a working shape, a pattern of small understandings. In this pattern my child had her place; for me there was none, and my arrival every evening was counted, I thought, among the many intrusions—the Orderly Sergeant's daily inspection, periodic searches by a security patrol—which had to be borne with as good a grace as they could find. The fault, I realize now, was entirely mine: against the hostility I secreted and cherished, no friendship of theirs could have prevailed. I gave them nothing except a common civility, and I had no right to ask for more in return. For your own distempers, however, you seek and find the cause outside. I expected from these people the very warmth and understanding which my heart was determined not to accept.

There was no more demurring when Wanda arrived, a minute later, with a loaded tray.

"I'm afraid I must have the table, Mother—I'll do the ironing myself later on. Yes, I must get supper going now, I've got to serve the N.C.O.s at eight o'clock. Henryk only gets into a mess if he tries to do it by himself. You might start setting the table, will you, Cousin Rosalia. I've got to go and hide these tins somewhere, they're a Mess issue. No, not you, Stefanie, you sit down! Mother, you'd like to go and tidy, wouldn't you?"

After working all day as general servant to the officers down-stairs, she must have been as tired as I was, but none of her movements betrayed it. She had taken to doing her hair in the strictly Polish style, as the Countess did; she wore a dark-blue overall throughout the day, and in this professional guise she appeared to be a creature incapable of any weakness. When we sat to supper it was she who took the end of the table, where Julius would have been, and who had an eye to every detail.

"There's no pepper, I'm sorry—I tried three times, but one of the batmen was always looking. I might have got a chit for it from the Adjutant, but I don't want to waste his good temper—that's more severely rationed than anything."

"The Adjutant?" Rosalia said. "I think he's a horrible man."

"No, he isn't really. (Would you mind if Mother had that cushion you're sitting on—it helps her back.) He's a devoted husband and father; he's got three children under four years old, and he says their total weight last month was five hundred kilograms. Oh, and he's famous for his wit—they say his joke is better than the Commandant's. Or, at least, it wears better."

"*Canaille!*" the Countess murmured, staring at her untouched stew.

[91]

"You ought to be careful, darling," Sandra said mechanically. "It doesn't do to be familiar with those men."

She had changed, as she always did, into the wine-coloured marocain dress which had once been kept for her receptions; I think its dignity soothed her a little, reminding her of days when the children had been young enough to be under her control.

"Of course," she said reflectively, "there was that Captain Seidentopf I knew at Kovna—he was a man of culture. No, you mustn't accept any favours. Only I think they ought to give us back those dessert dishes. I understood the Commandant had only borrowed them for some special occasion. I think if you just reminded him——"

"What do we want them for?" the Countess demanded. "There are more important things than dessert dishes."

"I don't want to get into slovenly ways," Sandra answered with a touch of unexpected firmness. "It isn't good for the children to think it's the natural thing to eat from any odd china that happens to be about. (Annette dear, do sit up—you'll get round-shouldered if you sit like that!) Of course, his mother was of the aristocracy—Captain Seidentopf. She was on friendly terms with my own family."

The Countess stared icily at her plate. "Aristocracy? Those Junkers?"

"One of the soldiers came into my bedroom when I was in my dressing-gown," Rosalia said with a trace of indignation, pulling at her necklace. "I said to him, 'Mr Soldier, I am in my dressing-gown.' "

But Sandra, whose thoughts would move in a wide circle, was speaking to Wanda again. "At any rate, I think you should avoid talking to any of them, except when it's absolutely necessary. It's better for us to live our own lives."

I saw Wanda prepare an answer and let it die.

"Only there are titbits to be had," she said.

"Not if it leads to familiarity, dear. We can do very well without pepper and things like that."

"That's not what I mean. I mean there are bits of news."

The word 'news' brought the Countess to life.

"What sort of news? Have they told you something?"

Wanda hesitated. "I pick up things." She spoke with a lowered voice. "This lot may be leaving us."

"That," said Rosalia, "would be a good thing."

"*May* be leaving?" Sandra echoed.

"There's been a lot of fuss about getting things washed for the Commandant. He said they might not be back in time if they went to the Base Laundry."

"That might just mean that he's getting leave for himself!"

"Does it make any difference?" I asked. "Isn't one lot the same as another?"

"Yes, probably. (Annette, be a darling and just look outside the door.) Yes, only there may be more to it than that. I got the Adjutant talking and I saw a letter on his table. There's a political commission coming at the end of next week. Something to do with boundaries."

"But could that make any difference to us?"

Again Wanda hesitated, and I saw—knowing her as only a teacher does—that she regretted having mentioned the subject at all. She said:

"I can't even guess."

"Well, *I* don't have to!" the Countess said stringently. "I know exactly what difference it would make."

I suppose that all of us wanted to ask her what she meant—except Wanda, whose percipience was equal to hers. But no one had the courage. For long periods the Countess would stay so quiet that we almost ceased to feel the weight of her presence, but at any moment a few words such as those would make us all into children. I watched her as closely as I dared. She was far from well tonight, as Sandra had said: the care she had taken with her appearance, the collar of Venetian lace which she was wearing as if for some great occasion, only emphasized her sickly pallor; but her eyes, now darting to Wanda's face, now still and reflective, showed me a brain that was not retarded by the body's weakness. There was something of Victor in those eyes, as I saw then; more of Julius, his intellectual certainty. She towers over us, I thought, not because she is aged and of a dangerous temper, but because her mental power outreaches ours.

Sandra said nervously, "I suppose Julius ought to know."

"Know what?"

"About anything that's going on."

"He'll know when he needs to," the Countess said with finality.

"Perhaps if there's any change in the arrangements, he'll be able to live at home again." There were tears in Sandra's voice now. "It's miserable, his being so near, and my not being able to see him—not once—day after day."

The pathos in that utterance was not cheap or shallow. I believe that it moved me when I heard it. I know it was some evil outside my control which made me say, shortly and drily:

"Well, you can change places with me!"

At once, in her lightest voice, Wanda said, "Oh, but they couldn't do without you at that billet, Teffy. I'm told you're the neatest table-scrubber they've got!"

I left that pleasantry unanswered. But when Annette, red and anxious, came round to me and pressed my arm, whispering "Mother darling, you're so tired, you ought to be in bed!" I said at large, with scarcely governed anger:

"Yes, I suppose it spoils things for everyone, my being here! It should be a purely Polish gathering."

I was answered by the Countess, in her quietest tone, "Oh no—everyone with good manners is welcome."

And then, as Annette started crying, Sandra in her turn came to put her arm round my shoulders.

"But, Stefanie, you know we love to have you! It's your home as much as ours. We want to make it nice for you, Stefanie. What do you want us to do?"

. . . *as much as ours.* The room was carpetless, since the Adjutant had taken a fancy to the old night-nursery carpet; the stove, this chilly evening, was empty, and I remember even now how coldly the light from one unshaded bulb shone on the scarred varnish of the nursery wardrobe, the wicker bookstand with its load of cleaning tools and outdoor shoes. Downstairs the Orderly Officer was mounting the night picquet, and the sound of his hoarse, parade-ground voice, of stamping boots, the butts of rifles slamming on the stone floor, reverberated through the house as if it were a shell. But Rosalia, back in her usual chair, was nodding over Stryjkowski's *Chronicles* as I had seen her nodding ten and twenty years before. Stooping gracefully, with the faint smile of some odd recollection on her mouth, Wanda had started to make coffee on the kerosene burner, giving the room at least a smell of old familiarities. As soon as Annette had cleared a portion of the table, the Countess spread the contents of an old attaché case and began to write in her minute, unwavering hand, as if she were still in charge of the business of the farm; while Sandra, arranging her cashmere shawl round her shoulders, keeping her sad eyes away from mine, moved with a certain flat-footed dignity about the room, to pull the curtains closer together, to shut a drawer.

"Perhaps—Annette dear—you could find some flowers to-morrow. There must be some dahlias where the Count used to have

[94]

his garden, I think the Duty Corporal would let you bring some in. I was thinking—oh, but how nice it will be when Adam comes in every morning again, bringing me the flowers."

vi

In her youth my mother-in-law had probably been bilingual—as an adult she often lapsed into German sentences—but in these days she took an obstinate pride in pretending that Polish was her only tongue. The pretence must have added a good deal to the exasperating nature of her interviews with the Adjutant, Captain Bautz.

Bautz was a youngish Bavarian of the middle class, a family man, as Wanda had said; the roughness of his manner—that crudely bellicose air which is attached to many amateur soldiers—concealed very imperfectly the sentimental and the self-questioning strains of his kind. It is not impossible that he had a mother who bore some resemblance, in looks or manner, to Sandra herself. Certainly he treated her with remarkable forbearance, and seldom refused the interviews she was demanding every day. The subject of these conversations (as Wanda often overheard and delighted to report them) was generally food. They resulted in no action of any kind; but I suppose that in some obscure way they gave as much satisfaction to her as annoyance to him.

Returning to his office after the morning round—which had doubtless brought him many vexations—he would find Sandra standing by the door, watched by a sulky and embarrassed orderly. Standing with her heels together, in an attitude where dignity and humility were perfectly combined, she would announce in her very guttural Polish:

"The wife of General Kolbeck requests a short interview with the Adjutant."

"Well, what is it this time, Frau Kolbeck?"

"It's about the vegetable ration. At the present time I have eight persons in my household. Yesterday the total amount they gave to my son at that depot place——"

"Frau Kolbeck, I have told you again and again that I have nothing to do with issues from the civilian depot."

"What I want to explain is that one of the ladies in my household is an expectant mother who——"

"You must go and see the officer in charge of civilian issues. It's

[95]

absolutely nothing to do with me. Give the officer my compliments and say that I recommended you to see him. Now, please, I have a lot——"

"That's very kind of you," she would answer imperturbably; adding with maternal kindness, "I think you speak Polish very well; naturally you make a few mistakes, but you have improved a great deal. In the end, you will be mistaken for one of ourselves."

"I have no wish," said the Captain frigidly, "to be mistaken for a Pole—or for a Chinese or a Hottentot. If you have nothing to talk about except my linguistic abilities——"

"Oh, but that isn't what I wanted to talk about at all. It's about the vegetable ration——"

"I've told you that I can't discuss that!"

"You see, my granddaughter is little more than a child, and you know how it is with growing children——"

"Frau Kolbeck, have you or have you not anything to ask me about except the civilian vegetable issue? Because I myself have a great deal of work to get through."

"Yes, Mr Adjutant, I do know that you're a very busy man. I think it's extremely kind of you——"

"Have you or have you not?"

"Oh yes!"

"What is it then?"

"It's about the bread we're getting. You see——"

"Listen—I am a man of considerable patience——"

"I know, Mr Adjutant—my daughter has told me a great deal about your kindness, I feel that if you were not a foreigner you might well be one of ourselves. Your improvement in Polish——"

"I've told you that I *don't want* to talk about that. I'm not here ——"

"Of course not! I'm afraid we older people are inclined to wander away from the subject. We were talking about the bread we've been getting——"

"*You* were!"

"Oh yes, we've been getting some, but when you think that there are eight people in my household——"

"Enough!"

"No, Mr Adjutant, *not* enough—that's what I mean—and it isn't the *sort* of bread——"

"*Will* you be quiet!"

And at last he would drive her away. And in an hour or so she would be back with a sample of the bread to show him, and the two dull-witted creatures would find themselves embroiled in a further passage of futilities.

Yes, if the house provided those men with a measure of physical comfort, it gave them little else; and if sympathy can be purely mental, I sympathized with them a little in what they suffered from their hosts. There was Sandra to be borne, her gentle persistence, her settled assumption that she and they were partners in a kind of welfare mission. And there was Rosalia, with a keyhole curiosity which would have tried the nerves of a Siberian ox. The warning which Bautz stuck up on every wall—*It is categorically forbidden for Poles to stare at Officers of the Reich*—made no difference to her: morning or evening, if any of our masters had occasion to go upstairs an elaborately dressed grey head would suddenly protrude from a doorway, its melancholy eyes would hold him for an instant in their foolish, questioning gaze, and then, as if worked by a spring, it would be sharply withdrawn. Even in their own territory they were not safe from this kind of persecution. It must have seemed to them that whenever they crossed the hall Rosalia found some reason for padding past the top of the stairs, and although her face was always devoutly averted there was a moment every time when those childish eyes of hers would bring their narrow, inquisitive beam to bear on them. Had they been insensitive to her behaviour (which they were not) there would still have been the Countess to test their moral fortitude. She, indeed, treated the order not to stare at officers with something more than literal obedience: she appeared never to see them at all. Walking along the middle of a corridor and meeting one of them there, this tiny, desiccated old woman would hold her course exactly as if the way were clear, forcing him either to step aside or else to collide with her head-on. In practice, he stepped aside. If an officer shouted at her to stop she would do so, and would answer his questions, but without the smallest movement of her eyes—as if it were a gramophone which addressed her. I can scarcely think of an insult harder to defeat, or more shrewdly damaging to their complacence, than this undeviating pretence of hers that as individual beings the Germans did not exist.

Even so, it was Wanda who must have hurt them most, for her weapons were the most delicately forged. The officers used her partly as housekeeper to their mess, partly as general servant, and superficially she was everything that a woman so employed should be—quick, reliable, as friendly in her manners as the menial position allowed. It was in her friendliness that her power to wound them lay.

"You're a pretty girl, you know!" Lieutenant Miethke would call out, when he was homesick and a little over-wined. "It's very nice, having such a beauty to wait on us!"

And she would answer, "Yes, for a Polish woman I am thought to be quite good-looking," with a radiant smile which, inexplicably, made the gallant youth look like a schoolboy who has forgotten the declension of *mensa*.

Or Bautz would ask her to admire the riding-boots he was so proud of, and she would say, charmingly, "They suit you perfectly, Herr Kapitän."

"You really think so?"

"Oh yes, they are wonderfully German-looking boots."

"What do you mean by that?"

"So strong, so durable! Nothing will ever make any marks on them."

That was said with perfect gravity. And for a few moments Bautz would bask in the sunshine of her flattery. Then, as he watched her seriously smiling face, hoping for some bonus of admiration, he would just detect a quiver of the mouth, a distant light in the reverential eyes, which would make him say sharply:

"I greatly dislike insincerity!"

"I, too, Herr Kapitän," she would answer, gracefully retiring from the presence.

And for the rest of the morning the poor fool would be biting his nails, cursing everyone who came within reach, and continuing to wonder whether the brilliant and entrancing *Polin* really did admire his boots, or adore his heavily masculine face, or—as he somehow feared—regard the whole assembly with a withering contempt. . . . I am not suggesting that these Teutons were among the more sensitive members of the human species. But they were males, males of peculiarly inflated self-esteem; and for such as they it must have been a subtle torture to suspect, faintly and intermittently, that a woman of the highest intelligence as well as incomparable beauty was secretly enjoying their pretensions as a ludicrous jest.

At first I failed to appreciate the situation. I used to be in the kitchen on some evenings giving a hand to Henryk, who was always hopelessly behind with his chores, and as Wanda flitted in and out it appeared to me that she was on increasingly amiable terms with every soldier in the house. For a time I supposed that she was simply working for favours, from which we should all benefit, and then I began to think she was playing this game for its own sake. This was nothing to do with me—none of the Kolbecks' concerns was mine; but in bed one night (she shared a room at that time with Annette and me), when I was in one of my sulkiest moods, I said:

"It must be quite a pleasant life for you, with all these admirers!"

To that she answered very soberly, "Yes, most of them are more or less in love with me. There's not so much in the way of competition—you go about scowling, and somehow they don't feel romantic about Rosalia." She was silent for a minute or two, and then she went on, in the same low voice, "You see, there's no way of doing any harm to these people. But one can hurt them. Once a man's in love with you, you can always hurt him, you can make his life a misery."

I asked, "Is there any use in that?"

"For me there is."

I did not press her to explain; she did so presently of her own accord. She said rather dreamily:

"They took the hospital, you know—the Germans did—the hospital I was working in. I've never told Mother—I told her I had started for home before they came. We had rather a time, really. Some of the other nurses got killed."

"But how did you get away?"

She ignored the question. "They wanted one of the house-surgeons," she went on, still speaking with a curious lack of tone, "a man called Sigismund Pacsalski, they wanted him to come and attend to their own casualties. He was quite young—he was just nineteen months older than me."

"Yes?"

"He told them he would go in half an hour. He said he must attend to his own patients first. They needed him, you see, Sigismund's own patients—some of them were in a bad state because of the bombardment. It wasn't Sigismund making anything up. Well, he could see that for himself, that man—the patients were all round him."

"What man?"

"What man? The officer, I don't know who he was; I don't know his name—why should I know his name?" She paused, and when she spoke again the faint note of hysteria had vanished. "He lost his temper, anyway. He got out his revolver and pointed it at Sigismund's stomach; he said he'd give him ten seconds. Well, he did. I counted them. Then he fired."

"He killed him?"

She did not answer that directly. She said, after a few moments, in a small, dry voice, "I went to kiss him before he died. I heard one of the soldiers laughing."

In those few moments I forgot about myself, and I forgot to think about her except as the child who had been my pupil and whom I had loved. I got out of bed and went to sit on the side of hers, where I found her arm and held it on my lap. I said incisively:

"Wanda—Wanda, you must try to forget about that! No, I don't mean forget—I mean, you mustn't think about it, you must keep on turning your thoughts on to something else."

"What else?" she asked. And then she said, "I *want* to think about it. With these Germans all round me it's the only sort of thinking I enjoy, it's the only pleasure I get."

"Wanda, it's stupid!" I did not speak roughly, but as a long-suffering teacher would. "It's stupid to have thoughts like that; it can't do you any good. And it isn't sense to talk as if all the members of one race are just the same——"

"Do you think anyone but a German would have done that?" she demanded.

And I answered, without premeditation, "Yes, I do. There are Poles who can do things just as cruel and cold-blooded as that."

Our voices had wakened Annette, who turned over and said sleepily, "Is anything wrong, Mummy?" I told her to go to sleep again; but Wanda and I could not talk any more. Wanda, indeed, was crying, as I knew from the shaking of the bed. I went on sitting there for some time, still holding her hand.

We never returned to the subject; but I can see in restrospect that our talk in the darkness created a new bond between us, of a curious kind. It had brought us back, for a little space, to an old relationship; but beyond that it had revealed to me—and intuitively, I think, to her—a certain analogy of emotion; an analogy, if you will, of unreason. She remained a Kolbeck, and I could no longer regard any Kolbeck, except Victor, as my friend. But to my admiration for her tireless fortitude something was added now. Of all the members of that household, fellow-sufferers in the debilitating boredom of a life which had lost all meaning, she was the closest to my sympathy; not for her grace or courage, the stoic patience with which she served the others' needs, but rather for the bitterness which her buoyant energy concealed. The rest, it seemed to me, accepted their subjection as they would a natural disaster; unable to raise a hand against the conqueror, they scarcely troubled any more to hate him. In the hatred which Wanda nursed with such cold tenacity, the counterfeit of my own, I saw the genius of rebellion. It could do no good. But in this epoch where collective cruelty had the upper hand and no one seemed ready to challenge that supremacy, I valued the resolution of those few who refused to let the anger of one memory be dulled by the climate of oppression.

vii

In this house, then, my child was going to be born, and the earliest scenes he would distinguish were going to be the ones that I myself had known first of all. But to me they did not look the same. The objects which had always been familiar—that cupboard in the night-nursery, Sandra's sewing-machine, worn books I had both learnt and taught from—had lost their associative virtue; they no longer meant anything more to me than the bric-à-brac of an auction sale. Even the view from the windows—the familiar pattern of roofs, the trees beyond—had so assumed the aspect of prison walls that I forgot how it had looked as the background of drowsy lessons, the invitation to picnics or games in the stable loft. The smell of the house had changed, and the ghosts, which may have returned now, had gone. One voice perhaps could have given back to my Setory the tincture of earlier days; but that voice, when I last heard it, had said, 'We aren't entitled to have a child', and now I could hope for no gentler echo from the silence which had fallen.

I say the ghosts had gone. But those of us who had lived there longer than I may still have felt them close. A shapeless rumour which was blowing about among the village people came to me where I worked, and presently penetrated to the house itself: that the Germans were uncomfortable here and meant to withdraw. Knowing little of politics or strategy, I could see no sense in that, and scarcely believed it. But I realized that the others received it with greater credulity—and with no relief at all: for only fools could imagine that we should be left to our own devices; and the fear that haunted them, who had lived through 1905, who had their own or their fathers' memories of '63, was not of any terror which came from the west.

viii

I found one refuge, from the others and from myself, where I should not have looked for it.

For many years now—indeed for a great portion of his long life—Count Kolbeck had been an invalid, suffering from paraplegia and from partial blindness. During my previous period at Setory he had already been confined to one room, where I had seen him only on special occasions, and so he had continued to exist, for me, as the shadowy personage, local deity rather than human being, which had taken its narrow place in the background of my infancy. If in this latest period I had thought of him at all, it had been as a vague appurtenance of the Countess: something which, like the poultry and the farm accounts, was necessary to the scheme of her existence, and as much a figure of the vanished past as Rosalia's admiral. So, but for the Countess's illness, he would have remained. When increasing weakness (due, I think, to the poorness of her diet) kept her in bed for several days, someone else had to take in the many trays which he needed; the duty often fell to Annette, and one evening, when I saw that she was poorly, I took a plate of kascha that she was carrying and went up with it myself.

The Count's small room was at the south-east corner of the house, reached by a short passage from the end of the main corridor upstairs. I remember how, as I turned into that passage, I had the curious feeling of having gone back in time; for the barrack atmosphere in which our visitors had steeped the house had failed to reach so far as this, and the room itself, furnished with austere simplicity, corresponded exactly with my earliest memory. The smell, I suppose, came mainly from the Greek cigarettes which the Count had smoked in great numbers throughout his life—especially at night, when pain often kept him awake; but on that visit I did not try to analyse it: I was conscious only that a segment of the world which I had thought to be lost altogether had somehow survived.

I had expected to find him in bed, and resembling other aged men whom Victor and I had sometimes visited in the Veterans' Hospital at Przedborz, shrunken, wax-like bodies which scarcely seemed to breathe. In fact, he was sitting in a chair, much enclosed by pillows and blankets, and his face, at my first glance, was not that of a very old man; it was rather the face of one in the prime of life, which time had bleached and thinned without weakening its structure or its vitality. Even the eyes, which were too weak to reach me when I entered, were not the dim or listless eyes of extreme age; his mouth, gently shaped, showed no feebleness; and I had the impression that he was watching with quiet amusement some scene which memory projected on the wall of shadow which surrounded him. I was surprised again when I went nearer. I had meant just to put the food beside him and go away, not thinking that he would be interested in who had brought it; but as, bending, I brought my face close to his, he spoke to me; and though the voice was very small, it was clear and unwavering:

"How kind! How nice it is to see you, Stefanie!"

I was too much astonished by his recognition to answer collectedly, and I only said something conventional: was he comfortable, was there anything else he would need? This he ignored, continuing to speak to me as if we were friends who had been meeting regularly:

"You've not had any news of Victor? No, of course—Jadwiga or someone else would have told me. Yes, news is one of the things we are short of now. For me it doesn't matter—it's the greatest advantage of being old, one loses so many appetites which are a plague to younger people. But it's hard for you, it's almost worse than anything, to have no news."

Seen closely, his body looked much older than at the first impression. The white, almost transparent skin, bound to his skull as if no tissue lay between, was caught about the eyes and mouth into tiny folds where silver hairs glistened in the light; a crumpled hand protruding from the worn sleeve of his dressing-gown, beautiful like a hand of Canova's, was slender as a child's; and the whole of his frame, like the structure above a ship's engines, was just perceptibly trembling. Yet the illusion of a young man's presence persisted. I do not know how far he could see, but at this distance his eyes seemed to hold me in focus without straining, and they were active, rather humorous eyes. He spoke without ever fumbling or losing his way, and even when his voice sank very low its inflexions were youthful—eager, full of light and shade.

". . . Yes, poor Jadwiga, she detests the Germans being here; she's always had such a contempt for those people. You see, she judges other peoples by the exported article. It's my fault, really—my being a crock all these years—the poor darling has had so few chances to travel. That's the only way, don't you think, to ease these little prejudices? In Russia, yes—we were together a great deal in Russia when we were young."

I wanted to ask if that had eased any prejudice of the Countess's about the Russian character; but I was not yet ready to take such a liberty. I only said, with caution:

"Those are curious people, the Russians."

And he answered seriously, "Yes—yes, I suppose the true

Russian is harder to understand than anyone in the world. But they are lovable people—those who have not been spoilt by alien contacts. Yes, love—it seems to me—is the only means of understanding them."

I was bold enough then to ask him, "Does the Countess think that too?"

He hesitated, and then he said, smiling a little, "She never knew them as I did. She was so busy when we were there, so busy looking after me. You know, it's been a wonder to me—more wonderful than anything I've heard of—the way she's devoted all her life to my well-being. Nothing, nothing for herself. If I'd read of such devotion in a book, I shouldn't have believed it possible—one human being sacrificing all her life to the life of someone else, someone who had so little to give in return."

He seemed ready to go on talking, but at that first visit, not knowing what his strength would stand, I did not encourage him; and when he saw that I was trying to get away, he released me gracefully.

"You will come again? Old people have no right to make claims on the young; but they always do, you know!"

Politeness alone would have forced me to accept that invitation. It became a regular evening duty of mine to carry up the old man's tray, and even when the Countess was well enough to look after him again my visits were allowed to continue. It was not a practice that she cared for, but she submitted to what must have been her husband's own wish.

"He wants someone to read to him," was all she said to me. "It's a young woman's job—my eyes aren't good enough."

So, late in the evenings, I found myself sitting in the little chair which always stood beside his own, reading from the heavy, calf-bound volumes of Sienkiewicz and Krasinski, which were kept, with big tins of cigarettes, in the iron trunk beneath his bed. And sometimes I read the *Pensées* of Pascal, and Zeller's *Plato*, and Colleville's translations from Dante; while he, smoking one cigarette after another, would listen as eagerly as a child hearing fairy-tales. As a rule, I paid little attention to what I was reading, but the exercise was enough to send my thoughts, which ran in the same grooves all day long, in new directions. In this room, where a man could hardly have taken four paces between the walls, I had the sense of space and liberty; and that, I think, was because my companion, living so far beyond the normal term, had lost the ordinary relationships with locality and time.

He was aware, of course, of the state of things in other parts of the house. He would ask how the soldiers were behaving, whether they made themselves troublesome to Sandra, to Annette. He talked sometimes of Julius: "Yes, my son is a good soldier, a great patriot —he is like his mother in many ways. He only lacks—well, it was hard for him, you know, being in exile so long—those years which should have been such happy ones." But since the past is more real to the aged, his mind was never fastened to immediate realities. He liked to have any scraps of news which had found their way to us; but these always led him on to paths of his own.

"At Saarlouis? That's where Ney was born, you know. Ambitious, yes, but it's so wrong to talk as if he was a soldier of fortune. My father nearly killed him once—have I told you? Yes, at Borodino, it was when my father was a young lieutenant; he was out with a reconnaissance patrol, and Ney rode past within a dozen yards of him. He was very quick, my father, he fired with his pistol, he would have hit him—because he was an excellent shot— only his horse moved just at that moment. My father's horse, I mean. He used to tell me about it. It was curious, because the horse was perfectly battle-trained; it should have kept absolutely still. I've often wondered if it wouldn't have been better for Ney if the horse hadn't fidgeted. He would never have had the title of 'Prince', which must have meant a great deal to a man of such humble birth. But then, it would have saved him from the miserable end he came to—miserable, I mean, for a soldier—having to accept a court's verdict instead of the verdict of arms. They live so much, these soldiers, on their conception of honour. A narrow philosophy, I am inclined to think. I was talking to Alphonse Daudet—oh, that must have been some time ago, it was when we were on a little tour in Puy de Dôme—we were talking about some military man, and he said, 'Soldiers have the virtue of supreme fidelity. They are not always very clear what they are being faithful to.' It was funny to watch him when he said that, he had such a look of despair. Such eyes he had, such compassionate eyes! And yet they were always laughing. Couvelier used to say you learnt more about Provence looking at Daudet's face than by reading all his books. I wonder if it's all imagination, the idea that a particular countryside imparts a special character to the men it breeds. I once paid a visit to Ibsen when he was living in Munich—such a depressing place, all that elaboration, all that weight of grandeur—and I put the question to him. . . ."

All this came as if from a young student, one of intelligent curiosity, delighting in the novelty of every fresh experience in which his eye or his mind is engaged. He had the specially Polish gift of making his lips play a double part, speaking by subtle gesture as well as sound; and his eyes, which tired easily and lost their focus, were constantly searching for my face again, inquiring whether his words continued to amuse me. The part of a young man that he lacked was vanity. As I try to recall his talk—with the liquid quality of his voice, the shadow-play his hand made on the yellow wall—I can scarcely find anything about himself, except as listener and spectator to his friends. I must have done my best to draw him out—what woman would resist doing that?—but he always gently evaded me. I knew, for instance, that a part of his second exile had been at Sakhalien, and I remember asking him directly on what charge he had been condemned to a punishment of such extreme severity. I had to wait while he felt about his memory for the answer, as if I had asked what shoes he had been wearing on a special occasion.

"It was to do with the Governor of Verkhoyansk," he said reflectively. "I had a disagreement with him, it was about some other *détenus*. But listen, I must tell you—if you can spare the time —about the Gilyak fishermen. I found them most interesting people, although their mentality is in many ways so primitive. . . ."

Once, when he had been speaking of his father's fabulous activities, he said a little wistfully, "And I—I've done nothing with life except to look at it, generally from a long way off. You see, to accomplish anything your vision has to be simple, and I've never seen things very simply." That, I think, was sincere; and yet I cannot accept it as a true and final portrait of the man who seemed to live so radiantly within this withering body. He was Julius's father —I saw it constantly in the build of his jaw and brow—and it was not to be believed that he had merely transmitted, or that Jadwiga alone had given, the stature which (unwillingly) I saw in Julius more clearly every day. Neither could I doubt, when something I was reading brought a sudden anger to his tired grey eyes, that both the generosity and the rebelliousness which I had worshipped in Victor derived from him. He had, after all, torn down a Russian flag from the Siedlce court-house roof at the age of sixteen; and the man with whom Garibaldi maintained so long, so intimate a correspondence, whom Turgenev in his last years had travelled a thousand miles to see, can hardly have been morally insignificant. His achievement, I suppose, was small; but how much of his powers must have gone to contending with the illnesses which enslaved him throughout life, and how much—according to my present

[106]

surmise—to controlling the factious passion which was part of his inheritance.

There were evenings when the Countess joined us while I was reading, slipping in very quietly, as experienced nurses do. Naturally I offered to go away whenever she came, but she always answered laconically, "No, no, the Count likes you to amuse him", and settled herself on the remaining chair with a blanket she was patching. Knowing how intensely she disliked me, I marvelled at such tolerance, but I saw very soon that in this narrow space she herself was a little altered in temper. Her self-sufficiency remained, there were no soft looks on that tight and weathered face of hers, no parade of gentleness; and yet she was at home here, as she never was in other parts of the house, and she revealed it by a relaxation of the tautened mannerisms, the invigilator's air, to which we were accustomed. The truth, most likely, is that she saw my presence in the room as of little consequence: there was a cosmos here which a servant's child who had attached herself to the family could scarcely disturb.

She spoke seldom. I doubt if she attended, as a rule, to anything I read, and though she turned her head a little when her husband started talking, I think she listened merely for the pleasure his voice and animation gave her, as the mother of a small boy does; she must have heard a hundred times what he was saying, and I suppose that nearly all the objects of her general interest had long grown cold, as they do with most old people. So, strangely, she and I, who had no trait and no impulse in common, shared the contentment of those calm hours. I remember only one occasion when the calm was broken. I was reading from Jouvain's *Pierre le Grand* the passage where he describes the Russian genius—the passage beginning 'That fierce ardour of the spirit which, lacking a true culture to absorb it, results in a tortuosity of mind . . .'—and I became aware that it had caught her attention. Putting down her work, she said abruptly:

"Yes, they'll always find some literary man to make elegant excuses for them, the Russians. They do the devil's work, and people say it's because they're intoxicated by religion!"

That outburst did not surprise the Count at all. He said with the utmost gentleness, smiling:

"You make things sound foolish, loveling, expressing them so simply as that!"

But the anger which Jouvain had roused in her was not appeased; to my consternation, she stood up, leant over me and pulled back the sleeve of the Count's dressing-gown, revealing his bare fore-arm. I did not look at it for long, only enough to see that the wasted flesh was circled some way above the wrist by a deep ravine, as if a wire had been tied round it in his childhood; but in a curious way this deformity in an old man's arm upset me more than the sight of an open wound would have done.

"Yes," Jadwiga said, addressing me with a kind of suppressed triumph, "he hung by that arm for eleven hours. That's one of the things the Russians did to him! In mid-winter—eleven hours!"

I had nothing to answer to this assault on my sensibilities. It was the Count who spoke, as quietly as before:

"My own, I've told you—so often, so often—the fellow was in misery all the time, he begged for my forgiveness. He was only a serf, he was under orders——"

"And who gave him those orders?" Jadwiga demanded.

"My own, they were given in a fit of drunkenness. That man had lived away from his own kind much too long. Yes, he was a drunkard, but there was a great deal of good in him."

Painfully embarrassed, I hoped that Jadwiga would go no further; but this eruption of an ancient sore had so wrought upon her that she had lost all her self-control. Her voice became as shrill and broken as that of a peasant woman cheated over a hen.

"Good in him! Would you say there was good in Nero, in Iscariot?"

That brought a silence, in which the Count looked at her for-bearingly, as a doctor watches a patient for whom he can do nothing until a spasm is over. When he spoke, he seemed to be dictating the answer to a problem his pupils had been strangely slow to solve. "There is a Christ in us," he said, "in every one of us—waiting to reveal Himself when we are willing." He smiled then, as if in tolerance of our simplicity; relieved that so elementary a theorem could now be left behind. "I agree," he said cheerfully, "that Jouvain becomes a bore sometimes—so terribly didactic! Perhaps dear Stefanie can find us something more light-hearted." But I saw that the contention had tired him, and I made an excuse to go away.

ix

I think it was on the following day that I had a brief conversa-tion with Julius which I particularly remember. I had brought him the usual letters from Sandra and his mother, and he had gone over to the fuel stack, as he always did, to read them in comparative security. "So they're going to move the cage!" he said, more or less casually, when he came back. "I thought that was coming. A pity, in some ways." Then, before I had time to digest this information, he remarked with something of his old stiffness:

"I hear you entertain my father in the evenings. I appreciate that kindness."

I answered rather primly that I found the Count's room more restful than other parts of the house.

"I am very fond of him," he said thoughtfully. "Of course he has been quite out of touch with realities for many years. That's perfectly natural, one accepts it in an old man. I find it unforgivable in younger people."

Even now I do not know whether that last remark was meant to have a special significance for me.

'Out of touch'; he was right, I supposed. From where we stood, beside the gimcrack cooking shed, I could see a portion of the house and the window of Count Kolbeck's room. There, kept warm by the blankets and the little stove which Jadwiga contrived to keep going, he would be sitting now; and even if he was in physical pain his clouded eyes would be faintly lit with amusement over something scratched from his mind's vast field. So long as food was brought when he needed it, could any of our lives concern him? During the night the first snow had fallen; it had thawed almost at once, leaving behind a raw, fidgeting wind and a lake of mud which the lorries were churning into slimy mounds. All morning a straggling train of old men and women had been trudging between us and the village with rubble from the ruined houses, carried in barrows and slings, to toughen the vehicle-standings; they were no hungrier or more raggedly clothed, perhaps, than such people had been in my childhood, but in their pinched and cheese-white faces I saw the settled apathy of those to whom life is only death's postponement. A dozen men in uniform, themselves rough labourers knocked into the pattern of soldierhood, were directing them with a boredom which crackled now and then into bursts of savage temper. In the eyes of these men, too, was a morbid hopelessness; and to this spectacle of shapeless, objectless existence the steely light of Polish winter gave the look of an untalented painting, each object equally defined against a uniformity of tones, chilled, watery and flat. . . . Of this the Count knew nothing; and within the wall which age builds round a man, protecting all his senses, it was easy for him to warm himself with gentle philosophies.

I said to Julius, as these thoughts were playing across my mind, "Are there any realities worth being in touch with?"

"Poland," he said almost casually, "Poland is the reality." And he went on to talk, in the sane and confidential way which somehow flattered me, about the news which his mother had sent him, the political strategy which lay behind it and what prospects it implied for us.

5

i

I DREAMED, in one of those nights, that my baby was already born; that he was crying, and that when I moved the shawl from his head it was Victor's face which looked up at me in piteous entreaty. This peculiarly vivid dream haunted me for a long time; superstitiously, I took it as a sign that Victor was still alive.

It may have had its influence on my plans; and certainly the news about the cage being moved gave urgency to what had been rather a wish than an intention. But I was only brought to action by a piece of information which Tytus gave me when he came one late afternoon, with a cartload of blankets, to the billet where I was working. No one else was about. He got down from the cart, stood with his back against the wall about a yard away from me, and spoke in an undertone without once looking in my direction.

"That Josef Mariek—you remember him? The cobbler's boy."

"Yes, I know him well."

"The cobbler's boy," he repeated, "Mariek the cobbler—he took a girl from the House—Yanka—a kitchen-girl she was——"

"Yes, yes, I know."

"And he got this Josef from her. A big lad, big shoulders he had—that was when he started growing up, you see. Well, they thought he might do as a soldier, a big lad like that——"

"I know, he enlisted in my husband's regiment——"

"So they went to Mr Victor—the Count's grandson, that was . . ."

I listened patiently while he told me everything about Josef Mariek that I had known for years, and by degrees my long-sufferance was rewarded. It appeared that three nights before, when Tytus had driven his cart into the cage and was unloading it as usual, a prisoner had come to him in the darkness, and had whispered a message for Yanka, the cobbler's wife: 'Tell her that Josef is doing all right.' Tytus could not be certain, but he thought from the voice that the man was Josef himself.

"And then, you see, Ladyship, I thought to myself—not that night, nor yet the day after, but only this morning, as it was—I thought to myself, 'The young Ladyship was saying about her husband's regiment—Colonel Victor's regiment—she was asking me if there were lads from Colonel Victor's regiment in the cage. Well now,' I thought to myself, 'if that man was Josef Mariek—this man that came to me in the cage—and seeing it was Mr Victor took him into his own regiment——'"

A voice from the other end of the building, shouting "Where's that—— cart?" cut short this dissertation. Almost as soon as the last word reached us he was back on his driving-board, lashing at the horse's quarter; and when I tried to talk to him again, a little later, he affected to be blind and deaf.

This was a Friday, and according to routine Tytus should be making his next journey to the cage that evening. In about an hour, if the Corporal was in a reasonable temper, I should be dismissed, and at that time Tytus would be loading from the ration store— unless he got away early, as I had seen him do once or twice. By Tuesday, the day when he should go again, the cage might no longer be there. It appeared, then, that I had just an hour to make up my mind. This gave me time enough to realize that what I had roughly planned was immeasurably foolish; it would put not only me but my unborn child to the gravest risks, which the chance of my finding Mariek was far too small to justify. So reason told me. But I left myself a loophole, as one does in such circumstances. 'I shall decide finally,' I thought, 'when the moment arrives.'

The time for dismissal came, and the Corporal was not to be found; Julius thought he had gone over to the N.C.O.s' canteen. To leave without his permission would involve severe punishment. I waited for five minutes, for ten. When he did come he was in his worst mood, and refused to let me go until I had taken down all the electric globes and washed them. (The poverty of light in the billet was one of this man's obsessions; the globes were perfectly clean— the current was feeble.) I was thus some twenty-five minutes late in getting away, and I might well have accepted this with thankfulness as fate's decision. Illogically, I felt thwarted and angry.

Then, as I started back towards the house, I looked over towards the ration store. One of the windows, screened with too thin a material, showed a faint rectangle of light, and against this rectangle I could discern a horse's head. My single chance of getting into the cage had not yet passed.

ii

I have thought since how a man like Victor would have planned such an escapade as this; how minutely he would have calculated the timings and prepared for every conceivable mischance. But then, if I had tried to act in that way I should not have acted at all, for such deliberation demands a bravery which I have never possessed. As it was, I did not make my way to the cart cautiously, as a person of even moderate intelligence would have done, but running as fast as my condition allowed; and instead of climbing aboard it with circumspection I almost threw myself inside. I cannot think what would have happened if the cart had been quite full.

I had, indeed, not much space to play with, and when I shifted a sack of turnips to make myself a little hiding-place another sack fell over, pouring part of its contents over the tail of the cart to the ground. Had it been a German who came out of the store just then he would at least have been suspicious; but it was Tytus who came, and to his peasant understanding there was nothing strange in the notion of inanimate objects rolling themselves out of a stationary vehicle. He stooped, cursing, and angrily hurled the turnips back into the cart, where a number fell on my head.

The journey to the cage may have taken twenty minutes—time which should have served for the planning I had previously neglected. But I did not use it so. I knew so little of how things would be at the end of the journey that I really had no basis on which to plan. No, as far as I remember them, my thoughts in those twenty minutes of painful discomfort were engaged in composing the speech which I should make if I were found. (I was inventing the absurd kind of story which people often use when caught red-handed—I had 'never realized the cart was going to the cage', had meant just to take a lift to the village to draw my rations, and so on.) These thoughts were accompanied by all the physical symptoms of fear, but not, I think, by fear itself. There is a special sense of unreality which protects the mind on such occasions. With a certain morbid fascination I was picturing my arrest, the rough-and-ready trial which might follow, even my execution. But I disbelieved those pictures. I said, as life has never cured me of saying, 'These things

[113]

have never happened, and therefore do not happen, to me. Even the present experience, of crouching on the dirty floor of Tytus's cart, half covered with vegetables, cannot really be happening.'

We halted at what was evidently the entrance to the cage and waited for some minutes there. I could hear the sentries talking together—they seemed to be scrutinizing Tytus's entry permit with that pedantic conscientiousness which German sentries will devote to the same papers, produced by the same man, five times in an hour. If equal thoroughness had been exercised by the one who flashed a torch inside the cart, this record would probably not have been written; fortunately, no army can waste its best human material on the staffing of prisoner camps. That, none the less, was a moment of sickening fright.

When we stopped again I received one lesson in the folly of acting without advance information. I had supposed that the scene of clearance would be much the same as that of loading, darkness broken only by a pale shaft from a doorway, perhaps a torch shining here and there; and in that scanty light it would be easy—I had thought—to pass unnoticed, in the brown boiler-suit which was my working dress, between the men unloading. But the regulation about showing lights evidently did not apply here, other risks being reckoned the greater, and the area where the cart came to rest was almost as well lit, from lamps high overhead, as a railway station in peace-time. Here again my naïveté helped me. My one clear thought was that I must not be found inside the cart. I waited till Tytus had got down, and then, when I heard him tapping at a door perhaps twenty yards away, I raised the canvas at the front of the tilt, squeezed through to the driving-board which he had just vacated and dropped to the ground beside the shafts. Straight ahead, at a distance of some forty metres, was a line of what appeared to be small, square buildings. (They were actually tents.) In a gap between them I saw two men talking. Without pausing to see if I had been observed, or to calculate the chances that the men I saw might be guards, I started walking towards them.

They watched my approach with the curiosity of animals, which increased palpably as they realized I was a woman: probably none of my sex had been seen in that encampment before. I went up to them boldly—there was nothing else I could do now—and said in Polish, "I'm looking for a man called Mariek—Sergeant Josef Mariek. Can you help me?" The answer was a wooden silence. And then the taller of the two, furtively but very swiftly, turned and slipped away into the darkness.

For a few moments the other one went on staring as if he were drunk. But at last he said, "Who are you?"

I knew then, with a flood of relief, that he was a Pole.

"It doesn't matter," I told him. "I'm looking for Sergeant Josef Mariek. Do you know him?"

There was another long pause. Then he said, "It's dangerous here, they can see you," and led me to where the nearest tent cast a shadow.

"Mariek, do you know him?" I repeated.

"Mariek? No." His voice was that of a townsman of some education. At the time I could not understand his infuriating slowness; I know now that one frequent effect of captivity is to retard the mental processes. "Mariek? What corps? What unit?"

I told him, adding a sketch of Mariek's appearance, and he began to ponder this information as if it would serve to pass the dull remainder of the evening. "Yes, yes, I knew some of those people, in the camp at Ciechanowiec. . . ."

"I've not much time," I said.

"There's a man in my roster—Roster IX," he said slowly, "a cavalryman. I think he sleeps in Tent 23. He might know your friend—what did you say his name was?—he might know this Sergeant Mariek. I believe he did belong to General Prystor's command—I'm not certain——"

"Could you find him?"

"I could try. Tell me, what are things like? Is the War over? We don't get any news."

"Will you go and try!" I said desperately. "Please—please will you see if you can find him, this man who may know Mariek?"

He nodded then, and went away, slowly, repeating 'Mariek' to himself. I thought it likely that as soon as he was out of my sight he would forget his mission altogether.

Alone, keeping in the shadow, I looked back to where the cart was standing. Tytus had returned and seemed to be petting his horse or perhaps making some adjustment to the head-harness. So far no one else had appeared. Farther, in the same direction, I saw something which had been outside my range of observation before, a little roofed platform, perhaps twenty feet high, on which a helmeted soldier was standing. He appeared—I saw him only in silhouette—to be looking the other way, but while I watched he turned in a quarter-circle, and at his next turn he was facing me. Indeed, I had the impression that he could see me clearly, and I even waited for him to call out—'You! What are you doing there?'

This man, I thought, must surely have noticed me as I moved away from the cart; but since I had been walking at an ordinary pace he had presumably seen nothing suspicious about me. Two or three men, who might be guards or prisoners, were even now strolling across the open space over to my right without attracting his interest. It seemed that one could move about this place with impunity so long as one did not break the rules; but that freedom left some anxiety for me, who had no idea what the rules might be.

The wretchedness of the minutes which followed was such that I can recall it distinctly, although I have experienced more serious discomforts between then and now. The snow had started again, large damp flakes which came in lazy spirals and then swayed sideways like a street crowd out of control, to fall and melt immediately on the bare, wet earth. They lent a theatrical, almost a dreamlike quality, to this scene where the garish yellow light, cast in overlapping circles, gave an artificial hardness to the nearer canvas walls and a falsity of shadow to the structures farther away. But I knew well enough that this was not a dream. I was cold, and my clothes, damp with sweat, seemed to hang on my body loosely; I felt, newly and strangely, the pressure of my enlarging womb, and my excited breathing gave me pain. Fear is quickened by inaction, and I think that even a person of some courage would have found that period of waiting hard to bear. At any moment someone would start unloading the cart; even if there were only one man on the job besides Tytus (who was a feeble-bodied creature), it could take no more than a few minutes, and directly it was finished I should have my single, slender chance of getting away. What if that moment should arrive before my helper returned, with or without Mariek himself? Should I go on waiting, in the hope that friendly men could hide me somewhere till Tytus came on another journey? Or should I concentrate on escaping, and resign myself to having risked my life for no purpose at all? There was in my mind a rational part which told me that no further risk was justified; for the chance that Mariek—if he came—might have some news was no more than an even chance, and I seemed to know already that the only news of Victor which anyone could give me would be that he was dead. But beneath this voice of reason, steady and clear, there was another which only repeated softly, 'I cannot live any more without some certainty; I have got to know, to know!' So my physical nervousness, the kind which any uncourageous person feels on forbidden territory, was intensified by the torment of indecision. Standing perfectly still, straining my ears, I heard only the ship-like sounds of ropes and canvas chafing, a burst of coughing from some uncertain distance, men's voices which reached me eerily through the shadowed emptiness of this phantasmal place. My feet were like ice and the whole of my body was shaking with the violence of fever.

Perhaps a quarter of an hour passed, and then Tytus went back into the hut. Presently he reappeared with two other men, and the three of them in a desultory fashion began the unloading; even at that distance I could see that the newcomers were men unused to this sort of labour, and at least a minute must have passed before they got the first sack on to the shoulders of the biggest man, who carried it inside the hut. I tried to think how many sacks there might be and to calculate the total time the unloading would take. For so long, I thought, this is just a performance which I can watch as in a theatre; but the moment is coming, it is nearer now, nearer, when I must mount the stage and take my own part in the play.

I counted the sacks as they came out: four—five—six—seven. There would be twelve or fifteen perhaps. Fifteen? Not so many as that.

"You want Sergeant Mariek?"

I turned as if something had stung me: I had heard no footfall, no faintest sound of anyone approaching. I gasped:

"Who are you?"

The voice, belonging now to a soldier's shape moulded from the darkness, whispered:

"He's dead, Mariek. He died last night."

The man stood only a yard away from me, but in the shadow which held us both I could see nothing of his face except a patch of grey, framed in many windings of a scarf. His voice seemed vaguely familiar: one that had never broken properly, an adenoidal and rather peevish voice. It brought, suddenly, a name to my tongue:

"You're Corporal Paviakowski!"

"Pajciekowski," he corrected, and then he said again, "Mariek—he died last night. They had him on the punishment diet—that was for giving them lip. There was nothing I could do."

Yes, Pajciekowski, a regular—regimental farrier or something of that sort; I had a faint memory of his narrow, Galician face. In the way of his kind he was starting to rumble along his own path, explaining and explaining about Mariek; and because I was afraid now —afraid of learning the truth which I had come for—I could find no way to stop him, no words with which to ask the vital question. I could only say in a feeble voice, when he paused for a moment:

"You know who I am?"

He came a little closer, peering towards my face. I think my voice may have identified me already; but from shyness or the perversity of simple minds, he could only answer in a roundabout fashion:

"You oughtn't to be here—gracious pardon—they don't let civilians come in here. A civilian lady like your Ladyship, you don't know what they might do."

I hardly needed to be reminded of this uncertainty. Looking over my shoulder, I saw that Tytus and his fellows were standing still beside the cart. They might be taking a short rest or they might have finished. I said rather frantically:

"You know my husband—Colonel Kolbeck? Can you tell me anything about him—what's happened to him?"

"Colonel Kolbeck?" he repeated, speaking with great deliberation. "Why, of course I know him—it was the Colonel took up my Service and Conduct paper. Captain, he was then—Captain Kolbeck. That was at Bialow——"

"Is he alive?" I broke in. "Tell me—do you know—is he alive?"

"It was Mariek knew him better than I did," he said. "Sergeant Mariek that I was telling you of—he was talking to me, well, not ten days back, he was talking about the Colonel. He was with him, you see, the last mix-up they had with the Germans. The way Mariek told me, they thought they were fighting the Russians, see, and they knew the Russians couldn't come in on the right flank because they weren't across the river, not then, see. Only, the Germans could come. Of course they didn't think the Germans had got as far as all that, they reckoned that 45 Brigade were holding them on that flank."

Over by the hut the three men were still standing idle; indulging, probably, in illicit conversation. But even as I looked that way the door of the hut was opened and an angry voice shouted something in German. The two loaders immediately broke away, and Tytus came round to his horse.

"Tell me," I said again, "is he alive?"

The desperation in my voice should have forced an answer from a dumb animal. But these men, trained to the special humility of rank and file, have a delicacy of their own. Never before, I suppose, had an officer's wife asked him such a question as mine, and he simply lacked the means to answer it directly.

He began, "The Colonel, you understand, he was a cavalry soldier of the old sort——" and then stopped.

Satisfied with his last adjustments to the harness, Tytus was climbing rheumatically on to the driving-board.

"Yes——?"

No force on earth would hurry Pajciekowski now, for he had found the channel where his thoughts moved with the greatest comfort. They were seldom greatly gifted in utterance, these seasoned troopers, but when their professional interest was roused it would move them to something in the nature of eloquence—the slow, charmed, confidential oratory of scholarship.

"The Colonel, you see, he thought there was nothing you couldn't do with horses. It was armoured cars the Germans had— a whole dozen of them coming over the crest, with the infantry close behind. It was good infantry work, Mariek told me——"

"Yes, but——"

"He could see it all from where he was standing—Mariek—he was with the Colonel, see. Well, what could he do, the Colonel? Armoured cars, you've got to have guns to deal with them, the automatics just bounce off them, and the guns over above the river were registering all the other way. He was cursing everyone, the Colonel. 'I've got to switch that battery,' he said. 'Where's the Gunner Officer?' he said. 'Where's the signallers?' Well, there wasn't a Gunner Officer, he'd got himself shot, the Colonel might have known—that's what Mariek said——"

"Look, I've got to get in that cart before it goes. What did happen to the Colonel? You've got to tell me——"

"I can't tell you more than what Mariek said. It was the Colonel's way, he could never stand by and let the others do the fighting, no matter what the General might have ordered him. 'B' Squadron it was that he put in. Captain Filipieski—I used to be with him—it was his squadron. 'Tell him to cut the infantry off from the cars'— that was the order the Colonel sent down to him. Well—but the way the cars were, they'd got to ride between them first, and that's no nursery play for horses, with nothing but their speed to care for them."

And now the cart was moving off, slowly, turning in a wide circle to face the avenue by which it had come. So, that much was decided; my last chance was over. For a moment I felt, curiously, a kind of relief.

"What do you mean," I asked in bitter weariness, " 'the Colonel wouldn't let the others do the fighting'?"

"Well, it's what I was saying. The Sergeant tried to stop him— Mariek, I mean—so did the other officers who were there. Well, what could they do? 'I think it might be amusing,' was what he said —the Colonel—and he was off away down the track before they could say the next word. Well, of course, Mariek went after him— he was the old kind of soldier, Mariek. But he couldn't catch up with him—there wasn't a horse in the Brigade could show its shoes to that brown mare of the Colonel's. Joined in with the second line —the Colonel—just as they were starting their wheel. And the next the Sergeant saw, he was right up ahead with the Captain— with Captain Filipieski—and then he was out in front of them all, going on through the cars as if it was a steeplechase." He paused, and seemed to be shrugging his shoulders. "Well, that's the old style of fighting. It's finished. There may be a use for horses—outflank-ing movements, long-range patrols—but you can't put them straight on at armoured cars."

"You mean—he was shot down? My husband was shot down?" He must have nodded; in the darkness I did not see. He said:

"Of course, I can only tell you what Mariek said. It wasn't easy for him to see, with the smoke and that—it may have been the Colonel was hit himself, or only the mare. And of course he hadn't the time on his hands to see a lot—Mariek—he'd got his own horse to ride. The way Mariek saw him, he was on his back, right down in the mud. He could see from the wheel-rut how the car had gone right over him. He could see he was dead."

'He could see from the wheel-rut how the car had gone right over him. He could see he was dead.' The news you have long ex-pected comes, in the end, in some slightly different shape, with a different feel. In advance, you think of all the ways in which it may reach you—on a sheet of paper this size or that, written by type-writer or by hand, spoken in one voice or another—but actuality accords with none of this prevision, experience cannot be rehearsed. The effort which the mind makes to forestall experience may not be wholly wasted, for the result is to sheathe the evil when it comes in a softening coat of unreality. The pictures you have made have all proved false; this, happening now, may somehow be false as well. *He could see he was dead.*' It was not possible, I thought, for so momentous a fact to be conveyed in a sentence as simple and bald as that; and though I caught my breath when I heard it, it became almost instantly a pattern of words which had no meaning. The death of the old is easy to accept: it could not be that a creature hardly older than I, in whose rich life so much of mine had been absorbed, was never to smile, to speak to me again.

Perhaps this incredulity was only of the heart. I know that I did not greatly suffer then. The heart, I think, which may be convulsed by lesser griefs, is an instrument too finely made to respond at once to the highest charge of sorrow; it will vibrate a little, and that vibration must continue through the years before the charge is absorbed.

I remember that I thanked Pajciekowski for his information with an absurd politeness, as if I had been seated in my drawing-room at Poznan, receiving from this soldier a message that Victor had sent me; so that he, in instinctive response, clicked his heels, turned smartly and marched away. I remember also that I stayed where I was for a minute or two; not so much for lack of a plan as because no plan for staying alive seemed relevant any more.

iii

Nothing that I did after that came from intelligence, as that faculty is commonly understood. If I had acted before with the audacity of fools, my movements now were those of the inebriate. I walked slowly—in the direction where the cart had disappeared—because there was nothing to make me run. I took a wide route, keeping at a distance from the observation platform, because I wanted solitude for its own sake. I have no recollection of being frightened or even faintly excited at that stage, or of feeling the cold or physical pain.

I met no one. It seemed that I walked for a great distance, as one walks in dreams, through the canvas streets of this empty city, where one rhomboid of yellow light, stippled with drifting flakes, was succeeded by another; where, in the intersecting shadows, a guy-rope suddenly came against my chest, or I stumbled against a pile of deals, or found the tailboard of a lorry barring my way. Here there were voices which came from some way off, muted and impersonal, like the random voices in a telephone. Here, fluttering with the snowflakes, were shreds of German sentences, a splutter of toneless laughter, reaching me as the sounds of reality penetrate into sleep. I moved without purpose, vaguely expecting that in time someone would stop me. Mechanically I repeated the sentences which I had prepared on the outward journey, 'I thought the cart was going to the village; I was tired and wanted a lift; I came here by mistake.'

Where the light was dimmest a wooden wall rose suddenly and brought the road I followed to an end. Here, as I turned, was some large thing which moved, which shook itself and stamped in the mud. And so, I thought as I went along, there are horses kept in this strange place. That was as far as my reflection reached, and I had wandered on some way before a whiff of lingering curiosity made me to turn to look at the horse again. With the light behind me now, I saw that there was a cart attached; a cart like the one in which Tytus had brought me.

And now intelligence was faintly stirring. I had seen Tytus drive away, but it did not follow that he had driven straight out of the cage; something might have stopped him, and the cart I was looking at now might be his. I was to know, later, that nothing out of the ordinary had happened: on these excursions Tytus had to deliver portions of his load at two different stores, and when I caught up with him he had just completed his second delivery; at the moment of my reaching the cart he was actually inside the hut, waiting for his receipt. But my brain was too sluggish at the time even to wonder what the reason for the second stop might be. At the same somnambulistic pace I retraced my steps, felt about the back of the cart, decided that it must be Tytus's and climbed inside with as little emotion as if I were boarding a Warsaw tram.

It is hard to recapture that torpidity of mind, and I marvel at the foolishness I manifested then. The cart was empty of vegetables, but a dozen empty sacks had been thrown inside, and with these a woman even of feeble wits could have contrived some sort of concealment. I did not attempt it. I sat with my back against a sideboard, my legs stretched out before me, my eyes closed. I think I may even have dozed before the cart started moving. It is a fact (if my memory of so somnolent an hour is to be trusted) that I had clean forgotten the sentries who would examine the cart on the way out.

When we stopped it was too late. I might, even then, have tried to cover myself with the sacks; but the shock of hearing voices close to me again—the offensive staccato of the sentries, Tytus's bleating replies—so reawoke my cowardice that I became incapable of any movement at all. One may decide that life has lost all use; but when danger suddenly comes close the primal instincts prevail over all philosophy. Just then I was an animal, trapped, almost paralysed by fear.

That was how the sentry found me when he came to the back of the cart and swung the beam of his torch inside. He saw a trousered figure sitting absolutely still; not, I think, trembling, because there is a stage in fear where trembling ceases, giving place to ice-cold stillness; and in the hard, narrow light from the torch he probably failed to see the colour of my face, which must have been white as chalk. I know that as he stared at me I gave him a sickly smile.

"You, who are you?" he asked in German.

I did not answer—my power of speech had gone. But when he repeated the question in Polish I said in a shrunken voice, totally unlike my own:

"Stefanie."

"What are you doing in this cart?"

I remained quite dumb. He put his head closer to mine, and although I saw it in a dimly reflected light I have a clearer memory of his than of a hundred German faces I saw at that time: the primitive, flat nose, great teeth projecting from foolishly parted lips, the eyes of a bull-calf just taken from its dam.

Again: "What are you doing in this cart?"

The sentences which had been running in my head—'I thought the cart was going to the village, I got here by mistake'—came almost to my lips. But they would not do, these people did not allow you to make mistakes. I could feel the idiot smile lingering on my mouth, and the words that came had the same fatuity:

"He told me to get in."

"Told you—who told you?"

Who? A German, it would have to be, a soldier, someone of importance. I said, still grinning feebly:

"The Commandant."

"*The Commandant?*"

A lie, once started, grows by itself.

"I've been to see the Commandant."

"Sergeant!" the sentry called, and another man came, bearing a more powerful lamp. "There's a civvy in the cart here."

"So I can see."

"She says she's been to the Commandant."

"Oh—so you've been to the Commandant?"

"Yes, sir. He told me to get in the cart."

The Sergeant hooked his lamp on to the tilt.

"That's interesting. How did you get into this camp?"

"I came in the car."

"Car? What car?"

"The Commandant's car."

"Oh—so you're a friend of the Commandant?"

"Yes," I said, "yes, a friend."

The Sergeant looked at the sentry, and a grin appeared on his pockmarked face. The sentry, young and slow of mind, did not understand that; but I did.

"The Commandant told me I wasn't to talk to anyone," I said.

The Sergeant nodded quizzically; he suddenly called "You—Polish fellow—come here—at the double!" and Tytus came. "Now, Polish bastard"—he had his massive hand on Tytus's neck —"who's that you've got in there?"

For half a minute (or so it felt) Tytus stared at me, his small, heavily whiskered face poked over the tailboard, his mouselike eyes glazed with incredulity.

"Who is that?" the Sergeant demanded.

"I never saw her get in there."

The Sergeant dug his nails a little farther into Tytus's neck and shook it.

"I didn't ask you that! I said, Who is it?"

"Sir—with gracious pardon—that's the Colonel's lady."

The Sergeant's grin appeared again. "It is, hch!" He gave Tytus another shake and pushed him away. "You, Krumke, stand by here —yes, keep the bitch covered! You—*Polin*—you move an inch and that rifle goes off, see!" He turned and marched into the guardroom.

I heard presently the whirr of a field telephone and then the Sergeant's voice, clipped and deferential, paying out short threads of information. ". . . difficult, sir, as she's spoken about the Commandant. . . . Exactly, sir. . . . Well, I should say, not ugly, sir. . . . Understood, sir!" His voice fell below the general chatter of the guardroom, from which a few words found their way to me: '. . . prisoner hiding in it. . . .' 'No, it's a Polish civvy—it's a tart' '. . . The Sergeant thinks she's the Colonel's whore.' By degrees the laughter gave place to silence, in which I could hear the nervous breathing of Tytus, standing beside the shafts. The face of the soldier Krumke had settled to the impassivity of duty, he had his wrists resting securely on the tailboard, his index finger along the trigger guard of the rifle, and I doubt if the foresight, held within a foot of my stomach, once shifted half an inch. How long the silence lasted I do not know.

It was broken by the sound of a small motor, which slithered to a standstill beside the cart. A new face now appeared by Krumke's elbow, rotund, grotesquely dutiful, the quite unmilitary face of an elderly lieutenant. "This is the woman?" he gravely asked, and Krumke, without moving, answered "Sir!" In the guardroom heels were clicking, and I heard, interlaced with the Sergeant's servile tones, a fluting voice which smacked of the Kaiserhof:

[124]

"Awkward, yes, very, I agree!"

When I saw the owner of that voice—his chin above the junior officer's head—I seemed to know him well: the soldier of opéra-bouffe who is found in every army, nature's recognized provision for the soubrette and for G.H.Q.s. I was not surprised by the smile he gave me, or by his first remark, made in a whisper that everyone could hear:

"I never thought the Old Man had so much taste!"

The Lieutenant eyed him anxiously; perplexed, as amateurs are, by senior levity.

"I haven't questioned the woman, sir. I thought you might prefer to do so yourself."

"Indeed, yes!" The Captain changed to Polish: "You, my dear, you say you've come from the Commandant?"

I answered, "If you please, yes, Mr Officer."

"And he gave you a pass, my sweet?"

"No, sir. He said I didn't need a pass, not if I was in the cart. He said I wasn't to speak to the soldiers at all."

That answer, born of desperation and given in a smirking twitter, seemed to afford him pleasure. He bent closer, so that I smelt the schnapps in his breath.

"Very right!" he said. "It's a wise rule never to speak to soldiers —only to handsome officers, like my friend here, for instance. Well now, I think we'd better take you back to the Commandant——"

"But sir," the Lieutenant interrupted, "the Commandant——"

"Shut up, Hechtel! . . . We'd better take you back to the Commandant and ask him if what you say is true. Don't you agree?"

That was the moment when I gave up hope. But my brain still struggled. What had the Lieutenant been about to say? Was it that the Commandant was out of camp, or too busy to be disturbed? Had he meant to suggest that an officer in the Commandant's position might not much care to see his subordinates producing—on a salver, as it were—his private affairs? From these speculations there emerged one certainty: to refuse would be to lose the match.

"Oh yes!" I said.

In the pause that followed, the Lieutenant turned another anxious glance upon the Captain, and then glared at me.

"How do you know it was the Commandant you saw?"

"I think I saw it on his door, sir."

(This was a guess; it was lucky.)

"And what is his name?" he demanded fiercely.

"He told me to call him Hansi."

"Hansi?"

But to the Captain this was the crown of happiness. "But, of course!" he said, nodding at me and then at his junior with a caricature of gravity. (And at that moment I breathed a blessing upon him and all his species, male animals of the common breed, living on the frivolity of their small and bawdy minds.) " 'Hansi', of course—it's always 'Hansi'!"

"Hansi did say," I added, "that he didn't want to see me again. Not till Saturday night."

"Not," the Captain repeated, "till Saturday night!"

The mask of earnestness cracked and melted away, his head fell back and from his raucous lungs there came three thunderclaps of gargantuan laughter. In the studious face of the Lieutenant the look of pain continued for a moment and then yielded to a deprecating smile; if a senior and professional officer could be amused without breach of discipline, then a modest joviality was permissible to Lieutenant Hechtel as well. His eyes puckered, he opened his mouth a little way and a titter escaped.

"Such temperance!" the Captain gasped. "So moderate, so respectable of Hansi! Only on Saturday night!"

The Sergeant, standing at attention behind the officers, had so far kept his icy composure. He, in his turn, accepted a hearty nudge from the Captain's elbow as permission to relax. It was not for N.C.O.s to share in officers' jests, but this was a joke which transcended every boundary, it was *the* joke, ageless and sanctified by age, blessed by the generosity of nature for the use of all malekind. He smiled respectfully; the demon of ribaldry seized its chance and he laughed aloud. Now the sluices opened wide, and now, caught in the torrent of primal emotion, the three inquisitors were laughing as one man. Rocking on his heels, the Sergeant was uttering volley after volley of pectoral snorts, the Captain with his head on the Lieutenant's shoulder wheezed and staggered, while from Hechtel's puckered eyes there rolled upon his quivering cheeks great tears of German mirth, honest, childlike, catholically obscene. Only the soldier Krumke was unstirred by this wave of merriment, which he was perhaps too simple to understand: as if he were at practice on the range his eyes remained intent, expressionless; his hands, white with the cold, were steady, his forefinger still rested stiffly against the trigger guard: and though my own eyes wandered once and again to the peculiar court on whose verdict my life depended —the three intrinsically commonplace creatures who rolled and spluttered in the pool of freckled light—they returned to rest on

Krumke's homely, disciplined face, as if he and I were privately engaged in an affair of mutual trust.

It was the Sergeant, naturally, who recovered first; he dropped his merriment as a man throws away a cigarette, his body clicked back to attention.

"Shall I put the female in the guardroom, sir?"

The Captain, pulling himself together, screwed his knuckles in his eyes and yawned. "I'm a tyro in this outfit—is that the drill for civilians?"

"It's in the Standing Orders, sir—anyone found without a pass, confine in guardroom, report to Duty Officer."

" 'Report to Duty Officer'—well then, it's up to you, Hechtel. Chance for your legal abilities, you can beat up an elegant Court of Inquiry if you like these things. I expect that's what it says in the book. Only I shouldn't call Hansi as evidence, I think he might not care for that."

I glanced then at Hechtel's face and saw that he was back in the miserable perplexity of civilian soldiers. He said, "I shall have to study the text of the Regulations——"

The Captain nodded amiably. "Of course! Only it'd save a lot of time and fuss if she'd happened to be 'shot while attempting to evade arrest', wouldn't you think?"

"You mean——?"

"Oh, God!" said the Captain, suddenly losing patience. "Are you sentimental about these bloody Poles? Here, someone give me a rifle!" The fit of laughing may have done something to clear the fumes from his head; he was showing now, at least, the genuine soldier's capacity to make a decision. "You can stand easy, sentry." He took the rifle which was brought to him from the guardroom, opened and closed the bolt, and then shouted at Tytus: "You, get up on your seat! . . . Now, drive on! And keep straight down the track, see!"

As the cart moved forward, and the wired barrier was pulled across behind it, I saw him come up to the aim, in the competent way of a practised game shot. I remember that I heard the Lieutenant tittering—that, I suppose, was a nervous reaction. We had made perhaps thirty yards—I do not know—when, flat on the floor, I heard my own voice screaming and the crack of the fired cartridge at the same time. From what Tytus told me later on, I conclude that the bullet went high above the cart; which means either that the Captain was more drunk than he seemed or that he possessed what answers for chivalry in men of his kind. It was enough, when I recovered consciousness (somewhere near the village, I think), to know that I still lived.

Tytus may have taken me to the house, or I may have walked there from wherever he set me down. From that point Annette or Wanda probably helped me, and it seems that I went to my work as usual next day.

That night and day are lost, but I know that the sense of wonder at being alive persisted, as the wonder of first love persists, and at least another day must have passed before this artificial light began to grow faint. In the common daylight to which it yielded, my spirit was like a house from which the children have gone away. The slender hope that Victor lived had been my reason for living; and now, when a pain I was familiar with attacked me on successive days, I thought that his child had ceased to live as well.

6

i

I TOLD no one of what I had learned. The knowledge of Victor's death seemed to me a part of himself, the last that I could claim as my own, and I would guard it jealously. Less irrationally, I did not want the Kolbecks to realize that my dependence on them was again complete, as it had been after Casimir's desertion. I had begun to hope, when the pains did not recur, that my pregnancy was saved. It was certain that when the child was born my father-in-law would claim him as a Kolbeck possession, and my only means of resistance would lie in the pretence that Victor might one day come to support my own claim.

Deliberately, then, I bore the grief alone, when so many were at hand to share and so to relieve the burden. But the instinct which had craved for certainty proved to have been no false one. With the acknowledgment of grief there came a tranquillity which I had not experienced till now.

Wrapped in this sombre calm, I found in the final investment of winter a kind of sympathy. In the weeks of rain and blustering wind the hills about us had been lost in haze, and the scene I was conscious of had been filled with the alien gear that shaped our discomfort, iron-roofed sheds which the invaders strewed about our fields, gaunt vehicles scarring the earth with their tracks, the fumes of kerosene cookers and the raw sibilance of the German voice. Now, when the snow had attacked in heavier force and the cooled earth could no longer absorb it, the contours of our valley emerged, freshly drawn on a blue-white sheet, and the world which they restored to us, wider but firmly defined, was impervious to conquest and to change. It was not to be left immaculate: a small army of villagers was set to clearing roofs and roads; over a widening area about the depot buildings the snow was furrowed and soiled; but away from the village, where the land rose into forest, the massive coverlet could no more be disturbed by men of any sort than the hills themselves. Made wretched by the cold, the soldiers increased in spitefulness—they shot a village woman out of hand for stealing a litre of oil—and they were always tightening their hold upon our lives. But they could not prevent the fall of snow, and a winter of this majesty, familiar to ourselves, imposed on them a tyranny greater than their own. Beneath the vastness of this white invasion, which hushed the noise of their wheels and turned their march into a drunken shamble, which trapped and sometimes buried the trucks with their supplies, they must have felt their smallness as well as their isolation. The wind, now, was a slowly flowing stream, sensible only by its coldness against your skin. The salt flavour it took from the snow diluted all the smells which they had brought with their campaign, it blurred their voices and tricked their ears, so that the sneering cry of marsh-fowl passing in hungry flights across the valley, the creak of burdened walls, a sudden rap from pellets of snow blown against a window-pane, must have been sinister to them. To them the voice of animals in the forest, which the stillness of these winter nights brought close, was strange and fearful. While to me it was just an embroidery on the quilt of silence; and an eerie light which the snow reflected through Setory windows only recalled, for me, the bygone safety of being a child.

We too suffered from the cold, and our food was insufficient for the demands of the work they gave us: But the purpose of my life, narrowed and stiffened by the knowledge of Victor's death, was enough to distract me from these incidental hardships. If the details of my existence were largely ordered by a man who formerly sold fish (as I discovered) to the housewives of Dortmund, an army of such creatures could not interrupt the force that silently, in one superb assault, had possessed our countryside. To that power I felt myself in service. Already, beneath its hardened shell, the ground was being prepared to yield new life; and in the fastness of my body I could feel a kindred work advancing. Though I suffered at this time from vertigo and other symptoms of physical weakness, I still believed that with so inexorable a force supporting my own resolution I should be ready when the time came to bear my son. Sometimes now I would talk to Conrad (as I already called him); whispering, with my face bent towards where he lay, 'We shall win, you and I! I shall find the strength to give you life, whether or not it costs us mine.'

Yes, the winter was too much for our masters, or so it appeared, and they had to retreat. In truth, the move was political. A staff car with an armoured escort came through the snow, filled with personages who, though uniformed, had 'Wilhelmstrasse' written in every wrinkle of their sallow faces. Someone who looked like a Divisional Commander came to join them, and there was a conference lasting half an hour in the Sub-Area Commandant's room. Talk in the mess that night was so free that even Henryk, on duty as bar orderly, picked up some notion of the impending move. It was coming soon, he thought, when we questioned him upstairs—tomorrow, it might be. "Tired of it, that lot!" he giggled. "Off home!"

Their departure, two days later, was like their arrival: abrupt, faultlessly ordered. The Germans are in one sense of a masculine nature: they believe that an action is sanctified by meticulous performance, regardless of whether it is worth performing at all. And in this instance they were doubtless as glad to depart as we to see them go.

Reporting before it was light at my place of employment, I found the barrack furniture already stacked for removal, the men hard at work: some dismantling the temporary fittings, some bundling their kits. With swift and clever hands a draper-like creature who appeared to be half asleep was packing light-bulbs into a case of shavings, a man with a limp was gathering every nail and screw into an ammunition tin. There was no confusion, scarcely an appearance of haste; they applied to their tasks, these riff-raff of an army with their squints and curvatures, the mechanical precision of the finest soldiers I have seen. Outside, the cookhouse and washing-sheds were being taken to bits, the numbered sections stowed in the trucks which stood beside them with their engines running. The trucks moved on; another purring up from the darkness was filled with tables and utensils, the next with kits and bedding, while an N.C.O. checked every item on his printed list. Ten minutes later, in the half-light, the men were parading in marching order, with their boots and equipment clean. For fully a quarter of an hour they stood at attention in the snow, motionless, impeccably aligned; then they were marched by details to the trucks which still stood empty. By nine o'clock the last of these had gone.

Up at the house some touches of ceremony were added to the routine of exodus. The Commandant went upstairs to make a little speech to the womenfolk in which he told them, with slightly lachrymose emotion, that his nation was not only the greatest in the world but also the most humane; while Captain Bautz, after a final snub from Wanda, got my poor Annette in a dark corner and tried to embrace her there. But the cars were waiting and industrious orderlies were about their business. This clutch of adolescents, Commandant and all, had disappeared before eleven.

There had been property of value in the rooms they occupied, household silver, the sword presented to the first Stanislas Kolbeck by the City of Cracow, miniatures by Prieur and Isabey. Not one of these things was taken. A walnut writing-desk which they had damaged had been skilfully repaired by one of their own tradesmen before they left.

So I returned, that morning, to find the lower part of the house empty; empty, and exhaling the chilled, sepulchral air of those long deserted châteaux which are kept for exhibition to inquisitive tourists. In the hall, where Wanda was scrubbing the tiles, there were a few wine bottles, and a pull-through belonging to some unusually careless soldier hung over one of the chairs. Those, with a few rubs and scratches, were all the visible traces that our visitors had left of their occupation. They had not materially altered the place, and it may have been only in my imagination that they had killed some genius which was there before they came.

The Kolbecks may have felt about it as I did, for they did not immediately take possession of the vacated rooms, as one had thought they would. Indeed, the cramped and inconvenient life upstairs seemed to be continuing as if no one could conceive a better one. Perhaps, in those days when every certainty had proved to be illusion, they merely clung to any mode of existence which seemed to function. This apathy had apparently caught the village people as well. When I went out in the afternoon I saw several cottages which the Germans had used standing empty with their doors swinging in the wind, and everywhere I came upon groups of people wandering as if they had no idea where to go. I spoke to some of them, and found that in their belief the German removal was only a ruse: one woman produced a circumstantial rumour that as soon as the inhabitants had settled in their homes again the village was going to be bombarded with incendiary shell. For the rest, everyone was celebrating the liberation by taking a holiday; but these holiday-makers so lacked the spirit of carnival that they had the air of children taking part in a play they do not even faintly understand.

There were special reasons for this look of bewilderment. However onerous the burdens which the invaders had laid upon us, however meagre the food we got in return, we had come to rely on them for keeping most of us alive. If their system was harsh, it was at least a system: you were given your ticket, you knew where to present it with the certainty of getting something in exchange—either food or the authoritative information that none was available that day. To this arrangement we had become accustomed, and its sudden removal left us like a ship without rudder or sails. The notion of returning to an earlier way of life did not occur to us. In our present isolation, the framework of that life had gone; and even had we been in touch with the authorities we were used to they would not have restored our former situation, for what we really needed at this time was not so much the moral force of government as something to eat. Some grain—I cannot say how much—lay hidden in outlying farmsteads, but every sack of it that our visitors could find had been commandeered. They had slaughtered cattle and poultry recklessly, and nearly all of what was left alive had been driven or carted westward. This was a high price to pay for the *pax Romana* with which they had indulged us, and it was not surprising that the simple country people were more impressed by the economic than by the political aspects of our new situation. The cold was now intense. As, trudging once more to the shop which they could not believe was out of business, they passed the charred remains of houses fired at the start of the occupation; as, with their backs to empty barns and deserted shippens, they looked out at the frozen countryside, they were, I think, to be forgiven for hailing their liberty less exultantly than men with heavier stomachs would have bade them.

Emerging then, from tyranny, we instinctively looked for some new tyranny to take its place; and were not kept waiting long. There was, however, an interregnum; in which some of our community might have perished, as much from lassitude as from cold and hunger, had not one voice sounded to remind us that neither human will nor the possibility of an ordered life had ceased to exist.

iii

As a labourer, my father-in-law had played his part so faithfully that I had sometimes come near to accepting it as the reality. Indeed, I had often thought of him simply as workmate, and felt for him

[133]

that kind of rudimentary affection which working-men will show for their fellows—an emotion unaffected by differences in age or temperament. So, when the play was over, I saw the return of his own personality with something of the incredulity one feels in meeting an actor of one's acquaintance just after watching him perform: an experience which is the stranger because the actor himself finds nothing strange in the metamorphosis. In the little tour which I made on the afternoon of our liberation I came upon signs of his emergence: a notice with his signature on the wall of a partly ruined house, *Danger, keep away!*; another against a pile of unsawn timber, *Not to be moved*. Then, as I was returning to the house, I met him walking energetically towards the village, still in his labourer's clothes. He turned, after he had passed me with scarcely a glance of recognition, and said:

"Oh yes—Stefanie—I shall want you. In the old bailiff's office at six o'clock. You can do some clerking for me."

He did not specifically claim his old authority, he merely wielded it. It was known in a matter of minutes that the General was in the Rent Office, and people came there to ask for advice. What they got was orders. At daybreak a team of men and women, those few who had strength to haul a sledge, were trudging up to the woods for fuel; others were collecting blankets from every cottage to furnish a stopgap hospital; and before nightfall, at the other end of the village, a rudimentary soup-kitchen was in operation under Sandra's management. These efforts of a hungry and exhausted people could not, I think, have been accomplished if a person of greater humanity than Julius had ordered them. He used no violence of gesture or voice; but he was pitiless. At some of the houses blankets had been refused, the collectors said; very well, they must go again, at least one blanket must be drawn from every house, if it was the last they had. A boy who was wretchedly ill-clad burst into tears when ordered to take a message to a cottage three kilometres away. "I want the answer quickly," was all that Julius said, and the child stopped crying and set off.

"Oh, Stefanie, one thing more! Ask my mother, will you, to collect all the foodstuff she's got hidden—I'm sending Tytus for it at eight o'clock. Yes, it's all got to go in the general store, the same as what we get from the villagers. Henryk will have to come and draw the ration for the House each day."

I hear him issuing that instruction—a harsh one for the Countess —in the voice he had used for a dozen others, bloodless and concise; and his face, as I recapture it, with the bored eyes and rigid mouth, is that of a duty officer roused early after a night's carouse to witness a defaulters' parade. Physically he must have been overstrained; for he was, after all, in his fifties, and a man twenty years younger might have faltered under the burden that he carried then. Day and night he was on the move, goading, adjusting, tightening the joints of his makeshift organization; rarely stopping to eat or drink, never (as far as I knew) out of his clothes. But the dullness of his expression covered something besides fatigue, and to me, who had come to know him a little, it appeared that beneath the boredom of a man performing some everyday professional duty there flowed, narrowly and deeply, a stream of satisfaction. For him this Command was not a large one. But it was independent. He was in bondage only to his own sense of duty, and that is a tyrant which men serve with love.

Perhaps my judgment of his mind was facile; I could not help reading it through my knowledge of the way that Victor had thought and felt; but I was again living closer to him than anyone else—he needed something in the way of staff-captain errand-boy to follow him about—and because of my inferiority he could relax a little in my company, as men do with their soldier servants. Occasionally he gave me confidences of a trivial kind—"My mother is very annoyed with me, she's an obstinate old woman"; "If it weren't for my wife's feelings I should let Rosalia starve, it's all she deserves!"—and there were private gestures, a nervous scratching of the palms, a movement of his tongue along the upper lip when some obstacle had been cleared, which he did not trouble to hide from me. Once or twice he even allowed me to see a wintry smile. I remember an occasion when he returned to the Rent Office at about midnight, having been on his feet since morning. I had waited for him there, knowing that he would want me to take down instructions on matters that had cropped up during his tour. Because he was so tired he would not sit down—he had foolish, masculine notions about repugning weakness—and I see him standing for a long time with one soaking trouser-leg on the table, his hands in the pockets of an old uniform coat, eyes staring morosely at the candlestick which lay between us. From that look of puerile sulkiness I knew that he wanted sympathy but would be vexed if it were offered. So, as a boy's mother would, I went on with my work, patching a blouse of Annette's; and presently his trouble came to the boil.

"These women," he said with conscious restraint, "they have roughly the mental range of farmyard geese. They're saying now they want to go into the town—to see the latest fashions, I suppose. They think there's nothing except a whim of mine to stop them."

I might well have thought the same, but it would not have helped me to say so. I asked, unconcernedly:

"How *are* things in the town, do you know?"

"Not yet," he said; "I shall soon. The Germans may still be there; but if they're not, the Russians are—you can be sure of that. The place has been a bargaining counter between the politicians—I don't know which way it went in the end."

"You don't think it could have been left unoccupied?"

"A place of that size? No! No one bothers much about a pocketful of houses like this. A place with factories and a railway station, that's a different bag of hay."

He was running through the latest memoranda in his notebook and at the same time cleaning his boots with a piece of newspaper—of such details he was still pathetically careful. In the way to which I was so well accustomed, he had ceased to be aware of me except as an audience for his thoughts.

"Yes, I'm in the dark at present, the channels are all closed. It doesn't matter, the system can't finally break down. In a few days' time I shall know something, I shall make a trip round and see my friends. As soon as I've got some sort of order into things here." Just then his busy hands came to rest, as if something had reminded him of an urgent duty he had forgotten. "For all we know," he said, "these few hectares may be all that's left of independent Poland."

His voice, when he said that, lost some of its impersonality, and he looked directly at my face.

"I suppose so," was all that I could say.

And now, still staring at my eyes, with a smile which had its source in bitterness, he said, "I suppose I'm the only person here—except my mother, perhaps—who can see any meaning in that. These people, these creatures who've been given the power of reason and choice, they're not interested in anything except their stomachs, keeping themselves alive. Our country—when it comes to it—our country means nothing to them."

Those words he said without anger, only with a simple grief which came near to stirring my emotions: here was a man who had suffered no trivial hardships; he suffered now, and he was lonely. To such a hunger for sympathy one would respond instinctively. But even at that moment, when I myself was hungry—for food, for warmth, for someone who could share my own distresses—I remembered that he was worth no murmur of pity from me. If compassion were wide enough to encircle the rest of mankind, this man, himself incapable of pity, would still be outside it. I said impassively:

"I don't see quite why you trouble about their getting fed and clothed, if they're not the sort of people who count with you."

"They're my own people," he answered.

"But not a marketable property, as things are now."

"No, I agree, not marketable." He was never offended by my sarcasms—the door of his mind shut quietly against the entrance of such vulgarity. "No, but they're the stock from which our nation has been reborn again and again. In one sense they are the world's finest people. They don't realize that; but I do." He was faintly smiling, but the smile went out like a lamp in the wind. "Now listen, the first thing for you tomorrow is to see Wanda for me. She *must* understand that if anyone dies in the hospital when she's drawn the day's food allowance for him, the next day's drawing has got to be two units short, not just one. . . ."

iv

My record of that last sentence may be verbally inaccurate. I do know that it was spoken at the end of this particular conversation; and it has made me certain, by process of deduction, that a small event which was to have importance for me took place on the same night.

This was a late visit by Jendrek, the former farm steward, who now had charge of the party detailed to collect any foodstuff which could be found in outlying farms. He had come to the office earlier, but had refused to discuss his business with me. It must have been towards one o'clock in the morning when he returned.

There was trouble, he said, with a peasant farmer called Pawczac (a man I knew a little; his wife had once been nursemaid to the Kolbeck children), whose holding was four or five kilometres along the Niezen road. This fellow had a locked storeroom at the back of his house, which he declared was empty except for old rubbish, and he was pretending to have lost the key. It was known locally that there had long been a bunker beneath the floor of this room, and Jendrek was convinced that several sacks of beetroot were hidden there. A long speech followed. Jendrek was one of those men so stamped with their occupation that one can hardly think of them outside its uniform; and I have a picture of the dour old man standing rigidly as far inside the room as his status allows, holding his sheepskin cap as if he were restraining a lively horse and keeping his respectful eyes on Julius's stomach, while his rhythmic voice with its faintly Kazak inflexion plods through the story again and again.

"He said the soldiers had taken the key. I told him he must have had a good crop, the crop was good this year, it lies very well for the beet, the lower piece he has. He said the soldiers had taken all his crop, he said they'd come in the motor-wagon and taken every root of it. I told him the soldiers wouldn't know about the bunker, I told him I was under your Honour's orders. He said the bunker was closed up in his father's time, he'd show me now for your Honour and for the Blessed Virgin except the soldiers had come to him to steal the key. . . ."

To all this eloquence Julius listened, I suppose, with patience— I do not remember. Intrinsically a man of many impatiences, he could yet show an aristocrat's indulgence to the slowness of people who lived near the soil. What I do recall precisely is the words with which he brought the interview to a conclusion:

"I can't go tomorrow morning—I've other things to attend to. In the afternoon—yes. Make a note of that, Stefanie: tomorrow afternoon I'm to go and see Jasiek Pawczac. Yes, Jendrek, I think I shall find some means of persuading him."

I was to have occasion, not long afterwards, for thinking attentively about those words. I have felt it necessary to record them, and I have done so with—I think—verbal accuracy.

Julius, in the event, was saved from the trouble of visiting Pawczac: he was forestalled by someone else who had faith in his own powers of persuasion. In accordance with Julius's instruction, I was at the 'hospital' early next morning, and was told by Wanda that Pawczac was her newest patient, brought there on a sledge by his wife and daughter. These two had found him, during the night, lying in the snow some way from the house, savagely mauled about the face and with a wound in the groin. I remember that when I gave this news to Julius later in the day his only comment was that under certain pressures people forget the laws of God. Whether it was established, at any time, that Pawczac had been hiding food, I do not recollect at all. The import of such questions was so soon to be changed.

[138]

The coming of our new controllers was undramatic: they appeared rather as mice appear in an old farmhouse during the winter months. The first arrivals, eight or nine of them, were brought by an antique American truck which had plainly suffered a villainous passage through high drifts of snow. They propped their rifles against the wall of the old Priest House, relit the stumps of cigarettes, and stood in a small circle, chattering, stamping their feet, grinning amiably to children who, loitering to stare at them, looked hardly more unsophisticated than they. After a while they trooped into an empty house and got the stove going with a wooden bedstead they discovered there.

Next day, at the House, we found the morning-room occupied by two more of their kind, who had evidently slept on the floor and had thrown their modest equipment on to Julius's desk. These, round-headed country fellows who looked to be about sixteen, offered us some of the black bread on which they were breakfasting. One of them produced a crucifix of solid silver which he wanted to exchange for eggs or tea.

If the cold had driven the Germans away, as some of our villagers imagined, it appeared to have an opposite action with their successors. The sky was again heavy with snow, at dusk it started falling, and with the grey torrent which settled on our fields, obliterating the last traces of the earlier occupation, there came from the darkness a new infestation of Russian soldiers. However poorly clad by the German standard, these men appeared impervious to the weather, and were no more troubled by strange surroundings than insects newly hatched. At every turn you came on a little party gossiping, some bareheaded, while the snow fell thickly on their shoulders; staring at passers-by with scant curiosity, turning aside to urinate, massaging each other's hands, or simply standing in silence with the tolerant smile of Orientals on their flat, leathern faces. These one could not think of as possessors. The majority were of no great stature, and no more formidable in mien than the creatures which emerge from the wainscot in a warm room. But their presence was pervasive. Curiously, they seemed more remote from our understanding than their predecessors, further from the rest of the human breed. The smells they brought were wholly foreign. The pitch of their speech and laughter was strange, and so were their moods of silence.

One memory of that period has remained peculiarly vivid. Since the newcomers evidently had no means to help us, we meant to keep our own organization going as long as they allowed, and in the evenings I was working with Sandra in her soup-kitchen. (This was not pure altruism: there were pans which could be cleaned out with the fingers before being washed, and even that small extra nourishment might be of some use to Conrad, growing in the darkness.) On the night which followed the first Russian influx I left the kitchen rather late, to return to the house alone. I was tired and rather hungry, and that may have been the chief reason why this short, familiar walk became all at once a menacing ordeal. The electricity had ceased to function when the Germans departed, scarcely a cottage had candles left, and those few Russians who needed light were making do with twists of tow stuffed into small tins of paraffin: these, through a naked window here and there, spilt strips of smoky light across the snow, chequered with the shadows of men moving inside, and on so dark a night such fillets of illumination transformed entirely the pattern of houses to which my eyes were used. Here, where I thought the road ran straight, a wall came right in front of me; here, where the bridge posts should have begun, my reaching hand found nothing at all. In the German period I should not have moved so far without being challenged, and my nerves were keyed for the sound of a rifle-bolt being opened, the light of a torch suddenly shining in my face: when a dog, perhaps more scared than I, brushed past my legs I started so violently that I slid and fell. But there was no challenge. Only, as I groped my way, a man coughed close beside me, and now what I thought was a thornbush moved, and now my hand as it felt along a wire fence came to another hand, belonging to a motionless soldier. Farther on, a man put out his arm to stop me, and feeling my clothes asked in a modest voice if I would sleep with him, for a silver trinket he had; but he made no effort to detain me, and other soldiers against whom I stumbled only grunted and moved aside. Harmless fellows they were, poor creatures who hung about for lack of any comfort to return to, and in daylight they would not have alarmed me; but when all the landmarks that I knew were lost, it was frightening to find the darkness possessed by shapes which kept so still, which seemed to feel nothing and yet were alive.

It was that night—or perhaps the next—that I found Annette waiting for me at the top of the stairs in a state of pitiful distress. Two of the soldiers had come into our room, when she was already asleep, and had settled themselves for the night, one on my bed and one on the floor. She had slipped away and, not wishing to disturb her grandmother, had been shivering in the passage for more than an hour. Although I felt, privately, that she had over-dramatized the situation, this news angered me. I found a candle and went straight to our room to expostulate.

The man I wakened first either would not or could not understand me; he was, I fancy, a Transbaikalian, he had little Russian, and mine was clumsy from long disuse; but his fellow, the one in my own bed, was very willing to converse. He had supposed, he said, that no one needed the bed, since he had found it empty. It had seemed a pity to leave it so, such a beautiful bed.

"I have never seen one like this, never, never. In pictures, yes. I saw one just the same in the American magazine."

"I expect so. Only this happens to be my bed."

"You paid for it yourself?"

"Well, no."

"Then it was a gift for some special service?"

"No. Really, it has only been lent to me."

"Lent to you?"

The boy was enchanting; his fair hair rather long, like a student's, his solemn eyes those of a child who hunts for delight in every shadow.

"You means, there is a rota?" he suggested. "Everybody in your working-unit has it in turn?"

"At any rate," I told him, "it is my turn tonight."

He pulled a face and then smiled.

"Understood, little friend! I take the floor with Dolka."

"But not this floor. This is my room."

"But there's plenty of space!"

"Not for you!"

We argued the matter without acrimony but at some length, while he hunted through his very dirty clothes for a greasy pamphlet which he wanted me to read. It talked of the glory of belonging to the people's army, the privileges which everyone should gladly give to soldiers. He simply could not understand my attitude, which he said, with a sad politeness, was 'unfortunately historic'. But in the end I persuaded him and his friend to take their things to a corner I found for them downstairs.

Just as we were getting into bed, he appeared again, and I have a clear memory of him standing barelegged in the doorway, a figure of curious dignity, with his handsome head wrapped in a grey bashlyk, and a filthy coat clutched about his shoulders.

"I only want you to understand," he said, "that you are free now, you Polish people—all of you. The Czarist slavery is over, and now the Pilsudskist slavery too! That's what we've come for, we children of the Revolution, we've come to rid you of your capitalistic overlords, to welcome you into our workers' family of freedom!"

It occurred to me, as I thanked him for this speech, that the rationale he offered was not one which my father-in-law would have received with much appreciation.

vi

But Julius had already disappeared. I can only make guesses about where he went and how. He was not a man who would run away for the sake of his own skin, and indeed there was nowhere safe for him to run to. At Setory his usefulness was virtually finished. I do not doubt that he had work to do elsewhere.

His mother probably knew something of his plans; he trusted her, for her intelligence and discretion, in a way that men do not often trust women. If Sandra, poor Sandra, had been told anything except that he was going away, she did not confide that knowledge to me.

Shortly before he left I came upon the three of them in the only room downstairs which the soldiers had not so far discovered. I saw that Sandra had been crying. Julius, wearing his old shooting-boots, was gazing out of the window with the exaggerated boredom which men use as armour when there is some risk of a demand on their emotions. He, perhaps, was relieved when my entrance broke up their conversation. A sentence begun by Sandra petered out, and she said awkwardly, "But Stefanie would not be interested in that!" While the Countess, attempting no finesse, picked up the shirt she was patching and stamped out of the room.

"You will come to my bedroom later on, Julius," she said.

I should have retreated, but Julius stopped me.

"It was nothing private," he said shortly. For an instant he smiled, as if at some joke we had between us, but that smile, as I knew, was nothing but a trick of his features. He was desperately tired. "I was only saying that history has gone into reverse now. Everything we've accomplished—everything that generations have given their lives for—the barbarians have got it back without the expense of a cartridge. Well, that doesn't matter to you. Perhaps it matters to no one except myself."

[142]

In that there was no rhetoric: he spoke rather in the flat, tired voice of one describing an accident in which he has been injured. In another man I should not have been surprised by such abjection; it is in the nature of men to vest their pride in symbols, and to be anguished when those images are overthrown. But this was one who, doing a scullion's work under a makeshift Bavarian N.C.O., had revealed to me the kind of bravery which oppression only brings to a finer temper. All that resilience had gone now. He had turned to look at Sandra, but I do not think he saw her, or the wall beyond, or me: his mouth was fastened as if the muscles there were locked, his eyes were like those of a long-term convict, vacant from final defeat. Perhaps all men come to those moments. If I could ever have pitied him, it would have been then.

Remote from us, he started moving towards the door. He said absently, "I suppose I'd better see what my mother's got on her mind."

Sandra said, "But you'll come back here? I was going to make some tea for you. Wanda's found me some tea."

"If it comes from the hospital issue, it must go straight back!" he answered.

But he did, an instant later, move towards her; even such a man as he cannot for ever evade the smaller, private demands on his devotion. I slipped away, for her sake and my own.

Some weeks were to pass before I saw him again.

He had been wrong, of course, in suggesting that no one but himself cared who were to be our rulers. Among the villagers, and those who had taken refuge here, there were many who had grown up under the old domination, and to these it must have seemed that a congenital illness which they had been cured of in middle life had once more taken hold of them. I visited Anusia, who was sharing a bed in Wanda's 'hospital' with two other old women; and all she would say to me, clutching my sleeve with her almost fleshless hands, was, "So—they are back, you see! We always knew they would come!" But younger people, as far as I could tell, were still not greatly concerned about historical implications. For the time, at least, they had forgotten that there could be any world but this, where soldiers came and gave what orders they pleased and took what they wanted: one's only care was to keep a wife or a mother alive as long as one could. While the children, understanding still less the significance of what had happened, but already aware that hunger was no less normal than the bitterness of winter, moved in ragged groups along the road, refraining from games and laughter as children do in the houses of grand relations; sometimes crying a little; but generally wearing on their narrowed faces a look of apathy which was curiously adult.

I myself was fortunate in having a single purpose which diverted my mind from lesser realities; for to me it always seemed that Victor's child was more important than people who were alive already. And perhaps I was not alone in finding the reality of immediate sensations diminished; for hunger, at a certain stage, has effects like those of intoxication, where a house nearby and distant hills are seen in the same plane, where you can feel the pain of a frostbitten hand and yet not recognize it as your own. I spent a portion of my time in Count Kolbeck's room, to which our new guests had not penetrated. There, as I listened to his piano voice, I could sometimes see in his perspective the fragment of time in which I lived; sometimes forget that the only precious parts were beyond recall.

7

IT was the Countess more than anyone who kept us from starvation. She had handled peasants all her life, and these soldiers had few mental quirks with which she was not familiar. So it was she who managed most of the barter on which we depended for supplies—for even when the Russians had introduced a system of civilian issues, it worked dyspeptically and was loaded against people like ourselves.

Congenital bargainers have their own esoteric rules which, like children or Englishmen playing games, they treat as the laws of God. These rules the Countess understood. More importantly, she had the appearance and temper which the game demands. She was never eager, never affable; and yet her workroom (itself recovered for her use by nimble bargaining) was visited at every hour by men who, I suspect, wanted to do business with the old woman as much for the fun of it as for anything they were likely to gain. These were her proper prey.

"I have nothing at all!" she would say testily. "All my valuables were taken by the Germans. The few little things I managed to keep, I've sold those already—you must know that, your friends have got them. There's nothing left except my old family album, and I should never part with that, it was given me by my mother and has sentimental associations. . . . No, I do not need any bread, the Russian bread is a thing I can never swallow. Will you please go away and do your drilling or whatever you have to do!"

At once the album became a legend, every day someone was asking to see it, and she would say that it was lost or stolen. At last she produced it: a thing of Magdeburg manufacture, with dreadful gilt embellishments, and filled with amateur photographs of dull relations in the clothes of 1902. But the Imperial regalia could not have been handled with greater ceremony than she lavished on this tawdry object, asking her visitors to shut the door, slipping the album gingerly from the velvet bag it was kept in, allowing no one to turn the pages but herself. And after resisting every offer for three weeks, during which it was carried up to her bedroom every night, she let it go to an imbecile trooper in exchange for a fine sable coat he had looted elsewhere, with two kilos of tea thrown in.

Deals of that kind were a sideline. Her main business was done with a man called Solitsin, whose military functions seemed to correspond approximately with those of a quartermaster-sergeant: evidently he had a large control over certain supplies, he was free from Apostolic notions of communal ownership, unaware of any legal or moral rules except the ones he made for himself. A plainer man I have seldom seen: his thin, cheese-coloured face was thickly scarred from smallpox, the shortness of his upper-lip revealed an immensity of purple gum sown raggedly with rotting teeth, his moist and bulbous eyes might have been held by suction in their narrow pits. And yet when he stayed for hours in the Countess's room, idly smoking, morosely observing the manœuvres of other bargainers, his presence seemed to offend her no more than that of a dog offends its master. "Solitsin?" she said to me in an expansive moment. "A rat from the Kostroma sewers! But I understand him." He understood her too; admired, and I think even liked her, in the way that one lawyer may acquire a sense of comradeship with another when they are for ever duelling in the courts. Otherwise, could she have won so much when all the bargaining power was his? Exactly how their business was done I never learned, for Solitsin was far too prudent to engage in it when a third person was present. I only know that most of the necessities of life arrived (in wretchedly small amount) in the Countess's bedroom, which served as larder for the house, together with such extras as a length of slightly scorched duffel, a pair of Kazak boots. For these she must have paid with treasures that she had kept well hidden: small things, some jewellery perhaps, articles of virtu. In Solitsin's eyes there was a shade which suggested Circassian blood, and I imagine that he had some instinct for value. That is all surmise. The man was abhorrent to me; but it used to fascinate me to see how that arrogant old woman, adroitly contriving to be alone with a more repulsive individual than I could have conceived for her companionship, betrayed now and then the complacency, even faintly the excitement, of a girl in love.

The rest of us, recognizing our limitations, left Solitsin alone. Our dealings were mostly with Sergeant Butusov, who, among the floating population of soldiers which now filled a great part of the house, remained a permanent lodger. This large and rudimentary creature served as billet-master—whether on his own appointment or that of higher authority we could never discover—and claimed particular privileges: a room to himself, sometimes a share of our meals (if they could be called that), unlimited licence to keep us in our place. "You!" he would roar at poor Rosalia, flinging open her bedroom door, "you're nothing but scum, you're a dirty, twisting Pilsudskist!" And he would slap her heartily upon the rump and then burst into laughter. He gave us lectures at all hours of the day on the simpler conceptions of political theory, he continually threatened us with nameless penalties, "You—I know you're plotting all the time, I know just how to deal with you!" and when drunk he was capable of actual violence. But like other blusterers of this juvenile kind, he liked to reserve such bullying for himself. "You leave them alone, these are *my* bloody Poles!" became his watchword, and in this way much of the annoyance we suffered was kept in manageable order. It was tiresome to have this fellow about us, especially as he was gross in his personal habits. But I could never dislike him. He was of Georgian stock, with a grizzled head that Rodin might have cut from sandstone, a quarryman's beautiful hands, the disjointed movements of an animal for whose bulk and power there is no longer a sufficient function. His mind was childlike, and I think he held us all in a child's affection, which his uniform required him to cover with gasconade.

Yes, we were much at the mercy of people of that sort, including some who were more innately vicious, and this was a disagreeable situation. By then, however, we had at least learnt the habit of self-subordination, for when you are greatly in want of food and warmth the demands of dignity grow less. Moreover, these men were seldom frightening, since their mental structure proved to be essentially simple. (In my own experience, soldiers out of battle are commonly the least alarming members of the human race.) The men who did frighten me were of another kind.

These, nominally, were soldiers too, and the uninitiated might have seen no distinction in their uniforms; but the difference in their faces was apparent to all but the blind. They were men of indoor breeding, and the army had not assimilated them in the way that armies turn a ploughboy into a gunlayer overnight. Their hands were those of tellers in banks, some wore spectacles and many others had those eyes which seem undressed without them—the meticulous eyes which I associate with the managers of luxury hotels. They appeared with various titles, such as 'Informationist' or with none. To the real soldiers they were known as 'The Politicals', 'Specials' or—where unpopular—'the Cribs'.

"I'm not afraid of the bloody Cribs!" was Butusov's cry when he was a little in his cups. "I'm as good as them, and they know it; they can't do anything to me!"

This meant, of course, that he was as much afraid of them as we.

The first of them that I remember was young—in the twenties, perhaps; not older. I found him alone in the Countess's workroom when I slipped in there one early morning, intending to hide some oil I had stolen for the Count's spirit-stove. He was standing with one of the old wage-books in his hand, as much at home as if he were in a public library, and he asked, hardly looking at me:

"Do you occupy this room? Do you work here?"

I told him, no.

"But you live in this house?"

"I'm staying here."

"This seems to be an old book."

"Yes, it looks like it."

"You don't know anything about it?"

"No."

"The wages paid here seem to have been very low."

"Oh?"

"This house belongs to a man called Kolbeck—that's right, isn't it?"

"Yes."

"A General in the former Polish army?"

"Yes."

"Was he a good employer?"

"I really don't know."

The questions were not asked in a magisterial tone, he seemed to be just a young man of vulgar inquisitiveness. Superficially, he belonged to a class I had been familiar with at the university, struggling students of several nationalities whose hunger for factual knowledge was informed by no distinction of mind; he had their physical insignificance, the exigent regard, the faintly supercilious air, which shows through a cloud of shyness. But to these commonplace traits there was added the suggestion of indomitable patience.

"You say you've never looked at this book before? . . . You

[148]

don't come into this room very much? . . . You were looking for
somebody when you came in?"

It sounded like a child's cross-examination, which comes from
nothing but the desire for adult attention. The difference, for me,
was that I could not evade him as one evades a child.

How long it went on I do not remember. I know that we were
interrupted by Solitsin, who, coming on one of his routine visits,
was ready in a moment with some story about a billet inspection.
His arrival gave me the chance to get away. As it happened, I never
saw that visitor again, though he returned to the house next day
and (as I heard from Wanda) put Sandra in a flutter by questioning
her as he had questioned me.

Thereafter they came, these soft-mouthed inquisitors, as frequently as the beggars and bagmen of other days, singly or in pairs,
once only or several times. They were seldom brusque, sometimes
faintly apologetic. What they had in common was a quiet insistence,
a forensic trick of returning again and again to the same question;
that, and a way of nodding upon our answers with half-closed eyes,
as if to show a connoisseur's approval of falsehoods which had been
correctly shaped. The harm they did consisted in a new disturbance
of our privacy. Previously we had supposed that we counted for
no more than the village people, and shared with them the comparative security of unimportance; our anxieties had been the
obvious and immediate ones. Now it appeared that we were under
particular surveillance, that our most private actions, past and
present, could be explored and used to damage us. So, by degrees,
we felt ourselves surrounded by a new and multiform danger which
could never be exactly defined. It was like spending a night alone
in an old house, where the scrape of a branch against the window,
the sound of a door closing in the draught, so work upon your
nerves that your daylight reason loses all power to control them.

ii

I want to be honest as far as I can; not to ascribe my actions to
causes outside my control.

There are, I believe, physical conditions in which the moral
sense ceases to work; but I had not come to those. The privations
which I suffered at this time were no more severe than those of
others in the household, while the village people were far worse off
than we. No, I did not lose all sense of right and wrong because I

was hungry. Yet when I try from this distance to study my motives impartially, I am persuaded that they were a good deal influenced by the situation I was living in.

I had been through two fruitless pregnancies. This, the third, would have been one of great anxiety even if I had been living peacefully in my own home, with Victor to care for me. I have shown that my actual state was different from that; and with so much to militate against my chance of giving Conrad life, the task became an obsession by which my mind was unbalanced. 'Unbalanced': I use that word with scrupulous regard to its meaning. My thoughts were often as clear as they are now (when it is morning, and the sunshine of a New England spring is falling on my table), and in those lucid periods I realized that there was neither sense nor virtue in dwelling on an outrage that belonged wholly to the past. But when the goodness of life has been withered, the ground so poisoned that nothing seems able to grow from it again, you may come to feel that morality itself is meaningless; and it is then that virtue, losing its command, gives place to impulses which have their source in the darker recesses of the mind, in half-remembered grievances, vengefulness pretending to be justice. One of the troubles which came from under-nourishment was a kind of lassitude, which retarded my faculties and made my ordinary relations with people a strain to me. My loneliness had increased. Instead of seeking help from those who were near me, I continued secretly to think of them as adversaries; and this image of enmity, pored over in the hours when I lay awake at night, took possession of my will in a way that I did not then understand.

I do not mean—let me repeat—that I was a virtuous being overwhelmed by circumstance. Others have found themselves in storms of equal severity and have ridden them out. I lacked that fortitude.

iii

It was about midday; I had returned from a visit to Tytus, whose wife was ill, when Wanda came to meet me in the hall. There was a new Special up in the night-nursery, she said; he had seen me coming in and wanted to question me. As we went upstairs, pushing through a group of soldiers who were passing time in gossiping and ragging each other, she spoke to me very rapidly in French:

"If he asks you anything about Jasiek Pawczac, Father had had nothing to do with him for years. Father hardly knew him, and hadn't given any orders about him. You're clear about that?—it's important! And about where Father is now—you haven't seen him since the Germans left. You think they took him as a prisoner into their zone. You've got that?"

Butusov was smoking a cigarette outside the night-nursery. "I know what you two tarts are doing," he said, "you're plotting! It won't do you any good."

"That's right, little friend!" Wanda answered. She stretched and ran her fingers through his hair, and we went inside.

Tedious as these interviews had become, they had often a flavour of absurdity which gave me some small enjoyment. Here now were Sandra and Rosalia, behaving rather as small-town ladies who have to entertain a celebrity; they had even produced tea, made à l'anglaise, from stolen rations. They sat side by side on the hard nursery chairs in attitudes of extreme decorum, and as the Special pursued his interrogation they nodded to him, almost in unison, with polite and anxious little smiles. If such courtesy seemed excessive, the Countess's behaviour went the other way; for she had Henryk by the window, where she could get the light, and with her back to the rest of the company she was mending a tear in his blouse. These incongruities, however, appeared to make no impression on the Special, who was perhaps insensitive to finer shades in etiquette. He was the least imposing of his tribe that we had seen; a small, asthmatic creature whom one could picture as the contented owner of an unsuccessful café-tabac. Hunched over the inevitable notebook, he looked as if he were wrestling with some small piece of arithmetic which gave him a different answer every time.

"But you tell me," he was saying to Rosalia, "that this Kolbeck, your relation, was a whole-time officer in the Polish army. Then why wasn't he with the army when the German advance was in progress?"

Rosalia gave him the smile she had used throughout her life as the answer to every problem, so innocent of meaning that it fell like a curtain upon all discussion. "But I think I've told you," she said daintily, "the General's movements were never anything to do with me."

"My husband——" Sandra began.

"Yes, yes, I know—I was asking your relation. . . . You must try to remember, it's most important that I should have accurate information. Where was Kolbeck when the German advance started?"

"Well, *I* was in Grodzisk."

"At Grodzisk, yes! And no doubt you were in correspondence with these people?"

"In correspondence? No, I don't think I was then."

"You must try to remember!"

I saw that he had jotted down the name 'Grodzisk', and was staring at it with the concentration of a feeble-minded child who will try every piece of a jig-saw puzzle in every position, regardless of colour and shape. This could go on all day! It did go on for another ten minutes, and I had settled drowsily into the rôle of spectator at a witless farce when he said, without looking up:

"Stefanie Kolbeck, where is your husband at the present time?"

I was too much startled to answer the question promptly. When he repeated it, I said that I didn't know.

"That is not an answer!" he objected.

"In all probability," I told him (since it did not seem to matter what I said), "he is a prisoner-of-war."

"In whose hands? . . . What makes you think that? . . . What was he doing when you last saw him?"

I went on answering patiently, in the level and apathetic voice which one came to use on these occasions; but the interview was no longer as boring as I should have wished, for the man was continually arriving—as if by instinct—at matters which I had no desire to discuss in public. He had learnt, perhaps through a previous interrogation of Annette, that I had been married twice. Now he wanted to know why Casimir and I had parted, what my relationship with Victor had been before and after that event, where my second marriage had taken place. As I dealt out my colourless replies—"We had been friends for a long time. . . . My Swiss lawyers arranged the filing of a suit in America. . . . In the Stadhuis of Amsterdam, by civil process"—I had the sensation of being searched for some shameful contraband.

"And this second marriage was approved by the father of your husband?"

"I—I didn't ask him."

"You had no communication with him?"

"Later there was communication between my husband and his father."

"And what did the father say then?"

"He disapproved."

"And yet you came back to live here in his house?"

"That was quite recently. I had nowhere else to go."

"He still disliked you?"

[152]

"I don't think he had any special feelings about me personally."

"And you disliked him?"

The questions were coming in the same prosaic voice—he might have been asking me my size in gloves and shoes—and this neutrality should have prevented me from losing my temper. It did not. I felt as you do when, pressed for money, you take a cherished possession to be sold, and a bored dealer twists it between grubby finger-nails. I said, with weary anger:

"I had no feelings about him at all!"

"Except that you were frightened of him?"

"Certainly not!"

"But you never dared to oppose him?"

"The question didn't arise."

"But you'll admit that he forced you to work for him after the Germans had gone?"

"Not at all. I merely wanted to be helpful where I could."

Wanda had made a signal to me, but too late. I realized now that the long procession of questions had not been aimless, and that the Special was not the fool I had thought. There was a moment of silence, broken by the Countess:

"Keep still, Henryk! I can't do this if you keep on wriggling!"

"I can't have interruptions!" the Special said sharply.

The face of Sandra, whenever I glanced her way, had been comatose, like that of a dull student defeated by a lecture on philosophy. The Countess's voice roused her from that trance.

"My daughter-in-law," she fluttered, "will tell you if you ask her that she has always been treated as a member of our family. Since her childhood. My husband——"

"Yes, yes!" the Special said, and turned to me again. "You were paid for the clerical work you did in the Rent Office?"

"Paid?" I said. "What could I have bought with money?"

He was not annoyed by that retort. Nothing could annoy him. "So you were not paid anything?"

"No."

"Not even when you worked very late?"

"I was not paid anything."

This answer made him hesitate for a moment, as if I had given him some cue which he could not see in his script; but the next question, which was put to Wanda, came smoothly enough:

"You told me that your sister-in-law came to see you in the nursing establishment on the morning of Monday the 28th?"

Wanda said, "I'm not certain."

"You were certain a few minutes ago."

"She often came."

"But you told me that on the morning of the 28th she came to you with a message."

"Did I?"

"I must ask you in your own interest to be straightforward!"

She seemed to be nonplussed; and I thought, as other fools have done in similar circumstances, that a bold lie would help matters.

"That's right," I said. "I remember going to her with a message from the Countess—she was to bring home a basket she had borrowed."

Inevitably I glanced towards the Countess to see if she would play to this lead, but she still showed no sign of taking the smallest interest in the proceedings. I need not have troubled.

"So you particularly remember," the Special said, "that you took that message on Monday the 28th?"

"I'm not sure of the date."

"You often took messages?"

"Oh yes."

"Then why do you specially remember taking that one?"

"I—I don't know."

"What made you connect it with the day we were talking about, the 28th?"

"I suppose I didn't, really."

"But you connected it with something else? With something you saw at the nursing establishment?"

"I suppose so."

"In fact, with seeing a man called Jasiek Pawczac in the nursing establishment?"

"No, I don't think so."

"Oh—it was a different message you took on the morning you saw Pawczac?"

"I don't remember."

"But you do remember seeing Pawczac?"

"I don't know. It's quite a common name."

"You may have made some note about it?"

"No, I'm sure I didn't."

"Your memory is not very good," he said. From the back of his notebook came a crumpled envelope with my handwriting on the back of it. He read out "'Monday hospital General to see Pawczac'. You made that note?"

My eyes turned from his face, and I saw the Countess biting off a thread. "And will you in future be more careful!" she said to Henryk. "I don't see why I have to spend the last weeks of my life mending clothes for grown-up grandchildren." That exclamation did not seem to break the silence, but rather to lie outside it, like a nervous laugh from the audience when an actor forgets his lines. In the stillness which lay upon the room like winter, I could feel that Wanda was staring at me with a fierce intensity.

"You made that note?" the Special repeated. "It's in your writing, I think."

I had come, as one does under questioning, to the state of weariness where one hardly knows what one is saying. But I did see clearly, now, the point to which the inquiry had been directed. I had not spent years on this side of Europe without learning what kind of information the Russians always wanted about people they did not care for. I knew that however little they were concerned with truth—as others understand it—they liked their files to be furnished with data which were concrete and precise. Someone had talked about the Pawczac incident. Someone else, perhaps, had connected Julius's name with it, and his was a name which had been on the files for a long time past. There was material here from which a case could be built, positive, popular in appeal; but it needed to be defined, and the definition was to come from me.

The grey-white middle finger of the Special was tapping rhythmically on the edge of the table. "You must know your own handwriting!" he persisted.

"Of course I do."

"Then did you write this or didn't you?"

"Certainly I wrote it."

It must have been some small gesture of Wanda's which made Sandra realize that a point of extreme danger had been reached. She said abruptly, but in a voice of greater calm than I should have expected:

"There is something I wish to tell you about my husband. I—I don't understand what it is you're trying to prove. I only know that my husband has acted throughout his life from the highest principles. He is—he is a man whose life is guided by principles of honour and justice."

The Special had tried to interrupt that speech, but the power of its simplicity carried it past his interruption. It gave me the few moments that I needed; time to see clearly which side a person of the smallest decency must belong to in this battle; to collect my wits.

"Yes yes!" the Special said. "Yes yes! . . . And you, will you tell me, please, what you had in mind when you wrote those words?"

"In mind?" I said. "Only what I wrote. General Kolbeck made a point of visiting every serious case in the hospital. It was my business to bring those cases to his notice."

"But he had some special reason, I think, to be interested in this man Pawczac?"

"No, none at all."

"You're certain of that? I must remind you that it's necessary to be straightforward."

"Quite certain!" I said.

The Special sat still for a moment, nodding, and then abruptly left the room. In a few moments he was back, and Jendrek was with him.

"You can sit down," he said, but Jendrek remained standing. "I want just to go over a piece of information you gave me yesterday. You were telling me about a conversation you had with General Kolbeck—it was late at night. You told General Kolbeck that a man called Pawczac was withholding certain foodstuffs from requisition?"

"Yes—but——"

"And General Kolbeck told you that he would go and deal with this man himself?"

"Well, the way it turned out, there wasn't any need for the General to go, seeing——"

"I didn't ask you that! I'm asking you if that was what the General said."

"Well—yes, he said something like that."

"And this woman was present? She was listening?"

"I think so."

"You didn't 'think so' yesterday—you knew! She was listening, wasn't she?"

"Yes."

The Special turned to me.

"You told me just now that General Kolbeck had no special interest in Pawczac?"

"Yes, I did. He hadn't."

"Are you pretending that the conversation which this man has described never took place?"

"No, I'm not pretending anything."

"Well?"

"It's just that he's got the name wrong. The man they were discussing was not called Pawczac."

"Oh? What *was* he called?"

"It was some name like Sobolka."

The Special turned sharply to Jendrek again.

"What do you say to that?"

"I—I don't know."

"Nonsense! You knew perfectly well yesterday. It was Pawczac that you and General Kolbeck were talking about, wasn't it?"

Jendrek said with dignity, "The Ladyship has higher scholarship than mine. The Ladyship would not make a mistake."

And to that point the old man stuck faithfully, under five minutes of remorseless cross-examination. Indeed, the fire of questions only increased his native obduracy. For his pride was at stake. He was obliged to represent himself as a man of such mental feebleness that his statements were wholly unreliable; in short, as an egregious fool; but to him this was far less shameful than contradicting any member of the family he had served from boyhood. What he thought of me I do not know, for beyond a certain depth you cannot read a mind like his. It was enough that I belonged to the Kolbecks, and that a stranger (for whom his contempt was written large in the set of his dour lips) had the impudence to question my veracity.

"Yes," he said, for the fourth or fifth time, "I was wrong about the name, as the Ladyship says. . . . No, I don't remember his name. Sobolka—yes, it might have been something like that."

Even at the time I did not suppose that the Special believed us; and since two partners telling lies without preparation are easy to expose, I thought he would have us trapped before long. I was taken by surprise, therefore, when he closed his notebook and said abruptly:

"Very well, that's all the information I need!"

With that his personal insignificance returned, and as he worked himself into his over-large greatcoat, smiling diffidently at the tops of our heads, I was already wondering how this small-town shopkeeper could have put our nerves to so much strain. Nevertheless I stayed quite still, as the others did, for several moments after he had left us.

It was the Countess who moved first, yawning lugubriously as she gathered up her sewing things.

"That was a very tedious person!"

"What was he saying?" Henryk asked excitedly. "He was a funny man. Why did he want to ask all those questions?"

"Because children and barbarians must always ask them!" the Countess said tersely.

But her voice was overridden by that of Sandra, who, damp-eyed, seemed suddenly to bring herself under command: "Because your father is a man who loves his country! Because he's incapable of any dishonourable action, and they've got to hunt for some falsehood to bring against him."

Embarrassed by her fierce emotion, I followed Jendrek out of the room.

Later on Wanda got hold of me, and I gave her the true version of what had passed in that late-night interview between Julius and Jendrek. She asked me then, just avoiding my eyes:

"It's right, isn't it, that Pawczac getting beaten up was nothing to do with Father?"

"I've told you all I know," I answered. "The time when it happened seems to show that he couldn't have been responsible—not unless he went straight to Pawczac's house when I left him that night on an impulse——"

"But that's ridiculous!" she said. "A man like Father—he wouldn't go off in cold blood and attack someone!"

Avoiding this challenge, I only said, "Well, there wasn't time for him to have done it, anyway, as far as I can see." And that provoked her to a burst of temper.

"You've always hated him, haven't you!"

"As a rule," I replied, "he and I get on very well."

"That isn't what I asked you!"

"Well, I've lied for him, haven't I?"

"Yes," she said, "yes—oh, Teffy, you were wonderful!"

She put her arm round my waist tightly, and like that we went along the passage together; she laughing a little tearfully, and glancing at my face, looking for the loving response which I should have given her had I been able.

iv

I think that all of them were grateful for the part I had played. Little was said, but I could feel that they were treating me with a new gentleness.

In a way their gratitude emphasized my estrangement from them. Since my marriage with Victor I had never been in their confidence, and now it seemed that they were newly determined to break down the wall of shyness and suspicion which lay between them and me. With what good sense, as well as kindness, for when we were living at the mercy of strangers there was everything to unite us! Their attitude did not fail to affect me. I was pleased with myself and with them. Had an effort of will been all that was needed, I might have become, in the days that followed that inquiry, as much a member of the family as I had been in childhood.

But the region of trustful affection is not one which the rational mind, or even simple sentiment, commands. A part of me longed more than ever to accept and to be accepted. A part of me, in this world where the stuff of delight had grown so thin, reached out towards the comforts of familiarity—the little jokes which Annette and Wanda had together, the feel of Sandra's homely clothes and the cadences of her stolid, maternal voice. But between that yearning and its fulfilment something obtruded: a semblance of loyalty.

Loyalty? To Victor? Surely my devotion to him should not have shown itself in continued estrangement from those who had also loved him, whom he had once loved. It was rather, I think, a fidelity to the bonds between him and me, the union for which he had sacrificed all other allegiances and which these others still rejected; for if I allowed them to take me as one of themselves, now that Victor was dead, it would not be Victor's wife they cherished, but a child whom they had once cared for and whose intervening years they were ready to forget. One's capacity for self-deception is infinite. The feeling I had may have been the crudest sort of pride, only pretending to have its centre elsewhere than in myself. But if that was the truth I had no power to perceive it then; and if self-love was all that kept me from the Kolbecks' affection, it had another source besides their discountenance of my marriage, one more potent because it issued from a greater depth.

By chance, it was Annette who revived that deeper spring.

She had not been present at the interrogation, and naturally she wanted to hear all about it: what had the Special come for this time, had he been the rude sort, why had he gone on so long? Tired, I answered these questions rather laconically—I was always forgetting that she was no longer to be treated as a child—but when she returned to the subject next day I gave her a reasonably full account of the business. Afterwards I could see that it was still on her mind, and she must have talked it over with Wanda; for one night, when I went to tuck her up in bed, she emerged from a fit of shyness to say impulsively:

"Oh, I'm so glad you told that man a lie about Pawczac! It was marvellous of you, it was so clever and so dear, inventing another name and everything!"

Taken aback, I asked her, "Why do you say that?"

She was a little confused then. She said, "Oh, it would have been so frightful if you hadn't! I mean, if they'd had that up against Grandfather, if they'd made people think he was cruel like that."

I could still not read her real thoughts, and I asked unguardedly, "Why—do you think he couldn't ever be cruel?"

Now I had made the opposite mistake, I had spoken as one would to a mind fully matured; and the effect was to send her farther back into the childish state. I remember poignantly the look of bewilderment and pain in her eyes as she echoed:

"Cruel! Grandfather?"

"He's a soldier," I said. "Soldiers have to maintain discipline, it's their business. You can't do that without sternness."

For a moment she pondered that statement helplessly, as a child would. But her childishness seemed to fall away once more when she said, in a harder voice than I had ever heard her use, a Kolbeck voice:

"Then you think that Uncle Victor might be cruel!"

I forget how I answered that thrust. Of course, I closed the discussion as quickly as possible; and next day she made me a touching apology for 'saying something I didn't mean about Uncle Victor'. There the matter seemed to end, except for a new, sweet thoughtfulness in her behaviour towards me. But the passage stayed in my mind (so that even now it returns to me with some of the surrounding details vivid, the colour of the rag her hair was tied with, the incongruity of her ripening breast with the childish moulding of her mouth and chin), as conversations often do when they have marked some stage in the progress of a relationship. I knew with certainty now that this creature of mine, still loving and still beloved, had ceased to belong to me.

Had she been two or three years older, I might have told her straightforwardly all that I knew about her grandfather; and then, I believe, her sympathy—however circumscribed—would have been of infinite value to me in the sickness of spirit which I was suffering. But I had not learnt to think of her as old enough for such confidence, and now the gulf between us was already too wide to be bridged. With that there grew a sense of injustice, and in hours of loneliness I was dwelling again upon the outrage which had first brought me into the Kolbecks' care.

When a week and more had passed and the Special did not return,

[160]

it was concluded that the Pawczac inquiry had been dropped. At that time, when we understood so little the mentality of our latest rulers, it seemed unlikely that they would take any further trouble with a defective and irrelevant charge against a man who was not even in their hands. It appeared, then, that my lying had been successful, and that a situation which might have been dangerous for Julius had thus been averted. I ceased, by degrees, to be proud of this achievement. The fact that Julius was perfectly innocent in the matter of Pawczac weighed less and less with me; I began to despise myself for having turned suspicion away from a man once guilty of a far more cowardly crime. When I thought how Annette had admired me for protecting him, how she had cooled towards me when I confessed myself no partisan of his, I felt a sullen, irrational anger. She is one of them, I reflected, and so she is guided by the idiot belief that a Kolbeck can do no wrong.

That was my prevailing mood, hidden from the rest and sometimes from myself by the shallower moods of every day. It was at night that the obsession chiefly plagued me, as if my mother's voice whispered from the darkness, denouncing the cowardice which let me spend my life at peace with those who had taken hers; while in daytime that murmur was subdued by the traffic of plainer voices, and I could believe that it came only from some point of weakness in the mind. Sometimes, sitting alone in my bedroom, when a failing light gave to the carved furniture the grotesque shapes I had watched in the old days, when the winter stillness and a chilled breath of the house brought back for an instant the sensation of childhood, I would feel an urge to be united with the others, whose talk like old, familiar music came to me faintly across the corridor. But when my body started moving in response to this impulse some force like that of conscience would be roused to stop me; as though by admitting my need for them I should surrender my own integrity.

v

But I hungered for friends. I had them among the village people, who were always glad to be visited, and unexpectedly I discovered new ones among the soldiers. The billet where Julius and I had done forced labour had been taken over by the Russians, and there I found some work, such as washing clothes, which brought me a few perquisites—occasionally a tin of milk or fat, things that were useful for Conrad's growth. The men I worked for had the simplicity and some of the charm of children; they were occasionally boisterous and boastful; sometimes naïvely serious, often homesick. Generally they treated me with unforced kindness.

There was an officer who used to come and talk to me as I worked, and sometimes, out of his good nature, to lend me a hand. Evidently he had no regimental duties, and from this fact anyone of intelligence might have drawn an obvious deduction. Perhaps, in truth, I drew it myself; but because I liked him I shut my mind against such speculations. By comparison with the ordinary soldier he was a man of education, and in those days of narrowed horizons I was simply grateful for the talk of anyone whose interests were not limited to home, livestock and the small coin of military routine. He was fifty, a man with grandchildren. At the university of Kharkov he had made a desultory excursion into European letters; he had become a lawyer, then a minor official in one of the revenue departments. After the Revolution he had made a living by writing for the newspapers, chiefly as an expositor of collectivist farming— "You must go where life leads you!" he said, with a gesture of his graceful hands as if he were scattering corn. "I came to realize," he told me on another occasion, "that all the earlier teachers had designed their philosophies for an elect minority; when I began to study Karl Marx with humility it was like the world of vision breaking in on a man born blind." This rather shop-worn statement came with a smile in which I detected a certain embarrassment, but I do not think it was cynically made. Intellectually, he seemed to be a butterfly which drew nectar from every flower, and found the latest the sweetest of all.

He was lonely, among men who could not appreciate the European flavours in his discursive mind, and he evidently enjoyed his conversations with me. Indeed, I think he became fond of me; not romantically, for my appearance then would not have stirred romantic interest in the monks of Athos, but in a paternal fashion. For my part, I found pleasure in the company of one so detached from my present background and from his own. He spoke a slightly démodé Russian with soft, agreeable pedantry. His looks, predominantly Asiatic, I should scarcely have admired at any time: he had the stoop of one who has grown too fast, his features were set unevenly in a head which might have been pressed between two stones. But there was in his heavily framed brown eyes the charm of an artist's curiosity, and the humour of his flexible mouth was irresistible to one who saw little but the bullock mouths of soldiers. If his dealings with me were not—as it proved—straightforward, it was because he lacked the sort of mind which uses only one road at a time. And were we to meet again now, I believe we should resume our former relationship without the least embarrassment on either side.

This Captain Vaninov (as I shall call him) was greatly concerned about my condition, which, at our earliest acquaintance, he spoke of with frankness and a grave sympathy. Very soon he was taking pains to see that I had opportunities for rest, and was making me presents of food from his own rations. It was the wrong time, he said, to be in such a case. My husband should surely have realized—but then, the forces of love, as he knew, were not to be governed by political sagacity. . . .

"It would be very much better," he said one morning, "if you were to get right away from here—now, when you're still fit to travel. Here, you see, nothing's organized yet, so our army can't look after people properly. We had to move in such a hurry, and we still don't know what the Germans are going to do—the political situation is very obscure. You ought to be in some place quite unaffected by the German–Polish war."

"Such as Sweden?" I suggested.

"Yes," he said seriously. "Sweden might do. Would you like to be in Sweden?"

"I should like to be on an island in the Pacific," I answered; "only I happen to have mislaid my private aeroplane."

"No, no; you must be serious! Surely the child will have an infinitely better chance if it's born in peaceful surroundings, where there's plenty of food for everyone!"

"You know perfectly well," I said, "that no one's allowed to move as much as five kilometres without a permit, and permits are just not to be had."

"That's not at all certain," he replied. "It's a case of knowing who to apply to. Yes, of course there are delays—an army on a war footing has a great amount of business to attend to, papers dealing with smaller affairs get put on one side. Still, there's always a chance. You ought really to put in an application to the District Commissioner for Civilian Affairs."

That was the kind of conversation which, in any context, leads nowhere. Of course it started a new daydream, or refreshed an old one: Sweden—safety, a modern hospital, perfect nourishment for Conrad and for me! But I should have had sense enough not to let the dream possess me if Vaninov had not returned to the subject. He came to me a few days later wearing that air of mystery and excitement which one associates with scandal-mongers.

"You must not be too hopeful," he began, "but I think we've made a start, anyway. I've put in an application on your behalf to the D.C.C.A.—he's extremely sympathetic, he's sending it forward with a personal recommendation of his own. Yes, for your removal to Sweden. You see, it's already recognized in high quarters that civilians who need special care ought not to be in an area like this. They've been working on a scheme already—the only question is whether we shall get co-operation from other countries. At any rate, negotiations are going on at a high level."

Did he, I have since asked myself, believe that? Well, there may possibly have been some general truth in it, which history has yet to bring to light. And did I believe it? *Enfin*, in times of hopelessness one believes what one wants to believe.

For several days I did not see him at all. When I asked one of the more intelligent soldiers if he could tell me what had happened to him, the man shrugged his shoulders, smiling quizzically. "He's busy, I expect. They've always got plenty to do, those brothers of ours. Nobody quite knows what it is." Then, when I got to the billet one afternoon, I found my friend waiting for me. He explained that he had been at Army Corps Headquarters for a conference on 'Moral Affairs'.

"I took the opportunity to see a man I know on the staff there—someone very high up—about your application. It seems to be going on all right, only there's a small technical difficulty. In the case of a married woman, an application of this sort has usually to be supported by her husband—that's because certain principles in international law are involved."

"But I thought I'd told you—my husband is dead."

"But you haven't any proof of his death?"

"No."

"Well, that's the difficulty."

So! It was no new experience for me, to blow a great bubble of fancy and see it burst on some pin-point of legal requirement.

"I never shall have any proof," I told him, "so I suppose that ends it. I'm enormously grateful for all the trouble you've taken."

"But wait a minute!" He smiled surreptitiously. He was an amateur conjurer now, boyishly pleased with his cleverness. "Sometimes there are ways of getting round these things—you haven't spent half your life dealing with officials, as I have! Listen: who is the head of your family—your husband's family, the people you live with?"

I told him—Count Stanislas Kolbeck.

"Very well then! What we have to do, first of all, is to get Count Kolbeck to Corps Headquarters. He will have to give testimony in person to the effect that——"

"That's quite impossible," I said. "The Count is a very old man, he's been a cripple and invalid for years."

"Oh!" He seemed utterly crestfallen. "And he is your late husband's father?"

"No, grandfather."

"And your husband's father—is he alive?"

"As far as I know."

"He's not living here?"

I said, "He's away on business. I've no idea where he is."

"But his wife or someone would know?"

"I'm afraid not."

"That's a pity!" he said thoughtfully. "If he were here, I could get him a pass to go to Corps Headquarters without much difficulty. If the authorities had his support to your application, I think it would probably prove effective. You don't think he's likely to be back here?"

At this point I saw no reason to beat about the bush. I told him that my father-in-law had at one time been closely associated with Pilsudski, and so had obvious reasons for keeping out of the way. "Least of all," I said, "would he suppose himself likely to be *persona grata* at a Russian military headquarters."

It seemed to take a few seconds for this statement to sink in. He said at last, "Yes, I see exactly how it is. Really, we could hardly be more unlucky. Well, I must see if there's any other way round." And curiously, at that moment it was for him that I felt sorry, as when one sees it dawning on a child that some grandiose plan he has made is utterly impracticable. He did appear as much mortified as if a scheme on which he had laboured in his own interest had suddenly collapsed. I said:

"I'm afraid I've been a great nuisance to you. Really, you should never have bothered about a person like myself."

And then I found, to my disgust, that I was in tears.

Vaninov put his hands on my shoulders. "You mustn't talk like that!" he said, gently shaking me, and smiling. "You talk as if all our chances were over! I'm not as easily beaten as that! Listen, I've made up my mind to get you to Sweden—before your child is born. I shan't rest until I've found some way. You really must believe that!" And he added, as on an afterthought, "If you hear anything about your father-in-law's whereabouts, you must let me know. Privately, I mean. I think I might manage things with him *without* getting him involved in any trouble. I have friends, you see! You understand—if you do get any news of him you must tell me at once. Send a message if I'm not about. You know Solitsin, the supplies fellow? He can always find me."

Those last sentences, beautifully acted as they were, should have told me everything: at that stage no one in her senses, certainly no one with a native understanding of Slavic ways of thought, could have mistaken his intentions for unalloyed benevolence. But by now the dream had assumed in my mind an empire that was not to be shaken by reason. In a thaw which lasted over several days the snow was turning into mists and slime, the majesty of winter had gone. The house was a prison where the smell from clothes drying over an oil-stove, the sound of Sandra's cough and of Rosalia's shoes along the passage, were sores upon one's sensibility; while here, standing about in the mud and the damp winds, faintly hoping for some soldiers' leavings, were the aged and the children, shrunken faces grey with hunger, the eyes of settled despair. Sweden! In Sweden there would be shaded lamps on freshly laundered pillow-slips, shops with gay jerseys for tiny children. And beside me was one who was striving to get me there; who had given me already what I had lacked so long, a man's simple affection.

I said, "It's very unlikely that General Kolbeck will come anywhere near Setory while the present situation continues. Even if he did, I should not be told. My husband's family don't regard me as one of themselves."

vi

There is a limit to self-deception, and if I needed further demonstration of the way in which I was being used it was granted me a week later.

It happened in my own room, one seemingly destined to be the frame of every small event on which, as on pylons, this length of existence was hung; that awkwardly proportioned room with its hybrid furniture, the dingy Perugino over Annette's bed: where Wanda, sharing it for a time, had once let me cross the threshold of her secrecies; where Victor and I had spent our last few minutes together. And like those other happenings, it came at night.

The day before, I had overworked myself at the billet, where there were sick men requiring special attention; this made me sleep heavily, with dreams like wreathing smoke in which Vaninov's voice continually sounded; and when, opening my eyes, I saw his face near to mine it took me some time to make the passage from dream into reality. He was talking just as he did in the daytime:

". . . So very tired! My poor Stefanie, you've been doing too much for those wretched soldiers—they told me. No, lie still, lie still, shut your eyes, I don't want to disturb you. It's only a little thing, a little service for a friend of mine, someone who may be useful to you. You can't have too many friends, can you—people who'll help you to get to Sweden!"

I let my eyes fall shut again, as he bade me; the lamp which he had placed between him and me prevented me from retreating into sleep, but it seemed that nothing was required of me, and I lay contentedly listening to his quiet voice.

". . . just to get it clear, what you told him. You remember, Jendrek came and told your father-in-law about Pawczac. You remember? It was late at night, and you and your father-in-law were together, and Jendrek came. Jendrek was worried, poor fellow —Pawczac had been so troublesome, wouldn't part with the grain he was holding. You remember?"

I murmured, "Pawczac—yes, I remember."

"And your father-in-law was angry—naturally, because that fellow was keeping his grain when people in the village were starving. Of course he was angry! He said 'I'll see that fellow, I'll deal with him myself, straight away!' You remember?"

"Yes—I think so. Yes, something like that."

"Yes; he said, 'I'm going to deal with him straight away.' He said to Jendrek, 'I'll come with you now, at once. I'll want something to threaten him with, a stick, a heavy stick.' You remember? And then he and Jendrek went out together—you remember?"

I said, "I'm not sure. I don't remember about the stick. I'm not quite sure."

"But we must get this clear." His voice was still gentle, but insistent. "You'll have to rouse yourself just a little. Just a little!"

By then I was fully awake; drowsy, but conscious of what he was saying. My eyes opened once more.

There was another man, whom I did not at first recognize, standing between Vaninov and the door. When I looked that way the lamp hurt my eyes, and I turned them towards Annette's bed, where they could rest more comfortably. Annette was lying in a posture which had been habitual with her from earliest childhood (when I had often been afraid lest she should suffocate), with her face buried in the pillow, her head framed by her arms. She appeared to be sleeping deeply, and for that I was glad, for even then I had some vague idea that she ought not to be witness of this conversation.

"You see," Vaninov continued patiently, "my friend has had a statement of great precision from Jendrek. Jendrek specially remembers about the stick, and he's sure you'll be able to support him."

His voice went on and on, now gently demanding, now soothing again. I listened only with a small portion of my mind, for my thoughts, refusing to be contained by this peculiar hour, were drifting back to the dreams I had lately come from, and to happenings of earlier days; I forgot, from moment to moment, who it was talking, and I was constantly surprised to realize that a man—not Victor or Casimir—was close to me in this familiar room. My own voice seemed to be doing what was needed, as on those occasions when I had been hostess to Victor's friends; and I scarcely noticed that now instead of murmuring "I don't remember," I was saying "Perhaps . . . I suppose so . . . Yes."

To the end of that interview Vaninov never bullied me; he was only sympathetic, persuasive; but there was a stage when his voice, becoming a little firmer, brought me farther into wakefulness:

"That's excellent, excellent, we seem to be clear about everything now! Now I've got a written statement here, I think we've agreed on every point in it, I want you just to put your signature at the bottom and then I shan't bother you any more."

The exact wording of the document I do not now remember, but I know that it was quite unambiguous. Up to a point it gave a substantially correct account of the conversation between Julius and Jendrek at which I had assisted. Thereafter it asserted that Julius had plainly announced his intention to deal with Pawczac by means of physical violence, and had started upon this mission immediately. (A less likely course of action for a man in Julius's position can hardly be conceived.) It concluded, again more or less correctly, with an account of my finding Pawczac at the hospital next morning, grievously wounded. While Vaninov waited, with the utmost patience, I read the statement through twice, understanding it perfectly.

"A lot of this is entirely untrue," I said.

He appeared not to hear me. He said, smiling as a sick-nurse would, "You'll have to sit up for a moment—just to sign," and with a nurse's care he raised my shoulders and put a pillow behind my back. I remember that what chiefly—and absurdly—troubled me just then was the indignity of being seen in an old pyjama suit of Victor's, much torn, which was all I had left to wear at night.

The other man had come a little closer, and now I recognized him as the Special who had examined me at length in the hearing of the family. His presence alarmed me. He had failed with me before, and I had recognized in him the kind of person, stubborn from smallness of mind, who would bear a grudge against me for such failure.

"I don't like your friend being here," I said to Vaninov, and I think the fear must have shown in my voice. "Will you ask him to go away, please!"

There was a quick exchange between the two men, of which I only caught the words—from Vaninov—"Just three minutes; it would be best, I really think." Then the Special went outside the door, but not, I imagine, any farther.

Vaninov returned to me "To tell you the truth," he said confidentially, "all this amounts to nothing at all, it's purely red-tape. The information you gave my friend the other day, it's all gone off to Headquarters Security—most likely it's buried deep in the files by this time. It's just that my friend—well, people in his line, nothing very much in the way of education, they suffer from the disease of pedantry. Signatures, they dream about signatures. It doesn't make a speck of difference to anyone on earth whether you sign or don't. Except, of course, our friend himself. *He* won't be happy till you *do* sign, and he's a man I'd like you to be on the right side of—in certain matters he counts for something. You see what I mean!"

I saw what he meant. I saw, as clearly as I do now, that my signature on this piece of shameless falsehood was to them a matter of first importance. I saw, also, that the burden of living could be made insufferable as long as I refused. I knew, in short, that they would force me to sign in the end.

But I should not, I believe, have surrendered at once if my inward battle had been fought on even terms. True, I was in feeble condition physically, oddly scared by the thought of that sinister person returning, engrossed in the chance of escape to Sweden which these people seemed to be offering me. But I had been educated at least to a common decency, and I could not have perjured myself so flagrantly for the sake merely of my own convenience. If the truth about my mother's death had never been made known to me, I should at least have resisted for a time.

[169]

Vaninov placed a pen in my hand. He smiled encouragingly. I signed.

"You will remember," he said, putting the paper carelessly in his pocket, as if that business were a long way behind, "you're going to let me know if there's a chance of my getting in touch with General Kolbeck? For the rest—don't worry, just leave everything to me!" Supporting my shoulders, he moved the pillow so that I could lie flat again. "And now I hope you'll go back into your dreams—if they were sweet ones. You've been so patient with me, so kind! Sleep well!"

Sleep?

As soon as he was gone I lit the candle which stood by my bed; and instinctively, when the flame settled, I looked towards Annette. She had moved. I could not see her face, but a tiny sound which came from her lips made me get up and go to her side.

"Annette! Darling, did they wake you, those men? Were you frightened? There's nothing to be frightened of, they'd only come to ask a lot of silly questions, the way they do. You weren't frightened, were you, darling? You're not frightened now?"

She did not answer. That was natural, for she had always been a child whom strong emotion held in absolute silence. She looked at me for an instant, then put her face into the pillow again, and lay quite still, as if asleep. She was not sleeping, however. Asleep, her body would have yielded to the tenderness of my arm about her shoulders, of my face in her hair.

8

i

ANNETTE, in her misery, confided in Wanda. I know that now; at the time I read it in Wanda's behaviour to me. No doubt Wanda tried to respect her confidence, but she must have given the others some kind of warning that I was by no means to be trusted. This, I also read—perhaps over-read—in a hundred glances, in their constant reticence.

They were in touch with Julius again, or so I inferred from the furtive arrival, now and then, of some old servant from the village asking to see Sandra or the Countess on private business. There was a certain flutter over these visitors, pains were taken to prevent my being present when the messages were delivered, and then there was much clumsy pretence that their errands had been of no importance. If the Countess could carry off this kind of thing effectively, Sandra could not, and sometimes I felt as mothers do when their small children are 'hiding' in conspicuous corners: it became almost a strain to play the part of the deceived. Why these precautions? Did they really think me clever enough to act harmfully if they told me outright that Julius was finding means to send them letters? To this question I found for myself, in time, the most likely answer. No man was more devoted to his family than Julius—in his own, unsentimental way—and he would probably contrive to visit them before long, even at great risk. If his letters had not already spoken of such a visit, the next that came might do so; it was therefore important that they should not be seen by me, better that I should not even know of their existence. Soon I grew positive that my surmise was correct. In a life so narrowly confined one is abnormally sensitive to others' moods, and I could feel that the temper of the Kolbecks was keyed by expectancy. More than ever, Julius was the corner-stone of their lives, the symbol of ultimate independence which the tides could not alter or diminish; and where so little else was to be hoped for, their thoughts were for ever upon his return.

Yes, the feeling of a house alters entirely when its master is away; there is a relaxation, sometimes grateful, of certain tensions, together with a sense of slackened purpose; and Julius was not less the master because his parents still lived here. It could be said that his absence brooded over his family, and from this obsession I was not excluded. I found myself pondering on the possibility that I should suddenly meet him; wondering how I should act if that occurred.

"I suppose your father will be back here sometime?" I said boldly to Wanda, one evening when she and I were in the kitchen together getting a meal ready for some soldiers.

If she was startled she did not betray herself—probably she had prepared for such a question.

"It's not at all likely," she said calmly. "For one thing, he's got too much to do. He hasn't stopped being a soldier just because there's no immediate fighting."

There was nothing unfriendly in her voice, but she kept her eyes away from mine; and I remember how I felt, at that moment, the bitterness of our estrangement. I said with gentleness, "But he must be aching to see you all!" and that did make her look at me.

"Why do you say that?"

"I know him a little," I told her. "After all, we were working together."

"If you knew him," she said distantly, "you'd realize that nothing, nothing, comes between him and what he feels is his duty. Yes, he loves us all. Even Henryk. That's ordinary—anyone's fond of his own family—it's so ordinary you can hardly call it love. Loving Poland, that's something different. There's no one left who loves Poland as he does, there's no one else large enough." She was faintly excited now. "You won't understand that!"

I answered, "Perhaps I do understand. I've been married to two of his sons."

"If you understood him you would love him," she said soberly; and then, making some excuse, she left me.

Those last words stayed in my mind.

The Julius I had known most intimately, the stoic labourer who had unobtrusively cared for my well-being in the days when we worked together, was already receding; that personality was a complexion of half-tones too delicately made to leave, in his physical absence, a clear image in my mind. The fading of this image was what I wished, for the thought of having given false evidence against such a man was a sore on the spirit which I could not long endure. I had striven to replace it with the earlier impression of a man whose very virtues were so coldly surfaced that they inspired only a formal respect. And here, now, was Wanda, no vehicle of cheap emotions, assuring me that the man was of one piece and altogether to be loved. Had I known either her or him less well, I might have dismissed her feelings as filial piety. It would not do. In her acceptance of her father, the man as he was, the whole man, I saw a likeness to my acceptance of Victor, which had the force but never the blindness of idolatry. Recognizing the quality of her love, I knew that the being who commanded it could not be small or valueless; and however often I reminded myself of the man he had been in earlier years, the sense of having acted viciously would not be subdued.

'If you understood him you would love him.' Had there been one voice only to echo in my thoughts I might yet have recovered in some measure the quietness of spirit that I needed, in those critical months, to offset the discomforts of living under alien domination. But another was still sounding against it: the cry—as it seemed to me—which my mother had uttered as she fell. Once more I was trying to persuade myself that so distant an event, the sordid climax of a young man's bitter anger, could not concern me; that every tie between me and the victim—probably some callow peasant girl— had been loosed by death and by the years which had intervened. That was a judgment of intelligence, and upon the heart it had no effect. The life this woman had given me, after travelling the wearisome road I travelled now, was part of hers. I knew, from the preciousness of the child growing in my own body, that the worst of what she had suffered in her dreadful end was the anguish of being torn from me; and that was a claim on my loyalty which cold intelligence would not dismiss. The revulsion that followed the night of Vaninov's visit had stilled it; but when nothing developed, when my action appeared to have been—as Vaninov said—a vacant formality, it returned with fresh and increasing force. If, in fact, I had done no injury to the man who had destroyed my mother as men destroy vermin, the debt which my own life seemed to demand of me was still unpaid.

On the fetid ground where these opposing claims made war no clean wind blew, none of the breezes of small pleasure and excitement which had come to refresh me in other stages, no gust of hopefulness. All I could hope for was that Julius would stay hidden, that the chance to injure him would not become an actuality. In time, if no decision were forced, the battle might wear itself out.

ii

"I am sure we shall get some news from Victor soon!"

This piece of vacuous optimism came from Sandra in the voice she had developed for bringing up her children, the maternal voice —I had fallen into it at times myself—which is not inherently far removed from the mothering cry of ewes. She was helping me to make Annette a dress from an old one of Wanda's, and while I intended to give the neckline as much of mondaine elegance as the stuff allowed, she was gently pressing the case for extreme modesty. "I do feel, Stefanie dear, that now she's getting so grown-up we ought to be careful about these things. With all these soldiers about. I do feel—don't you?—that Victor would want you to be careful." And then that trite remark, "I'm sure we shall get some news from him soon. You know, Stefanie, I have a feeling all the time that he's safe and well. He is in God's hands."

However conventional, the observation was not insincere; it came directly from a piety which was never cramped by reason; and it made me realize afresh how much she would be impoverished if I told her that I knew Victor to be dead. For her, uncertainty was the lesser evil; it would enable her to continue for months or years to have Victor as part of her life, an imagined presence to supply her need for a son's devotion, a small, sweet spring of hopefulness.

Of us all, she, I think, was the least dejected by the havoc of our fortunes. She lived, as animals do, chiefly in the present, and the climate of anxiety was one to which she was accustomed. Of course she suffered from the lack of every physical comfort; but the disappearance of the gentle decorations of living did not too harshly affect her, since, lacking all subtlety in her own physical senses, she had regarded these things merely as part of her duty—the business of keeping Julius's house as a General's dignity demanded, of dressing the children so that they should do credit to Julius before his friends. I believe she still imagined that the present inconveniences were something that would shortly pass, like the childhood ailments which had periodically ravaged her nursery. Indeed, I came to wonder at that time whether intelligence, in a world where women exercise so little direct control, is a blessing to us at all.

Her eyes, which had been nervously scanning my face, went back to the long hem she was unpicking. "He will scarcely know Annette," she said, her stubby fingers working like grapnels, "she has grown up so much since he last saw her. Even these last few weeks. Of course Victor himself grew up very fast, he was just a naughty little boy one day and a grown man the next, there really seemed to be hardly any time in between."

I listened to this prattle with a kind of contentment. It was some time since she had talked about Victor, and the others seldom mentioned him at all. Just to hear his name, lovingly spoken, was to feel a glow from the fire whose warmth I had lived by. But it was not Victor who held her thoughts for long.

"Victor's so like his father," she said, as if she were speaking to a stranger. "You know, so many people only think of Julius as a great leader—people who only read about him in the papers or meet him on official business. They only see his sterner side—and you know, Stefanie, no one could do the work that he's done, no one could occupy his position, if he let people think he was weak and easy to influence. I don't suppose you've ever quite thought of it like that."

I answered non-committally. And now her voice became a little tearful, for she could never speak of Julius without emotion:

"People don't realize how good he is, how much he sacrifices himself for others, how gentle he can be!"

She stopped her work to glance at me again; she was appealing to me now. But there was nothing for me to say.

"Of course, I know that he was vexed about your marriage. But you see, his religion means so much to him, it governs the whole of his life. And then you must realize what a shock it was to us, Victor not telling us anything, just running away."

Oh, why should they talk to me like this, as if I were still too young to grasp the obvious! Why must they speak at all of Julius, for ever raising afresh the issue I wanted to avoid! Wretchedly embarrassed, I could only say:

"Surely that's all past history now! I don't suppose he's actually forgiven me, but——"

"Oh, but that's wrong!" she said. "He may not say anything— that would be against his principles—but Julius has never been the kind of man to harbour a grudge against people. If you only knew it, he really has an affection for you, he has often spoken of it to me."

It was she who was embarrassed now; and while I was groping

for some topic which would draw us away from this awkwardness my private thoughts took hold of my tongue:

"I've been meaning to ask you—have you any idea whether Nilniewicz is still alive?"

"Nilniewicz?" Of course my abruptness had startled her. "Why do you ask that? Nilniewicz—that was all before you were born."

"Someone told me," I said rather lamely, "that a man of that name once did some harm to my father-in-law."

"Some harm!" For a moment her face showed an anger which I had thought impossible in so dull a woman. "That man—he was a devil in disguise, he had the devil's pride and cunning, he was utterly evil! It was that man who sold Julius to the Russians. If Julius had killed him, it would only have been justice."

Inevitably I asked, "But did he try to?"

"We never saw him," she said, beginning to stumble in her speech as emotion ceased to carry her; "he had disappeared before Julius was released. We heard he was hiding in one of the Ruthenian villages—I think it was only a rumour—no one ever saw him again." Slowly as her mind worked, she was coming now to see obscurely what had made me think of Nilniewicz, and she said suddenly, with a new distress, "Stefanie, you don't understand! I don't know who's told you about that man—it wasn't a personal grudge that Julius had against him, it was only his sense of justice! Even if he *had* found him he wouldn't have hurt him seriously, he wouldn't have given him more than the punishment he deserved."

The ingenuousness of that outburst, inconsistent as it was, confirmed for me the fact of which I had long been all but certain: that Julius had concealed from her the whole story of my mother's death. But although she had told me nothing new, she had increased the pain of my isolation. This creature of simple affections, who had known me from my earliest years, was one to whom I might have confided the misery that darkened my inward life. She, humble enough to ask my sympathy, would not have refused me hers if she had understood—though only with the heart—the moral burden I was carrying. But how could she understand at all unless she knew of Julius what I knew; and how could I even start to persuade her of that truth about a man whom she had idealized so myopically and so long! We sat side by side, each pretending to be making some purposeful use of scissors or needle: two women at sullen enmity who needed each the trustful love which the other could not release. It was actually a relief to us both when the Countess came in.

She, stumping over to the cupboard where she kept her work-things, paused to survey us with the sardonic interest she had once devoted to her poultry.

"Are you still quarrelling over that ridiculous dress?"

Sandra said feebly, "No. No, we weren't quarrelling. No, Stefanie was only asking me about that dreadful Nilniewicz. She wants to know what happened to him."

"Nilniewicz? He's still at Przedborz, for all I know. With the Prussians to look after him, I trust. Julius gave him a farm there—it was a stupid piece of quixotry, I always said. If your time is not too occupied with historical researches, Stefanie, the Count would like you to read to him now."

iii

Did I read to him that evening, or did I make some excuse? I cannot remember. There were times, now, when the pleasure of being with him was spoilt by a sense of obliquity; for of the many rooms in his mind there was none that he would not open to me as I wanted, while I could not invite him into all of mine. Yet I could not altogether keep away from the one place where it was possible to escape from the others without facing the ordeal of solitude.

The period of physical weakness which sometimes occurs in middle pregnancy was curtailing my walks abroad, and indoors the area of comfort was now as much restricted as in the German days. The house had become a barrack of the less creditable order, inhabited upon no system one could follow by men for whom the use of houses seemed to be a new experience. No piece of furniture was regarded as different from another, no door was ever closed. The walls had ceased to be a rampart against winter, which, when you returned from the village, followed you inside; there, with a gale blowing from the kitchen quarters to the upper passages, with muddied snow across the hall and even on the stairs, the feeling of 'indoors' possessed you no more than in a covered market-place. You steered your way between men who were sleeping in odd corners, apparently impervious to the cold, past a group who were idly stripping a machine-gun, another throwing dice for cigarettes; from these and the mess they spread about them, their monotonous laughter and their rancid smells, it was a relief to retreat into those two or three rooms which—except when Butusov and his intimates were in a mood for civilian company—the Kolbecks managed to keep to themselves. Relief? A physical relief, I mean. With the wood which Annette and Henryk scratched from the countryside we could generally keep at least one stove alight; the carpets had been recovered, things were clean. Yes, and there was kindness, for Sandra would always stir herself when I came in, putting a chair for me near the stove, forging the little smile of welcome which was unlike the one she produced for Butusov and his friends: while Wanda, looking like a middle-aged woman with her white, drawn face, was never too busy or tired to think of some small service to my comfort. Only, I could not be at ease where nobody talked to me except in chosen sentences. So often someone—it was likely to be Henryk or Rosalia—would utter some chance remark relating to Julius, and a draught of awkwardness would chill the others, and Sandra would make clumsy haste to lead the talk on to some safer path. What refuge had I then but to slip away and find warmth in my bed? It was not home, a room where the light of intercourse flickered so wanly; a room where Annette fell into un-childish silence when I entered, and where I was for ever catching furtive glances from her pitifully anxious eyes.

None of the ordinary soldiers—as far as I know—had found their way even now to the Count's bedroom. The Countess may have arranged the matter through Solitsin; but you could have lived in the house for a long time without knowing that such a remote, small room existed at all. It was partly for this reason that it continued to escape the infections which had come to the rest of the house; and partly, I think, because, like an old suit of clothes, it seemed to be a component of the fragile creature it had sheltered for so long. Here the past flowed into the present so smoothly that it seemed impossible for any coming event to disturb that stream. Here, loosed from the day's frictions, you felt yourself whole and unchanged. And I should have found peace here but for the obdurate inner voice which forbade me to enjoy it.

Only in this room could I feel sure that there would be no sudden awkward intrusion of Julius's name; and so, perversely, I found that I was constantly bringing it in myself, or steering the talk towards him. I asked the Count, on one of those evenings:

"Do you remember a man called Nilniewicz?"

And to my surprise he answered at once, "Ah yes, poor fellow! I made a mistake about *him*."

"A mistake?"

"Yes, I encouraged my son—my son Julius—I encouraged him to take over that man and give him work of a confidential kind. He was so very able—Nilniewicz—we had given him an excellent education; able and deserving; I thought he was completely trustworthy."

"And he turned out to be a bad lot?"

"No—no, I can never think that. My wife thinks so. And Julius too, I've no doubt. I think myself that he had just a streak of weakness in him—a streak of vanity. Possibly he was venal as well, but I've always supposed that conceit was the main trouble. That's the difficulty, you know. You find a gifted child, you educate him, and his education divorces him from his own people. He belongs nowhere then. Because he has inherited no wealth he finds himself subservient to richer people, and that seems to him wrong, because he knows that his brain is as good or better than theirs."

He looked at my face intently, rather as a boy does when he has said something risky and expects his parent to be shocked. Then he began to laugh. His laughter did not startle me, since I was accustomed to his swift changes of mood, to the gaiety which was never far from his surface; his thoughts had drifted, as I found, to a corpulent priest who had been charged with the early stages of Nilniewicz's education, and with whom he had once spent much of his time in boisterous disputations about the Lutheran heresy. And with that the subject of Nilniewicz seemed to have passed out of his mind.

Unexpectedly, he returned to it of his own accord. I think it was on my next visit that he said, as if we had never left it:

"No, Stefanie, you mustn't think too harshly of Nilniewicz! The temptation may have come to him at a moment of special weakness. If that hadn't happened, he might have proved a faithful servant. You must try to make Julius realize that when he comes home—he will listen to you as he would never listen to me."

I did not immediately understand why he should make that curious suggestion. But when he said, after a silence, "It's hard for you, having him away so long!" I began to realize how his mind was working. That mind was rarely clouded; he said nothing that was blurred or meaningless; but the area which came alight was small, and since he enjoyed his memories for their own richness his brain no longer troubled much about sorting them into the right compartments of time. (Of one of his friends he said, "He wears the face of the hunted; he's terrified of overlooking some chance to be kind, or of being caught in an act of kindness. . . . He comes to play chess with me quite often." And what did it matter to him—was it, indeed, relevant to absolute truth—that the man he spoke of had been dead for twenty-eight years?) I knew, then, what pattern his thoughts had taken when he continued:

"You will find him changed, you know. Some of my friends, my best friends, have been there for a time—in the Kadorka prison. I think it affects a man more powerfully than the other places one is taken to—in Yakutsk there is always the sky, which is often beautiful, and you wait for the season when the birds will come. In the Kadorka they miss all that; it's a much more difficult place for God to find."

He was feeling about for my hand, which I gave to him to hold; this was the means by which he steered his eyes back to my face when they had lost it, for when he was a little tired they would not keep their direction for long. He seemed, now, to see me as clearly as I saw him; and it was strange to feel myself so close to the old man, so free from fear or confusion, when the regions where his thoughts and mine were moving were almost forty years apart.

"Yes," he said, "it won't be easy for him to start the life of a free man again. A part of him will be left behind for a few years— perhaps for always. You mustn't let that hurt you, you must be patient—if you are beautifully patient, you will find your way to the part of him you seem to have lost. You, only you!"

He spoke those words slowly, searching for them as a vinegrower will pick out bunches of grapes to give to a friend, and smiling to me as if the task gave him both pleasure and pain. Because I knew that he had mistaken my position for Sandra's and meant his counsel for her, I allowed it to pass from ear to memory without much stirring my mind. My thoughts were upon the Count himself; and I remember clearly how, while I listened to that curious appeal, I was wondering what feature in this calm, aged face evoked the transient likeness which I saw between him and his son. It was not the eyes themselves, and it could not be in their regard; for while the tranquil light of the one man's gaze seemed to flow unhindered from his self to mine, the other's, in his gentlest mood, would be broken by shadows of resentment. They had no gestures in common, no wrinkle of the brows or shaping of a smile such as you often find in parent and child; and now, when I see them in the truer perspective of distance, I can still detect no physical sign of their affinity. Yet the likeness did not come from the play of my imagination on their relationship. Just as you see in the faces of the newly dead something which tells you peculiarly of their shared humanity, so I saw in the faces of these two men, the reflection of a common experience; of years in which, detached from every vestige of human gentleness, they had watched despair advancing as cancer advances.

But I saw without understanding. You do not interpret, you do not make calm judgments on the questions which concern you as each day unwraps them; you look, rather, for something to say, for an argument or instance which will shape the issue to fit some prejudice of your own. Perhaps I had vaguely hoped that the Count would help me to resolve my dual feeling about his son; but now, remembering that what I knew about Julius was unknown to him, I was attacked by a wave of impatience. Here was a senile tolerance which, measured against the facts of Julius's life, had no validity. I forgot that his words were not meant for me or for the time I lived in; and I said abruptly, letting go his hand:

"There isn't only Julius to be thought of. If he's dangerous to other people, one has got to think of them as well."

Although I did not raise my voice, that gust of feeling would surely have shaken another man; and I looked instantly at his face, fearful of the pain I should have given to one so vulnerable. The fear was needless. Depending for so long on his own resources, requiring so little the commerce of words and sentiments which for other minds is daily food, he had come to live where the shocks of discord and petulance could not reach him. He did pause for a few moments, as if some breeze had brought to his mind a dust which had to settle. Then, smiling, he said distinctly:

"Julius—yes—Julius has chosen the profession of arms. A narrow one, I often feel. And yet, you know, a soldier if he's any good can't be without virtue. I mean, in other trades you offer your services on a limited contract. Not in soldiering—there you put your life itself at the disposal of your fellow-creatures." I thought he was faintly troubled now; perhaps he realized, remotely, that his thoughts had slid past a tract of history, or perhaps the effort to shape them was a greater tax on his powers than I had supposed. "Virtue, yes!" he said. "Of course, that isn't the same as love. But it can be a road towards it. Love is achieved through so many roads. And don't you think it's the only valuable achievement?"

Answering mechanically, "Oh yes, of course!" I moved the neck-pillow to get his head in a better position. From a slight trembling of the cheek-bones I knew that the pain which generally possessed him at night had started, and I did not encourage him to talk any more; but when I had lit a cigarette for him he seemed comfortable enough, and content that I should stay at his side.

The minutes that followed were imbued with a pleasure warm

enough to keep them in my memory. If his last words had come to me without meaning, his silences were like cool water on tired feet; he continued to observe my face, but I was too well used to that quiet gaze to be embarrassed, and in the calm which enclosed me I could study as I wished the beauty of his head. Perhaps it was only in my fancy that the flesh had thinned still further in the last few weeks. I know that as I saw his face now it seemed to have nothing but a cover as fine as silk about the framework of bone and vein, and I felt as if I watched a mechanism of exquisite structure displayed with sides of glass where the solid walls should be. This ethereal shell, carved faultlessly to allow the tiny plays of muscle and nerve, was all that was needed to house a human mind; and just as he had discarded every physical redundance, so he seemed to have left behind him all thought and feeling which were not intrinsic to his wisdom. He had never been less aloof; seldom does one being offer another so whole a sympathy as he was offering me then, as he leant forward rather painfully to hold my wrist, his very thin fingers tracing the veins in my hand. But I had not learnt to breathe the air which the years had made natural for him. Between a creature who, looking within, would find no corner shaded, and one such as I, there could be no unity of understanding.

iv

It is not chance which rules us. The opportunities which come are the ones we have prepared for, knowing it or not.

It was chance that I returned a little earlier than usual from one of my regular visits to the village, to find Henryk alone in the night-nursery; chance, I suppose, which made him say, "I don't know what she does there all the time!" But the fact that the words caught my attention, as few of Henryk's did, was not accidental. I had noticed in the last day or two that Sandra and the Countess were frequently absent at unexpected times, and this had stirred in me something more than curiosity.

"What *who* does?" I asked. "Where?"

"Who? Mum!"

"Does where?"

"What? You know. That place. Place where Aunt Betka used to live."

"Is that where Sandra is now?"

But he declined to attend to me any further. He had started

spelling out the words in an old newspaper which was lying on a chair, and he would no more return to a subject he had tired of than a bored dog will repeat its tricks.

So: it was Betka's cottage which the Kolbeck women were visiting so assiduously. Why? It had become a billet for senior N.C.O.s, and none of the Kolbeck servants lived there any more. Would there be any place in so small a house for someone to hide without the other occupants knowing? There was the attic, of course, with its gable-end window. And now it came back to me that Victor had once got in that way, climbing up by a pent-house roof, to frighten me by making weird noises above my bedroom. For a man of Julius's physique it would not be too hard to make such an entry.

Late that night I caught a glimpse of Wanda going downstairs with a parcel under her arm and a lamp in the other hand. From a window at the end of the upper corridor I watched her leaving the house by the dairy door, and the flicker of the lamp enabled me to trace her progress along the road which led round the back of the stables. Betka's cottage was beside that road.

I woke next morning, after sleeping poorly, with a limited intention. I meant to take a walk to a spot where I could comfortably observe the cottage and look for some evidence that the attic was being used as I had surmised; it seemed to me that I was merely trying to satisfy a normal curiosity, begotten by the secretiveness of other people. This was self-deception, as the outcome proved. Having chosen a time when I could leave the house without being noticed, I got ready for the expedition and was actually on my way out when I met Solitsin in the hall. We had come to be on fairly amicable terms, and he stopped to favour me with one of his thin, oblique witticisms about the Countess and her bargaining. Without reflection, I interrupted him to ask if he had lately seen Captain Vaninov.

"Vaninov?" he said. "You know him?"

"Yes—has he gone away?"

"Why?" he asked. "Do you want to see him?"

"Not specially."

"I might get a message to him."

"It's nothing special," I repeated. And then, caught in a fresh wave which I had not seen approaching, I said, "Oh—perhaps if you do see him any time—I'll just write something."

He found a piece of paper for me. Whether he had any notion of what might be in my mind I cannot tell; a faint slyness in the set of his underlip had been with him, one imagined, from birth. I wrote, without pausing, 'I do hope Sweden is not altogether forgotten. Possibly there is someone who can help in cottage beyond stables here. My kind regards'. Solitsin took the folded note and put it in the lining of his cap.

"I might run into him," he said, "but most likely not. There's a little brooch you used to wear with a blue stone. Not very valuable. I know someone who likes that sort of thing."

"The message is of no importance," I said.

I tried later on to persuade myself that I should never have sent that information but for the chance meeting with Solitsin. But that was not the case. Somehow, in time, I should have contrived to send it.

v

The period in which I waited miserably to know if the note had reached Vaninov, and whether he would act upon it, was not a long one. I was at supper that evening when Butusov barged in and said I was wanted downstairs. In the passage he told me I had better put on a coat; then he led me to a ration truck which was standing ready at the front of the house.

I have an oddly salient memory of the man who drove me, a tiny creature buried in an ill-fitting greatcoat who appeared to wrestle with his wheel as with an angry beast while the truck floundered and skidded on the snow. Was I comfortable he asked —leaning over so that his minikin voice should reach me through the dreadful uproar of his engine—and not too cold? Did I like the truck, which he himself regarded as his personal friend? In its own country, he told me, the truck would not behave so boisterously as this; in Poland the roads were miserably bad because all the money was used to build houses for rich landlords. His ingenuous chatter diluted the flavour of nightmare in that short drive, and I was grateful, too, for a certain callow ceremony with which he helped me down when, at the far end of the village, we stopped at a two-storeyed house.

"One day you will ride with me again, little friend?" he said, holding my arm to lead me to the door. "In my own country, perhaps—everything is nice and homely there, not like this. You would love my mother very much, she is a little sweetheart; she can eat a raw parsnip with only her gums."

The house had formerly been occupied by the land surveyor, an uncle by marriage of Jendrek's; in the room where I was taken I recognized a table and sideboard which had belonged to him, while half the rest of the floor was covered by ammunition boxes with German markings. From these, and a folded coat, a man who looked like a Dutch trooper had made himself a seat, and with an ancient Blickensderfer propped on the piano he was laboriously typing a report. Catching sight of me, he threw a cigarette over his shoulder.

I said to this man, "I hope I'm not going to be kept here long."

"So do I!" he answered rather sourly. "How do you spell this word *kvitantsii*?"

I told him, and asked, "Perhaps it's Captain Vaninov who wants to see me?"

"How should I know!" he said.

It was, in fact, Vaninov who presently arrived. He gave me a friendly smile, but he seemed in a hurry and rather preoccupied.

"This business of your emigration," he said without preamble. "I'm afraid it's been held up a good deal, but everything seems fairly clear now. I've got the formal application here, it just wants your signature."

I remember the document as being immensely wordy and very badly typed; most of it seemed to be concerned with my identity as the wife of Colonel Victor Kolbeck and daughter-in-law of General Julius Kolbeck, formerly of the Polish General Staff, and so forth. It asserted, with a cheerful disdain of logic, that the signature below was my true signature. None of this troubled me much, so quickly does the habit grow of signing as one is told. I put my name where Vaninov pointed with his finger.

"And now," he said, with a carelessness which I recognized even then as counterfeit, "we must get your father-in-law to endorse it."

He unfolded a section which had been tucked underneath, and on this was typed—'As father-in-law of the above-named Stefanie wife of Victor Kolbeck I hereby signify my consent to this application'. He said to the soldier who was with us:

"Tell Vladimir I'm ready for the General now."

We waited for perhaps five minutes—I do not know. Vaninov, in that interval, was making conversation with his old pleasantness, but I paid him little attention, since my mind was transfixed by a feeling of unreality. So much was familiar here: the marquetry of the Leipzig pianette, which the surveyor's wife had often played for us when Aunt Betka brought me to visit her, the portrait-engraving of an earlier Kolbeck, Vaninov's amusing mouth—familiar but grotesquely juxtaposed. In the fluster of leaving the house I had thrown round my shoulders an old marten cape which had still the air of Paris about it; and it seemed to be outside the channel of experience that I should be sitting on a pile of grenade boxes wearing this garment, and smiling politely at Vaninov, while between us, in the lowering light from the kerosene lamp, lay the sheet of periphrastic nonsense which was supposed to represent our business. The sense of illusion was not diminished when the soldier returned with another, and with Julius, looking thin and ill, between them.

He was in a mechanic's clothes, but not otherwise disguised. What I found strange in him was that he appeared to be completely unaffected by his surroundings: he was neither nervous nor hostile, neither resentful nor embarrassed. When he saw my face he gave no sign of recognition; and although he had sometimes treated me almost as disdainfully when we were constantly together, the effect of this completely neutral glance was to make me doubt for a moment whether it were really he or a man with identical features. Vaninov may have read that in my face. He said, with a smile:

"This *is* your father-in-law, isn't it?"

And I answered, "It's someone who looks like him."

At that point Julius himself seemed to come to a sudden decision. He said to Vaninov in his most military voice—that voice which finished a sentence as if a trap was sprung behind it:

"Well, I think we needn't argue over that. Everyone knows me about here. What is it you want at this moment?"

"I don't want anything," Vaninov answered. "It's your daughter-in-law, she wants you to support her application for emigration to Sweden."

"*My* support? What authority have *I* got at the present time?"

"It's a formality," Vaninov said.

He had picked up the application. Julius stretched and took it from him as if he were dealing with a subordinate officer, ran his eye through it and turned to me.

"Stefanie, you're not such an incredible fool as to think this means anything?"

My voice, when I answered, sounded as feeble as I felt, "It seems worth trying, if there's only one chance in a hundred."

Ignoring that, Julius spoke to Vaninov again.

"Have you really taken all this trouble just to get an up-to-date copy of my signature?"

Vaninov, with a restraint that was perhaps remarkable, said, "I haven't asked for your signature, General Kolbeck. It's simply a

[186]

question of whether you want to do a service to your son's wife. Well, perhaps you'd like to talk to her about it."

He made us a little bow—he belonged, I still think, to the old order, he was never really at home in the galley where I found him—smiled in a friendly way and left the room. We heard him going upstairs.

The soldiers stayed; and while the one who looked like a Dutchman went on with his work the other, a cadaverous youth with the zealot's joyless eyes, stood watchfully against the door. His duty, I suppose, was purely a military one; neither of these men appeared to have any special interest in what might pass between Julius and me, and though Vaninov may have posted an eavesdropper somewhere close by I do not think he had. The lamp was flaring. The men's faces, thrown intermittently into hard, sculptural light, showed like museum effigies. Against the winter silence which enwrapped the house the sound of the typewriter was like the tapping of a nuthatch's beak.

In this makeshift of privacy we were free to talk as we pleased. Its effect on me was paralysis; but it needed only a few moments for Julius, in the way I knew, to shake off the superfluities from his thoughts; and then he spoke to me in French.

"Yes," he said reflectively, "the idea is to have your signature and mine on the same document, they get a neat identification that way. They like that sort of thing. It's odd, they forsake all logic but pedantry survives." His lips came together as he savoured this observation. Then the bleak amusement in his voice faded. "Tell me—I gather you've had no news about Victor?"

Taken by surprise, I had no chance to consider whether there was anything to gain from continuing to withhold the facts.

"He's dead—he was killed," I said.

I should not have thought—had there been time to think—that the news would come as a great shock to him. It was he, surely, who had told me some time before how small were Victor's chances of survival. To all of us death had become a thing that was near and commonplace, and to him it must always have been so. I had forgotten that people do not expect the laws of probability to apply to themselves.

"Killed?" he repeated. "Victor killed?"

"One of his men told me," I said. To me the fact of Victor's death had lost its edge. It was like a rheumatic pain which possesses you dully through all the hours of wakefulness. "A man I met— a friend of his had seen Victor's body."

"Dead?" he said once more. And then, "How? What happened?"

"I don't know exactly. He was crushed by an armoured car, it went over him. But he must have been shot down before that. I think he was shot off his horse."

Again he echoed my words, as people of feeble mind do. "Shot off his horse?" He closed his eyes, and when they opened again I had the impression that he had laid the subject aside, as a busy, conscientious man will push away some paper of lively interest which has no immediate bearing on his work. Abruptly, a little hazily, he said, "This—this document—you really think it means something, you think that fellow will try to get you to Sweden?"

There was no sensible answer to that question. I said, "I'm not going to bother about it any more. I don't really want you to sign it—it was an idea of that Russian's."

He had the application in his hand again, turned to catch the light. He was reading it right through, but only with his eyes, as I could see. "You," he said in Russian to the soldier-clerk, "give me a pen," and to me, "I'm afraid I don't think so, I don't think you'll ever get any favours from these people."

While he was speaking he took the pen which the clerk had given him and put his small, aggressive signature in the space that was left for it; carelessly, as officers sign documents of routine. I murmured, "It's very good of you"; but again he did not seem to hear me.

"I wish I could believe it," he said remotely. "Sweden, yes, I'd like to think the child was going to be born there; it would give him his best chance as things are now. It's a pity that neither his father nor I will ever see him."

That prosaic observation came from near the surface of his mind. I knew he had far more to say could he but find the means, and I saw all at once, as I glanced at his face, the strain to which this interview had put him. As a young man he had needed to govern and conceal his emotions. (How intense were those emotions I realized only much later than this.) That practice he had continued throughout life; and now, when his spirit's overflow required some physical escape, the channels were all silted from disuse. Some small surrender, some softening of his looks or voice, would have been to him like the release of weight from an injured limb. He was incapable of such self-relief. And the pity which had suddenly risen in me could not dissolve such barriers as his.

There was much that I, on my side, wanted to say. I wanted above all to talk of Victor, for at least we were partners now in the knowledge of Victor's death, and we both had loved him. But we had never talked of things so close to ourselves as that. I became aware that the clerk had finished his typing and had turned to stare at us with an idler's curiosity. Our time must be giving out, and the tongue struggles hopelessly against that handicap.

A sentence tumbled out of my mouth almost of its own accord, "I think you ought to know that I was closely questioned about the business of Jasiek Pawczac."

"Pawczac—yes!" he said apathetically. "I've been hearing a good deal about him. I fancy that's the charge they're going to bring against me, if someone insists on legal forms. It makes no difference—I'm a person they've got to get rid of, one way or another. Well, yes, it does make a difference. If they're going to use a specific charge there'll be a lot of delay, most likely they'll take me to Kartushka—they work a standing tribunal there. I should detest all that!" he said with sudden vehemence. "I loathe delays and verbiage and mumbo-jumbo."

"But if they don't?"

He looked at me as if he thought this a foolish question. "Well, they'll finish the business here, as soon as possible. They use the orchard, I imagine."

Yes. Yes, of course. Yes, that was what I had foreseen, what a part of me had hoped for. But I had not pictured it like this. In the scene of my mother's death there had been no grandeur; and yet I had vaguely imagined some grandeur in its retribution. Not that it should happen to a man who looked so tired and old, who talked so quietly; not that it should start from this shoddy parlour-room, or be witnessed only by strangers to whom it would be meaningless, men too commonplace to provoke a memory or to hold one, whose very conjunction was merely casual.

Turning my eyes away from him—because there were likenesses I did not want to see—I said in a voice which surprised me by its steadiness, "I'll take any message you want. You'll want me to say something to Sandra?"

Although he failed to answer it, I do not think that question passed without touching his intelligence. For when he spoke again his voice was gentler, and I felt at last that we had returned to one of those intervals of friendship which belonged to the German days. This I remember with pain but also gratefully; as when, on the day of leaving, the sun comes out to light once more a countryside which has stirred one's affections. He said, feeling his way from step to step:

"You know, Stefanie, if this had happened a few years ago—what's happening to me—I shouldn't have minded more than any other man. To have seen the resurgence, that was enough, I shouldn't have made a fuss about dying then."

He smiled. I did not want to see that smile, but I could not look away from him any more. He had fallen into Polish; I doubt if the soldiers understood, even now, more than a word or two of what he was saying, and yet I knew without turning to look that both of them were listening as intently as I.

"I don't mean that Poland's finished," he said. "I could never believe that. Poland means too much—to the world as well as us. It's not just a country, it's a shrine, it's a faith. They can grind it to bits, but it can't be destroyed." Those words, spoken from compulsion, must have cost him what it costs a man of his kind to make a declaration of love: his voice was controlled, but through the table on which his arm and mine were resting I could feel the passion which induced them, and though he was scarcely addressing me I found myself responding as one responds to love when one is suddenly confronted by its power and violence. There was nothing for me to say. I only moved my hand and held the sleeve of his coat, tightly, as one might support an invalid; and as if he were not aware of it he suffered that grasp without moving. "But to leave it like this!" he said. "With everything to be fought for and built again!"

He fell into a silence then, keeping perfectly still, while the soldiers curiously watched him: I think he was as much in solitude as if none of us had been there. But presently he came to see and recognize me again, and the smile which was a flag of pain returned. "You see, there should have been Victor to follow me. And his child—I don't know what will happen to his child." He leaned forward, staring at my eyes as if his own were failing. "Stefanie," he said, painfully, with that humility which comes when the spirit is bared from its disguises, "I can't make any claim on you now. But perhaps you no longer have any claim against me. Listen, Stefanie, I can only ask you now—for Victor, not for me—I can only beg you to teach the child that he is a Pole, to teach him what Poland is—what history and suffering have made her. At least you'll bring him up in the Catholic Faith—I beg you, I implore you to do that. If he's a Catholic he will know what he owes to his country, that truth will be born in him, he'll find it for himself."

'Perhaps you no longer have any claim against me.' Later I was to recall and ponder that phrase, but in those moments the relations between him and me were of no more importance than the room we were in or the soldiers staring at us. Death, at the bedside of the aged and sick, may be only a tranquil presence, but when it stands close to one whose body and mind are unimpaired it lends to him some part of its stature and authority. 'They use the orchard, I imagine.' This man, possessed of all his faculties, had accepted the near approach of death; and if the shining surface of men's loyalties hides an alloy of selfishness, the private hungers and conceits which seem to order their lives are of no more use to one whose life is at an end. Here, diminished by the loss of every dignity, was a creature intrinsically like myself; who yet, belonging to my kind, had far transcended it, because having done with life he was no longer bound to the shape of life's exactions. Here humanity was naked, and of all that this man had believed in only the nucleus remained. If that had no more value, then humanity itself was meaningless: the valour that I saw in this tired face, in the abnegation of these eyes, was only one more illusion.

I have thought since then what kind of answer I might have made. I should have told him that if ever my child came to years of understanding and to physical freedom he must have full liberty to follow his own course; but that I should not let him be ignorant of what part his fathers had played, of the charge that Julius had laid upon him or the circumstances in which that charge had last been given. All this I could have said with honesty, and not without gentleness, had we been talking at our ease. But actuality gives no room for ordered speeches. I had broken the silence with only a few words, halting and ambiguous, when Vaninov's return brought a cold wind into the room. The soldier at the door relaxed as students do at the end of a difficult lecture, the clerk returned to his typing, while Vaninov himself, tactfully pretending to ignore the paper which still lay open on the table, merely asked with a stagey politeness if we had finished our talk—the car was waiting to take me home, he said. There, untidily as it had begun, the interview ended. And this irruption of conventionality, which affected me with a feeling close to hysteria, was at once accepted by Julius with palpable relief.

"It's a closed car?" he asked, speaking once more as if Vaninov were a junior officer on his own staff. "You must see to it that this lady is wrapped up warmly, she's in no fit state to be out at night at all." Then, with a little nod, he wished me good night, adding, "You will tell my wife, if you please, that I may be away for some time. And will you, please, give her a message of affection from me."

As quickly as that, these two men had re-created the masculine world, the world where reality, which lies in the heart's knowledge, is counted as something immodest, and where every relationship must be reduced to a familiar drill. I don't think I spoke another word before I left, except to the clerk, who, noticing that I hadn't smoked the cigarette he had thrown me, asked me to give it him back.

vi

Some instinct—I should not exalt it with the name of charity—made me ask the driver to set me down when we reached the other end of the village; and from there I went on foot to the cottage some three kilometres away where old Father Rosciewski had lived since his retirement eight or nine years before. Him I roused, and when I had made him understand my father-in-law's situation he agreed to get up and to return with me to the house I had just left.

In a calmer hour I might have shrunk from inflicting such hardship on a man of his years: his limbs had long been fettered by arthritis, and although he rested a great part of his weight on my shoulders, each step must have been agony for him. Once, where the steeply descending path was covered with ice, we slipped and fell together, while the ciborium which I was carrying rolled away into a drift of snow, and it was a long and painful task to get him on his feet again. But of that difficult journey I have only a fragmentary recollection, since it stands in the penumbra of an experience which had impressed me more deeply: all I remember is how, when the darting wind had flakes of ice in it, my body was soaked in sweat; how Conrad seemed to kick out in anger at such usage; and how Rosciewski, between the little cries he uttered as he lurched and stumbled, kept murmuring, "We shall manage, my child, we shall get there at last!" Miraculously he did get there, but the struggle was wasted. A few yards short of our destination we saw the lights of a car moving away; the house, when we reached it, showed no glimmer of light, and a man who materialized from the shadow answered my questions by repeating, in the terse and sulky fashion of his trade, that he would shoot us if we moved another step towards the door.

9

---

i

IT was reckoned that about a quarter of the people in the village and outlying farms failed to get through the winter; but of these a good many were old ones who, even if they would not have died in normal times, had not much to live for. That was how Jendrek put it to me, in his own fashion. For myself, I had expected the wastage to be larger. I think it was not only I who had a sense of achievement, even then, in having remained alive.

In that country the retreat of winter is screened. When the scathing wind gives way it leaves between the hills a wadding of white mist, as if a rainstorm were held in suspense. The intensity of cold abates, but the earth cannot immediately respond; chilled far below the surface, it stays like the bodies of those villagers who have sometimes been lost in the Setory hills and lain there stiffly all the winter through. It is the sound which changes. Besides the altered noise of footsteps and of wheels, now passing through slush instead of the firm and silencing snow, there is a new, soft tide of noise, constant as that of traffic in urban houses, which must be curious to a stranger. This is a watery sound, but different from that of fast-flowing streams; it is built out of many noises, drops that fall continuously from the branches of a thousand trees, countless rivulets trickling on every slope, brooks that set up a rustle from the frozen grasses edging their path. Where men go about there is only discomfort; paths are rivers of slime, the dulled light gives a flatness to the dripping houses, and the moisture which hangs between them finds its way beneath your clothes. But go towards the woods—as I did on a job that was allotted me—and the invisible stir of all those waters will enthral you. The pupal skin which has shielded the earth's fresh life is dissolving, and the first sounds of the liberation carry the excitement of tumultuous applause.

There were many days to go before we should see the sun; the warmth we felt, more positive than the blunting of the wind's edge, seemed to come from the frozen earth itself. Before there was new growth the smell from the ground and from the woods altered, it became a salty smell and then like that of newly rotted leaves. Wakening in the mornings, I knew from the draught which reached me from a broken shutter that the woods were alive again.

Optimism dwindles in those who have been hungry for a long time: it was instinct rather than any hopeful belief which made us feel these signs of the defeat of winter as if they meant some revolution in our own state of existence. Yet there were shreds of material for arguing hopefully. A moody personage of Siberian extraction arrived and made himself known to us as the Zavkhoz. This glorified peasant, who could change his temper in a moment from boisterous camaraderie to sullen vindictiveness, called some twenty villagers to a 'council for agrarian production', a body designed for accepting, in a haze of esoteric verbiage, his own orders. A map was made, and a dated programme: a man who for forty years had won a living from his ancestral holding was detailed to work a dozen kilometres away on a slope that faced in the opposite direction with a different subsoil; while his own land, merged in a larger area, was to be managed by a gang of woodmen and carters. But in spite of organization it seemed that work would be done and something got from the ground. It was a favourable omen that the Countess was found to be in possession of a brood of pullets, procured for her by the invaluable Solitsin; and about the same time a few small, black heifers, miserable creatures with almost concave flanks, were brought to nibble at the moss and frozen turf on the banks of the old dyke. More wondrous still, a scarlet tractor, American and almost new, was decanted from a huge transporter into a hollow beside the village road, where it lay as promise of the fuller life, collecting admiration and rust. There was still no excuse for complacency. News was filtering through that districts on either side of ours had been stripped of people like ourselves, while here at Setory there were disappearances: a truck came in the night to carry off an elderly veterinarian, and not long afterwards the entire family of a former village teacher was removed in the same way. Yet in me, at least, the significance of such events could not repress that quickening of spirit which came with the first lengthening of the days.

Behind me the view had fallen into calm. If I had acted shamefully in Julius's regard, I had not done it wantonly or for ends of my own: an obligation imposed on me had been discharged, and if conscience had not been silenced, at least it no longer plagued me with a dual voice. There were no decisions to be made now. I was free to absorb myself in the task which carried all my hopes and which no extraneous happenings—I thought—could interfere with.

I was suffering a good deal of sickness, and Conrad, grown heavy, was a difficult burden when my legs had become so feeble. Yet how gladly I sustained it! I knew that his body was already perfect; and I had the feeling that it was he, of us two, who responded more urgently to the excitement of this season, to its warming breath and rustling noises, the sense of forces massing in darkness to sweep forward in the earliest light. I never doubted that he was a man, this being whom Victor had left to take his place; already I seemed to know him as companion rather than child, and I waited for his coming almost as one awaits a friend's return when long absence has dimmed the memory of his face. It is hard, that kind of waiting: you thrust yourself against a wheel which is made only to turn more slowly as your pressure increases. But happiness, as I have known it, is a current flowing slenderly at great depth, where it is not disturbed by the strains and commotion of every day. However stubbornly time loitered, it was carrying me with certainty to the end of my loneliness.

There was an evening when the restlessness of my body overcame fatigue, and a little before the hour of dusk I set out on the short walk which Victor and I had often taken, to the farther slope of a hillock where, in summer, one could look across to the Dunik hills. This evening there was no distant view, for although the roof of cloud was higher a ground mist had come with the waning of daylight, making a belt of larch a hundred yards away appear as a solid wall; with the air so raw, the boundaries of the visible world closing in, you could have felt that winter was still to come. For a time it was grateful to me, this chilled and melancholy scene. Solitude is the frame that comforts loneliness: it was easier to imagine Victor's presence here than in the gentleness of summer, and I felt it right that Conrad should taste such an evening as had often matched his father's mood. Then something happened as startling as any event I have witnessed: the wind that was feebly stirring the hair against my neck had been powerful enough to tear a gap in the cloud-bank, and the sun, whose existence I had almost forgotten, was suddenly shown bare. It was a wintry sun, low on the horizon, and the light it shed was thin. But that was enough to waken a whole range of colours in the turf about me and in the misted slopes to which my face was turned—I seemed even to feel a warmth on my skin from its pale radiance—and it so enflamed my spirit, this startling irruption of light, that the dull resolution with which I faced the physical ordeal of Conrad's birth was changed in a moment to exaltation: in the brief space while the sun lasted I was released even from the pain of Victor's loss; for where the lifeless earth was so wakened by illumination I could imagine that death itself had no finality. So is one moved by tricks of the senses. It must have happened often, in many places, that the sun after long imprisonment should break loose on such an evening in the last minutes before nightfall; yet this experience— perhaps because it was later reflected in one that influenced more profoundly—found a place among those which become a part of oneself. It lasted, I suppose, for hardly more than a minute. The pale gold which tinged the haze, the liquid green of terraced clouds, faded as if an electrician's hand controlled them; a plover which had risen noisily to fly in bewildered circles dropped back to its hiding-place in the bracken. There came with the succeeding veils of darkness a different wind, bringing the clean, moist smells of a night in spring.

ii

"Stefanie! Stefanie, I think the Countess wants to speak to you— she's in her workroom."

They could have come from one of several periods in my life, those words, spoken in that particular voice of Sandra's, faintly monitorial, tinged with maternal anxiety. They are separately impressed on my memory—with Sandra's tired eyes looking up from the sewing-machine—because they make the starting-point of a stage in the journey.

Obediently I went to the workroom, and with the Countess I found, as usual, Solitsin. "He's got some message for you," she told me curtly. Solitsin said, "It's nothing that matters," and continued to sit still, picking his teeth.

For several minutes, then, we played an absurd parlour game, we three: Solitsin pretending that he had no word for me of any importance, and I that I expected none, while the Countess, aware that the message was to be kept from her, enraged by this affront to her dignity yet determined not to reveal her fury, made a show of being intensely occupied with a wage-book which had been closed ten years before. Two or three times she went over to a rack of files by the window and fidgeted there with her back turned to us, hoping, I suppose, that Solitsin would whisper to me and that she would manage to hear; and during these performances Solitsin stared at my face with one side of his hideous mouth stitched in a tight gather—the only means that nature had given him for expressing a modest delight. In the end she gave up. She knew Solitsin, and—to a hairbreadth—the limits of her influence with him. After one false exit, when she returned quickly to say that Wanda would be needing my help with the soldiers' dinner, she left us alone.

It pleased Solitsin to continue tantalizing me. For another minute or two he talked idly about the food situation, and what he called 'the non-realistic attitude of you wealthy Poles'; and when he started wandering towards the door I concluded that the message he was supposed to have for me was nothing but an abstruse bargaining device. Just as he was leaving, however, he turned and said casually:

"Oh, Vaninov thinks you may as well get your box packed. You may be travelling soon."

"Travelling? Where?"

He gave me that sniff which corresponds, with people of his kind, to a shrug of the shoulders.

"That was all he said!"

But I needed nothing more. Sweden! I had tried to suppress the hope, the very thought of that escape, but it had never left me. Again and again I had told myself that only a woman of crass stupidity would take Vaninov or his promises seriously; but there had always been another voice to whisper: miracles may happen, they have happened before, Vaninov has some friendship for me and I have done him a particular service. . . . Those few words of Solitsin's were spark enough to set the hope alight, to change it into perfect faith. The thing was settled, fate after all was on my side. I scarcely considered any hindrances—the hardships of a long and roundabout journey for a woman in my state, the entanglement of formalities and delays which hedged the frontiers even in normal times. All I could think of now was my arrival in Sweden, the freedom waiting for me there, the security in which Conrad was to take his first independent breath and to see the light of his first day. Absorbed in the vision, I became detached from my surroundings. My hands must have done what I had taught them, giving some help to Wanda as usual; I vaguely remember sitting through a family meal at which my mind would not be brought to answer intelligently a single remark addressed to me. As soon as it was over, I went to my own room.

The cabin trunk which Casimir and I had once travelled with was under my bed, I had a battered dressing-case and an old valise of Victor's: to pack my small possessions would be the work, I thought, of a quarter of an hour. But in that state of exhilaration I found my hands and mind to be clumsy. The jewellery which I should have to sell and live on until I could work again—how could it be stowed most safely? Was there any sense in taking all the clothes which appeared in astonishing profusion when I started to ransack the tall cupboard—the tennis-dress, discarded but still serviceable bodices, evening shoes and openwork gloves? I found, as ever, that there was hardly a pair of stockings fit for wear. I began some darning, left it to repair a broken shoulder-strap which caught my eye, and then, remembering some letters of Victor's that I wanted to pack in a safer place, put that aside as well. I came at last to sitting idly on my bed, strangely exhausted, with the cases still half-packed, a great confusion of clothes and oddments all round me; and as the cupboard door swung on its faulty hinge I saw in the glass there that I was idiotically smiling. At that stage Annette found me.

"Mother—what are you doing?"

"I'm busy," I told her. "Is there anything you want?"

"No, but can't I help?"

"No, darling."

The problem of Annette was one I had solved already in my mind. If I were given the chance to take her with me I should naturally accept it. If not, I could only leave her with the Kolbecks, who had come to command almost the whole of her devotion. I had at least set her some way along the road, and my duty to the child still to be born must now override my duty to her. But such decisions are easier to take than to explain, and when she persisted, "Why are you packing, Mother? Are we going somewhere?" I became flustered.

"Annette, I wish you'd leave me alone! I may have to make a short journey—it isn't settled."

She stood her ground; and I saw in her face, then, a trace of the Kolbeck obstinacy. She asked, presently:

"Are you going to see Grandfather again?"

The question should not have surprised me. The account I had given the Kolbecks of my meeting with Julius had been perfunctory—the N.K.V.D., I told them, had merely wanted me to confirm a statement of Julius's own—and this lack of candour had naturally increased their distrust. But it angered me to find such suspicion in the mind of my own child. I said, with a foolish ill-temper:

"Why are you asking that?"

The sharpness of my tone might well have put her to confusion, and perhaps tears. It did make her turn her eyes away; but she answered me in a voice that was quite steady, as a grown woman's might have been.

"I want to be some use," she said. "I want to look after you. I can't if you keep everything away from me."

I could find no answer, and soon she left me to myself.

The memory of those words was to bring me a pain which I feel afresh even now. But at the time that feeling was not strong enough to sour my optimism. I was like a prisoner counting the hours to the time of his release, and a part of the freedom to which I looked forward was a final severance from the Kolbeck faction, to which Annette belonged. When Sandra, in her turn, came with kindness and humility to offer her help, I rejected it with a bare politeness; and when even Wanda showed me great consideration, asking if I meant to take food for my journey, I shook her off in the same way. All my plans were very uncertain, I said.

Plans? The absurdity of that understatement became more obvious as the hours passed. By early evening the packing was finished. I had convinced myself that some instruction would come for me that night, and in this expectation I stayed all but fully awake. When morning came I found my excitement blunted, and throughout the day my hopefulness was steadily leaking away. I was looking a fool now. The Kolbecks, finding it impossible to talk to me, treated me with a tactful forbearance which I found harder to bear than any cruelty. A second and a third day passed. Solitsin was not to be found, there was no one to give me any news. Things I had packed with too little calculation had to come out again, the physical shape of daily life was returning; I began to teach myself the difficult practice of resignation. But even Annette could no longer show me any active sympathy. I was isolated from the rest as never before, and having ventured all my hopes on a bright, fond dream, I found there was no real life to retreat to. I knew in those strange, still days how ghosts must feel.

And then the summons came. It was early in the morning, I was alone in my room starting to make my bed. A young soldier, sulky from stupidity, marched in and said he had brought a cart for me. I asked who had sent him and where he was to take me, but he seemed unable to bring his mind to bear on those questions. I must come quickly, he said. Might I take some things with me?—I could pack them in five minutes. All right, yes, only I must hurry. He watched me gloomily while I threw things higgledy-piggledy into the cases, and then he relaxed so far as to help me fasten them. I asked, would he carry them down for me—I myself was in rather a weak condition. Well, it wasn't his business, but he would carry the valises. The trunk, no! Nobody needed to travel with a box that size, it was wrong for anyone to have so many possessions. Just then, luckily, I heard Henryk's step in the passage. I called him in, put him at one end of the trunk and with copious flattery persuaded the soldier to take the other end. In the fashion of two circus clowns, the one man giggling inanely and the other blaspheming, they dragged the awkward burden down the stairs and out to the cart.

"And now, Henryk—quick—I want you to go back and get the valises!"

"Valises?" He leant against the tail of the cart, puffing and dribbling. "Where are you going, Teffy; why do you want all those things?"

"I can't wait!" the soldier said angrily.

"Quick!" I repeated to Henryk. "I'll tell you everything another time. Hurry, please!"

He shambled back indoors. I thought that fortune was treating me unusually well, in that none of the Kolbeck women had appeared; but Annette must have seen me from a window, for at that moment she came hurrying out of the house. She ran right up to me, and then stopped abruptly, as though she had mistaken me for someone else. It was an awkward meeting for us both; for me one of poignancy. As if a match were struck in a darkened room, I saw for an instant the face of a being who was precious to me and whom without reason I had made to suffer. But the soldier was urging me on to the cart, I had neither time nor the quietness of mind to respond to my own emotion. I said, disjointedly:

"Look—Annette—I may be able to take you with me. I shall see. I'm going to try and get it arranged."

I should have kissed her, but she did not come close enough. She said tonelessly, "Yes, Mother!" and turned and went quickly back into the house.

The soldier by this time was on the driving board and pulling me up beside him. I said:

"If you'll let me go back for a minute, I can make my brother-in-law hurry. . . . I can't go without those cases——"

He nodded, smiling, as if he understood that perfectly, and then cut viciously at the horse's quarter.

"And I can't wait any longer!" he said.

The place he took me to was the house I had visited before. On this occasion I was led upstairs and put in a small bedroom, to the normal furniture of which had been added a trestle table and a number of wooden boxes stuffed, as far as I could see, with pamphlets and letters; by moving two of the boxes I made a space on the bed where I could sit. Here, foodless, I waited for just six hours. At the end of that interval I heard a car being driven to the front of the house, then footsteps on the stairs, and presently the sound of a man coughing in the next room. This, I thought, would be Vaninov. When another twenty minutes had passed and no one came near me, I started knocking on the wall and continued until the man came to unlock the door and take me into his own office.

It was not Vaninov after all, but a considerably older man, an obese and rather anxious creature with that lack of co-ordination between narrow eyes and fleshy mouth which one associates with homosexuals. He behaved and spoke with a distrait affability. I was who? Kolbeck? Yes yes, he had heard the name. Colonel Kolbeck —the wife of Colonel Victor Kolbeck—yes yes, he had seen a memorandum, somewhere, last night perhaps, life was full of so many things. And what question had I come to ask him?

With counterfeit assurance I said I understood that arrangements had been made for me to travel to Sweden; presumably I had been brought here to receive the appropriate papers.

"To Sweden? You mean—let me see, let me see—yes, Sweden!"

"Captain Vaninov was good enough to say that he would arrange the matter for me."

"Sweden, yes yes! Vaninov? You are a friend of Vaninov?"

"Yes, Commissioner."

"I too!" He smiled and shook my hand. "Vaninov, yes yes, an excellent fellow, I know him well, a man of wonderful capacities. You know how it is, a man like myself, I work all day long, most of the night sometimes, and yet compared with Vaninov I am a mere idler, I do nothing for the Party at all. And you are a friend of his?"

"Indeed yes!"

"Excellent, excellent!" he said, shaking my hand again.

"I thought perhaps I might see him here."

"Here? Vaninov? But you must understand, if Vaninov was here

I should take you to him immediately. We are old friends, Vaninov and myself. A man of wonderful capacities. A man like myself, I work all day long——"

"But he's left here now?"

"Left here? Vaninov? Oh, yes yes yes!"

"You don't know where he's gone?"

He looked at me sadly, as if I had spoken of some bereavement with insufficient tact.

"Difficult times!" he said. "The Germans and all that—nothing is normal, no one knows exactly what movement will come next, you lose sight of your friends, they appear again, or sometimes they are gone for ever. Vaninov, yes, I like him very much!"

"Perhaps he has left some instruction about me?"

"Some instruction? Yes, yes, he may quite well have left some instruction. You must tell me your name. . . ."

He began to hunt in a feckless way through the papers littering his table, stopping now and then to smile at me with a boyish amiability while he relit his cigarette; and very soon, as I supposed, he had clean forgotten the object of his search. I was wrong. He came at length upon a sheet of close-spaced typescript, triumphantly showed me my own name at the top and then took it nearer the window to read.

"Yes yes! . . . Yes, it's all perfectly clear. They want you at Kartushka, yes, they want you to give some evidence there. You have to travel as soon as transport can be arranged. That's what you wanted to know?"

"Evidence?" I said dully. "What evidence?"

He examined the paper again. "I can't quite read the name— Kol—yes, Kolbeck. Ah, of course, that is your own name! Some relation, perhaps. It says you have agreed to give evidence in the case of a Julius Kolbeck, he seems to have murdered one of his labourers."

"But one minute!" I was still too much shocked and dejected to talk sensibly. "Is there nothing about my going to Sweden?"

"Sweden?" Patiently he began to read right through the document again. "Sweden. . . . No, there's nothing about Sweden. . . . Wait, there's something written in the margin—'Applicant for emigration permit on grounds of pregnancy'. Would that be what you had in mind?"

"Well, perhaps so—roughly speaking."

"And someone's written something against that. I can't quite read it—wait—yes, it says 'Evidence to be satisfactory'."

"And that's all?"

"Yes. Yes, that's all."

His vacant, undirected smile came on again. He looked towards the door in such a way as to indicate that the interview seemed to have exhausted its usefulness.

I said rather desperately, "But do you think that means I may be sent on to Sweden when they've done with me at Kartushka?"

"To Sweden? Yes yes, it's quite possible, almost everything is possible nowadays. One hardly knows from day to day what will happen. Yes, I should say it's quite possible—extremely likely."

"But you can't tell me when I am to go to Kartushka?"

"It might be any day," he answered, with the air of a booking-clerk anxious to earn a reputation for good service. "Transport conditions alter from day to day, sometimes there are great improvements, it often astonishes me."

"And what is going to happen to me in the meantime?"

"In the meantime? Oh, I'm sure nothing will happen to you in the meantime, everything in this district is in very good order; they tell me it's a place that never gives any trouble." Again that glance towards the door. "But you must always come to me if there's any question you want to ask. I am in my office here all day except when I am out on some business. Really, I like people to come and see me."

I thanked him for this courtesy.

Outside the house I found a soldier leaning against the wall whom I presumed to be on picquet duty. The same man had been there when I arrived, and I asked if he could say what had happened to the cart which had brought me. He answered with civility and with some intelligence: the cart, he thought, had probably returned to the area transport lines, where all vehicles were controlled. Could he, by chance, tell me anything about the trunk which had come with me? No, he could not; but if I were to send a written application to area headquarters, to the department for civilian property, the matter would undoubtedly be investigated. . . . Yes, my return home would have to be on foot—he could see that I was suffering from weakness, but unfortunately there was no arrangement for the transport of Polish civilians.

So, such outings as this had to be paid for: the trunk contained, in value, perhaps a third of my total property. But physical weariness can sometimes serve as narcotic against worries of that kind, and if I was going to look a greater fool than before when I arrived back at the house I was sufficiently insensitive to that anxiety as

[203]

well. The light, which had been poor all day, was now giving out, my vision was confused, and more than once I collided with a wall or tree which I had thought was some way to right or left of me. There were not many people about, however, to observe my drunken progress; and soon after total darkness I had the lights of the house in sight, having made half a mile in perhaps less than an hour.

iii

My return was not, after all, the cause of a major sensation. The Kolbecks had matters of their own to care for.

Serjeant Butusov met me on the stairs. A little drunk, as he often was at that hour, he greeted me with his usual, artless buoyancy.

"Ahoy, fat bitch! Glory, here's a fat one for you—triplets, I say it is, you've got tucked up in there. Heard the news, fatling? You heard Butusov's news?"

I tried to get past and away from him, my spirits being too low for conviviality; but he pursued and cornered me.

"Listen, pretty!" he said hoarsely, smiling with the ardour of friendship and breathing hard on my face. "Butusov's got a secret for you. Just you and me—just a little piece of advice from an old military comrade."

"All right, Butusov—tell me!"

He became still more conspiratorial, he put his arms round my neck, his mouth against my ear, while his voice sank almost to inaudibility. "Listen, sweetie, little old fat bitch that you are, God bless you! You know old Butusov, you know he's your friend! Well, now take it from poor old Butusov and don't tell a soul that he told you—*get your boxes packed up!* You might be moving on in a hurry. Understand?"

I did not trouble to explain to him that all my things were packed already and that half my luggage had begun to travel on its own account. I thanked him as well as I could and escaped.

"And don't you blab to anyone what I've told you!" he roared after me.

I was ready to respect his confidence, but there proved to be no special occasion for doing so. I met Wanda coming along the passage with an armful of clothes. She did not appear surprised to see me, and would have passed me without a word, but when I gave her a cursory greeting she turned and spoke in a tired, colourless voice:

[204]

"You've heard, I suppose—we're all going."

"Going? Where?"

"I don't know. They say we'll be joining Father, but that may be just an invention."

"But when? Tonight?"

She shrugged her shoulders. "It comes from Butusov. I don't know how much he knows. It may be all his fancy."

The kind of disorder which had filled my bedroom a few days earlier had spread now over all that part of the house which the family still occupied. There were travelling boxes open everywhere, trunks that I remembered only from childhood, damp-furred portmanteaux with rusty locks; along the passage stood untidy piles of clothes, miniatures in leather cases and an ivory crucifix among sandalwood boxes and tins of condensed milk. Lacking the energy to go as far as my own room, I turned into the night-nursery and cleared a space to sit down. Here Cousin Rosalia came to me.

"I want you to tell me," she said anxiously, "that afternoon dress I was wearing on Wednesday—the blue marocain—do you think it looks too young for me? I want your honest opinion, I don't want you to say anything just to please me. I've been asking Wanda, she says it is all right, but I don't believe she really thinks what she's saying."

I myself, just then, was lacking in concentration, but she stood waiting patiently for my answer. She had the look of one who has scarcely recovered from the first shock of a bereavement, the doors of whose mind swing idly on their hinges.

I said, "I've always liked you in that dress."

"You see," she said, "it packs very easily, and I always think that when you're travelling the great thing is to have something ready to slip on quickly the moment you get to your hotel or wherever it is. It makes you feel a different person."

"Yes, I'm sure that's right."

"Only Sandra keeps saying I ought to use all the space I've got in my small valise for warm things."

"Well, perhaps Sandra knows best."

"I asked Annette, and she says she likes the blue marocain very much."

"Yes, I know she does."

"Rosalia!" The Countess's voice, as she stumped into the room with Henryk carrying a trunk behind her, was as stony as a music-master's. "Rosalia, I've told you already, there's no room for you in here. Go and get on with your packing, and when you've

finished go to bed. . . . No, Henryk, not there—here, on the table!
Yes, move those things—I told your mother to move them half
an hour ago. . . . No, it's not likely to open if you stand it upside
down. . . . Stefanie, I should have thought if you had nothing to
do you might have helped Annette."

That was all the notice she took of my dramatic reappearance,
and her sarcasm was not enough to shift the weight of lethargy
which, fastening on my body, had gripped my mind as well. In this
long day when I had been both hustled and bored to no purpose,
when my hopes had been gigantically swelled and casually deflated,
I had reached a kind of apathy in regard to my own fortunes, and
I found it incongruous that these others should still be busily concerned with theirs. Could they really be so put about by a rumour
from a drunken soldier? Such abundance of paraphernalia scratched
from the nooks and crannies, so little chance of transporting a
tenth of it: so prodigious an activity, so little being achieved! Only
the Countess herself appeared to know exactly what she was doing.
Grey, expressionless, she was stuffing her small possessions into
one case after another with a factory-girl's precision, while she
kept the wretched Henryk at her bidding with the minimum of
laconic, razor-edged commands. "Over there! Over *there*, I said!
. . . No, come back, *at once!* . . ." Beside this molecule of energy and
purpose the rest were mere encumbrances, to be thwarted and
shooed away. More than once there were bitter passages between
her and Wanda, for tonight even Wanda's self-possession had left
her, and as she drifted in and out of the room, alternately febrile and
listless, she seemed to do nothing except change the position of
things that she or someone else had put down a minute before. The
feebleness of the light increased the opportunity these women had
to embarrass each other's operations. Teased by the draught from
a broken shutter, the flames of candles placed about the room
bowed and fluttered, upon the disorder of half-packed boxes was
imposed a confusion of shadows which quivered and swung, which
hardened and grew faint. In the half-light at the doorway you saw
for a few moments the damp and hairy face of Butusov, vaguely
smiling like a timid host at a successful party; or Rosalia's troubled
eyes would appear, would turn upon the Countess's head and
instantly be withdrawn. My sense of time grew hazed. Watching
drowsily the recurrence of this clouded pattern, I felt that I assisted
at some industrious performance which for ever lost its way and
started again.

"Surely we can leave it for a while! If you'd like to sit down,

Grand'mère, I could do some of it for you. . . . I'm sure we should all be the better for resting a little."

Four or five times Sandra must have used almost exactly those words, till they became a part of the pattern, like the regular chiming of clocks. They won no attention. The pitch of her low, Teutonic voice was designed to rouse no one but children, her anhelose and creaking presence provoked only a mild irritation.

"Wanda—are you there? Wanda, couldn't you rest a little now?"

"Presently, Mother!"

"I'm sure they wouldn't ask us to leave in the middle of the night like this. Not people like ourselves! . . ."

Most of these appeals were uttered from the doorway, and it was a long time before, venturing into the room, she caught sight of me. Then she stared at me as if she doubted her own senses.

"But, Stefanie—I thought you'd gone! They told me—Annette said you'd gone away in a cart. . . . No, don't move—you look so tired! Stay there and I'll get you something, I think there's some coffee that Wanda left this morning, you'd like some coffee?"

"Yes, Belle-mère, yes, please!"

"She can surely get it herself!" the Countess said between her teeth.

But here Sandra was not to be diverted. She padded off to her own room, and returned after some time with a tray. As well as the coffee, there was condensed milk smeared on pieces of stale bread.

"I'm afraid it's not very good, I couldn't get the water hot. I told Annette to go to bed, she looked so tired—she's been so unhappy. I was going to tell her you're back, but I thought she ought to sleep. I expect you'll go and see her yourself?"

"Yes, presently."

"You—you've had a tiring day?"

"In a way."

"Yes—yes, it must have been." She became confused and turned her eyes away. "There wasn't anything special that happened? You didn't—I suppose they couldn't by any chance have taken you to see Julius again."

"No, Belle-mère—no, I don't think he's in this district at the present time." And then I added, "But a man I spoke to seemed to know about him. I gathered that he's quite well."

That much at least—that edition of the facts—I owed her. Had she once failed in her kindness to me!

"Quite well?" It was as if she took the phrase into a quiet corner and stared at it, like a lover with a long-awaited, ambiguous letter. "And—that was all? He didn't say if Julius is free again?"

[207]

"Free?" The Countess, preoccupied as she appeared to be, had evidently been listening to every word that passed between us. "Do you think that Stefanie's friends would know anything about him if he *was* free!"

"They're not my friends!" I said shortly.

"Stefanie's tired!" Sandra said. "Tomorrow, when she's rested, I expect she'll tell us anything more she managed to find out."

But was she not tired as well? At the time I had no mind to give to that, I saw her only as some children see their mother—a person whose movements are always slower than theirs, her face always a little foolish with anxiety; one who can scarcely find sadness hard to endure, since she wears it every day.

It was Wanda who came to me next, with the cold face of a nursing orderly. "Mother thinks you ought to be in bed. She told me to help you if you want me."

"I thought we were all supposed to be moving somewhere."

"Possibly. Butusov may have made it up. It doesn't look as if they're coming tonight. Are you going to bed?"

"Soon, I expect."

"Mother says you've had some news of Father."

"Only that he's alive."

"Why do they tell *you* that?"

"Oh, God knows!" I said.

I meant to go to bed as soon as I was alone, and so avoid the indignity of being helped there. But when they had all left me I found myself still powerless to move; it was, I think an impotence rather of spirit than of body, derived from the feeling that no kind of exertion would ever again be worth making. I was not unhappy. With my mind dull and empty I sat perfectly still, hearing without attention the dwindling movement of the house, watching the candles grow shorter; feeling no inclination to fall asleep. I should record that I did not even close my eyes, except that this impression, were it true, would leave a strange phenomenon unexplained: for as I looked across the room I thought that Victor was standing on the other side of the table, observing me with the sulky expression he always wore when something was on his mind. His appearance there did not surprise or puzzle me; and when he said, "You're coming to see me, aren't you?" I answered quite naturally, "I don't know yet, I don't know where we're going." He said something else which I did not hear, and then, "You'll bring Conrad with you?" to which I replied, "But of course, of course Conrad is coming!" I am almost sure that my own part of that interchange was spoken aloud, and in memory the whole of it is no less actual than any other occurrence of that evening, so powerfully can imagination work when the senses are slack from fatigue. I was still not conscious of anything abnormal when Victor's face, blurring for a moment, changed to that of Wanda, who came towards me saying laconically, "They've come for us now."

So this peculiar day—the day which had opened with the summons to set out, as I supposed, for Sweden—never came to an end. Or that is how I remember it. In truth a new day had begun when Wanda came to rouse me, as I should have realized from seeing the altered appearance of Wanda herself, who was wearing a heavier skirt and shoes and had redressed her hair; but my brain was not equal then to making such deductions. The candles had burnt out. The window, where someone had half-opened the shutters, gave already a feeble twilight to the room. I thought, confusedly, 'It is not so late as I had supposed.'

Had Wanda slept? Her tiredness had not left her, but she seemed to have brought it under control: her movements now were exact and economical, like those of an actress in a part she has deeply studied, and in the set of her white face I saw a striking reflection of the expression which Victor always wore on parade. Her voice, too, had taken on a quality of Victor's:

"You'd better go straight down. We've only got ten minutes. Annette's taken your cases."

I leant against the table while my legs slowly came to life, and then I followed her to the head of the stairs. Here there was no air of urgency. Under Butusov's light-hearted direction our own Russians (as we called the men billeted in the house) were wandering up and down in different degrees of undress, carrying any piece of baggage that came to their hands; four of them who had been tumbling a cabin trunk of Sandra's down the stairs had got it jammed between the newels and were standing round it laughing like over-excited children, while Butusov himself, carrying another trunk with Henryk, stood a few steps higher up and jovially cursed them. But there were other soldiers, strangers, who seemed to be unaffected by this spirit of end-of-term festivity. One, armed with a carbine, stood correctly at attention at the door of Sandra's room, and in the hall below I saw two more who had a look almost of German efficiency about them. It needed no intelligence to see who had given the order about ten minutes, or to judge that it was meant to be obeyed.

I found that Rosalia was beside me again, dressed as if for a fashionable excursion in the earliest kind of motor-car. She was talking partly to herself and partly to me with a pale, monotonous dignity:

"I'm afraid I can't make Cousin Sandra understand! It really doesn't seem unreasonable that I should want to have my little blue valise close to me. I've told her that the hat-box can go just where it's most convenient. The blue valise has my night things, and my little sal-volatile phial and my cachets Faivre."

Had there been substance in this complaint, Sandra might well have answered it herself, since she was standing no farther away from Rosalia than I was; but all she said to her cousin was, "Yes, Rosalia, yes, I'm sure that everything will be all right," and then she turned to me.

"I told Annette to wear her cardigan underneath her coat, it may be cold on the journey. I've given her some bread to go in her pocket, I should have got some breakfast for everyone but the corporal is being very awkward, he won't give us any extra time. Perhaps you ought to go down and see if Annette's all right."

"Of course, Belle-mère!"

But I was still incapable of reasoned action, and since I never identified myself with the Kolbeck women, I could not fully grasp the fact that I was included in this exodus. There was a question which had sounded close to the wall of my mind in the night's long idleness: it came more clearly now; and when I had detached myself from Sandra, and squeezed between the clustering soldiers, I found myself walking slowly along the corridor towards Count Kolbeck's room.

There the Countess overtook me, with the usual glass of tea on a tray. She went ahead of me until she was nearly at the Count's door, and then turned to look at me as if I were a total stranger.

"Yes—what do you want?"

I could not answer her collectedly. I said in an evasive way, "I only thought—I just wondered what was going to happen. They won't try to move the Count as well?"

Her lips moved, but nothing came that I could hear. She went on staring as a peasant does when he doubts the value of some animal offered him in the market. In my torpid state I was not much affected by this behaviour, but it seemed that my only course was to retreat. I had actually turned away when she spoke, in the voice she had used for giving orders to the farm-hands:

"Yes—you—you'd better take it. This! You can take it to him. He is to drink it all—you understand?"

She had pushed the tray into my hands. I nodded, and carried it towards the door of the Count's room, feeling that her eyes were following. I thought, indeed, that she would change her mind and come after me, but when, turning to open the door, I glanced over my shoulder, she was standing perfectly still.

Inside, the shutters were still closed, and the only light came from a small lamp on the table. The Count, whom I was used to seeing in his chair, was of course in bed. He was awake, however. When I went to his side he recognized me quickly, and received me with the courtesy he would have used in a drawing-room. "But how kind," he said, "to think of me like this!"

I told him it was the Countess who had sent the tea, and that she hoped he would drink it.

"Tea? But it's so early—it can't be morning yet!"

When he said that, I thought the Countess must have lacked courage to tell him what was happening. But a moment later he asked me, calmly:

"Shall I see my wife again? Or have they taken her away now?"

It was a question which had to be given some answer. To gain a little time I went to open the shutters, letting what day there was possess the room. I said:

"I'm not sure if she's started. I expect she's told you—she has to make an excursion. At least, I think so. I fancy she may be away some days."

He nodded. "And you?" he said. "You are going as well?"

"I don't know, no one's told me. But I expect so. I should have liked to stay and look after you."

"To look after me? You are so kind, Stefanie! But it's all arranged for, my wife arranges everything so well. After all, I've not many needs now. There's a man called Solitsin—an ugly fellow, Jadwiga says, but I find a great interest in people with peculiar faces—this Solitsin is going to do what is necessary, Jadwiga has found him very reliable. You say that I have to drink this? As a rule I don't have anything so early."

He drank it slowly, making little grimaces, as children do with medicine; and this reminded me how much the contentment of the old depends on the precise observance of their simple routine. His needs were so few now—a hot drink four or five times a day, cigarettes beside his chair, the known face; it was hardly possible to think of him without the Countess near at hand to supply these things, to imagine the hours and the days passing when the only voices he would ever hear belonged to strangers. His thoughts must have travelled almost side by side with mine, but they came to another destination; when he spoke again his voice was coloured with the diffidence he had often worn with me:

"You will be able to look after Jadwiga a little? There'll be some small things that have to be done for her. You see, I think of her as a young woman—she was a girl when I married her—but really she is getting old now. And you see, she's used to having me nearby—not to be any use, no, but to say something when things are vexing her—all those people, those foreign soldiers—to tell her that everything's all right."

He smiled then, as men are accustomed to smile over the small anxieties of their womenfolk; so that his words did not seem pitiful, but rather those of a shrewd doctor who gently belittles some small complaint. I believe that he fully understood what was happening to us, and what it implied for him, but had lived so many years in a place of his own that immediate and material happenings had ceased to involve his interest. It was not that he had grown feebler in sympathy; only—as I see it now—that he had come to that last maturity where compassion burning in the spirit can no longer scorch or crimp it. For a moment he had lost sight of my face, but he recovered it as he always did, feeling about for my hand and using it for a way-mark. When our eyes were in communion the light in his grew warmer. I felt as if I were a child facing the ordeal of leaving home for the first time, and he a father who would give me if he could the courage of his years.

He said thoughtfully, "Yes, Jadwiga will be lonely. But the other one will be with her—what is her name, the kind woman my son married?—yes, Sandra will be with her. She came to see me, to say good-bye, she came with the young woman—sometimes I don't remember names very well. Yes, I think I have seen them all. And you, little Stefanie, now I have seen you as well!"

He laughed then, as the old do in delight at some accomplishment of their own. Perhaps he was pleased that my name, at least, had come to his mind; or perhaps it was only that his zest for the small, bright facets of experience—the day's beginning, the curiosity in a child's eyes—would never diminish. Almost at once, but still amusingly, he frowned, like a schoolboy struggling to control his levity.

"Poor Jadwiga! Those Russians, she has never cared for them. You see—are you there, Stefanie?—you see, they've been cruel sometimes. I think I ought to tell you—it's better, I think it's always better to be ready for times when one has to suffer. Then you deliver yourself into God's hands and you're released from the burden of anxiety. Do you see?"

"Yes, I see."

See? I did not understand. All I saw was the tranquillity of his regard, the consummation of his own understanding.

He laughed again, mocking my dullness: he had not the power to laugh loudly, but his laughter was fresh and easy, like a boy's.

"I'll tell you," he said, "why you don't understand! It's because I've got old—old men always forget what younger ones are like, how important life is to them. Life—you know what I mean, finding things to occupy your senses, troubling whether people admire you and love you—all that industriousness, it makes the day so much more real than the eternity it belongs to. I'll tell you something," he whispered, "I myself, I should not be brave enough to be young again; I couldn't stand the weight of all the things a young man believes in."

He was playing with my fingers, as he often did when talking: his mind, I thought, had lost touch with circumstances, so that this visit of mine appeared to him the same as any other, to be protracted as we wished. He had not wandered far, however; for a moment later he said reflectively:

"Yes, there are people who make us suffer. But the Christ who lives in us is in them as well. We can love the Christ in them, and He can absorb our suffering in His own."

From somewhere that seemed far off a voice—I think it was Wanda's—was calling for me. "Stefanie, where are you? There'll be trouble if you don't come!" He heard that too, and he said briskly, "You must go, my love, you must go now!" But his hands would not immediately respond to his will, he continued to hold my fingers, and when we had stayed like that for a few moments more, he, smiling with a lover's authority, he stretched and took my arm. I knelt then, so that my face could come nearer his, and with a power that surprised me he brought my forehead to his mouth. This was such an embrace as I had not known before, and it was strange to feel the pressure of the broken lips, fragile as dried leaves, yet alive and sensitive like the body of a bird. He gave me a blessing, the words of which I did not hear; and then, when he had damped his finger and crossed the place where he had kissed me, he let me go.

I did not want to leave him without any words of farewell or of gratitude; but even if I had found such words I could not have uttered them, since the nerves which empower speech had fallen slack in me, like a spring overstretched. I stood, then, staring stupidly about the room, and thinking how I ought to have put these minutes to practical use; for the place was in a state no woman should have tolerated, with some of the bed-clothes on the floor, linen and utensils lying about which needed to be washed, the air stale and sour. The time had gone, however; my name was being called once more. I meant to avoid looking at the Count again, and so to guard myself from emotion which would have no usefulness; but as I moved somnambulantly towards the door my eyes must needs return to the bed, and I saw then how much of his strength the leave-taking had cost him. He lay quite still, with his hands where they had fallen when he released me; his eyes were open, but they no longer searched for me or showed any light of their own. I need not have troubled about my feelings: what appeared in this face and these hands, where the lamp's halo over-spilt the dull light from the window, was only such an image as photography reveals, the sober beauty of lit and shadowed planes, of the skin's frosted texture, the fine delineation of crevice and vein. Here was an object which held the eyes by its worn dignity: no more than that.

Yet after the door had closed behind me my mind lingered in that room, and as I made my way between the men still cluttering the stairs I seemed to have returned from reality into a clouded dream. When a soldier barked at me, asking if I thought they'd got all day to wait, I smiled absently as one does with a demanding child; and to a friendlier fellow, who came in his shirt and boots to beg a souvenir, I only murmured, "Presently—I'm busy now!" Would the old man be disturbed, I wondered, by the sound of all this traffic? So many people, such confusion, in the distorting twilight of this vaguely familiar house: so profuse an activity, to no purpose that I could recognize: so very long, this day.

iv

Outside, a drizzle had begun, retarding the daylight. There were two uncovered lorries, one with passengers from some other village, who had settled themselves as well as they could among the heaped baggage. Even at this hour a small crowd had come to watch our departure, and I caught sight of faces that I knew well, old servants and labourers. But these only stared at us apathetically, with no sign of recognition; abashed, I suppose, by the strangeness of the occasion, or by the soldiers with fixed bayonets who were there to keep them at their distance.

"There's a place for you beside Annette," Sandra told me. "Look—there—Wanda will help you up. Annette's got a coat of mine, you can share it, perhaps—you ought to have it over your knees. . . . Yes, Rosalia, I'll find your blue valise in a moment."

"You'd better get up yourself, Mother!" Wanda called sharply.

But Sandra was too busy to pay attention to such advice: she had, after all, ordered the details of Wanda's life for a number of years—her behaviour, clothes, the preparations for her first journeys away from home. And now, after months in which her normal activities had been perplexingly curtailed, there was so much for a woman of her experience to see to. "In a minute, childie!" she said pacifically, and returned to me. "I've seen the driver, I've told him about your condition and I've asked him to go very slowly where the road's bad. He looks like a married man, I'm sure it will be all right. . . . Yes, Rosalia, it looks very nice. What, dear? . . . Wanda, that coat of mine, give it to Cousin Rosalia, she's worried about the men seeing her legs. . . . What is it, Mr Butusov? Yes, I'm sure we all hope that; indeed we hope to see you again, the acquaintance has been a pleasure to us all!"

I saw tears in her eyes when she said that: it was evident that Butusov was much affected by the occasion, and she was one who responded quickly to any call upon her emotions. So, while this rather unfinished soldier held her hand in his gigantic fists, and told her that all the joy of his life would vanish with her departure, she submitted to his attentions with a liberal kindness added to the squat dignity of her usual bearing. She fluttered, she smiled moistly, she answered with a tremulous and wistful embarrassment. Indeed she would remember him! How grateful she was for the many little services he had done the family during his stay in her home! "And now, if you will excuse me, I have some little matters to attend to, my daughter-in-law is not really in a condition for travel, I want to make her as comfortable as I can. . . ."

By this time the rest of 'our own' soldiers were crowding affably about us, to wring our hands, to deliver solemn, ingenuous speeches or to make a final bid for perquisites. They climbed aboard and scrambled over the luggage, laughing like schoolboys, Annette was boisterously embraced, from sheer exuberance a youthful trooper snatched at the cigarette which Wanda was smoking and transferred it from her lips to his. It was, considering the hour, a generous farewell.

So far the escort which had come to remove us had seemed to accept such frolics as a normal procedure; but their patience could not last for ever. Someone chanced to kick over a case of Wanda's, which fell to the ground, and a guard who was standing by called out that it could stay where it was. Either failing to hear him, or from simplicity, Henryk climbed down to recover it; at which the guard, reaching him in three easy strides, swung the butt of a rifle against his thigh with sufficient force to send him sprawling, whimpering like a child. It was perhaps an ill-tempered rather than a vicious blow: the soldiers round about saw the incident as comic and broke into fresh, uproarious laughter. For us it served as a hint that we should be under more positive management from now.

Fortunately Sandra did not see it—she was busy with some trouble of Rosalia's. Wanda did. I saw her stiffen, and I thought for a moment that she was going to jump down and attack the guard, as Victor would have done without hesitation. She controlled herself, however, and a moment later, with her hand perceptibly shaking, she was lighting a fresh cigarette: experience had done more for this once wilful child than any of my earlier teaching. It was Annette who, calmly and efficiently, helped her uncle back on to the truck.

At the time I myself was not much moved by this affair, since my senses were clouded and my responses feeble: I continued to accept whatever happened as one accepts the occurrences of a dream. The question where I should find myself when the time came for Conrad's birth was naturally important to me, but the business of departure had lost its significance—one seemed to be for ever starting some futile journey. The drizzle was turning into a steady rain, that rain which, in the Polish spring, might last all day: it began to quiet the ardour even of our soldier friends. This hour was one I could not identify, for there had not been one of the same smell and feeling in any day I had known: with the light remaining feeble, the little crowd of civilian onlookers so silent and still, I felt as if I were part of a tableau which, exempt from change, would presently lose even the outward semblance of reality.

At the last moment half the escort climbed on to our lorry, some of them taking the places we had carefully made for ourselves; so that when we started, with a sudden and tremendous jerk, we were all thrown off our balance. Recovering, I found that the Countess was now close to me, standing to face the front of the lorry and supporting herself with a hand on Annette's shoulder. Her head, indeed, was only a few inches away from mine; but even when she spoke to me our eyes did not meet. She asked abruptly:

"You gave it him, the tea?"

I told her that I had.

"He drank it? *All of it?*"

"Yes."

She nodded with a quick satisfaction, as her son might have done on hearing that some order of his had been properly carried out. That was all. Her eyes were still fixed on the driver's cab, she did not turn to look back at the house where she had spent nearly all her life—the house of which she had always seemed an integral part—or at the villagers whose lives had been fastened to hers, or any of the landmarks which, as we shook and swayed, were showing in a grey half-tone beside us and being snatched away into the obscuring rain.

i

OF the faces that are woven in my memory of the goods
yard, a few which belonged to children have stayed the
most distinct. There was a girl of perhaps eleven years,
overgrown, with long, coltish legs; her head might have been an
Italian's, with the olive skin and the very dark, thick hair, and she
had that sad sublimity which Italian masters have given so often to
their madonnas: not, however, the fullness of flesh—in its long,
narrow, spade-like structure hers might have been an El Greco face.
Her strangeness—the look she had of experience wisely secreted—
made her a leader; and you never saw her without half a dozen
other children, the smallest clutching her hand, the rest filing in her
wake. They went up and down the yard, these urchins, playing a
game of their own. The tall girl would advance upon any group or
individual and announce with perfect gravity, "We have come to
Warszawa to do our shopping, we want a basket of bread and a
sack of onions" or "We wish to buy a wedding-gown for a lovely
bride." When the 'shopkeeper' was willing to play his part there
would be some decorous haggling and the transfer of goods and
money would be mimed with great attention to detail; but if he
stared woodenly, as many did, the tall girl would say with unaltered composure, "I'm sorry, but that is not exactly what we have
in mind," and the troop would move on to try their luck elsewhere.
It appeared to me that the 'shops' where they drew blank gave them
as much satisfaction as the ones where they were successful: there
was something so convincing in the leader's polite refusal that it
made this the more real transaction, and rich in humour: a breathless, frog-like little boy always burst out laughing, and his laughter
was reflected in demure smiles on the faces of the sage small girls
beside him. Day after day the sport went on. You met the little
band picking their way across the sidings, or emerging from be-

neath the loading-platform, or promenading round the edge of the dense crowd which converged twice a day upon the ration truck; so much absorbed in their purpose that they did not seem to mind when they were jostled or to notice the rain. Their progress was slow, since one of them wore surgical boots and the skeletal, bandy legs of another were hardly able to transport the balloon-like paunch which overhung them; but in the course of a morning the troop might get from the broad to the narrow end of the yard, having made a dozen or twenty calls, and when you vaguely thought of them as shopping the area where you last saw them, half a kilo-metre away, they would appear close by from behind the sheds which the earliest inhabitants had made their home. In arrow for-mation they would slowly advance, serpenting between the piles of baggage which littered the ground, reminding you absurdly of a flock of ducks, with the waddling gait of the smaller ones and with the wind fluttering the sacks and newspapers they clutched about their shoulders. Yet the tall girl, always a few paces ahead of her platoon, walked proudly, disdaining the use of any improvised cloak or hood, and in the bearing of her lank, child's body, which the sodden dress showed as if it were naked, you saw the dignity of queens. Presently she was standing before you, courteous but aloof, commanding your attention by the deep sincerity of her still, dark eyes. "Good morning, I am looking for a pair of dancing slippers for my little girl here. Perhaps you will be good enough to show me your range."

Were those children always wet through, as I see them in recol-lection? The rain cannot have continued without a break for all that time; yet the picture that remains is one where the fall of rain is permanent, the medium of all sensation—not a heavy but a saturating rain, a vault of humid smoke where near and distant objects, the sheds, the baggage piles, the loading-platform, show in the same flat monotone. To the north there were hills, not far away, but we never saw them: we hardly saw the outlying houses of the little town which sprawled towards us on the other side; according to the eyes' record, the pennon of ash and mud which we inhabited was cut from a plain as featureless as the deserts of Iraq. That was perhaps the source of our complaisance. We were crowded, and the trucks were bringing one or two hundred fresh arrivals every day; but if an opening had been made in the many-stranded fence surrounding us, and left unguarded, I doubt if many would have used it. In practice, there seemed to be nowhere to go.

No doubt the altered circumstances of living had weakened the spirit of adventure in most of us. We were concerned only with immediacies. Since we had arrived too late for any space in shelter, the first business of our party had been to make it for ourselves, and to this Wanda and Annette gave much ingenuity. With our baggage piled to serve as walls, coats and blankets fastened as a roof, we had a habitation no smaller and not much cruder than those which serve a family's needs among many primitive peoples; and if it failed to keep off much of the rain, it gave us at least a place of our own, a point to return to, some sense of being indoors at night. In short, we were better off than families which had no such contrivance, and slept on top of their cases, wrapped about the legs and shoulders with whatever they could find. We were fortunate, too, in having secured a site some distance from the field latrine which served the whole population, and which spread its offence over an area larger than I should have believed. Here, then, we occupied ourselves, on a reduced scale, with those details of personal comfort which make up a great part of more conventional living. We were always conspiring to get the older members into positions where the 'roof' was not dripping, and to give them some make-belief of privacy. We found, each for herself, devices to cushion elbow or hip-bone against the hardness of the ground; we tried incessantly—with string or safety-pins—to close the gaps through which new darts of cold, wet air were aimed at our faces with every shift of the wind. These were fretful occupations. They passed the time, but one could see no purpose in its passing. To me, suffering from the nerviness which precedes confinement, the tent (as we grandiloquently called it) was often an object of repugnance: I disliked being so close to other people, and the unnatural heaviness of the moist, pocketed air. I grew impatient over small annoyances —a coat-belt flapping against my head, Rosalia's voice and Sandra's tactful smiles, the experience of waking from troubled sleep to find a damp shoulder or heel pressed against one's cheek.

Mainly for this reason I took my share with the younger ones in outdoor duties, though these excursions put some strain on my physical resources. At least once a day I joined the throng at the ration trucks, which meant long periods of standing, with the risks of being dangerously jostled; and when I felt strong enough I helped in shopping at 'the market'—a group of traders from the town who took their stand each day along the outside of the fence to barter soap and cigarettes, illicit news-sheets, occasionally some scraps of food, for anything of value we had to offer them.

That fence—the length opposite the railway tracks—provided a social centre, like the main street of a village; for besides the traders a number of people from the town came out there every day. A few had friends on our side, some brought simple comforts for us or took letters to be posted, there was an aged priest who regularly stood there to administer the Sacrament, passing his hands through the wire. Of the rest, the majority came with no apparent purpose but to loiter in straggling groups and gaze through the fence with the unchanging curiosity of animals, while the rain obliterated every visible distinction between their state and ours. We were vaguely glad of these dour spectators. In some way they reduced the gap between our present existence and what we still thought of as reality, and the value of any rumours they had to offer rose steeply in a community where normal interests were in short supply. For larger fictions we depended on new arrivals: each morning, when the trucks drove in with a fresh consignment, a crowd would gather at the off-loading point to greet them; always hoping, I suspect, that these bewildered immigrants from the older civilization would have apocalyptic tidings among their baggage—that the Russians had decided to let us manage what was left of our country, or that Poland after all was about to jump up and win the War.

Yes, that was the chief event of every day. The next was nightfall. You might have no hope of physical comfort, and little of sleep, but the darkness was always grateful. It eased the load upon your senses—the shingle of dulled faces, the wide, half-toned confusion. It narrowed the boundaries of your world, giving it at least the smallness of a familiar room.

My own trouble was the habit of wakening some time before first light. I used to keep still as long as possible, believing that all the rest I could get would be good for Conrad; but the discomfort of lying there awake was hard to bear: my cramped limbs fidgeted like children, and every movement was a disturbance to Annette, who lay beside me. At this hour the tent was full of small, distressing sounds: the Countess, who spoke hardly a word during the day, kept up an incoherent chatter in her sleep which turned sometimes to childlike whimpering or to sobs of anger, while Wanda would argue in a clear, bitter voice with some imaginary opponent, and Sandra, her face buried in her shawl, was often crying. This restlessness about me made the recovery of sleep impossible, and in the drowsiness which came as substitute I would imagine that Victor watched me from the darkness, reproaching my treachery to his father. More than once a sudden internal pain made me think my labour had begun prematurely, so that I returned to full consciousness with a cry of fear; and then, no longer able to endure the tent, I would wriggle out and move about the enclosure until morning.

They never lost their strangeness, those walks through the dark encampment. It was like making one's way across heathland, where there are only narrow paths between straggling clumps of bramble and gorse; but here each hump was faintly animate—from this low mound came the sound of smothered coughing, from this the keening of a child, here an old man's voice flowed steadily, as if he were lecturing to a class, here, when your foot came against some object you had not seen, you were startled by a cry of alarm. Often I could not locate the source of these noises, which were faint but clearly shaped, and I came to feel that all the ground I walked on was alive, calling to me in a hundred tones which I had known in childhood, the voices of forgotten friends, servants' and teachers' voices. They troubled me, these presences, and at the risk of falling I would go on as fast as I could to where the ground was less thickly strewn. At the apex of the enclosure, where wagons trellised with wire blocked the outrunning tracks, I would stòp to rest my legs, sitting on a stack of timber. Here the wind blowing across the cinders put a shield of silence between me and the nearest bivouacs, and in such solitude I could imagine I was again on one of my lonely walks at Setory. This fresh illusion lasted when darkness had begun to weaken. Perhaps my vision was inert from the cold and from shortness of food; in the first grey light, stippled with rain, the ground before me seemed void of life, only ridged like a sea frozen in storm; and even when the nearer outlines hardened, describing separate hummocks of blankets and clothes, the quilted bundle where a family slept together, the shape of a man's knees stuck up beneath his coat, I could still detect no movement to suggest that any creature breathed here: this was a wilderness which the dead inhabited. But now, over to my left, the dark mass of the sheds was stabbed by flecks of light; here and there shrubs of smoke grew stealthily to form a livid sash which lay almost unbroken across the camp, and against the sombre colours of this drifting screen there appeared to be upright figures moving. Presently, through the portière of rain, I could distinguish separate forms, someone who stooped and stretched, a woman holding out a shivering child. Men started to move about the enclosure, on some small errand or to warm themselves, women were joining with their neighbours to talk of the night's discomforts, and as all the thousand groups began to break and mingle, the scene evolved from shadowed landscape to a vast intricacy of action. Even this had only a surface resemblance to the life of streets and markets. You observed, threading your way between these people, that all their movements were cramped and sluggish, as if sleep still possessed them: you could fancy they were peepshow models which a coin sets in motion, puppets with oddly lifelike faces whose limbs would joggle in small, purposeless actions until the machinery ran down.

ii

My trunk was restored to me—or rather, I found it for myself in a heap of rubbish near the latrine. At least it had come to the right camp, and that was remarkable, for there was not much evidence of reason in the way our affairs were managed.

One aspect of the place to which one grew accustomed only by degrees was the anonymity of its direction. There were, of course, some soldiers to keep an eye on us, but most of these, coming from eastern republics, spoke an almost incomprehensible Russian and in any case knew nothing. (Only Rosalia thought it worth while to go on asking them questions.) At varying intervals an officer of sorts went round the enclosure on a tour of inspection—I do not know what features he was meant to inspect—and he was approachable and patient, but ill-informed. A peasant woman whose bivouac was close to ours used always to accost him, holding one small boy in her arms while two more clung to her skirts, and she would reel off the same questions every time as if she were taking them from a written list: why had they brought her here—when could she go home again—what had these children done, to be treated in this fashion? The officer replied, with the air of a shy philanthropist, that everything was receiving due consideration; all such questions were being referred to the Council, who would make their decisions at the earliest possible moment. And who were the members of this Council, Wanda once shot at him. The officer, nodding gravely, made a note of her question, and promised to refer it to the Council for their attention.

There was another enclosure a few kilometres along the railway-line. That was for people charged with sabotage of the democratic front and offences with similar titles—or so we understood from neighbours who had a reputation for good guesswork. But the chance remained that the classification of détenus had been imprecise. The initials by which our own enclosure was officially designated proved to stand for 'Assembly-point—United Co-operative Agricultural Volunteers', and there were not a few among us who felt that our physique was better suited to the easier kinds of sabotage than to work in the fields. In time the authorities might regroup us; meanwhile the topic served well enough for those discussions which usually formed the staple of our entertainment.

'What are you—do you know?'

'I'm almost certain that I'm a voluntary agricultural worker.'

'. . . Yes, they say the food is much more plentiful in the other camp, and better still at Kartushka. I think I shall apply for imprisonment as a voluntary co-operative saboteur.'

All the official guidance we had came from the area propagandist, one much lower in intelligence than most of his kind—a rough burlesque of the old-fashioned Swiss evangelist, whose handy smile, displaying lustrous and unwieldy dentures, gave him the dreadful unreality of a marionette. I doubt if he commanded more than a sentence or two of Polish for private use, but when he had gathered a small group about him he would deliver a word-perfect recitation about the injustice of the traditional agrarian system of Poland—in the Soviet Union, by contrast, every farm-worker enjoyed a full share of the products of his own labour, with free training in modern technical methods, model houses to live in and the joy of recreation in a free co-operative community. Polish brothers and sisters—regardless of their present status or legal involvements—were invited to examine the system for themselves, and to take a part in it for a limited period, entirely at the expense of the Union. . . . A few listeners rather furtively gave him their names.

Ludwig Radznowski, who had been sent to our camp, used to come and talk to Wanda in the evenings—partly, I think, to get away from his wife, who coughed incessantly and whose suffering he could not stand for more than a certain length of time.

"I have made all my plans," he would say, in his high and rather precious voice, "I am getting myself registered as a ditcher. They say that digging ditches calls for nothing but intelligence, and am I not a professor of radiology and other intelligent subjects! Apply to me, dear Madam, for any ditches you require about your voluntary farm!"

And balancing himself on his one leg, and on the crutch he held beneath his remaining arm, he would perform a peculiar mime of digging. These antics might have distressed us, but there was often such a boyish good nature about this man—then in his fifties—

that his ferocious humour was not offensive. He had, besides, a certain elegance. In these days he was, like the rest of us, villainously dirty, and his over-long grey hair was plastered by the rain about his neck and ears—I have seen beggars in Warsaw who looked far more presentable; but even now his faintly ironic smile, the mannered delicacy of his gestures, made you feel as if you were talking to some gilded attaché at a diplomatic party.

"Tell me, Radznowski," old Commander Sulkiewicz said one evening, "what do you think they're *really* after, these bastards? Is it political? Do they just want us out of the way? Do they think if they keep us here long enough we'll toe their line—and if so, what line? You're supposed to be one of these intellectuals, you ought to know!"

Radznowski gazed at him patiently. "I don't want to be snobbish about it, but I don't really belong to this camp, you know. I am an intellectual, as you say, and I've had a proper charge brought against me. What was it? I don't remember exactly—espionage, counter-espionage, something of that kind."

"Well, there's been no charge against me!"

"Exactly! I hate to press the point, my dear Commander, but you are really just a member of the potato-gang—you're a voluntary agriculturist."

"But how the devil can I dig potatoes! I can't stoop more than this much—I couldn't if they threatened to hang me. I've said so forty times to that fellow who comes round, that counter-jumper dressed up as a Japanese policeman."

"And has he written it down?" Wanda asked.

Radznowski smiled. "Really, Commander, we must do something about all this. We must think of some charge and get you to sign a confession. Then perhaps they'll move you over to the other place—I am assured that you get a far better class of prisoner there."

Wanda said, "I'm not sure that I find that very amusing. It's quite likely that my father's there—he's accused of something or other."

"Something important?"

"I don't really know. My sister-in-law knows more than I do——"

"You take life too seriously," Radznowski said with acerbity. "It really makes no difference, except as a matter of taste. I myself should prefer to be shot or hanged—I feel that there's always a certain dignity in accepting punishment, even when it's not quite

[225]

clear what you're being punished for. So I envy your father a good deal. But practical people may prefer to leave the world in a more conventional fashion—to die in harness, as they say."

"I see no obvious reason why we've got to leave the world at all," Sulkiewicz said crossly.

"Oh, but my dear Sulkiewicz, surely you've answered that yourself! The reason is that neither you nor I can dig potatoes. If one has a horse that's no use for work, one disposes of it. These people are only applying the logic of political economy."

"Nonsense!"

"Dear Commander—forgive me—your head is stuffed with bourgeois inhibitions! And now, if you will excuse me, I must see what I can do about some supper for Sofietka."

"Is your wife any better today?" I asked him.

"Well—thank you—I can hardly say she is. Really I think the camp doctor ought to see her. But I understand that the camp doctor has yet to be appointed."

Wanda, putting her hand on his shoulder, said, "There's nothing I could do?"

"Well, really, I don't think so, thank you." He turned his eyes away from us, and I saw in his mouth an expression that was new to me. "Of course," he said, addressing the ferrule of his crutch, "it's supposed to be a good thing in the treatment of pulmonary cases, plenty of fresh air. It's just that the dampness is a complication. But you know, she would not have been happy if I'd left her behind."

When he had hobbled away a number of our neighbours—people who were shy of approaching Radznowski themselves—came round us to ask if he had brought any news: they seemed to imagine that because he was a well-known man, and had the knowledgeable air which is common among scientists, he must be privy to all kinds of cryptic intelligence. When we explained to them that Dr Radznowski had no sources of information which were not common to us all, they only repeated their questions: He didn't say how long we've got to stay here? He couldn't tell you what's going to happen?

I was troubled, on those occasions, by my own inadequacy. We belonged to that small portion of this camp's inhabitants who had once given orders to people like these; our business had been to make decisions which greatly affected their lives. Something of that ascendancy clung to us, perhaps in our bearing, our voices; not unnaturally they took it for granted that we still had means to help

[226]

them, and it seemed to me shameful that I had no reserves to meet their confidence. But if Wanda felt the same embarrassment, she never betrayed it. I cannot believe that she, once so quick and generous in her compassions, lacked sympathy with these bewildered fellow-prisoners; and yet she often behaved as if they were fractious children with imaginary grievances.

"No, of course Dr Radznowski knows no more than we do—how could he! . . . No, I don't think it's at all likely that things are going to improve. I don't see any use in complaining."

This coldness did not discourage them. It increased her stature; and while it relieved them to recount their troubles to Sandra or Annette, who would listen with endless patience, I believe it was Wanda's presence in those days which prevented the final extinction of their courage. At the ration issue one morning there was some kind of fracas, in which an old man was severely kicked by one of the soldiers—I think he died not long afterwards—and for the rest of the day the population talked of nothing else. In the evening our party was visited by a kind of deputation, who wanted us to prepare a written indictment of the soldier concerned, to be formally presented to the inspecting officer on his next round; and as a matter of course it was Wanda who received them. I see even now the stilled passion in her statuesque face as she leant against a telegraph-pole, in one of her father's attitudes, to give them audience.

"Can't you see," she said when they had finished, "can't you see that protests of that kind are utterly useless!" Her voice, almost without inflexion, would have lost its cutting force if she had raised it. "No—worse than that! You make speeches to these creatures—write letters to them—and it only shows that you take them for people like ourselves. We—we aren't that sort of people, we don't deal in words and phrases. Until we can fight we suffer. That's a business we understand, we Poles. We get our greatness from suffering."

They cannot have found any reason in that statement, these people whose furthest reasoning could be expressed in a few worn sentences. And yet I am certain, from what I saw in their faces, that her voice had discovered some region in their spirit which was more cardinal than that of understanding. At the least—as I believe—such words relieved the loneliness which was not the smallest of their miseries; for even those who had their families about them were homesick for the places they came from. Many belonged to the poorer quarters of cities like Pinsk and Vilna, and to these it was not the wire fence that mattered but rather the absence of the boundaries they were used to—the walls of houses pitched close together in their own narrow and stifling streets. It scared them, this roofless, featureless place, as the feel of a ship scares those who have spent their lives far from the sea; and I can understand how the onset of darkness increased its terrors for them, so that rather than hide themselves in the shelters they had made, to lie awake like children in an unfamiliar house, they would go on standing together in the rain, saying the same things over and over, sharing those stillnesses in which the noises of the wind, the sound of an engine starting somewhere towards the town, were strange and frightening.

iii

These were not groundless apprehensions.

During a night when wind and rain had slacked, so that other sounds were magnified, the jangle of wheels and couplings came into my dreams; the noise half-wakened me, but I fell asleep again. As usual, I was abroad early. I had then forgotten the night's disturbance, and at first light I had the impression that a wall had been built along one side of the enclosure. As the light strengthened I saw that the railway-track—so long empty that we had ceased to think of it as having any function—now bore a line of freight wagons which stretched the whole length of the camp and out into the country beyond; wagons of unfamiliar shape, dark green in colour and seeming to be of gigantic size.

Here was something new to stare at and discuss all day. Among the simpler folk a certain optimism prevailed: it got about that the Council of whom we were always being told had come to hear of our desperate shortages, and that these wagons, holding a huge quantity of food, had been sent to remedy our needs. The fact that authority took no steps to get them opened did not, for some time, interfere with this hopeful opinion: we had discovered long before that the methods of our guardians often called for an interval between preparation and performance. In the event, the vans stood idle and untouched for three whole days.

It happened that on the third night I turned in early. Conrad's weight had seemed more burdensome than usual all that day, and although I was conscious of some bustle in the camp I fell quickly and deeply asleep. I suppose I had slept for an hour or so when Annette roused me.

[228]

"Mother! Mother, you've got to get up, *you've got to get up*! We've got to join the queue!"

And as if in echo there were voices from every side—Russian voices: "The queue, come on, get moving, hurry, get in the queue!"

"Perhaps you can carry this case!" Annette was saying. "This one—it isn't heavy. Wanda and I can manage the rest."

The tent had been dismantled already, and I was lying with only the sky above me, but I did not immediately grasp that fact; the night was one of peculiar darkness and I saw no stars. I got slowly on to my feet and took up the small suitcase which Annette had placed at my side. What now? People were moving all round me, I did not know whether they were our own party or strangers, things were bumping against my legs. A scarf that Annette was wearing showed as a triangle of paleness in front of me. I would follow that as long as I could.

The queue? Where was this queue, what did they mean by that, the men who were continually shouting? There was no queue here, no shape or alignment, only the figures made from darkness, solid for a moment when they lurched against me, dissolving into the darkness again. Yet now, as the pressure increased, I could feel that everything tended to move in the same direction. We were making for something, I and all these people, there must be some common objective. I asked dully, of a shape that I felt beside me, "Where are we going?" and surprisingly it was Sandra's voice which answered: "To the train, I suppose. They're putting us on the train."

Something which felt like a heavy stone struck me on the arm, and the voice which came with it said, "Get in the queue, you, keep in the queue!"

The blow did not rouse me, the pain only increased my sleepiness; but my eyes were becoming adjusted, and soon I began to realize what the queue they spoke of was. It was a wide river of which I could just discern one frayed margin, a stream of clotted shapes, shapes of darkness more intense than the dark country through which it flowed; a sluggish stream, now moving just perceptibly, now ceasing to move at all. Here I could sleep, leaning against a man who walked at my side, or dropping to the ground, but the sleep was always spoiled, for the heavy baggage which people were dragging forward at each move would come violently against my arm where it was bruised, relighting the pain, and one voice or another would always attack me, "Stefanie, is that you? You must get up, we're moving again, you can't sleep here!" For

[229]

an hour perhaps they let me be, then Annette was imploring me, "Mother, you must come on, they'll hurt you if you don't keep in the queue!"

'I can't go on any more.' 'I've got the chickens here.' 'Is that you, Hanka, is that still you?' 'Yes, Henryk's pulling your trunk, he's not far back.' 'I can't go any farther.' 'Mother! Mother, I've lost Zoya, I've lost her!' 'Are you still there, Hanka, is that you?'

These were not obtrusive voices. It was a quiet company, drowsy or a little frightened, which behaved with no less patience than animals would have shown. At such an hour there was not much inclination for talk, and those who had to speak did so in lowered tones, as if they were in a house where children were sleeping; but in spite of that restraint there was from so large a concourse a steady tide of sound; not a tumult, only a murmur of many subdued voices which, interwoven with the shuffle of feet and the scrape of heavy cases dragging along the ground, made a noise so close and smooth in texture that it had the feel of silence. Out of this carpet of sound your ears picked a few stray threads from near at hand, a woman who begged to be left where she was, the child asking again and again for leave to go back and look for her doll. Beyond, there were always voices so foreign to ours that they seemed to be irrelevant: some oddly gentle and persuasive, some loudly virulent: 'Get up, you bitch, if you don't want this in your ——, get back in the queue!' From those we were protected by our weariness as well as by the bodies pressing against us on every side.

And now the stream was tightening, as it was forced into a narrower channel: we seemed to be on a rising slope, with timber under our feet.

Some way forward a few electric bulbs had been strung on a high cable, and these going on and off as they danced in the wind threw splashes of yellow light on the thicket of heads below them, on the stark wall of wagon sides. It was a light too feeble to reach ourselves. In the total darkness where we stood we were only spectators of a shadow play that was at once unreal and oddly sinister, where a waving arm would suddenly protrude from the black sierra, where the glint from a bayonet showed like a falling star. Our advance had dwindled to a halt, but from farther back some impulse still pressed the crowd upon us with the slow force of an engine, till all independent movement was impossible, and one who found himself with his legs astride a hold-all or jammed between two cases could only stay as he was. That situation was frightening, and not least for me, who had Conrad to protect from being crushed. But my neighbours, conditioned already to strange experience, were keeping themselves under fair control, and what I chiefly heard was the voices, only a little tremulous, of those who had lost touch with their friends: 'Hanka! Is Hanka there?' 'Is Maria Czerkowna there? Will someone tell Maria Czerkowna her little girl's with me, she's on my shoulders, she's quite all right. . . .' After a time these voices became less clamorous, as people were assured that those they wanted were not too far away or that it was hopeless to make further effort in the dark. When the rain started again its noise on the wagon roofs crushed out all feebler sounds, and then—as it seemed to me—the several hundreds of us sank together into a kind of sleep, where consciousness remained but where our faculties brought us only crude sensation—a plateau of darkness spattered with moistened light, the body's tormenting weight and coldness.

Beside us the wagons stood with their doors still shut and barred. Had someone lost the keys? At the time we did not speculate: a force like that of nature had brought us here, and at some hour in the natural course the wagons would be opened to give us their shelter.

But the feeling that human reason had ceased to operate on our concerns was partly at variance with facts. Someone had arranged the movement of the strong detachment which had come to reinforce our regular guards; someone, making a soldierly calculation of risks, had ordered the construction overnight of a new barbed fence to run the length of the loading-platform, isolating it from the rest of the enclosure.

We had sight of this at the first easing of darkness: the fence itself, with the top strand not much higher than our feet, and the soldiers who irregularly lined it. They looked excessive, these measures of security: in the grey morass which stretched before and behind me, drenched bodies held like faggots in a bundle, heads lying at queer angles, I saw no signs of the capacity or indeed the will for rebellion. But here my understanding of the situation was imperfect. I was supposing that the whole population of the enclosure had been driven on to the platform. With so thick a crowd about me, and in such meagre light, I failed to see that a great number had been left behind: the new fence was an equal safeguard against their intrusion and our escape.

Whether or no the time of loading had been deliberately chosen, it might have proved fortunate. The job was almost a success.

The loading party consisted, I think, of fewer than twenty men, who must have been shrewdly picked; they were business-like and very quick. A detail of three pushed their way along the edge of the platform, sliding open the wagon doors. The rest, following up, were cordoning thirty to forty people at a time, herding them into successive wagons and sliding-to the doors again. It was done firmly but without roughness, and so comatose was our condition that we hardly realized what was going on: far in front, where the lamps still broke into the half-light with a faint, unnatural radiance, we could see that heads were moving, but at first that seemed to be no affair of ours—we were merely relieved to find that with the easing of pressure we could shake out our limbs. So, a dozen wagons or more were filled without trouble, and the operation might have been completed just as smoothly but for one of those physical mischances which spoil the most careful plans. One of the sliding doors jammed and remained half-open. This gave time for the group which had just been loaded to consider their situation. A woman, shrilly calling out some name, struggled back on to the platform. One of the loaders instantly raised the butt of his rifle and struck her down.

Annette saw that. I, lifted off my feet in the backward surge of the crowd, had a glimpse of the woman sprawled on the ground with the soldiers closing in. The scream I heard, which continued high above the other screaming, above the shouts and blasphemies, may have been hers. The voice I remember more distinctly was some other stranger's—the small, insensate voice that beneath the uproar was demanding peevishly, "What is it? What is it? Is something wrong?"

These noises presently were subdued for me. As I lay at the platform's edge, where the toppling wave had thrown me down, the heel of someone still on his feet struck me between ear and temple, and from then the din became remote and blurred, like the tumult of a city heard through a high, closed window. Something heavy lay across me so that I could not move, but I felt only a little pain, no fear at all: my field of sensation had contracted to a narrow circle of objects which needed no response from the understanding, a striped petticoat with a neatly hemmed patch in it, the upturned face of a man who appeared to be smiling at some joke of his own. There was, outside these things, a dimly lighted spectacle which the mill of legs and arms about me revealed for a moment at a time: along the wire were the grotesque and floundering shapes of those who had fallen from the scrimmage and been caught by their clothes there, once and again there were figures running frantically towards us through the rain, a girl in a yellow coat who pitched herself against the soldiers, a rifle going up and down like a flail. But this confusion seemed to be far away and came to me void of actuality, like some fragment of a moving picture where the sound has faded out. At the time it was unreal to me, the contorted face I saw—not far from mine—of a child flung from the platform, whom a stalwart soldier with his bayonet stuck in her clothes lifted and sent hurtling back.

By stages sensibility returned. Someone had dragged me to my feet, and now with returning terror for Conrad's safety I was striking right and left with my elbows, trying to keep the crowd away from me, till a whipping rebuke which came in Wanda's voice brought me to quiescence. Now the shapes about me were people like myself, a peasant woman I had talked to in the ration queue, another who seemed to be sleeping on her feet; I caught sight of Radznowski's face, and now, as the turmoil began to subside, I found that Annette was once more holding me by the arm. It was the soldiers who had won this battle. People were shouting that they would not go in the vans, a few still tried to make their way against the stream, calling for a wife, a son, who had been torn away in the skirmish; but the whole crowd of us were moving back towards the train as if drawn by gravitation, and the faces close enough for me to read, pallid and smirched with blood, the sick, the petrified faces, were those of the defeated. There was a moment of fresh danger when we were tightly squeezed at the entrance to the wagon and one of the women started struggling again to get back to her child; but the force of the incoming tide overcame her. In that vortex I was twisted round, so that I had a last glimpse of the world I was leaving, and I curiously remember the crowded spectacle as if every part of it had been motionless—not only the shapes of those who lay unnaturally along the platform, but the curving line of soldiers' heads and beyond that battlement the straggling throng of the discarded, now spent and helpless witnesses of our departure, reaching back and back to where rain and shadow absorbed them. This picture (where the strange, sub-toned colours are scarcely faded now) was not before me long. I was dragged aside, while a load of baggage was thrown in after us, and then with a clang of finality the great doors came together. Here, at this hour, we were in almost total darkness. Comparatively we were safe; but many saw no use, indeed no meaning, in this version of safety.

In one sense, the haste seemed to have been needless, for the train did not start immediately when the loading was completed. When a few hours had passed there was a jolt which told us that an engine had been attached. I am not sure how long we remained stationary after that, but I know that the twilight in which we now lived was changed at least twice to total darkness during the waiting period.

The delay was not without advantage to us. Although we had grown accustomed to irregular conditions, there was much for us to learn about living in so small and awkward a frame, and these new difficulties could be studied better while we were, so to say, in still water. There were perhaps sixteen of us women, almost as many children, and I think seven men. We had to settle who should have places on the broad shelves at either end of the wagon, there was baggage to be sorted out, things to be stowed. A little motor mechanic from Piotrkow who was in our company did much that was useful in this period; he even contrived a screen of sorts to hide that hole in the wagon's side which was all we had for evacuation and which was inevitably the main focus of our discomforts. In the nature of things, a life physically so confined was more troublesome to us than to the men; for myself, I largely subjugated those instincts of modesty which a civilized upbringing imposes, but older women like Sandra—and particularly Rosalia—could not do so, and I believe the wretchedness they suffered on that account never grew smaller. Yes, it was a help to us to have our surroundings steady while we made these adjustments—while we arranged positions to sleep in, found places where the scanty light would catch a borrowed hand-glass and enable one at least to comb out one's hair. Outside, the weather had become cold again, and draughts found their way disagreeably through our clothes, which would not dry: for that reason, too, we were glad to be still.

On the other hand, there were drawbacks which became more serious as the period of waiting lengthened. One was the stercoral smell, which increased until one found oneself trying to take only shallow breaths. Of greater importance was the nervous strain which attends any act of waiting, and which was increased now by many uncertainties. There were several among us who had lost their families or friends. (From our own party the Countess had disappeared, and we thought it likely she was dead, since the riot on the platform could easily have been the end for a woman of her great age.) The absentees, if alive and unharmed, might have been herded into other wagons, or they might have been left with that large body which was now held at some distance from the platform, and would probably be loaded on to other trains, not necessarily for the same destination. This, for many, was the question on which existence was centred. Until the train started there was some hope of it being answered. But the hope grew more precarious.

Once or twice in the day the doors were slid open a few inches for a pail of watery soup to be pushed inside, and were promptly shut again. For the rest, the only view available of the world outside was through two grated apertures close to the roof, and to use them one had to kneel on the upper shelves. There were difficulties about this. Sofietka Radznowska, separated in the skirmish from her husband, had been borne into the wagon with us: Commander Sulkiewicz and others rightly insisted that she should have one of the top-shelf places near the opening—it was her only chance to get the fresh air on which her life depended—and her presence there put that 'window' virtually out of use. The other was largely occupied by one Maria-Josefa, whose baby son had been swept away from her and who knelt there day and night, incessantly calling the child's name. From time to time someone would get up beside her and shout an inquiry to any of the guards who was nearby, but these were hostile or stupid fellows, who at best would only answer vaguely that there was no need to worry—anyone who had missed this train would follow by the next. Sofietka Radznowska constantly threw out notes addressed to her husband, and there was at least one among the soldiers who said he would get them delivered. But similar notes were being thrown from one wagon or another all the time, and Sofietka herself saw scores of them, she told me, lying on the platform and being trampled into the mud.

I can remember how Sofietka looked as she lay there; how, in the calm which possessed her between long spells of coughing, all her grief for Ludwig was submerged in a gentle dignity, like that of a very young bride. And I recall, capriciously, how Rosalia was for ever complaining that so dangerous a source of infection had been put to travel with ourselves. Maria-Josefa's shrunken face has stayed in my memory as well, with its grief so differently worn, the stained and bloodless cheeks, the animal look of eyes that misery had emptied; and among the sounds that filled my ears throughout those hours, the continuous shouting of names along the train, the savage and despairing voices, the whimper of children, Maria's voice remains distinct—that cry of hers, toneless and unchanging, *Josef! Where are you, little Josef! Josef mine!* There were some who became so fretted by this monotonous call that they lost all pity for the distracted creature. One girl, in particular, whom Annette called 'the Star'—she was a hairdresser from Lwow whose pretty, commonplace face was always faultlessly made-up—became so infuriated that she would attack her with crude invective and almost with blows. There were others, however, who preserved their sympathy. I recall the stolid patience with which Sandra told the poor woman again and again that someone would undoubtedly be caring for the little boy: would not Maria herself be happier, Sandra suggested (perhaps with greater kindness than insight), if she gave herself for the time being to the care of this little girl, the youngest of several children among us who had got detached from their families? To this Maria-Josefa made no answer at all: I doubt if she heard with her mind any word that was spoken to her.

In truth, the little girl, who called herself Issa and was something under three years old, would not have let Maria-Josefa touch her, for she had a will of her own. From the several people who were ready to mother her she made the odd choice of Henryk, and he, applying himself to the duty with surprising diligence, became both master and slave to the child. I doubt if anyone else was so contented at that time as he. His senses were too dull to be much affected by bodily discomforts, and with so narrow a mental horizon he was not oppressed by physical confinement. There were children to play with, whose humour and speech accorded with his own. And now the task of amusing Issa, wiping her face for her, putting her to bed between two holdalls, gave him all the satisfaction his own simplicity required.

It has not been easy to recollect these things, which I observed as if from a distance, with feeble sympathy, as one sees a play too tame to usurp the place of one's own anxieties. My brain was slack. Sometimes I could not remember what had brought me to the gaunt shed we lived in, and then I could make no sense of this half-lit scene where the crowded pieces shifted and vanished and always appeared again—a girl's fair head on the legs of a labourer who snored beneath the lower shelf, a mother wearily supporting the head of a vomiting child, the soiled, emaciated faces of children who sprawled among the heterogeneous bundles and tumbled over the old peasant women trying to sleep. Often it seemed strange to see friends of my own enmeshed in this confusion; I was startled when they addressed me and found it burdensome to reply. How had they grown so unreal to me, these who had shared so much of my experience, whom I had known so long? It was, I think, that I had ceased to make the smallest effort to participate in any feeling of theirs. At no stage in my life had I been so wholly self-centred as I was at this time: my mind was occupied by one thought alone, one passion—a cancerous impatience for the train to be on its way.

I wanted the journey to be over. I did not care about its destination, so long as I reached it in time for Conrad to be born there. I had dreamed of Sweden. Now I needed only a sheltered, motionless place, a place where I could be alone, and still.

v

"They'll get us moving in the middle of the night," Sulkiewicz said, "then or at dawn. They always choose one time or the other, these maniacs. God knows why!"

But Sulkiewicz was wrong. This time it was late afternoon.

The light—so much of it as reached us—had started to weaken. A few minutes earlier the day's delivery of soup had come, and as usual Wanda and Sulkiewicz together were supervising the distribution (no easy task in that crowded van, where there were always some who tried to get more than their share). The first warning we had was the sound of couplings successively taking up their loads; this, I think, went unregarded by many in the wagon, who had almost forgotten that their prison was a thing capable of movement, and hardly anyone realized what was happening until we received a jolt which threw us all towards the after-end, even jerking a man and a sleeping child off the forward shelves. So sudden and violent a shock brought upon us a moment of peculiar silence; then Maria-Josefa, who was at her usual place and who saw the platform beginning to move away, uttered a cry like an animal's when its neck is wrung, and at the same time there was an outburst of shouts and screaming from the wagon in front of ours. With us, everyone seemed to be scrambling for a place at one of the apertures, in the last hope of catching a glimpse of friends left behind.

Wanda was close to me, and I could see from a movement of her body that this impulse had reached her as well. She mastered it; and on her pallid face, which I saw in profile against a man's dark coat, there came a look of irresolution, as if a decision of great importance were being forced on her. I thought, an instant later, that she was speaking to someone on her other side; and then I realized that she had begun to sing.

She sang *The Krakow Guard*, that artless, haunting rodomontade which every soldier knows and which Sobieski's men were perhaps the first to march to. I should not have believed that a voice as soft as hers would be audible in the pandemonium, but this was not the voice of her childhood; sexless, it seemed to have its source outside herself, perhaps in the passion of lives which had engendered hers, and it broke upon the turmoil as if ancient bells, long silent, were pealed for a city's liberation. At once another voice burst out. That was Annette's. And now I heard the tuneless bass of Sulkiewicz, and now the engineer had joined them, and the girl from Lwow was singing with all her strength:

> *What could our lives gain more than this—*
> *A Poland where our sons are free!*
> *Can dying shake the hearts in us*
> *Whose death wins Poland's liberty!*

It was curious how it took hold, this simple tune, on a truckload of dilapidated people, creatures who had seemed to lose even the desire for the dignity of their kind. The children, of course, had learnt the air in village schools: I saw a sickly boy stirring two others, who, in the little space they could find, stood straight and stiff and bellowed the words as if they would tear their lungs apart. But there were old people who came to their feet as well, women who clutched each other and sobbed and yet could make their wheezy voices sound enough to swell the tide. Even Sandra, even Sofietka, tried to sing. I watched these people dumbly, a stranger to their fierce emotion. And then the fire that had caught them flared suddenly in my own breast and loins, so that leaning against Annette, with tears flowing, and overwhelmed by a feeling of release and triumph, I found my weak voice joining theirs:

> *Long though it bear the pagan heel—*
> *By all the blood of Poland's slain*
> *Our Polish earth is sanctified:*
> *Poland shall rise, shall rise again!*

The wagon walls could not contain so furious an assault, the raging sound leapt as a heath-fire does and we heard it breaking out in vans before and behind. Then like a muffled echo it came back to us from the crowd beyond the fence, and it seemed as if the countryside, as if all Poland, were joined in that farewell. The soldiers were yelling at the crowd to shut their mouths, I heard the rataplan of rifle-fire, but the wave of sound which answered, which broke across the guards' shouting and the clangour of our wheels, was higher and more violent still:

Poland shall rise, shall rise again!
Poland shall rise, shall rise again!

We were moving at a foot's pace, the engine rebelling against so huge a load; it felt as if more than a minute went by before the shadow of the weigh-house passed across our roof. We were clear of the goods-yard then, but after we ourselves had fallen silent, our voices spent, the others' corporate voice reached us once more, till we in turn gathered what breath we could and in several times and keys flung out our last salute against the walls that held us:

Poland shall rise, shall rise again!

So, we had gone some distance before our ragged voices petered to final silence, and for some way farther still the chorus hung like a sunset in our minds' emptiness, so that even our bodies were warmed. But as daylight drained away we were left intensely cold, the wagon rumbled on as if it were climbing a stony hillside, and already, falling into a state that was neither sleep nor wakefulness, I had the sense of journeying without a destination in space or time.

i

SANDRA made a berth for me on the lower shelf, forward. That was the night we moved off or the night after. This place was against the side of the wagon—a very good place, one that Rosalia had first claimed. I took it because Annette made a fuss when I tried to refuse.

Here I enjoyed the nearest approach to privacy that was to be had, and the position gave me a special advantage besides: where the framework of the sliding doors was bolted to the wagon wall a piece of clumsy workmanship had left a tiny aperture which served me as porthole, so that when the drab confusion about me tired my eyes I could turn them upon the outer world, or what counted for such in this longitude. For the rest, I found relief in the presence of Sofietka Radznowska, who was my nearest companion in those days. When the train was under way the upper shelf had proved too cold for her, and Sulkiewicz had moved her down to the place next mine. In other circumstances I should have been dismayed, for Conrad's sake, at having one in her state so close to me, but when all the conditions of existence are disagreeable, you are saved from troubling about minor dangers. At least she was scrupulously careful about using the rags torn from an old nightgown which Wanda gave her for the sputum; and in spite of the effect which the long bouts of coughing made upon me, I was glad, in a peculiar way, to have her beside me. She was still in her twenties. It brought me refreshment to look at one whose beauty kept her apart from our surroundings; a beauty which had survived the wasting of her body, and would not change.

We stopped, by night, at a place which I afterwards identified as the Benylniez camp. There was nothing to see except a few electric lights, strung high above patches of what appeared to be scrub but may have been clusters of people. Here, with much shunting, we took on more wagons, and I believe a second engine.

ii

Once there was a town. This was at night as well. I woke to see a long, high wall, with lighted windows, which may have been a factory or a row of houses. Next I was looking down into a street, where people were walking in the lamplight. I saw a man and woman strolling arm-in-arm.

I thought in the morning that that had been illusion, a scene from some older journey. Nothing had changed. The sun rose in the same quarter on the same flat sea, a waste of black earth patched with sand, with mist on the grey and purple distances. The timber cabin which had crossed the view the day before passed by again; now, as yesterday, the pines began and gathered into an unbroken wall. They ceased towards evening, leaving the country naked once more.

But the sun was strengthening. The heat in our box increased: in the daytime we lay sweating, and the dank smells we had brought with us changed to the more pungent smells which summer gives to the cramped and sunless rooms of peasants' houses. That was the measure of our advance, the sign that this day and yesterday were not the same.

There was a night when I thought that Sofietka was dead, she kept so still; she had hardly once stopped coughing the day before. But when the night had gone on for a long time, or else when another night had come, I heard her laughing. I asked her timidly:

"Sofietka, are you all right?"

"I was thinking of Ludwig," she said. "He's so foolish sometimes."

"I've never heard anyone else say that."

"You know," she whispered, "he spent the whole of a day trying to propose to me. We were sledging together. In the end he said he would write me a letter, an important letter; I was to be sure to read it. So I said I would. But it didn't come, not for two days. Then he came himself, with a piece of paper—all he'd written was 'Darling Sofietka'. He said I'd have to write the rest for him."

"And did you?"

"Of course! I just put, 'Since you love me so much I think you had better be my wife.' " She laughed again, and then, turning herself painfully, she put her mouth close to my ear. "Stefanie! Stefanie, if he *did* get in the next wagon, you don't think he could possibly hear me coughing?"

"Of course not! Not a chance!"

Then she said, with the simplicity of children, "I keep on praying that he may be kept from thinking about me. For the time being, anyway. That's reasonable—don't you think so? I don't think one ought to pray for too much. And if it's for something that goes against yourself, or partly, that's better, isn't it?"

"Perhaps. I don't really know."

"I think there's quite a chance he may be in the next wagon, don't you?"

"Yes. Yes, more than a chance. I expect he'll find his way in here as soon as there's a proper stop."

"Yes. Listen, Stefanie—will you do something?"

"Of course!"

"If you see him again—and if I don't—will you tell him something?"

"Tell him? Yes, what?"

"Tell him that I didn't get any pain. Not for the last part. Tell him it all happened awfully easily—like going off to sleep. No pain."

"But you'll see him again. I know you'll see him again."

"But if I don't, you'll tell him that?"

"Yes, I'll tell him that."

The demon which was always waiting in her body took hold of her again, and I helped her back to the position she found best during these attacks: it was easy to move her, she had no weight at all.

That, as far as I remember, was the longest conversation I had with her; measured in days, our time together was small, and I think I never saw her face in a clear light. Yet the place she occupies in my memory is larger and more deeply graven than that of many people whom I knew for long periods. Lying so close, I came to feel the power within her gentleness; often she seemed far older than I, for she had learnt already how to accept her day.

Sometimes the train stopped, for a minute, for four or five hours; as a rule at night. It was in the long halts that the disease seemed to increase its grip on her, and then the sound of her coughing, diminishing and breaking out afresh like a baby's cries, would rob me of the sleep I should have gained. ("I'm sorry, I'm so sorry!" she would gasp. "It's stupid, it's a little tugging thing in my chest.") But sleep and wakefulness were only relative. As the train limped on through an endless day its broken rhythm, like a pupil's first piano-exercise, was hammered into you till it felt like a function of your body; dulling your faculties it brought a kind of drowsiness, and when it stopped you felt as when you wake in an unfamiliar room. The partition of time in days and nights became less palpable than this division between two kinds of endurance, the dull distress of the train's motion, the hours of listening half-awake to the tempest by which Sofietka was shaken and torn; when I would slip my arm beneath her body, hoping faintly that the pressure of human flesh might give her some relief, when her hand, childishly small, would find its way to mine and stroke my fingers. But those dual faces of experience are themselves merged in a tract which memory will only partially illumine: in a skein of blunted sensations, framed by the hardness of the shelf, by the smells of illness and sweated clothes, the creaks and undertones which filled the vibrating twilight.

For most of those days there was a trunk standing up-ended close to where I lay, with the gaudy label of a San Sebastian hotel. That, and the hole in the wagon's side where the pines eternally jogged past, and Sofietka's curly head, were boundary marks to the field of my intelligence. In the penumbra beyond I sometimes recognized Annette's or Wanda's face; I would see among the dark shapes the flutter of cards that the engineer was dealing, and from the web of listless talk, the stertorous whimper of old people drowsing, my ears would pick the demanding voice of Issa followed by Henryk's foolish laugh. But only now and then would my brain be stirred to put those fragments of sensation together, relating them to the half-forgotten time when people had moved in and out of houses, chosen whom they would see and whom avoid.

iii

Since the second or third day the feeding halts had been fairly regular; I mean, we did not often go for longer than twenty-four hours without one. You heard the doors sliding in succession, the repeated order coming down the train, "One man out!" and then we had to be on the alert; someone was put to stand against the door holding the two empty buckets, ready to jump the moment it was opened—only a second or two elapsed before it was slammed-to again. Outside, a man stood by with a machine carbine cocked; when they said 'one man' they meant just that.

The jump—more often than not in darkness—must have been a

considerable ordeal, and for a man or woman living not far from starvation the carriage of the filled buckets (one with soup, the other with water) was not a light undertaking—to say nothing of the climb back into the wagon. Yet nearly everyone who could move at all wanted to go. To be out of the wagon for ten or fifteen minutes, to feel one's feet on solid ground, perhaps to evacuate in the open—these were rich rewards; and the hope of finding someone in the queue who had news of missing friends was worth all the exertion, worth the chance of a blow from a rifle-butt or of a broken leg. There were quarrels in consequence; on one occasion actual fighting. Then Sulkiewicz organized a system by which names of candidates were kept in a box and one drawn for every halt. This worked quite well.

For Sandra the drawing was always a time of suspense and then of bitter disappointment. Supposing that she was quite strong enough for the excursion, she had put her name on a slip and believed that it was in the box; not knowing that Wanda had managed to abstract it. Even so, she made her own use of those halts. She always got to a place by the door, and the moment it opened she would deliver her speech to one of the men below:

"Mr Soldier! Mr Soldier, I want you please to take a message to your Commandant, it's very urgent—it's absolutely necessary to have a doctor, there's a lady seriously ill in this wagon here, and also an expectant mother. . . ."

She seldom got so far as that before the door was shut, but she never gave up trying.

When the halts occurred in darkness a fair distribution of the ration was virtually impossible, even with the scheme of tallies which Wanda had invented. The confusion in which we lived was always intensified by the emissary's return; for while half the complement swarmed like animals upon the buckets, which Sulkiewicz and the engineer were desperately guarding, the rest, more ravenous for news than for any food, were struggling to get the ear of the person who had brought them. Often the turmoil had not abated when the train started to move, and an hour or more after the halt I sometimes heard the same questions being asked all over again.

"A *little* boy—somebody would have told you if you'd asked them. . . ."

"You did remember to ask? Did you see anyone from the wagons up in front, did you ask them?"

"You're sure you had the name right—Bronislas Mudinski?

Anyone in the same wagon would know him—a tall man, with very deep eyes, he's quite different to anyone else."

"You say that she's come from the Benylniez camp? And she's in one of the rear wagons? But she hadn't even heard of my father?"

The time came when Annette's name was picked from the box. The halt which fell to her was in daylight. I should not have let her go if I had been strong enough to exercise my will.

She was, of course, quite exhausted when she got back—she had spilt a third of the water, to the anger of many—and for some time she had no breath to answer any questions at all. It was much later, when everyone had settled down again and many were asleep, that I heard her talking in an undertone to Wanda:

". . . whether to say anything to Granny or not. . . . Yes, one of the last trucks. No, this woman didn't know his name, but she knew he was somebody high up in the army, a General, she thought he was. It could have been Grandfather, from the way she described him. . . ."

The train was gathering momentum for one of those short bursts of speed which it achieved once or twice in a day, and the loudening rattle overwhelmed the rest of what Annette was saying. 'Grandfather'? It was no affair of mine. The grey horizon had begun to dance more violently, a rudimentary village appeared and became the mainspring of a shapeless dream. Julius—did she mean Julius? I had seen him in some poorly lighted room, he had told me—I thought—that that was to be our last meeting. That was in some previous life, and surely no concern of his could interest me now.

iv

At intervals I lost faith and thought that Conrad was dead; for it seemed impossible that the pauper's fare on which I had subsisted for so long now could have kept us both alive. But even in those periods of despair I went on talking to him, in a foolish way, trying to give him courage. The country we had come to, I told him, was not all forests and naked steppes. Ahead of us were cities, with houses well built and properly warmed; there people took a special pride in their care of the sick, the hospitals were as well equipped as any in Europe. We should be looked after, I said, in a clean, still place. He had only to be patient, to lie safely as he was, not to start struggling for his separate life too soon.

[245]

That was a good deal to ask of him. It was on the day of his expected birth that we had been loaded into the train.

In those shapeless but vivid dreams which come when sleep is shallow and disturbed, Victor was sometimes close to me: not clearly seen, but so lively in presence that more than once I thought, on coming awake, 'How foolish, to imagine that he was dead—whoever told me so must have been mistaken!' There was nothing of warmth or colour in those elusive meetings; they took their tone from many small encounters in our married life, when Victor, with all his mind on his work, had come home for a hasty meal or to attend to some domestic business before hurrying back to the camp; yet the brief sense of his companionship was strangely heartening to me at a time when so little of the goodness of life seemed to be left. To this there came an exception. In a night when the engines seemed almost too weary to drag us any farther, when the train repeatedly stopped, jerked on again, crawled for an hour as if there were heavy chains on the wheels, I found that he was beside me once more. He did not speak, and I could not see his face clearly; but I knew he was vexed with me, impatient for Conrad to be born. I tried to explain that we were waiting, Conrad and I, to get to some quiet place, somewhere less crowded than the shed we lived in now; but my voice fell silent beneath the noise of the train and I could not make him understand. Now he made a move which was new and alarming. He bent very close, and stretched as if he would seize Conrad from me; and I thought that Conrad in response began struggling to reach him.

I woke, crying out with fright. There was a pain in the lower part of my back which might have accounted for the dream and for my alarm; but this pain was a small one, like a twinge of rheumatism, and I could not remember that Annette's birth had brought me anything of that kind. Half reassured, I think I dozed again; but after a short time—perhaps an hour—a new pain started, and then I was no longer in doubt.

Some movement that I must have made unconsciously roused Sofietka; I felt her fingers on my wrist.

"Stefanie, is anything wrong?"

I told her, "No—I had a dream—that was all. I'm afraid I woke you."

"I don't sleep much. You're sure you're all right? There's nothing I can do?"

"No, I'm quite all right. Do you think it's nearly morning?"

"Morning? I thought the night had only just begun."

The effort of moving set her coughing again, and I think the attack continued through most of that night, depriving me of her companionship. But not of her presence, and that was what I most needed then. As long as I could I would keep it private, this affair of Conrad's and mine; but I had not courage to be quite alone in the darkness.

This was the climax of the long vigil which I had held in jealous solitude, this was the battle itself. I was frightened. The pain at its first assault had not been severe, but it recalled as memory alone can never do the ordeal I had suffered twice before. I had been young then; I thought of the strong, well-nourished body which had once been at my use, and compared it with the instrument which had to serve me now—would it suffice, this scantling of slack muscles and impoverished flesh, for the violent task of forcing a portion of itself apart? Yet fear was matched by an obstinate self-will. As soon as the Kolbecks knew my case I should be under their close protection, and from that moment Conrad would cease to be altogether mine. Until I reached the limit of my powers I would fight this battle by myself.

But suppose he were born before morning: would someone hear his cry if I were past crying, would he find himself alone in this sightless, quivering place? How long, till someone discovered him? How, in this intensity of darkness, would they find and sever the cord; how feed him? And then, what future was there for him if he lived? Live he must! It was not thinkable that my own life should peter out—here, in the corner of a cattle-truck—with its purpose unachieved, that my last gift to Victor should be only the shell of his child. Was it possible that I should survive as well? Or could it be that all I was, the knowing, the feeling, the remembering, must pass into extinction an hour from now because the weak receptacle was broken? I had looked at death with cowardice before—when bombs were falling on the city, when a drunken officer had aimed a rifle at me in the entrance to the prisoner cage. It was not death that I feared now, for—while the second bout of pain was fastening like a toothed trap inside me—I saw it as a merciful presence, ready to hide me in oblivion when I reached the limit of endurance. Only, the thought of it overcame me with such grief as one feels from the death of friends, so that when the pain had drawn off again I found my eyes filling with fresh tears. That Conrad should never hear my voice, that he should go without me on the fearful voyage! What use to give him agonized birth in a world on which the final winter had fallen! Did he want to live, this son of mine, this being I should never know? Would he forgive me for endowing him with life when I had nothing else to give? If the train would stop, if I could have an hour's silence, then my mind would come clear and still; then he might hear my quiet voice, lending him courage, persuading him to accept my gift for the love which had created it. But the wheels below me, which had slowed for an hour, only jerked into fresh animation, and my very thoughts were broken to the jagged rhythm in which my tired head jolted, jolted on the crumpled skirt I had for pillow.

The bubbles of pain returned, withdrew, returned again. Their hold upon me was more powerful now, as if the screw of a letter-press were being turned with increasing strength and clumsiness, and the intervals seemed to be getting shorter. In a moment when I was taken off my guard I let a cry escape.

Almost at once there were movements about me, and soon I felt a hand searching for my head. Then I heard Sandra's voice:

"It's all right, Stefanie; it's quite all right!"

Seldom has human utterance sounded more foolish; and seldom can the power of touch have been more perfectly used. With infinite caution her hand came to rest against my neck, her thumb, which had the coolness and the slight roughness of a stone, began to stroke me beneath my hair.

"It's begun?" she said. "Never mind, liebling, it won't be long; it'll all come right."

She must have roused Wanda, whose voice, a little tired, wholly without emotion, came to me presently out of the wagon's noises —"How long have the pains been going, about? . . . About how often now?"—and who, turning me on my side, began to do a nurse's work on me. "Keep still, Teffy! (It's all right, Mother, they're very blunt.) All right, I'll wait a bit, only then you must keep still." There was reassurance in the authority of her voice, in her professional hands, working in the total darkness as surely as if her fingers had lamps of their own. But it was Sandra who gave me comfort. She used no conscious skill. Mine was an experience she knew, and such understanding as hers needed no other voice than the wrinkled fingers which tirelessly caressed my skin.

I asked Wanda if she knew what time it was.

"Time? I might find the Commander's watch—he's under the other shelf——"

"Do you think it's long till morning?"

"I don't think so, not long."

Perhaps she was right—I don't remember. That night was not

to be measured by the familiar scale of time. I do know it was not long after this exchange that a bout of pain I was expecting seemed to be late and then failed to come at all.

I felt—to begin with—only a serene relief; it was Wanda who fussed, asking me again and again, "Do you feel it now? Don't you feel anything?" In time, feverish and sleepy as I was, I realized what conclusion she had come to. Then I was crying again, in a weary and hopeless fashion. With the train continuously shaking me I could not be certain, but it seemed as if the movement inside my body had entirely stopped; which must mean that Conrad had ceased to struggle, not wishing to live.

v

The darkness divided into moulded forms, along the high shelf on the other side patches of paleness showed, a hand or part of a face. From the ravelled mass below a man got up and picked his way across the rest, hunting for a space where he could stretch his limbs and put on his boots. It became an ordinary day.

Very early the women knew. Here at last was a business each one of them understood, something—the only thing—which could take their minds a little way from their own state. There were some who had hardly stirred from their places on the floor or shelves since the journey began: even these, as soon as it was light enough, hobbled over to get a look at me, and after that there was never a time when I could not see at least two sallow faces peering with lugubrious curiosity from the edge of the shelf. Occasionally I caught sight of Henryk, grinning fatuously but without unkindness; and once I heard him explaining to Issa, "Yes, poor Teffy's having a baby. . . . Yes, it hurts a lot."

These faces scarcely troubled me; they belonged to a life which I seemed already to have left behind. I was suffering new discomforts, an ache in the neck and shoulders, a very great thirst, and these kept me from falling asleep. But the night of wakefulness, and the misery of failure in which it ended, had brought upon me a drowsiness which made all but the closest things appear unreal. It had not yet come home to me that if Conrad had died I must soon die as well; but I had the peculiar feeling which I think may come to the dying—that all reality is contained within themselves. In the narrow sphere where things were still intelligible, Sofietka had first place. When she was not coughing she lay with her face towards me, and now and again, raising herself on her elbow, she managed to straighten the clothes that were rucked under my head or to wipe the sweat from my face with a piece of cloth torn from some garment of her own. She hardly spoke; but whenever I looked that way her eyes would open, and she would smile serenely, as if I were doing something she admired and believed in. This made a difference to me. Her face was colourless, and it must have been soiled with dirt and sweat as the other faces were, yet I remember it as if it had been untouched by illness or by the grime all round us; for these were irrelevant to its power and radiance. I was aware of Sandra's presence too, although it was never obtrusive. All morning she leant against the shelf, silent, seldom making any movement, but keeping one hand lightly pressed against foot or knee, and nodding to me in a simple, confident way when my eyes met hers. Beyond her grey, familiar head, the bunched shoulders in the torn jersey, my senses found nothing that my brain could master. These figures which stayed upright for a time and then flopped on the floor, the man-like faces with unlit eyes, sprawling shapes that still bore a likeness to children, what were they waiting for, crowded together in this shadowed room?

Someone who should have been here was missing. Victor? I had not seen Victor for so long, a man had told me in some field at night that he was dead. Annette—where was Annette? I thought I had seen her face, but that was yesterday perhaps. Someone wearing a jacket I had made for Annette had brought me some water in a little medicine bottle. Was that yesterday too?

Yesterday there had been woods and hills; these had been taken away now, and there was only the brown plain, where the folds of a wide stream showed like tarnished bronze between banks of blackened sedge. A building came which appeared to have strayed from some other country, a cluster of giant pepper-pots, with box-like houses strewn among the ash-heaps for a minute or more on either side; but when these had gone no sign of life remained, no village or farmstead, nothing but a file of concrete poles which drew by degrees towards the blurred horizon. The wind must have followed us that way, for the air seemed still. The sky that I could see, dull white, was naked, and as the sun came to our flank it bore so fiercely on the wagon's side that I had to keep my arm away from the wall. The stench of dried secretions which we carried with us ripened in the increasing heat. The sour, torrid air became more difficult to breathe.

As my thirst increased, my wish to die became as simple and

prosaic as one's longing for a holiday. I never thought of what death might mean. It seemed intolerable that my life, which had no purpose any more, should have to go on so long.

vi

The murmur that went on all day, audible through gaps in the noise of the train, came mostly from women's voices. Only a few words reached me fully shaped.

"It's dead, they say. . . . Well, that's what the old lady told me."

"I don't see how she can. Not without they get a doctor to her."

"Just as well for the poor little thing. What could anyone have done with it?"

"But it's sad, don't you think!"

That was Rosalia's anæmic voice, and it was answered by another that I recognized, the voice of the Star, which vibrated like a tautened wire:

"Well, we've got enough in here, haven't we!"

More than once I heard the gruff voice of Sulkiewicz, "There's nothing I can do?" and Wanda's reply, "No, there's nothing anyone can." It was Wanda, again, who kept asking me a question which at the time I found meaningless,

"Do you feel anything now? No? You're sure?"

She belongs to my recollection of that day less as a person than as part of my material surroundings. She seldom left me; and for long periods her slender, sinewed hands were gently kneading my sides in a way that gave me curious relief. I suppose I was glad to have her there, to know that in this time of utter weakness I was under someone's management. But she remained so impersonal that I felt no gratitude. Her companionship meant nothing to me in those forlorn hours.

I did notice her absence when, for one interval of perhaps half an hour, she did not come near me, and I realized that something out of the ordinary was happening; but my mind explored no further than that. Much later I had some account of the affair from Sandra. Wanda had determined that at the next food halt she should be the one to go with the buckets: she had just a chance, she thought, of approaching the train commander and getting medical help or possibly having me put off the train at some village where a doctor might be found. But the Star had been successful in the draw, and would not be persuaded to give up her turn. A halt came, early in the afternoon. Both women had got themselves near the door when it opened and a scuffle took place. The Star, who was the younger, managed to get free and jumped down, but before the door was slammed Wanda had squeezed through and jumped after her. It was, of course, a useless action. The door was opened again a few seconds later and she was hoisted up and violently forced back into the wagon. It must have been one of the mildest of the guards who was on duty at the door that day: the remarkable thing is that he did not kill her.

As I have said, I did not realize at the time what was going on: people always crowded towards the door at the food halts, there was generally some bickering and much confusion. When I saw Wanda again I could not fail to see that one side of her face was swollen and livid with bruises, but even this did not rouse me to any speculation: people were always bumping their heads against the shelves, one did not see faces in those days which were healthy and clean. She was asking me the same senseless question:

"You still don't feel anything? No new pain?"

Perhaps I should have asked her why her face was bruised, but Rosalia, I remember, came between us just then: her face, appearing beside Wanda's, was solemn and anxious, her damp eyes had the look which had settled there at the start of the journey, that of a righteous woman whom no one would understand. I heard her voice dimly:

"I'm sorry—I don't want to be a trouble, Stefanie. But it isn't easy to look after one's things. You remember—at that camp we were in—I lent you one of my little hankies?"

vii

More than once I recognized among the inquisitive faces the stone-like face of Maria-Josefa, her deeply sunk pale eyes fixed upon me with that look of hunger which often shows in the eyes of the insane. I was relieved when the others elbowed her aside. At times when Sofietka turned away, coughing, the only face I could look at restfully was Sandra's; hers made no demands on me, it was free from curiosity and even from pity as pity is generally seen; she had, rather, the look of an experienced partner, waiting with patience and comprehension till her help should be needed.

When the heads became mere outlines, featureless, in the falling light, the pattern of voices was sharpened to take their place; inquiring, speculating, advising. For a time my brain distractedly pursued them, and then their sound, like a retreating tide, loosened the foothold I had kept on the shore of wakefulness all day. I passed into a garden I knew well. It belonged, as I realize now, to a single-storied house we had lived in near Nowy Sacz when Victor was stationed there. I saw only dimly the brown roofs of the cavalry stables, and the comb of hills beyond, but the pillars of our verandah were near and sharp, the autumn sunshine fell serenely on the stunted pear-trees and the coarse turf where I lay. Here I was trying to explain to Victor that my failure to give him Conrad was not due to my cowardice or lack of will. But the facts refused to be arranged, and while he stood a yard or two away, and watched me steadfastly, I could see that he thought it not worth listening—his mind was always on some business of his own. In desperation I called out loudly:

"Listen! You must listen!"

Once more the answer came in Sandra's voice, "What is it, Stefanie? Have you got the pain again?"

I said, "I can't make him understand!"

"Make who understand?" she asked gently.

"Victor—he won't listen, he never listens to me!"

She said soothingly, "You must be patient, liebling—he'll understand in time."

And at that—I remember—I called out, "He can't—you know he can't! You know that he's dead!"

Were those words a shock to her? Or did she take them for nothing but the froth of delirium? Even now I was hardly awake; but as I recall it the short-breathed voice which came rather wearily was placid, almost devoid of emotion:

"They're not like us, Stefanie, you mustn't expect them to be like us. They don't think like us, they don't ever tell you if they understand. You've got to get used to that when you're married to someone. You've got to be satisfied with the other things he gives you—you mustn't expect him to understand."

That portion of my mind which stayed above the cloud was working with febrile intensity, and I must have realized even then something of what she meant. The huge unhappiness which possessed me, as I drifted back into the sunlit garden, came not from the loss of Conrad alone, but rather from the feeling that my life, sinking now like a starved flame, had been spent without bringing me any return; and as if the picture had at last come into focus, I seemed to see more clearly than ever before that the total failure was due to my total dependence on another being, one who had never the means to respond. But what could I have done? You make yourself, and you cannot enjoy what you have made; you offer it entire for another's enjoyment, and if at last the gift is one he cannot realize, it returns to you lifeless. Was Victor to blame? Or had I been lacking in some talent, some virtue, which love needs for its consecration? Surely there was something I had missed at every stage, a knowledge which should have given experience its meaning, some kind of wisdom which should have gathered and made lasting the warmth and colour of all the separate hours I had delighted in! This sorrow, I thought, was final. Mere mournfulness recedes with bodily change; from the process of loss and failures the mind finds new distractions. Here, in the revelation of life as happiness still-born, wasted endurance, I had come upon grief itself; where the heart's cry is answered by nothing but the echo sounding in its own emptiness. The sunlight was failing now; not as of old, when the long summer evenings passed into sunset, but as in a theatre, swiftly, with the colour draining away. So this was how death came, this was all that happened! I thought that Victor was still near me, but I could not see him any more, and I knew he could not follow me into the darkness. Did no one care enough to come with me as far as this, was there no one on whom I had any claim? I had borne a child once, I had called her Annette. Had someone taken her away? Had she forgotten me, had she died?

"Annette!"

"I'm here, Mother, I'm here!"

"Good-bye, Annette!"

She cried out, "No, you mustn't! Mummy, you mustn't!"

Was it that appeal which had power to recall me? The train had slowed, its noise as I returned to the level of sensation was as if it laboured on a gradient. Not far away a thread of lights was passing.

"Are you awake? Mother, are you awake? I've saved some water for you, I've got it here."

I felt the bottle against my cheek, I drank a little.

"Annette—is that Annette? Where are we? Where have you been?"

She said, with her voice strained and tremulous, "I didn't think you wanted me. I wanted to come, I wanted to all the time."

I could not answer. I was sleepy, I did not understand what had happened. But I found her head close to me, I put my wrist against her cheek, which was hot and damp. For a time we stayed like that, in silence; and it was Sofietka whose voice I heard:

"Stefanie, are you—are you awake? Oh, I'm so glad, so glad!"

Then Sandra again: "Are you all right, Stefanie? Is everything all right?"

I knew that if I slept I should fall still deeper in the darkness which had come upon the garden. That was frightening; but it was easier to yield than to stay in this palsied body which the train was mercilessly jolting. I said bemusedly:

"I'm tired, I can't stay in this train. Did Conrad come? You'll look after Conrad if he comes? Please, Annette, you will look after him?"

"Yes, Mother, yes! Until you're better——"

"I'm tired!" I said again.

She had raised my head to slip something soft beneath it; her small hands seemed to have become curiously strong. Was this Annette? Her voice was a woman's, the face it brought me was the strong, sad face of many young Polish women; here was a stranger, and yet one closer to my understanding than the child Annette had ever been. I wanted to tell her of my gratitude, my love: if there was any barrier between us a word would have forced it now. But when the heart is nearest truth the tongue will no longer serve it; my weariness hung on me like a weighted hood, and the time seemed to have gone.

"Annette!"

"I'm here—what is it, Mother?"

"You'll stay with me?"

"Mother, of course!"

The lights had drawn nearer, moving still more slowly, for a second or two the brilliant beam of a high arc-lamp shone into my eyes. A camp? A mining settlement? The houses labouring into view, growing taller, came close against our track, in fleeting squares of bluish light I saw a man working at some machine, a woman combing her hair. Here our noises hardened, trapped against the walls, and a townish odour, thick and acrid, crept in to join our own. Presently the train pulled up like a horse viciously reined, and began to slide back.

Then a marvel happened. The pains started again.

The first assault was lenient; overwhelmed by relief and thankfulness, I was able to bear it in silence. But the interval which followed was short, and before I had steeled myself for a new attack it came upon me with such violence that I cried out loudly. With the train at rest there was none of the usual noise to cover this cry, and the whole wagon was roused: a babble of voices started, and some of the older women began to whimper in artless sympathy. I heard Sulkiewicz barking "All right, all right, keep quiet there—keep away!" The noise, the sense of emergency, must have filtered through to wagons ahead of ours, for while Wanda and others fussed about me I heard from that direction the sound of people shouting hysterically to be released and thumping on the doors. This kind of uproar had broken out from time to time in earlier stages of the journey. But now there was something new and startling: the sound, close and boisterous, of music.

That bout lasted for a long time and was very severe. It left me exhausted and dazed, as if I had been thrown from a horse at full gallop. Perhaps I was actually unconscious for a few moments: I know I was puzzled to see that fillets of light had appeared on the farther wall.

It seemed that Wanda was once more in control; amid the senseless hubbub the very quietness of her voice made everything she said distinct:

"Mother, hold this, will you! Annette, you must move. Get this behind her shoulders. Get Sofietka moved, can you—turn her the other way!"

My head had slipped from the improvised pillow, my forehead was against the wagon's side, and I seemed to be dreaming again: I saw, not more than a dozen feet away, a lighted room where people were dancing to a rag-time band. Had the journey, after all, taken me back? The student dances in Madame Baudry's basement room had looked much the same as this; there had always been a couple who stood together like those by the window, merely tapping with their feet, and surely the girl in the green silk blouse whose tight skirt stopped at her enormous knees was a fräulein I had known. They seemed so close, the pair now frisking towards me, this soldier with a glass in each hand, that I fancied they must see me; I thought that if I called to them someone would bring me a drink of water. But when the music stopped the only voices I could distinguish were those of my friends, there was Henryk asking sleepily, "What—is Teffy bad again?" and the terse voice of Sulkiewicz— "Anything I can do?"

The pressure of Wanda's hands was shrewd and confident, someone with delicate fingers was stroking my cheek: in the scant light from the gratings above I could just distinguish Sandra's face, a head which perhaps was Sofietka's, figures like rock carvings moving spectrally behind the flattened hillock of my own thighs. These shapes I saw as a falling wrestler must see the gaping crowd, they had ceased to be personal to me; for now there were only two protagonists—myself and pain. The pain, when it took me in its

[256]

hold once more, had turned from senseless force into an animate cruelty, which seemed to be enraged that I had survived so long; and now I should gladly have surrendered, since nothing which eases the body's life was left—all that my senses brought me was nauseation and hardness and thirst. I twisted violently, I screamed. The scream only hurt my lungs, it came to my ears as a fresh and needless ugliness of which I was even then ashamed.

There were voices that broke into the ensuing silence, a woman who sobbed, "It isn't right, I say it isn't right!" and the Star's infuriated voice, "Stop it, I say! I can't stand that! Someone for God's sake stop her!" Then Sulkiewicz's "Steady there! Keep quiet!" But Sandra's voice, which seemed to flow with the rhythmic pressure of her hand upon my side, was perfectly controlled, "Not long dear, now, not long!" I caught the sound of Wanda's quickened nasal breathing as she worked with hands which had grown like steel; I heard her say almost fiercely:

"Go on, Teffy, go on trying—*you must keep on!*"

I gasped, "I can't—it's killing me!" but she scarcely seemed to understand.

"That doesn't matter!" she said.

The spurt of anger pricked by those words did more for me than any kindness: when the will has failed, anger alone will find a residue of strength in a body from which it seems to have drained away. I would see this battle out! The music, growing louder, had changed to the tempo of men victoriously marching, some part of me responded, and I clutched at its power as a surf-rider mounts the incoming wave. Now, as I fought with neck and shoulders thrust against the forward wall, as I yielded and fell limp and rallied and strained again, it seemed as if pain itself was on my side, that the pain and the music were furious horses which I alone could hold together and drive. Time was hostile. In a moment when pain reached the climax of its violence I knew my body was close to the limit of toleration, I knew that darkness was in pursuit and that when it caught me I should not emerge to fight again. This was the last ordeal, to end in victory or total loss: this, if my endurance held, was the terror and triumph of creation. I shouted voicelessly, and the cry resounding through the darkening arena was like the shout of a relieving army: 'I can! I *can*!'

The darkness came as when a lamp is doused by a gale of wind. I do not know what time elapsed before that night was invaded by sensation; but I remember how I thought it strange that even here, beyond the edge of life, you caught some image of the old perceptions—a sense of corporeality, the distant reverberation of drums. That image, growing by degrees more vivid, remained unfocused and liquescent like the substance of hallucination: here was the grey silhouette of a woman's head, here, brightly lit, were the weaving red and green of figures that approached, combined, receded, here a soldier's shape and here a hand that grew immense as it came to wipe the sweat from my eyes. Now, stealthily, pain returned, with the scorching thirst; but this was pain that anyone could have borne, it was only the hot pressure of a tool from which the twist and edge had gone. Was it over, then? Could you die and continue suffering; could you fail and yet live? Through the resurgent music came sounds familiarly shaped, uncertain in direction and strength, ownerless voices: 'A knife will do.' 'Another piece—quick as you can!' 'Keep back—she needs the light!' And afterwards a heavier voice: 'Any chance—the mother, I mean?' My mind received those words only as paper receives the impress of type, but the sound that followed them awoke my understanding: it came to me as the flourish of trumpets, as the sound which broke first upon eternity's silence—a pinched and strident animal cry, the agonized utterance of a human creature brought newly into life.

In the shred of memory which holds that cry there is another human voice; Sofietka's; a whisper as fragile as a flake of snow: "Stefanie! Stefanie, I'm so glad for you!"

viii

I saw the lighted room once more, with the bright dresses floating, then it was drawn away, and the feverish music was crushed beneath the renascent uproar of the train. It seemed as if the continuity of darkness and vibration had not been broken. As the stir within the wagon subsided, there were scraps of talk which stood out like names you recognize in a newspaper— '. . . got milk, she told me so—she was nursing her own child' ;'. . . do something about the body. Yes, she can't have been more than twenty-five'— and these, always evading my tired intelligence, recurred incessantly while the weighted hours laboured across my head. With the slow return of twilight the forest began again. For a while they put Conrad in the curve of my arm, so that his downy hair was against my chin, but at that time I was too weak even to stir and kiss his head. There were faces peering at me all day long, much jabbering. I was happy, though still in pain.

i

THE wagons containing political detainees should not have been attached to our train at all—or rather, they should have been taken off at Kiev. That, at least, was the conclusion of the passengers themselves, some of whom I talked to months afterwards. A patch of fog in the mind of a junior official may have led to a wrong order being given, or the order may have been wrongly transmitted, or a railwayman instructed to uncouple the wagons may have been confused, lazy or drunk at the time. When you are moving a great quantity of people over large distances a mistake of that kind, whereby a few score of them are sent a thousand miles or so beyond their destination, is no great matter. It can be rectified. The order for uncoupling the wagons caught up with the train at Laza-Natinsk, where the rest of its population was being off-loaded; and these wagons had only to wait for eleven days before a westbound train was found with the necessary margin of power to haul them back.

My father-in-law should have made the return journey with the others; and the circumstances in which he avoided doing so, though not so curious or dramatic as many incidents of that time, amused me a little when I came to hear of them.

There was a small factory close to the siding where these 'political' wagons stood, and the Workers' Committee in this factory complained that the smell from the wagons was lowering their productivity. When one considers what the Siberian nose will usually tolerate, it seems a curious complaint; but the N.K.V.D. officer in charge of the trucks evidently took it seriously, and in consequence he arranged for the prisoners to be let out for an hour each morning and evening, in a small enclosure beside the line which was hastily wired for the purpose: the temptations to escape offered by Laza-Natinsk were not overwhelming. Julius, of course, was the one who made the fullest use of this concession: as often as possible he would bribe a passer-by to get him half a bucket of water, and standing at a corner of the enclosure he would take off his shirt for the luxury of a thorough wash. On the third or fourth day a convoy of lorries, tightly loaded with 'agricultural volunteers' from the train, was passing along the road which ran beside the enclosure when one of them came to a stop. The engine had petered out. It was not in Julius to ignore the miscarriage of an operation, however little it concerned him. Naked to the waist, he leaned over the fence and began to give advice to the Kalmuk driver, who had opened the bonnet and was staring at the cylinders, after the fashion of his kind, with an expression of helpless abhorrence. The passengers, many of them children, took no part in the affair; few of them were in a state to care whether they went on or stayed where they were; but during a pause in the discussion, which a passing soldier had joined, the small, hoarse voice of an old woman was suddenly heard saying acidly, "Yes, the Russians mishandle everything. They always did. They always will." It was not hard for Julius to recognize that voice, which was his mother's.

Another man would instinctively have looked up and called to her. Julius did not. He said to the driver, "Wait—I'll get some tools I have, then I can do it myself," and went back to the wagon to get his valise. Then, with a friendly smile to the soldier, he got through the wire and went round to inspect the engine from its other side. The only tool in the valise was, in fact, a pair of nail-scissors, but the driver had at least a spanner, and the fault in the mechanism—something to do with what they call the 'petrol feed'—was not serious: in three or four minutes Julius had the engine running. There were smiles and handshakes, the driver gave a cigarette to Julius, Julius gave it to the soldier. The driver climbed back into his cab. As casually as if he was boarding a train in peacetime, Julius handed up his valise to a man on the lorry and climbed after it himself.

The Countess had watched these proceedings without word or movement. When, with the lorry under way, Julius came to her side, she said, "Is the machine all right now? I thought it was you I saw, only someone had told me you were dead. You'd better put on your shirt." Her voice, he told me afterwards, betrayed a faint acrimony; whether she experienced any other emotion at that time, one cannot tell.

This burlesque of Samaritanism which brought Julius to No. 5 Distribution Camp had another consequence: back at Kiev, where a list of the prisoners despatched from Benylniez was available, and the loss of one of them inevitably came to light, the officer responsible was charged with negligence and shot the same day. By all accounts he was an agreeable if rather stupid fellow. I cannot pretend ever to have felt deeply about the fate of N.K.V.D. officials. But the fact that some clerk in an office fourteen hundred miles away from Laza-Natinsk kept accurate lists of names was to prove important for Conrad and me.

ii

I do not remember the occasion when Julius again became part of my surroundings. For that matter, I have virtually no recollection of No. 5 Camp at all. The road journey which took me there started in darkness, and the picture I retain of a long file of headlamps must belong to the moments when Sulkiewicz and Henryk were lifting me from the wagon into the lorry. Close to that, but in sunlight, comes the fleeting memory of a high gate made from many strands of wire—like that of the Setory cage—with soldiers of Mongolian appearance standing beside it. The rest has gone from me.

We were there, I suppose, for three or four weeks, but in all that time my hold on life was slender, and I still enjoyed the calm which death affords to those who sail close to its shore. There were no demands upon me, not even the duty to stay alive; and in that peculiar liberty I would not exert the will-power needed to reinstate my ties with former experience, to put names and meanings to the faces which came into view. I know, for instance, that in those days Wanda was constantly beside me (or rather, above me, since there was only a blanket between me and the ground), but had I been told, afterwards, that she was absent throughout this period I should have accepted that statement without question. There were but two presences which came within my understanding, in such a way that I knew them without the effort of recognition—Conrad's, and Annette's. These seemed to be part of me, as my body was; no nearer or less near, neither more nor less necessary.

The flow of time was so gentle that it scarcely seemed to be moving, and the alternation of night and day affected me no more than the quiescent pain to which my body was still yoked: the variation which mattered was between the hours of solitude and those when Conrad was brought to lie at my side. There was little animation in our companionship: I had no milk for·him, and since my body had lost its obedience my caresses came to no more than a touch of the fingers against his skin. But we did not need such activity to express our understanding. I think that my love for him was less possessive, less purely maternal, than the feeling a mother generally has for a child newly born; for this was someone I seemed to have known for a long time. Asleep, he was comparatively a stranger: his head, peculiarly small, was almost elderly in the shape of cheeks and brow, and with the fairness of his scanty hair, the tiny mouth's severity, he often appeared to be no more than an amusing miniature of his grandfather. But when he opened his eyes, and the wizen face became alive, that semblance vanished: now—always with a fresh surprise—it was Victor I saw watching me, and the lips which tightened and relaxed as if he were trying to speak to me were Victor's. He did not often cry—you could not have expected tears from this, the grey, wise face of a creature born to privation; but behind his stoic solemnity I thought I discerned a latent vigour, a trembling impatience to be freed from the bonds of babyhood. Here was the very look that Victor had worn on days when he came home, sullen with rebellion, after some abortive battle with authority; the inarticulate anger, the desire for understanding which pride forbade him to ask for. In these smoke-coloured eyes, in the wrinkled brows, the faintly twitching underlip, I saw a person who knew and needed me; and this was all I needed.

I have wondered since then whether the deaf and the feeble-minded enjoy a peacefulness which compensates them for the experience they are deprived of. How little I suffered in those days from the lack of what we think of as communication. I did not want to talk to Conrad, my pleasure in him did not need to be defined. And although I realized that Annette often spoke to me, sometimes asking me questions, I suffered no disquiet in failing to identify the sounds she made. When her face came close to mine I felt myself smiling in response to her gentleness, and I was conscious—dimly, as perhaps small children are—of gratitude, for she seemed always to realize what I wanted; if I felt her hands behind my shoulders I knew I should be moved to a position of greater comfort, and again and again when I was thirsty I would find her holding a tin of sweetened milk to my lips. I had no anxiety about making a return for so much goodness. Lacking all power to do so, I accepted my feebleness as children accept theirs.

It was only at a later period that I realized, piecing these cloudy memories, the extent of what she had done to preserve my life in those critical weeks. I asked her then, with curious shyness, how she had procured so many comforts for me—the blankets, medicines, palatable food; to which she answered rather constrainedly that she had put my case to the commandant of the camp, who had been sufficiently sympathetic to release special supplies. This seemed to me an odd statement, since the others spoke of that man as of a miniature Genghis Khan. I assumed that she had stolen the luxuries; and I was surprised that she should be so reticent about the achievement, when we had long ceased to think of theft as anything but a virtuous practice.

iii

It must have been at Czennik, the place we came to next—four or five hundred of us, shifted by lorry in relays—that my mind and body began to resume their old relationship; for although we were only there for a few days, I left it with a clear impression of its general appearance. It was the last town we were to see.

'Town'? It was a large place: from the hutments which for centuries (I suppose) had cluttered the river bank a more recent growth of wooden dwellings was spread like lichen across the steppe; and where a lately gravelled road broke through to the barge wharfs, a line of market booths between the police barracks and the new, one-storied concrete houses gave you some faint semblance of a Polish urban scene. From the mudflats on the other side of the river, where we were corralled, the life of that dingy street looked busy and cheerful, if a little unreal. Turning your eyes up-river or down you saw, in the clear light, so huge an extent of naked country that it seemed to be limitless, and you had the impression that all the litter of boats and hovels before you was the wrack from a tidal bore, which the river would presently recover and bear away.

In the early mornings the fetid mist that lay upon the water hid most of the town as well, but in those few days we must have had a measure of sunshine: the most persistent memory they left with me was of a warm, level wind which, as it drove small waves of dust and rubbish across the flats, brought with it an odour of soil and space, luxurious to us who had lived in exile from the earth's sweetness. Besides that recollection there are fragments, grotesquely magnified like the images of a dream—the weatherbeaten portraits flapping from the underside of a wrecked omnibus, slogans scrawled immensely on a rusty iron fence—which must owe their ascendancy in my mind to another season. I was to see Czennik again; and among the places which have counted for something in my life, that perfunctory extension of the civilized world so dominates the rest that it gives them almost the pallor of insignificance.

Others to whom I spoke of it a year or two later scarcely remembered the place, though a number of them told me of friends who had died there, from a kind of weariness which was attacking people at that time.

13

i

YES, when I left Czennik for the first time I knew intuitively that I should return there. Or at least I believe so now— it may be nothing but imagination, influenced by the special nature of those years. The mechanism which, in any backward view, brings the landmarks closer together operates more powerfully when the spaces between are almost featureless.

At one stage of our eastward journey, when we had passed through two or three days without seeing a village or a tree, I had Ludwig Radznowski beside me in the lorry, and he was talking about Sofietka with that mordant gaiety which never ceased to make me uneasy. ". . . . I expect the body is still lying where they dumped it off the train. They're wasteful, these people, they're careless about raw material." Sandra—I think it was—leant over and spoke to him.

"You ought to remember, Doctor, you and she will be together again in Eternity."

"Eternity?" he said. "Surely that's where I've arrived already— and my wife has dodged it. Surely eternity's the very thing one wants to avoid—if I were a man of any courage I'd escape from it straight away. I see no point whatever in an existence which has no boundaries. Do you, Stefanie?"

I did not answer. No one understood his meaning better than I, no one knew more acutely how, when the centre of one's life is extinguished, the passage of time becomes a futility, as if one sailed on a borderless sea; and here, with the framework of what we understood by living left far behind—the work we had once been used to, letters, news—one was almost persuaded that time had ceased to move. Yet I could not see the future entirely with his frozen eyes, as a space with no possible horizon. Puny as Conrad was, I could feel already the increase of his body's weight and firmness. I was not convinced that there would be no world into which he should grow.

I think he had some pleasure from the summer. He was not one who smiled often or who crowed as other babies do; but when the day was clear, and the sun not yet very strong, he would turn his face towards the sky and his body would stretch a little—hē seemed to open himself as flowers do to the generosity of light. At those times the nervous restlessness which so often commanded him was stilled, and I could see he was content.

He was not beautiful; the look of an old man that he had been born with was slow to leave him. But I had not desired a pretty child, to be petted and adored, I had wanted a human being formed to belong to me, a man in little who would accept by degrees the service of my love that Victor had left so little used; one who would grow to be my companion, to discover and fulfil the purpose of which my life had been defrauded. He satisfied that need, as far as so small a person could; so well, indeed, that I sometimes fancied he was dimly conscious of the part I had designed for him. In the frown that he wore so often I saw an incipient determination, his grip on my fingers seemed intimate and urgent, he had a man's way of suddenly shaking his head as if to clear his brain of some obstruction. Once, when I was being beaten up by a Kazak foreman, I saw his whole body stiff and trembling as he lay on the ground a few feet away. That, I suppose, was from natural fear, but at the time I thought he was raging at his impotence to protect me. I believed— I still believe—that he knew me as someone distinct from all the other bodies which came into his experience.

It was well for him that Maria-Josefa's milk, poor as it was, continued for so long. Naturally I was jealous, but I had just enough sense and gratitude not to betray such feelings, or to make a fuss about her slovenliness. It was Rosalia who complained.

"I'm sorry, Stefanie, but I think it's wrong! I think it's quite wrong that a woman like that should be allowed to feed your baby. You don't know what she may have. Her hair—have you really looked at her hair?"

This was foolishness. If Rosalia's person was free from every kind of parasite at that time, then nature must have made her of material different from ours, and I doubt if her own hair would have borne close inspection. To be fair, though, she kept it in good order; she guarded comb and pins as others guard a talisman, at every halt she was gathering the wisps that had strayed and dexterously replacing them in the many-storied chignon which seemed to symbolize her rank, her attitude, her century. You would not have mistaken her even now for anything but a lady, in the fin-de-siècle use of the term. Her shoes, like ours, scarcely hung together, and the shapeless gaberdine coat she wore (once Henryk's property) was dirty and torn; but she had her brooches still, and the remains of a grey tulle scarf which must have belonged to the early days of motoring, and as she stumbled back to the lorries from some hovel where we had spent the night she would hold her garments close to her in the way of a gentlewoman crossing the pavement from her town house to her carriage. She was a lonely member of our society, but then she had always been so; and I have an idea she was less unhappy than she had been for a long time, because the part she played had developed into one where she could lose herself. She felt, I think, that she was guardian of sanctities which the rest had forgotten; that however little we followed her lead she was performing a transcendental duty by remaining what she was, a woman of birth. Her eyes had become a little vague, the eyes of one who waits with aristocratic patience for some small trouble to be rectified; and the gentleness of her speech had grown into a certain preciosity, as if she were caricaturing her own refinement.

"Of course, Maria-Josefa may be an admirable woman of her kind. And you know I never interfere with any of the Kolbeck arrangements. It's only that one has special feelings about a Kolbeck child. Perhaps my cousin Alexandra doesn't feel exactly the same. Of course I shouldn't dream of mentioning the matter to her. . . ."

But it was Janina, the girl we called the Star, who really detested Conrad's nurse. I cannot imagine what reason this foolish creature had for regarding Conrad as belonging in some way to her; but she did. She talked to him as *her* little one, *her* precious, she never missed a chance to manage him, to carry him about, and once when she thought I was asleep I even saw her putting his mouth to her own small, arid breast. Naturally she hated to hand him over to another female; and while Maria-Josefa was nursing him she would stand a foot or two away, biting her nails and glaring at the honest woman with sullen fury.

"Why do you let her!" she demanded of me one night. (This was in the squalid camp at Zetnizinsk.) "That dirty creature! What good do you think it'll do him, anything that comes from her!"

[267]

"I think I can decide what's best for my own son," I told her.

"Colonel Kolbeck's wife," said Rosalia virtuously, "must make her own arrangements."

And for some reason that mild interjection provoked the girl to a more dangerous anger.

"She can't," she snapped, "she isn't capable! Look at her, she's hardly sane! He's finished now, anyway. Here, you, give him to me! At once—do you hear!"

"No!" said Maria-Josefa, quietly but stubbornly. "He isn't ready!"

"Oh, isn't he!"

At that time I was still too feeble to risk a struggle with Janina. She would have tried to drag Conrad away, and Maria-Josefa might have fought with her, had her voice not roused Wanda, who was sleeping at the other side of the shelter. In an instant Wanda was on her feet.

"What's that? What's all this?"

"It's all right!" I told her.

"That lady," said Maria-Josefa, carelessly nodding towards Janina, "she wants to take the baby away."

"Filthy creature!" Janina said under her breath.

"That'll do!" said Wanda. "You're to mind your own business, do you understand! Stefanie, if she makes herself a nuisance you're to tell me."

She said that tonelessly, and the eyes with which she looked at Janina might have belonged to the dead. It was enough. No one argued with Wanda now.

Later on there was more than one scene of the same kind, and I was often afraid of Conrad's suffering physical harm from Janina's jealousies. But in truth Maria-Josefa herself was strong enough to protect him. She was a creature of extreme simplicity, normally so silent that I often found myself addressing her by signs, as one would with a foreign servant. Some said that she imagined Conrad to be her own, confusing him with the child she had lost at the start of the journey. I do not think so. In my view she accepted him not even as substitute but simply as a means to use the capacity with which nature had endowed her. The most vivid picture I have of her belongs to an evening when our convoy pulled into a wired enclosure. (It was a transit station with a large floating population of deviationists and ordinary civil and military convicts, as well as Polish 'volunteers'.) We had been moving since early morning—

sixteen hours, perhaps—and when we halted Maria-Josefa had just begun to give Conrad his evening feed. As usual, we were ordered to get off the lorries smartly, and I told her that she had better interrupt the feed and continue it when we were settled for the night. She shook her head: no, that would not be good for the child. I stayed beside her, and presently the Tartar corporal who had charge of us at that stage arrived with a lamp. This man had a face so pocked and scarred that it was scarcely recognizable as human, and I had seen him laying about with his rifle whenever he felt inclined. What were we doing, he demanded. Hadn't we heard the order?

I said to Maria, "We'd better go. There'll be trouble."

"The baby hasn't finished," was all she replied.

I thought the Tartar would go for her, and I got ready to put up the best defence I could. But he didn't; he stood where he was with his lamp shining on her, as a farmer might stand to watch his animals at the trough. She, for her part, took as little notice as if he were not there. With her eyes fixed on Conrad's head she was practising the nurse's craft with the slowness it demands, sometimes skilfully pressing her lank breast to increase the flow, now and then raising Conrad to her shoulder to bring up his wind; when her straggling hair fell against his cheek she jerked it clear, but the rest of her broad, squat body remained as still as if it were modelled in clay. From her face, as I saw it then, you could have guessed her age as twenty-five or fifty; a primitively stupid face, heavy, square-jowled, where cheeks and eye-pits might have been cut from the skull with mallet and wedge. But in this close, yellow light, which hardened all the shadows, I did not see its coarseness, I saw only the dignity which belonged to its power and quiescence, the absorption of the desolate eyes.

This image, intrinsically no more unusual than a sunrise, remains with me just as my first view of certain masterpieces remains. For the rest, I have no general recollection of that station, which had the same feel as half a dozen others where the trek was broken; but it was the theatre of one more incident, an affair of seconds only, which a narrow beam of memory still lights distinctly. We were being herded past a line of men who stood with their backs against a fence, tins in their hands—I suppose they were waiting for a food issue—and who, though some wore remnants of Polish military uniform, appeared too ill and apathetic to notice us at all. To this there was an exception. A man who I think was young, though his hair and beard were grey, looked up as I came near him, took a step towards me and peered at my face. He said, with something like a stammer:

"... Kolbeck—you're the Colonel's wife!"

I said, "Yes ..."

He hesitated, still staring at me as if at an apparition. I realized that he was someone I had known—perhaps a subaltern who had once attended our dinner-parties at Nowy Sacz; but I could not identify him, and I cannot do so now.

"I was with him——" he began. But he got no further: a guard who had seen him step out of the line came up at the run and pushed him back against the fence with a jab in the groin, while I was hustled on with the rest of my party. I made some effort to find him again next morning, but with no success. Probably he had been moved on already.

It was really an unfortunate encounter, because it set my imagination working in a way I did not wish. For months afterwards I wondered what he had been going to say, so that the memory became an itch upon my mind, a fine thread pulling my thoughts back to the life which there was no hope of recovering.

iii

Was I alone in that? Were the others still feebly hoping that at some time to come the wheels would start turning the other way, restoring to us that bygone existence which, however remote, was always more credible than this?

"When we get home," Sandra said, "I am going to turn my little room downstairs—you know, the one near the kitchen—I am going to turn it into a new study for the General. The one he uses now has always been a draughty room."

The cart which sometimes collected the feebler of us women had failed to appear that day, and she and I chanced to be side by side as we trudged back to the settlement from the field where we had been stooking all afternoon. I remember that—I remember how it looked, a sharp bend of the rutted track which we were approaching, and the expression of schoolma'am importance on her tired face as she spoke.

"It wouldn't be very expensive, there's the carpet that used to be in the morning-room, that could be cut down, it's only the border part that was worn." She grew doubtful then. "I suppose I shall find it again. I can't remember—those soldiers, that Captain Bautz, the one who was nearly a gentleman, he came and asked me to find him a carpet. I'm not sure which one I gave him."

She talked very often of that little plan. In the shieling where a score of us were quartered during those harvest months we could never get rid of bugs; they gave us restless nights, and often, in the earliest morning, one would find Sandra moving about and holding conversation with anyone who would listen. "I was discussing it with the General yesterday. I don't feel quite sure that he likes the idea; of course he's got used to his old room. . . ." But I never knew if she really believed in what she was saying. When she talked to me her eyes were usually directed away from mine, but when she glanced at my face I saw a look of uncertainty—one which, in another person, I might have described as sly. It was perhaps a kind of challenge, this chatter of Setory, an obstinate refusal to accept the statement of events; or she may have felt, in the abstruse workings of her mind, that if she could draw us others into her kingdom of illusion we might give it some kind of substantiality.

She had no encouragement from Wanda, who answered all such talk with the careless tolerance that mothers show to the romancing of young children. From Annette and from me she won at least a respectful hearing—we did our best to treat her chimerical problems as if they were serious. But Rosalia, who was surely of the age to show some sympathy, would never trouble herself so far as that.

"No, Alexandra," Rosalia would answer listlessly, "no, I can't remember the carpet you speak of." And she would add, almost without a pause, "I remember a very beautiful carpet my mother had, it came from Kerman, very valuable; it was given to my grandmother by the Archduke of Saxe-Weimar-Eisenach. One of my governesses spilt some ink on it—that was a terrible distress to my mother. Of course, you find girls of very good character taking posts as governesses, but then they have no appreciation of artistic things—naturally, they have never been taught to value them."

For if Sandra looked to us for reassurance, Rosalia had no need of it. Governesses and their shortcomings were a subject much on her mind at that time, but if she had graver anxieties her face did not reveal them. *Her* world was secure. There were disturbances of which she must have been conscious, but, following to the extreme the custom of her sex and generation, she never dwelt upon matters which seemed to be outside her understanding. Her attitude resembled a little that of cattle in the auction ring, which are so much accustomed to the alarmingness of men that the noisy crowd escapes their observation.

Sometimes she did complain about trivialities. A trench had been dug close to our hut for everyone's use, and she made a fuss with the Settlement Overseer about the smell that came from it. This man was a native, perhaps not fundamentally ill-natured, but cruel in the boisterous fashion of schoolboys; if the trench offended her, he said, she could empty the contents into another one, thirty yards away; and since I was on the punishment list (for some offence I have forgotten) I was detailed to help her, together with a girl called Nonolka, a Russian civil convict of tough physique who had piqued the Overseer by voluntarily sleeping with one of his rivals. This Nonolka was as good-hearted as a perfectly brainless creature can be, but she belonged to that fervent, primitive school of Leninist-Marxists which has no use for such as Rosalia, and through the five hot hours in which we toiled she did not cease to jeer at her.

"I suppose where you come from, the trenches all smell like flowers! I suppose the workers aren't allowed to use them at all—only allowed to come and have a sniff on Celebration Days!"

Her mockery had as well been addressed to the demented Uzbek youth who was supposed to be superintending us: Rosalia appeared not even to hear it. She was making no attempt to carry the loaded bucket, but on every journey she walked beside me while I did so, waited for me to empty it, and politely carried it back. Standing at the edge of the noisome trench, with her face discreetly averted, she delicately lowered the bucket into the sludge, and then, with a small, gracious smile, as one who hands her horse's reins to a stable-boy, passed the rope to Nonolka to haul it up again; talking to me all the time.

"Of course they're very strong, these young girls. This one is Russian, I think. These Russian girls, they can be trained as nursery-maids, as long as one has patience—sometimes they get to be quite satisfactory. But not as governesses! Oh dear, no, you must never have a Russian governess! I mean, they have no culture, you couldn't expect that. And of course what they regard as their religion is just as wrong as the Lutherans'."

And late that night I heard her going all over the subject again with Annette: "... I was helping one of those girls, those Russian girls—some of them are quite nice-looking and very willing—one ought to help them as much as one can. I think she would like to come to me as a governess, but I've had to say 'no' to that. I'm not sure if your mother quite agrees with me, but then, you know, I have seen a great deal of the world. I mean, living among a particular kind of people—the diplomatic circle and so on—one can't help acquiring a certain savoir-faire. . . . Annette dear, you do realize, don't you, how tremendously important it is—you really cannot be too careful in the matter of choosing governesses. . . ."

You would have said there was opportunity, in that torrid and sterile summer, to know one's friends. In this colony of perhaps three hundred souls, the majority alien to us in either blood or manners, we were much in each other's company, we who had been hatched from the same railway wagon. Through most of the daylight hours we moved together, a ragged platoon, in the track of the Kleinschmidt reapers, we stood together in the food-line, slept in two narrow rooms. Besides, there was not much else to explore, for the field we worked in was bounded only by the junction of haze and ashen sky, while the settlement itself was nothing but a string of hovels lining a single road. Yet I doubt—from that experience—if either propinquity or boredom is the gateway to understanding. It may be that intrinsically people do not alter: that the changes in their circumstance only discover attributes which were there already, putting others out of use. But here the landmarks had all gone; and as you acclimatized yourself to the life of a lower creation—looking for no other luxuries than sleep and some refuge from the sun—while your friends were doing the same, you had to learn them afresh, as if you were meeting in later life the companions of your childhood. We took some pride, perhaps, in preserving our secrecies: there was little else that remained of our title to individuality. And perhaps it shows some virtue in the human creature, as well as vanity, that he will not expose the cancers of his mind, lest he put his fellows to the risk of infection.

That sense of obscured familiarity, most palpable in my dealings with Julius and with Wanda, entered no less into my new relationship with Annette; which, in the main, was easier than the old. With a child—which she had been when I had taken her to Setory a year before—you pretend to be the kind of person he or she would expect: as far as possible you disguise your mediocrities. The time for such pretence was past now, and we could associate almost upon equal terms. Certainly she had ceased to need my care and protection. I did not resent that. Only, as with other changes which life imposes, I wanted time to get accustomed to her independence.

Strangely, starvation had not checked her upward growth, and she had nearly reached my own height. You saw, of course, the results of privation in her lack of flesh, the bones of her face were far too prominent, her chest and thighs pitifully lean; and yet there was strength in the thin legs and arms, and her skin, browned by many weathers, gave sometimes at least the semblance of robustness. From her earliest days her head had been of the Kolbeck cast, the cheeks flat and high, the brow protrusive; and now the poverty of flesh served to emphasize the nobility of its structure. I thought her beautiful, in the Polish way—with the sad severity of Polish women, who have nothing passive in their femininity. This was not the kind of creature with whom an idle man would fall in love, but a perceptive one would choose her and be rewarded by no commonplace devotion. To me she was companion and support, a person to laugh with when any thread of amusement could be drawn from the large futility surrounding us; in our gentlest hours a beloved friend. Intermittently our shyness continued. We walked sometimes warily, in the way of someone still learning to trust a leg which was recently broken. There were times, indeed, when I was hurt a little by the way in which she seemed to hide from me. But I told myself that if the sickness between us was not yet fully healed the fault had not been hers.

Our small society, as I see it now, was one that lacked structure and cohesion. This was because we had no leadership. In everyday affairs—in the bargainings for food and house-room, the incessant wrangles with our keepers—we generally had Wanda as our spokesman, but she was not concerned to bind us together. It was Julius who should have done that, and he appeared at this time to have neither mind nor heart for it. In the weeks of separation he must have experienced a solitude which we had been spared, and something was lost of his power of communication. He took at least his share of work and of discomforts, he attended—if more slowly than before—to practical things. But at other times he was wont to look at us, in silence, as the very old or sick do; as if he could not remember what claim we had on his attention.

iv

Often he seemed to prefer the society of a Lithuanian priest—a sorry specimen quartered with a native family along the road—to that of his own people. He was considerate with Sandra, who perhaps had never learnt to ask more of him than that, and with his mother he exercised a greater patience than any of us commanded. But it was—I thought—the soldier in him who discharged these obligations, as soldiers are trained to follow their routine even in a state of exhaustion: the man himself was far away. Surprisingly, he behaved more humanly with me than with anyone else; he had more than a grandfather's normal interest in Conrad, and it may be that he attached some value to me as Conrad's custodian.

There was a kind of illness which afflicted a number of men (but fewer women) in that settlement; it was talked of as 'the dullness', and you recognized it in the sufferer's face, in the emptiness of his eyes, the loosened mouth, sluggish responses. Most of us must have wondered if Julius had become a victim of this disease. If so, he was finished: in the physical sense he might live for a while, but the person he had been a year before, the man who commanded himself when all other authority was denied him, would not return.

We wondered, I say, if he had come to that condition. But I myself was inclined not to believe so. Even if I could not see the former presence, I felt it; and something that happened towards the end of our time at that place was enough to tell me that my intuition was not mistaken.

It must have been early in September that we were visited by one of the Organizational Sections which travelled round the settlements, mainly to collect particulars about us—our former lives, capacities, political affiliations—which had been recorded a dozen times before. They arrived early in the morning. At that hour every able-bodied person—a term which embraced both Sandra and the one-legged Ludwig—was supposed to be at work in the fields, while a handful of very old women was left to look after the babies and younger children; in practice, we always managed to leave one or two competent people behind by muddling the dull-witted fellow who counted us into the carts, and on this occasion Wanda, suffering from carbuncles on the hip, was released by those means. In the evening we were all assembled in the wagon shelter for 'political education', and while we waited for the lecturer I heard Ludwig asking her if she had seen anything of the Organizationals.

"Those people?" she said. "Oh yes, two of them came nosing about."

"All the usual questions?"

"More or less. Names and occupations. I gave them a list for the house."

"What did you tell them I was? I nearly always say 'Professional Wrestler'. They accept that, as a rule."

She almost smiled. Those two had formed the habit of treating

[275]

each other as if both were men, and he, who himself had lost the power of smiling, was the one person who occasionally drew a smile from her. But she said bleakly:

"I don't play the fool with those cattle. It's wasting time."

They were talking in low voices, and I thought that no one else was listening. We were all startled when the Countess, who seldom seemed aware of anything that was happening around her, asked sharply:

"What did you tell them about my son?"

"I said he'd been moved somewhere else," Wanda answered shortly. "I said I didn't know where. It'll be something to occupy them, following that up."

"But they'll check up with the Overseer," I objected.

"I've seen about that," she said. "Anyway, it's none of your business."

Julius was close to us, sitting on the ground with his head between his knees. He suddenly looked up and stared at Wanda as if she were some underling who had come into his office without leave.

"You'll please correct that!" he said. "You'll please find the Overseer as soon as possible and tell him you made a mistake."

Wanda, startled, said, "I don't see why, Father."

"And in future," he added, "you will not make any decisions of that kind without consulting me."

Just then the civil convicts began shouting at us to be quiet—the lecturer was arriving. Julius dropped his head, and I did not hear the subject discussed again.

Next day, when he was working near me, he had relapsed to his former insensibility; it was hard to believe that the outburst had ever occurred. But the memory of those few angry words convinced me that his apathy had not become inherent, and—leaving aside a small, malicious satisfaction in hearing Wanda so snubbed—I was curiously glad of this assurance. However little I had cared for his autocracy, I could not wish that he should cease to be a man at all.

It was not long afterwards that the wall of silence in which he kept his inward being was breached more widely.

v

Early in autumn—at the close of September, I think, but we were without calendars and the weather in that longitude is no guide—we were moved north and eastward again. There was work for us, they vaguely said, in the region beyond Kysnansk. About seventy people—the majority Poles—were ticketed for this destination, and we travelled in carts, all the serviceable lorries in the area having been allotted to other migrations. It made the journey a long-drawn affair, but this did not seem to matter; towards the end of the second day's travelling the birch plantations ceased, and in the featureless extent which followed time once more lost all significance.

There was a constant northerly wind across the steppe: it blew so evenly that in the daytime (when one's senses were mostly occupied with the various discomforts of the springless carts) it was hardly perceptible; but when the sun went low this wind grew very cold, and at places where we bivouacked our escort of Kirghiz-Kazaks made fires of dung and scrub for their own comfort which —since they were not incapable of humanity—they let us share. Had I been well fed I should have enjoyed those hours. To be still was pleasure. The vastness of the steppe, forlorn and hostile in daylight, was brought by dusk at once to majesty and gentleness. I could imagine that the dead were there, that in this infinity of space Victor and I might at last be together, at peace; and even when darkness closed upon it, leaving only the sound of the wind drawing ceaselessly across its surface, I could feel its presence, like the presence of the sea, surrounding our shrunken world. A world becalmed. The incessant voices of the Kirghizi, clustered all together, made a stream of sound as patternless as the wind itself, and the desultory talk of the prisoners, numbed from hours of merciless jolting, was gradually subdued by sleep. Even the child Issa, for ever fretful and demanding, would allow Henryk to soothe her then, and would fall asleep with her head on his thighs. Only Conrad was wakeful, and he contented; wrapped against me in a coat of Julius's, he gazed soberly at the dark display in the triangle of smouldering fires, at the flags of smoke curling above an intricacy of muffled bodies, faces which showed for an instant, still and strangely, in a spurt of flame.

On those nights I came to doubt if Ludwig slept at all. He used to limp off by himself into the darkness and return very late to join our group, using his crutch so skilfully that I did not hear him until he was beside me; then he would wrap himself in a blanket that Wanda kept for him, and lie on his back, quite still, but if I saw his face during the night his eyes were always open. At any hour he would start talking, as a rule to Wanda, in the inconsequent way of a child delaying its bedtime; and it was his chatter, once more, that pierced the shell of lethargy in which Julius was living.

"I suppose," he was saying, in the thin, drawling voice which had lost all its humour for me, "I suppose all this is doing some sort of good to the Russians. What good I can't quite see—but then I suffer from having no intellectual equipment beyond the narrow mind of a scientist."

Julius was in his usual position, sitting with his back against a pile of baggage. Without moving he said abruptly:

"Good to the Russians? What are we doing for Poland, that's the question I'm asking."

"Ah, Poland, yes!" Ludwig said gently, in no way discountenanced. "There used to be such a place, I remember. I believe I once lived there. An agreeable country; a pity it was found necessary to abolish it."

Wanda said rather sharply, "That's a silly joke, Ludwig. You know perfectly well that we shall be back there one day."

"Indeed?" he said. "You think we shall all just carry on where we left off?"

Julius said deliberately, "It's not a question of opinion, Dr Radznowski. Poland is eternal, its soil is waiting for us. And until we go back we have Poland with us here—here, in our hearts."

"I'm sorry," Ludwig said, "but for me Poland belongs to the past, it no longer exists."

(I suppose we all knew what he meant. But could anyone else trace his thoughts as closely as I did, I who had lain beside Sofietka through so many nights, feeling the touch of her fingers, hearing her small voice?) There was nothing to be answered. It must have been Janina who said naïvely:

"But of course we shall all go back to Poland after the War!"

The War? That consolidation of *Wehrmacht* on the western side of Europe, of which some gossip had followed us as far as Czennik, did that concern us still?

"By then, please God, we shall all be dead," Ludwig said shortly.

As if he were talking to himself, Julius murmured, "After the War? I'm not going to wait as long as that."

"What do you mean, Father?" Wanda asked.

"I don't say I shall get back to Poland. But I shall go as far as I can. I don't mean to stay in these pastures."

"But what else can you do?"

"What else? It's simple enough, isn't it! There's a charge against me. I've only got to tell the next Jack-in-office who comes along that I got through the fence at Laza-Natinsk."

"As likely as not," Ludwig said, "they'll express their keenest interest and leave it at that."

"Well, perhaps you know the Russians better than I do! Only I was in Russian prisons before you were born."

"But what's the good?" Wanda asked wearily; and then with anger, "Father, whatever good do you think could come of that?"

The slight rise in her voice was enough to stir Sandra, who was sleeping close to Julius's feet. She sat up at once.

"What is it, dear, can't you sleep? Look, you must have this blanket; I don't need it, I'm perfectly warm now."

Wanda said, "I'm not cold, Mother." Then, "Father says he's going to report himself as soon as he gets a chance. He wants them to take him back."

Sandra lay down again. She said drowsily, "You must leave all that to your father, dear. You're sure you're quite warm?"

We both, Wanda and I, were affected by that voice as in our earliest years, when we had taken as absolute her authority and wisdom. There was nothing more to say. My eyes closed, and I drifted back to that clouded state which serves the hungry in place of sleep, the gently coloured country which my mind had conjured for Victor and me to enjoy together: the rumbling voice of the Kirghizi only soothed me, as the noise of shingle raked over by the sea, the sound of fidgeting from the horse-lines was safe and familiar like the scrape of a dog's chain outside your home. But the ponderous wheels of Sandra's mind must have gone on turning, for after a little while I heard her speaking again:

". . . But Julius, I don't understand! You know what they're like, those people—they don't mind what they do. It's only by God's mercy they didn't kill you before. You can't *want* to be killed."

And afterwards Julius's voice, weary, like that of a boy who is too much scolded:

"I've got to get that business settled. I was a fool to run away."

They spoke as if in private—they may have imagined the rest of us were asleep. But much of the need for privacy is a habit belonging to life within walls, it diminishes beneath the open sky. In the current of sensation where the murmur of uneasy sleepers, the horses' bickering, were wrapped together by the scouring wind, I did not feel it strange to hear Sandra saying with naked simplicity:

"I know it doesn't mean anything to you, my wanting you to stay. It never counts for anything—our love—women like me."

Those words sank into a silence which might have let me drowse again; but Wanda was awake—I suppose she had not slept—and her voice, however quiet, was never one to which I could close my ears. She said, as if reflectively:

"So Poland isn't to matter, Father, after all! You only want to settle some business of your own."

"What do you mean?" he asked.

"You know what Poland's like now—you know at least as well as I do. You know it's in ruins, it's a dead country. Well, dead men are not going to bring it back to life."

"No!" he said.

"Well?"

"Neither are old men. I count myself old now. It will be done. But not by us—not by me. By another generation."

"Me?"

"You'll do your share. What a woman can."

"And Henryk?"

He let that pass without reply.

"Victor's dead," she said. "He must be. It's no use trying to imagine he's not."

"There's Victor's son."

"And Poland must wait for him to grow up? Do you think if he ever gets to be a man he'll even realize what Poland is, what it has been?"

"He's a Kolbeck," Julius said. "You don't learn to love your country by reading books. Poland's a mystery, you learn it with your heart."

"But you yourself," Wanda said acridly, "you're bored with it, you want to give it up!"

I thought—although I could scarcely see her face—that Sandra was weeping. She spoke, now, with her voice under control, but I could feel the strain she suffered to keep it so.

"Wanda, it's no use!" she said. "Your father—he'll always make his own decisions. They don't explain these things to us."

As a rule men answer such an attack—a direct demand upon their sympathy—by retreating behind a barrier of silence; and I had known that to be Julius's way. Now, indeed, it took him a little time to find his voice. But he did find it: a voice which revealed neither resentment nor patronage, almost the voice of affection:

"No, Sandra, I don't think we do make our own decisions. I thought so once. I thought so when I broke away at Natinsk, I fancied I was taking my own line again—defeating the plan that other people had made for me. It lasted for quite a long time, that notion, it encouraged me a great deal. It showed me—or so I imagined—it showed me I hadn't lost my power of making decisions—all the weeks of being treated like vermin hadn't made any difference. I thought I'd still be equal to the task I'd set myself—to do for Poland once again what Josef Pilsudski did before. Yes, I felt certain I was the one man living who could do that."

Wanda said quietly, "You are! As long as you stay alive."

"That's what I can't do!" His voice was tired now, as if the subject had begun to bore him. "Why they didn't shoot me in the first place, I don't know. They wanted a case, I suppose—a piece to put in the newspapers, something to help justify the occupation according to their own ideas of morality. Well, it doesn't matter. The thing's got to happen in the end."

"It hasn't!" Sandra said distractedly. "Julius, it hasn't!"

Fluttering for the first time, Wanda said, "Even if you *had* been something to do with it—that ridiculous business about Pawczak———"

"That?" he said quickly. "That childish invention! No, I wouldn't let myself be shot for that."

"Then *why?*" she persisted, with a note of desperation. "In God's name, why do you want to throw away the very life that Poland needs above all the rest?"

"I don't," he answered prosaically. "It's only that God demands it."

"Father, what do you mean?"

"I think Stefanie could tell you. Is she awake?"

I had been listening as one does to the conversation of strangers in some public room, and the sound of my own name startled me as if a light had suddenly been directed into my face. My voice must have sounded like that of a servant-girl accused of eavesdropping or of theft:

"I don't understand! I don't want him to be killed!"

For a moment there was silence between us, the silence that follows the fall of a slate in a quiet street. Then Julius said patiently, "But you haven't forgotten, surely! You do know what happened to your mother? I thought Zygmunt's daughter had told you."

I answered, "That was so long ago. It doesn't mean anything to me now."

(Was this the truth, grown like plants in darkness below the ground? Had I travelled so far from the time when the reality of my mother's death had ruled my mind as if I had witnessed it with adult and comprehending eyes? Had a winter's and a summer's passage blurred my sense of its ugliness—or had death itself dwindled in stature as it became the casual companion of our journey? From the bounded life of Setory I had looked at the crime as one man's responsibility, to be judged in simple terms—I had not conceived that violent action might be an abscess where the widespread foulness of a sick body is gathered and exudes. In the months since then, overcharged with new experience, the lifelong process towards maturity had moved at an unnatural pace. Was I wiser now? Or only less trustful of ideas which had seemed to be simple and assured? . . . Conrad was stirring, troubled by the increasing cold; as I held him closer to me, feeling faintly the working of his heart and his warm breath against my cheek, I could not think of death at all, except as the lapsing of majestic opportunity.)

One of the tribesmen stood up and knocked his heel against the smouldering fire, a piece of brushwood caught and blazed. In that access of light I saw that Annette was sitting up, her face turned towards me, that Ludwig's eyes, as ever, were open; and a movement from the huddled figure at Julius's side—a gesture of the hand across the forehead—showed me that the Countess was awake as well. But among our own people I observed no other sign of wakefulness, and the furrowed mound in which the Russians lay all together was motionless, as if one looked upon a recent battlefield where only the dead were left.

"What does she mean?" Wanda asked dully.

Sandra, as if with one breath, said, "I don't want to know—there isn't any need to know these things!"

That was not the Countess's mind. Perhaps, living so far from us, so far from the wilderness through which her body was transported like a bale of rags from place to place, she could hardly be said to have a mind at all; but as an ancient musical-box will still play its tunes when the spring is wound again, her brain receiving certain impulses would once more limp through an old routine. Her voice came through a barrier of phlegm, I could only just hear what she said:

". . . foolish child! 'Don't want to know!' Anyone would know —anyone could have guessed. That Nilniewicz, I'd have done it myself, I'd do it now."

Sandra said impetuously, "He didn't do anything to Nilniewicz! Julius, you told me—Nilniewicz ran away."

The flame from the kindled branch gave out, restoring to our eyes the black immensity of land which came to no boundary but the curve of stars. Julius was on his feet, and against the glimmer from the stagnant fire I could see the shape of his head turning as a sailor's does to scan the distances. Like me he may have felt as if we few were survivors on an earth which the wind had stripped of every life but ours—as if, brought close together in this curious hour, we had escaped from our own secrecies to an unimagined freedom.

He spoke as one who searches by candlelight in the deepest recesses of memory: "I made up my mind when I was in the Kadorka. I was all by myself for seven months—yes, I think it was seven months—that was after the second time I'd tried to escape. The first time it was only one month—five weeks, perhaps. Seven months, that's eternity when you're young and quite alone. Not even an old newspaper to read. My food came through a spy-hole, the man never spoke to me, he never answered anything I said to him. You've time to plan things when you're alone like that; you come back and back to small affairs, things that seem to be personally important. I was always thinking about Nilniewicz, I knew he was the man who'd sold me. It was like an open sore on my mind, I got to think of it as a kind of duty—to get the world rid of that creature. You won't understand. There are plans that grow in one's mind, one can't uproot them."

Sandra said feebly, "But you told me he ran away! You told me you never found him. And afterwards you gave him a farm."

As if he had not heard her, Julius said to me, "You know what happened, Stefanie—you must have got it all from Tilka." His voice was completely toneless now, the voice of one who has spent a long day dealing with people of extreme stupidity. "I didn't know that Nilniewicz had a wife, or anyone hiding with him. You can believe that or not. It doesn't alter things—it makes no moral difference that I killed your mother instead of him."

I remember very distinctly the strange sensation of hearing those words; it resembled that of seeing in print something you have said in private long before. But the night's vast quietness, the flow of wind and the tribesmen's monotonous voices, could absorb that strangeness; they engulfed the shallow, impetuous response which came from Wanda—"It was right, whatever you did! That's all I know or care!" And now, like the first reality that breaks a dream, I heard Sandra speaking in a voice to which passion gave only a strained simplicity:

"You could have told me. All these years you could have told me. I suppose I've never been worth it—a person of my sort—I've not been worth as much as that."

Those words, too, return to my mind's ear exactly as they broke from the darkness that night, and I can almost recapture the emotion they roused in me: no tears, no anger, could have affected me so poignantly as their naked humility. I was thankful when the wake of silence they drew behind them was broken by Ludwig's voice, dry and faintly querulous:

"Does it really matter so tremendously—something that happened years and years ago? I should have said it was our principal luxury—those of us who've mismanaged the past, one way or another—that we've left it farther behind than anyone else. It's not only finished, it's cancelled, it's out of sight."

This was a recognizable picture of our state. Somewhere in the world which we had left behind us our names and descriptions might still be recorded, but nothing seemed to connect such records with this cluster of almost useless bodies spilt on a piece of earth that no map would identify; objects too slight to interrupt the flow of wind, which would carry for a few yards only their smell of sickness and animality. This wind was colder, as the night moved nearer dawn, and beneath the overload of discomfort a bundle here and there was stirring; there were murmurous, childlike cries from those returning to the ache of consciousness. We should wake, shivering, to physical hunger, hoping for a place in the cart where there would be room to move one's legs, no bolt or stanchion to rub against one's spine: we no longer had any concerns but these, we looked forward at one day's journey, backward not at all.

"You think that?" Julius said.

Wanda said, "*I* think so. What does it matter, what's happened up till now! There's no Poland any more, we know that. But there's going to be. Isn't that what matters to you? It is to me."

"It isn't a solution, just saying that the past is over and done with."

Ludwig said wearily, "Life has no solutions. How can there be solutions to something that's got no meaning!"

But Julius did not seem to hear him; it was Wanda or himself he spoke to. "Without the past we'd be no different from those horses there. We've got the whole of our past within ourselves, it's what we're made of. Surely that's obvious enough."

"We don't depend on it," Wanda said. "We needn't let it rule us."

"Not only our own past—we contain much more than that. The people that came before us, we're the object of their lives, their only

[284]

fulfilment, they look to us for their immortality. You, Radznowski, you say that life is meaningless. Of course it is, if you take it a second at a time. That's what the beasts do—and nothing has any meaning for them. I say it's the past that gives our lives the whole of their significance. We can claim the dignity of being human just so far as we accept it."

"Accept it? Accept what?" I asked.

"The past," he repeated, "your own past and its responsibilities. Pretending that things didn't happen, pretending they can be cancelled out, that's childish, it makes morality a farce and then our lives are senseless."

I heard a sigh from Sandra, the sigh of a mother brought to despair by a fractious child. "But what good would it do," she asked him weakly, "punishing yourself for what you did when you were young? That Nilniewicz—of course it's dreadful that the woman had to suffer——"

"I'm telling you," he said restrainedly, "there's no importance, there's no value in life when you blind yourself to the part that would hurt you. I see no argument for living as anything less than a human being. And you can't be that if you deny humanity's obligations."

"I should have thought," said Ludwig almost inaudibly, "that there wasn't much opportunity for performing obligations—not on this excursion."

"Obligations to whom?" Wanda asked quickly. "Do you mean, Father, that because of Stefanie—because of her mother——"

"Your father owes nothing to me!" I said. "I thought so once——"

"Yes," Julius said with decision, "we shouldn't have to worry much about our duties if God was merely a glorified human—if he changed from day to day; if he had a short memory."

Those words, quietly as they were spoken, released in Ludwig a spring of violence.

"God?" he said. "What in God's name has God got to do with it! What do you mean by 'God'? Isn't God supposed to have made this world and everything that moves upon it? Isn't he supposed to have 'redeemed' it? Do you think the results are very impressive? Do you think that God is entitled to talk to us about morality?"

Sandra said, "Dr Radznowski, you mustn't speak like that!"

"I'll tell you who believed in God," he said. "Sofietka did, my wife Sofietka. She prayed to him, she trusted him absolutely, the worse her illness got the more she seemed to love him. I find that

[285]

most interesting, looking back on what happened. Your advice, General, 'Never turn your back on the past!' Well, I suppose it was me that God was punishing—she was just the Divine Instrument? I find that more interesting still.''

His vehemence was rousing the whole encampment. I heard Nonolka's querulous voice, "It's the bloody Poles—idle bourzhui —they've nothing to do but shout at each other all night!"

Sandra said, "God may forgive your blasphemies, Dr Radznowski, because He knows you don't understand what you're saying."

"Surely," I said to Julius, "God would not be more vengeful than we are—than I am!"

"You, Radznowski, you are a clever man," Julius said slowly. "If it were possible to discover God through one's intelligence, then you would be the one to find him. I cannot find God myself, I cannot understand his reasons. I only know that I can't escape his intentions—the intentions he has for me. I thought that he meant me to be the saviour of Poland. I was wrong—that's clear to me now—that work is for someone else. You're perfectly right, there are no solutions. There's no meaning that any of us can understand. All I know is that in the end I have got to do what God requires."

"And that means—in simple terms—letting the Russians shoot you? For some crime you didn't commit."

"The Russians—I suppose so—yes." He seemed once more to be speaking his private thoughts aloud. "I have a certain amount of amour propre. Or discipline—you can call it what you like. I should rather be obedient to God's will than let him hunt me down."

I think I was at the edge of sleep when those words were spoken: I remember none that may have followed. When the first light came —that Siberian morning light which gives a stone-like quality to the earth and to every object that it finds—I woke to see that except for Ludwig, who lay staring at the sky, my fellow-travellers were all in heavy sleep. The fires were dead, and even the Kirghizi slept, lying with the shoulders of one against another's side, as if a gust had blown them over where they sat. In those moments of wakening I imagined that all the talk I had heard had come to me as dreams come, the effluvium from some chamber of the brain where fears and longings make fantasy of experience. Those voices in the darkness had been joined but distantly to people who, known from my childhood, had kept for me the stature of a child's protectors: they belonged still less to the creatures I saw now. Amongst the flotsam of blankets, hessian, ragged coats, where a girl's brown leg protruded, where a man's hand appeared to lie by itself as in a dissecting-room, the faces of my friends looked little different from those of the drabs and pilferers a few yards away—unless the Countess's, shrunk like a raisin, seemed farther from human life than theirs. This sickly, peasant's face with the grey hair draggling over flaccid cheeks was Sandra's, the tousled head which might have been a kitchen-maid's, jammed against Henryk's sprawling bulk, could barely remind me of the grace and power that Wanda had brought to Setory a year before. Tilted back, where he lay by his wife's feet, the wasted face of Julius with its coat of stubble, the open mouth displaying morbid gums, showed less of the individual, less of human dignity, than the effigies of the Grévin museum. Above this litter of outcasts the monstrous birds which the natives call Poaching Priests were circling avariciously; it began to rain, and soon, at a petulant shout from our commander, the prostrate figures, like the dead summoned to judgment, were struggling all together to their feet.

Did the talk I have recalled take place, in fact, in the course of more than one night? I cannot now be certain. I happened to remember that Annette was very sick in the cart on the day after it ended, and that where we next bivouacked, some fourteen hours farther on, there was sleet falling.

vi

With the others—with his wife, perhaps with Wanda—my father-in-law may have come back to those confidences on some occasion when I was not in their company. But I do not think so: I got the impression that having once unburdened himself he neither needed nor would be able to communicate his feelings again. Below the apathy into which he had withdrawn I seemed to discern a resignation which came near to contentment— the relief men evidently feel when they have sealed a decision by making it public: he had arrived, perhaps, at what Ludwig had talked of as a 'solution'. This change in him I regarded with a peculiar sympathy. Although I no longer supposed (as the other women seemed to) that we should recover the kind of existence we had lost, I never saw this voyage as one which could only end in a darkening stagnancy. Each sign of Conrad's growth, his hunger and need for warmth, the searching of his eyes, appeared to teach me that life was not purposeless. But if we were at one, Julius and I, in refusing to accept the future in its obvious terms, how far were his thoughts removed from mine when he looked on death itself as life's sufficing purpose. I suppose that it was natural for him, as well as for Ludwig, to look for every interpretation in the mind alone: it was not natural for me, who believed that the heart's knowledge is a necessary part of understanding. To me it was not conceivable that mere ideas—of duty and sacrifice, of atonement—could be used to cover humanity's nakedness or satisfy human hungers.

But in the iron workings at Mikirka, to which that journey brought us, we ceased to talk or think about the future. Here winter returned; not with the majesty, the evolving drama, of Polish winters, but with the swift cruelty of a disease. At first there was no snow. On a night when the sky was clear and the wind had fallen, it grew colder so rapidly that I fancied there must be some new disorder in my own body, and when I woke in the very early morning I was convinced for a few moments that the shelter we lived in had been flooded—that we were lying in cold water. A little jar of watery broth I had made for Conrad, which stood on the ground near my head, had turned into solid ice. The working party I belonged to was out as usual before it was light. I found it difficult and painful to breathe, and I could not touch the brake handles or the points lever with which I controlled the movement of the coasting trolleys—I had to pick up my woollen skirt and protect my hands with that. When day came there was still neither wind nor cloud; the ravaged hillside we inhabited was in steady sunlight; but this light had a new, rare quality, a paleness, as if the sun's rays themselves were frozen, and it gave to the slashed escarpments, the sprawling forest of gear on the upper terraces, the barrack of iron-roofed shelters below, a gelid unreality like that of a tinplate scene under blatant electricity. In this cold radiance the faces of my work-fellows, Yakuts and Finnish prisoners, were changed; and even they were silent, moving their bodies stiffly, and looking at each other with wonder, as people look when dawn comes after the night of some disaster. I thought—as far as I could think at all—that so merciless an attack must be over in the course of hours; a week or more was needed to teach me that this extremity of cold was a settled state, that there would be no day's respite, no other air to breathe than this, no wakening but to this petrified earth and sky.

We returned, then, to our old preoccupation, the task of staying alive. It was a matter of using from hour to hour what energy one could squeeze from body and mind; of making draught-breaks in the long shelters with earth and slag stuffed between boxes, of neglecting no chance to steal things—kerosene for the drip-stoves, straw, any bits of rag to bandage arms and legs. This industry was enough for the part of our brains which still functioned: we neither spoke nor thought about days to come.

For me, of course, the body to be kept alive was Conrad's, and that also was a business where I could see no more than a day ahead. His life had not been long enough to give him the strength he needed for such a winter as this, and though he bore it bravely it seemed to deprive him of the power to grow. I realized that such retardment was natural, for I could not let him have the opportunities that babies are normally given to kick and roll—he had to lie all day, heavily wrapped, in the travelling case which did for cradle—but it troubled me that he seemed to have no use for the modicum of liberty his wrappings allowed him; whenever I got back from the trolley-yard he lay exactly as I had placed him six or seven hours before, and though his eyes always turned to greet me they would go back at once to their favourite objective, an old red jersey of mine which served to stuff a gap in the roof. Then, too, he was constantly hungry, but would eat very little of anything I could find for him. Everyone helped me. There were few days when Wanda failed to bring him some morsel won from the guards, whose practice was to round up the younger women for their comfort at night. Janina, grown listless from the cold, would still arrive in her hours off work to sit and hold him against her skinny body, sharing with him the little warmth it retained; but she could not match the service of her rival, Nonolka, who risked (and sometimes suffered) the harshest punishments for leaving her shift to attend to him. To her devotion he owed more, perhaps, than to any of the others. Throughout the winter he suffered no serious illness. But he lost palpably in weight, his motions were never healthy, and he had no colour now.

For many weeks I did not see Annette. She had been assigned to another part of the workings, several versts away, and all the news I could get was a rumour that she was dead.

One of those who died at this stage was Issa, whose hands and feet had become gangrenous from frostbite. I remember that occurrence because of its effect on Henryk, who had come to regard the little girl as his own child: unable to accept the fact of her death, he continued for a long time to hunt for her all over the workings, with eyes which reminded me acutely of Maria-Josefa's, and it needed brute force to get him back to his job at the stone-face. But to me the remarkable thing was that so many of those who did not die were people who had appeared least able to withstand the Mikirka climate and régime. The Countess still lived. It was life by definition, scarcely anything more: like Conrad, she stayed in the same position all day long, outside our aid, moving nothing but her animal eyes, and because her old, sick body was so slackly commanded, her presence close to us was not the least of the hardships of that time. Doubtless she longed for death, for there cannot have been one moment of ease or satisfaction in that existence; but she, whose life I had always seen as the delineation of absolute will, had come to a toll-bar where the will has no authority. I marvel hardly less—as I review that winter from the present calm—that Annette survived. For the rumour of her death proved false. A little after midnight (on a night early in February, it must have been) she arrived in our shelter in a state of extreme exhaustion, after walking by herself through the snow. It was then that she told me, with misery and shame, what I could now have deduced for myself: how, to get the comforts that I needed, she had been prostitute to the Commandant at Staging Camp 5. From this time I kept her with me, using one of my last trinkets (a sapphire-and-diamond brooch that Victor had given me) to square the Overseer of our detachment; and so, a fortnight afterwards, in a day and night of agony and fear, I was able to care for her at the birth of her son.

Those events are less alive in my recollection than many more remote in time, because they are in a plane of experience different from any other I have known. Pictorially, I can return to that amphitheatre floored with snow, the tremendous arc of terraced cliffs which, as you emerged from the shelter in moonlight, might have been part of the moon itself, blue-white and stark and desolate. I see like a company of ghosts the straggling train of men returning in the half-light from their twelve-hour shift, faces like crimpled hide, bodies that appear to drag on tensile wires; I see—too clearly —the stretched mouth of an old man fallen in the snow, the bored eyes of the guards belabouring him; and against a litter of women's clothes and the fluttering shadows thrown by a tow-lamp on the sacking wall I see Annette's white face, grown round and soft again in her crucial hour, the innocent, the patient face of a child. Yes, but I cannot recover (if I would) the concert of sensation which made me part of that arena and which would restore to me its actuality—the reek of oil smoke colouring all existence in the shelter or the pain, outside, of breathing air that felt like a cautery in nose and lungs; that lethargy, that deadness of the flesh which, if you collapsed on your way to the trolley-yard, would make you suffer a dozen blows before you would struggle to your feet and go on climbing the slope of ice and shale.

14

IT was not by my own choice that I returned to Czennik. But
the decision to take Conrad with me was mine, and mine only.
In saying that he would take the first chance to declare his
'legal' position, Julius had not been speaking idly: he did report
himself as soon as we reached Mikirka. The result was not sensa-
tional. At Mikirka, Authority was concerned with problems of
man-power in relation to tonnages of ore, not with the case-his-
tories of individual Poles, and a labourer's manifest wish to be
ceremonially hanged was a decoration of circumstance for which
they had—they implied—no time. Julius's statement would be
transmitted to the proper quarter, together with that of a Russian
prisoner who had declared that he was a reincarnation of Peter the
Great.... From time to time the Detachment Overseer, a youngish,
able Caucasian who boasted a certain humour, had us paraded for
his inspection, and as a rule he would halt when he found Julius
facing him.

"This—yes, yes—this is my friend who wants to play the star
part in a splendid trial at Moscow! But you know, Mr Kolbeck,
Moscow is very dull at the present time, there's no longer anything
of what you would call Society there. Well well, we must see how
things pan out, I expect the Department of Justice is considering
your application from every possible angle. One has to be patient,
in a country like ours there's rather a lot of things and people that
have to be seen to. Perhaps in the end you will get to like Mikirka
so much that you won't want to leave us...."

Events rebuked his flippancy.

To me it seemed unlikely that in a government office two or three
thousand miles away there existed someone with time and energy
to exhume a personal file from a year's accumulation of dust;
impossible that such research could light a spark of action powerful

enough to leap the gap between his world and ours. I had forgotten (as Julius had not) the measure of Slavic tenacity, the tradition of rulership acquired in centuries which annihilates physical space. The statement had gone forward, as the Overseer said. It had to reach the desk of a clerk who was paid to be conscientious, and no file was ever closed. About mid-winter a commission reached us— a dozen officials in all; they seemed to be mostly technologists, small men with spectacles and blunted finger-nails who were almost lost in their furs, but among them were the usual politicals. Julius, with some others, was taken to the Overseer's office late at night. "A question of identity," he told us when he returned. "They tried to convince me that I'm really a Jewish photographer from Ponevyej." But doubtless a record of that interview found its way to the file as well. By March the industry of distant bureaucrats had achieved results. The plant came into flower.

Our party was collected in the women's shed for an unofficial meal: a Russian friend had killed one of the half-savage dogs which roamed about the workings, and Wanda had managed to broil it. No one knew where Julius was, but after we had been sitting for some time he arrived and stood behind Sandra, as usual speechless and absorbed. We had been talking quite cheerfully— it was a long time since we had enjoyed such luxury—but his presence brought us to silence. He himself did not appear to notice this. Still on his feet, he slowly ate the helping I had given him, cleaned out his tin, and absently crossed himself as he did at the beginning and end of every meal. Then he said casually:

"I'm leaving tomorrow. Tomorrow early."

I looked at Sandra's face, and saw in its stillness how recurrent grief inures the heart's defences: her lips came together, and that was all. It was Wanda who first spoke.

"Leaving? Where for?"

He shrugged his shoulders. "Kiev? I've no idea. I don't know where they handle Polish political cases now."

Rosalia began weeping—it was a habit of hers in those days. "We shan't have a man!" she said pathetically. "Not a man who can do anything. We can't be without a man!"

"Why not?" Wanda snapped at her.

Sandra observed her cousin distantly, as she might once have regarded an importunate tradesman.

"It is for the General," she said, "to decide what is his duty."

I understood what Rosalia was feeling. We were all sensible, I suppose, of a need for his protection, however little it would avail us; rather as people too nervous to stay in an empty house will be satisfied if only a servant girl or a child is with them. Apart from that primitive cowardice, I was sorrowful that he should be leaving us. He had contributed little that was tangible to our fellowship, but among exiles in a barren country the mere shape of their society has a peculiar value. We should be impoverished; I no less than those who could call him their own.

Constrained by his old shyness, he stood gazing at Conrad's head, avoiding all our eyes. He said, with a note of impatience, "You were talking of something, Wanda, when I came in—I didn't mean to interrupt you. . . . Someone had better explain to my mother if she asks about me. But I don't suppose she'll notice I've gone. I don't think there's anything else to be settled, is there?" He surveyed us abstractedly, like a schoolmaster who has set some work to his class and is impatient to get back to his private studies. "I'll see you again, of course, before I go."

With that he left us and went off to a group of sheds on a lower terrace half a mile away. (He had found a Priest there, a Roumanian, and I believe he spent much of his off-duty time with him.)

In the event, he did not start his journey till two days later—no movement ever occurred at the time arranged—and by then my own interest in it had been given a new direction. One of the older guards wakened me in the middle of the night for what seemed an imbecile conversation. (On such occasions my Russian practically deserted me and I myself talked like a baby.) Was it true, this man wanted to know (screwing his eyes over a foolscap sheet of type-script) that my surname was Kolbeck? Was I, in fact, the wife of a Colonel Victor Kolbeck of the former Polish Army? Was I quite sure of that? Had I reported myself—had I taken any steps to make my identity known to the Commissioners of the Mikirka Co-operative? . . . Very well, then I was required by the Department of Justice to give evidence in the case of one Julius Kolbeck, a Polish fugitive, indicted for the murder of a Polish agrarian worker. I must prepare myself immediately to leave Mikirka. Clothing and portable possessions up to one and a half poods might be taken—it could not be guaranteed that I should be permitted to return to my present employment. Yes, a child, if sufficiently small, might be scheduled as a portable possession. No, it was impossible to say at what time the journey would begin, it might be in half an hour from now, it was a matter for the Local Administrative of Transportation.

I have sometimes been partly grateful to life's vulgarities for their power to dilute emotion. This was not my first separation from Annette, but one's capacity to be tormented by partings is never dulled by their recurrence. I think it would have needed physical force to get me away from her, in her state of pitiful dependence, if my sensibilities had not been confused by something like a market brawl.

The trouble came first from Janina. It had not occurred to me that my right to the close possession of my own child could be disputed by anyone. Janina disputed it. While I was getting Conrad wrapped up for the journey—this was about four o'clock in the morning—she was at the other side of the shelter, preparing to go out on the early shift. She suddenly came over to my corner, stared at me for a few moments with venomous anger, and said, with her lips almost closed:

"What are you doing? You're not thinking of taking the baby with you?"

I said, "What do you mean! Of course I'm taking him."

"You're mad," she said, "you're crazy! You can't imagine he can stand a journey in this weather—he's not fit to go outside the shelter at all."

Annette, raising her head, said weakly, "Please, Janina! Please don't interfere—it's nothing to do with anyone but my mother."

Janina's answer was to go to the other end of the shelter and take hold of Wanda, who had been on the night-shift and was getting thawed out; I heard her say, "Your sister-in-law's gone completely crazy. . . ." Wanda, I thought, would give scant attention to such nonsense—as a rule she had no use for Janina; but a spell of seven hours at the stone-face left no one in a state for sober reflection. She followed the raving girl to my side.

"Janina tells me you've thought of taking Conrad with you."

I said, "He happens to be my son."

"And so you think you've got the right to let him die of exposure! Do you suppose that between us we can't look after him here?"

Someone else—Sandra, I expect—said, "You know, Stefanie, really he will have a much better chance, staying here with us."

And then, with a bitterness that startled me, Wanda went on, "I'm afraid it's no use talking. Nothing ever counts with Stefanie except her own ideas. Conrad's got to be her own property, that's all she thinks about—his life doesn't count for anything when it's a question of her personal vanity."

It was left for Janina to add the small-dog's nip, "Selfish beast—she doesn't care about her child at all!"

I pretended to be deaf. One business claimed me at that moment, to say farewell to Annette. I knelt on the floor beside her, she stretched one arm and caught my neck and hugged me, weeping, while I kissed her eyes and the tiny head of Paul which lay between her puny, laden breasts. And because she looked so frail, so much a child, because we had travelled so much together in difficult country, I could say nothing at all. I had to tear myself away with violence, as one wrenches the plaster from a wound.

A moment later I saw, incredulously, that Janina had seized her chance: while my back was turned she had swooped upon Conrad, and now, standing a few feet away, she held him tightly in her skinny arms, watching me obliquely and smiling, tight-mouthed, with a diabolical malice. It was a moment of utter helplessness, of nightmare. In the feeble light which came from the end of the shed the whole of its population seemed to be gathered about the space where Janina and I were facing each other like cocks in a main—a circle of dishevelled women clutching coats and blankets round their shoulders, fascinated and stiff with alarm. I glanced about for Wanda, thinking that even in her present mood she would hardly assent to such an outrage as this, but she had moved out of sight. Sandra was supine with bewilderment and tears. In the crew of palsied creatures gaping at my predicament there was no one with the strength or boldness to give me help.

I said, "Will you give him to me, please!"

"You're not fit to have him!" Janina said. "He's going to stay with me, he's going to be looked after."

"Give him to me this minute!"

"You'd better keep off! I'll drop him if you try to hurt me!"

I took a pace towards her; not a firm pace—my legs were like jelly. She backed, screaming as if I had stabbed her: "Keep off, you filth! I'll kill him, I'll kill you both!"

I cannot conceive what I should have done then if help had not come. It came in the person of Nonolka, returning from the night-shift: a formidable figure, with her square head and breadth of shoulder, eyes puffed and watery, face matted over with the grime of quarry dust and frozen sweat. With the instinct that belongs to children of the streets she made her way at once to the centre of the affray, looked inquiringly at me, then turned and saw Janina; she asked no questions at all.

"You!" she said softly. "You Polish scum, you little —— bourzhui thief!"

She did not strike the girl, or did not appear to; she moved towards her in a quiet, almost a friendly way, and then her action was too quick for me to see—I think she must have slipped one hand between Conrad's body and Janina's, and simultaneously caught and wrenched Janina's hair. Next moment she was facing me, grimly complacent, with Conrad on her shoulder.

"And now, Stefanovna, little love, it's time for you to go?"

Yes, I suppose it is better that our partings should be like that, so void of dignity, so tangled in life's untidiness that the scars they leave are broken-edged. I managed to smile at Annette, and she to return that smile, as if we were playing parts we had carefully rehearsed. Then, glad to be so confused, so scared, I followed Nonolka, through the litter of bemused women and their possessions, out of the shelter. At least I felt no sentiment in abandoning the building which for several months had been my home.

It was Nonolka, then, who conducted me down the broken track to the old posting-house, while the official escort stumbled along behind us, leaving Julius and Sandra to follow him; Nonolka who, with Conrad on one arm, carried the greater part of my baggage as well, plodding as sturdily as if she came from a night's comfortable sleep, and chattering blithely all the way:

". . . And then, if you give your evidence cleverly, they'll find some high-grade work for you—you may be a clerk in one of the government offices! And one day, I suppose, you'll go back to your own country, and you'll tell them about the Soviet Union—how all the workers are free and happy here. And you'll teach the little Conrad all you've learnt in the Union, and perhaps he'll grow up and be the Lenin of Poland, to bring freedom to the Polish workers. . . ."

While I answered, "Yes . . . yes. . . . And you, Nonolka, you'll do anything that's possible to help Annette? You'll try to stop them sending her back to work just yet?"

Surprisingly, the sledge was at the post-house already, and a man like St Nicholas was backing the second horse into position while his blear-eyed wife or daughter clung fiercely to the head of the first. "They're no use, these old screws," the driver informed us, spitting to right and left, "you get nothing with any wind in their bellies these days. It'll take three days to the railway—four, I wouldn't be surprised."

"Four days, yes yes!" the escort said, nodding indulgently, relighting his home-made cigarette. A little apart from us, Julius watched the operation with faintly sardonic interest, while Sandra, looking smaller in a soldier's coat and bashlyk than I had ever seen her, talked fitfully to me in a voice which she kept almost entirely under control.

"You will do what you can for him, Stefanie? He forgets about his health when I'm not with him." For an instant her weak, embarrassed eyes were raised towards my face. "I know—of course I know it will be difficult for you. But perhaps you will have a chance now and then—in little ways, I mean—a chance to look after him."

I could not listen with much attention. The metallic wind which drove unhindered along the frozen Olna was savagely whipping our faces; my mind was still absorbed by the relief of having Conrad in my arms again, and when she said, "You're sure it wouldn't be safer, after all, to leave the little one in our care?" I did not trouble to reply. Our backs were turned on Mikirka now. Here, among the squalid hutments, there was an overflow of Mikirka's hideousness, discarded winding-gear and broken shafts, the spur of a giant slag-heap, while the poisoned smell of Mikirka still reached me in a backflow of the wind. But behind the stygian hills the sky had become a furnace in the sunrise; ahead, where the river turned, a soft-fleshed shoulder of the farther heights had caught from this fire an unearthly, roseate glow, and in the thorny scrub which lined the river's edge that fluorescence was broken into shimmering gold by a million particles of ice. I was cold, weak from the winter's long fatigue; but in the magic of this burnished morning my feeling of release came near to the exaltation of freedom; you do not picture in advance the long unravelling of a journey, and I could not think despondently of its destination so long as I was travelling with my son.

"At your worships' pleasure!" the post-house keeper called satirically.

"If you are ready, Comrade Prisoner?" the escort said with his amiable shyness. "And the gracious witness, she is ready too?"

Four days was an under-estimate: it took us six to get to Popelsk. Alone, I could not have kept Conrad alive for those six days, for the life that flowed in him was like the trickle in the bed of a stream which summer has almost dried, aud I myself, still possessed by the endemic sickness of Mikirka, had spells of lethargy in which I was not even capable of holding him closely. The going was rough, as the Olna bears a heavy traffic in winter; each driver steers for unbroken snow, and in the end the whole surface is a web of ruts which go down to the river's crust; but the jolting was scarcely harder to bear than the monotony, the softly undulating desert of snow which travelled past us on either side, unchanging, for hour after hour. This, and the bitter wind which seemed to blow always across the river, so dulled my senses that at times, if Conrad had fallen from my arms, I should scarcely have found energy to recover him.

It was not so with Julius. Since the care of his grandson was the only business he had on hand, he brought to it the whole of his resources in will and reason. For a great part of the journey he was holding him himself, fastened inside his coat, and he was for ever thinking of some means to encourage his circulation: he would work his arm up the inside of Conrad's jacket and massage his back with a woman's gentleness, he would carefully unravel the small hands, one at a time, hold them cupped in his own and warm them with his breath; then, without disturbing Conrad's body, he would take hold of his thighs and—as it were—set him marching, moving his legs up and down in an easy rhythm. It was he, too, who made himself responsible for Conrad's feeding. Wherever we stopped he hunted about for milk or for any foodstuff that the peasants would sell him; this he stored in small bottles in his baggage, and at any staging-post where a stove could be got to work he set himself to concoct a little broth which could be fed to Conrad with his own spoon. In these matters he scarcely consulted me, and with other people his behaviour was magisterial: he seemed at this time to have forgotten he was no longer a general officer with a staff to whom his smallest word was an edict of God. Generally they bore it. In my half-toned, almost featureless memory of that passage there is one picture which has stayed in focus: the fuliginous interior of a one-roomed timber house, with peasant wayfarers asleep in family groups all over the earthern floor, where Zukol the escort is squatting patiently with Conrad bundled in his arms; nearby, the grizzled driver holds a little pan against the stove to keep its contents warm, while Julius, stooping between them, dips the spoon, tests its heat, and cautiously brings it to Conrad's obstinate mouth, issuing brusque directions all the time:

"Steady, Zukol—let his head go lower! . . . Yes, it's going to be a long job, I can't help that . . . It's too warm now, driver. Don't hold it quite so close!"

I think gratefully of Zukol. He had fits of severity, when he would tell us that prisoner and witness were not allowed to communicate with each other—here it was, he said, producing his crumpled orders, we could read it for ourselves. But when we ignored such commands, he had sense enough to drop them. "If you try to escape," he said from time to time, looking fiercely at us and then at the limitless expanse of snow, "I have the authority to shoot you on the spot." The authority, perhaps; but the German revolver he carried must long have been choked with rust, and really I think his only wish was to oblige. He was a young Volhynian—in the early twenties, I suppose—and a prodigious moustache did little to disguise his schoolboy innocence: his face was of the English cast, with large and candid eyes, and that pugnacious chin which nature supplies as the buttress of simplicity.

Not only was Conrad alive when we reached Popelsk: he seemed to have regained some loss of ground. He was moving his legs a little, and more than once he stared about him as if he was conscious of his new surroundings. I like to think that it may have given him some small pleasure, the excitement of seeing different shapes above his head.

Popelsk, as it appeared, was a place whose staple industry was the expectation of trains. Between the long iron shelter which did for railway station and its single, slatternly povarnia was a rhomboid, flanked by market stalls, where a brocade of horse-droppings and motor oil was thickly spread across the frozen snow. This was the Lenin Square. From one end to the other there stretched, all day and night, a broad, untidy queue which can seldom have numbered fewer than a thousand souls—bagmen, soldiers, guarded convicts, Tartar families of three or four generations; and this concourse seemed to be unified by one topic of debate: would there be a public train today, tomorrow, this week? You had a better chance of getting a place, they said, if you held an Official Pass; and among the swarm of hawkers pestering the queue there was more than one who offered to trade an Official Pass for a wrist-watch or perhaps a set of teeth. But the knowing maintained that those passes were worthless—to buy the genuine kind you had first to join a different queue, on the other side of the square. . . . For us it would be easy, Zukol said. He held an Official Pass already. But the pass had to be date-stamped by the office of the Regional Executive for Transportation, and at this office there was another queue which did not appear to move at all.

It was hard on our friend. In exalted moments he had let us know that he was an officer of considerable standing in the police hierarchy. Now, returning to us three or four times a day, he had to find a new excuse for each occasion:

"Of course, the traffic's abnormally heavy at the present time; there are people of great importance travelling; naturally they must be given the highest priority of all. . . . At the present time there's a great deal of military traffic to be handled. . . ."

Sometimes he made a show of success:

"I've seen one of the Deputy-Controllers this morning. I made my official position known, he spent a quarter of an hour with me. I'm glad to say he entirely understands my problem, he realizes I'm in a special position and must have priority. . . . Of course it's all a question of justice. In the old days only rich people were able to use the railways. That's all abolished now—under the Union everyone has an equal chance. I've told the Deputy-Controller I agree with that absolutely."

And later his note altered a little:

"The Deputy-Controller has been into the matter with me very carefully. There are certain questions of permit-fees which were not fully taken into account at the time when I was appointed to this duty—otherwise those fees would have been allowed for in the expense allotment. As it is, I shall have to make arrangements to borrow a small sum for the time being. . . . There's a little crucifix I saw in your baggage, Comrade General. I was wondering if it's really any great use to you now?"

Happily there was no fresh fall of snow during those days of waiting, and in exchange for what we could offer them—a locket with seed pearls, a pair of nail-scissors—the pedlars brought us most of what we needed, sacks to lie on and to cover us at night, soup of a kind which they cooked over braziers along the square. The peasants near us in the queue showed me great kindness; one of them even gave Conrad a little of her milk—she had too much, she said, having lost one of her twin babies; and a woman who looked to be the wife of some official presented me with an extra shawl for him. Trains came, and some of them stopped, but they were always military trains. Old people sometimes cried with disappointment, yet soon there would always be laughter and even singing again. It was a friendly gathering, and when a child died, somewhere near the head of the queue, I saw all kinds of gifts being passed along to the child's mother as tokens of sympathy.

Conrad was taking food less reluctantly, now that we were still. I was constantly troubled because he seemed to have no wish at all to use his body, while other babies not much older than he were actually trying to struggle out of their mothers' arms. But what I can only call his 'wisdom' seemed to increase. He wore at that time a look of settled patience, as if he had reasoned out that I was not to blame for the discomforts he suffered. Once, indeed, he smiled to me, as to a friend with whom he had perfect understanding.

That is not a gloss upon memory. Against the promiscuous façade of iron and timber houses, amidst the chaos of squalid bundles, children sporting in the ordured snow, I see it exactly, I see it for ever, that smile.

iv

"They may build some more trains in the summer or autumn," Julius said tolerantly. "We can be sure of getting where they want us to be in the end. But in this country it's one of the technical problems they've never quite mastered—how to get their criminals hanged before they die of old age."

I myself was sick with impatience to be moving again, for I felt —unreasoningly—that life would be better for Conrad and me if we were nearer Europe by only two or three hundred miles. And for Julius the strain must have been beyond endurance, but for moral reserves that I had hardly appreciated even then: reserves which may have derived partly from his calling (if exhaustless patience is a quality which distinguishes as much as any other the paramount soldier), but which had, perhaps, a further source in his early experience of captivity. Like other faculties, it needs to be acquired in youth: the power to remain an integral being without the nourishment of freedom.

"I cannot stand delays!" he had said on the night when we spent a few minutes together in Vaninov's ante-room—the night which had seemed likely to be the last for him. But even then he had scarcely shown the physical signs of agitation. At Popelsk I recalled that curious interview, for here an aspect which I had not seen since then appeared in him again, as when a chance fall of light reveals in a familiar portrait some look you have long forgotten. It was one more firmly defined than resignation. "We can be sure of getting where they want us to be"—there was more in that remark, I thought, than its superficial sarcasm, and yet it was not an admission of defeat: Mikirka had not broken him. Rather, it was as though, since the night with Vaninov, he had been wandering in unmapped country, and had finally returned to the route on which he had first set out. Delays did not matter now. He knew where he was going.

He became more detached from his surroundings—but not less accessible to me. I think I lost in those days the last of my old, instinctive fear of him.

v

And I needed his companionship on the last stage of that westward move, because the task of keeping Conrad safe was one of peculiar anxiety. Zukol, early one morning, had returned to us in triumph.

"It's just as I said—I told you the Executive would make special arrangements as soon as my position was properly understood. The Deputy-Controller has been in touch with the District Military Headquarters—by telegraph, of course, by telegraph, you understand—he has obtained verbal authority to issue a permit, a special permit for my party to travel by military train."

And this was no flight of Zukol's fancy; for thirty-six hours later, when a train arrived with its open trucks stuffed with soldiers, the three of us were squeezed with our belongings into the last truck but one. There, indeed, we had every privilege enjoyed by the soldiers themselves, even sharing the rations which were issued to them twice a day; and no one could have shown us greater kindness than these stoical boys and men. But few spoke any Russian that I could understand.

Because of the cold, one could never stand up for long, and as the floor of the truck was deep in filth Julius made me sit on his knees with Conrad cradled, as it were, between our bodies. In this position we spent a great number of hours, by night and day, and so it is that my clearest memory of Julius's face belongs to that time. The flesh was thin now, anæmic, furred with a dirty grey; months had worked upon it as in easier lives the years do; and yet this face appeared no older than on the day when he and I had been train companions first of all, for its lean virility must have altered little since his early manhood, and his eyes, when freed from the stress of decisions, were always young. For a man of his kind it must have meant much to be done with the business of parting, and I think he may even have been glad that no one who meant anything to him was there to witness this final progress. He sat, as if contentedly, enclosed by his own reflections; sometimes, I think, in a state of coma; blind to the white monotony of the tundra drawing away behind us, to the swaying confusion of serge, the grey, frost-galled faces: and all the attention he had to give, all the unlooked-for gentleness, was for Conrad and at times for me.

"How's it going, petit-fils? Look, Stefanie, raise his head a little, I want to tie the scarf again. We must keep the cold out of his ears, that's important, a man's ears are always vulnerable. Yes, you're very good, petit-fils, you're patient, you're a brave lad! Your father would be proud of you, yes! . . . It's a pity—I should like his father to have seen him."

"He's all right, the little one?" the bearded corporal asked from time to time, grinning down at me. "It's a boy, yes? A Polish boy? Well, it's all the same, we'll make a soldier of him, he'll fight for the Soviets, yes? He's small—yes?—he's small to be making a journey. It's not too good, a train like this, not for a small one. . . . And the old man, he's Polish too? He's the father? Is he stupid—just a little? He looks sleepy, he talks to himself, I heard him in the night. I don't think he knows where he's going."

"Does anyone know?" I asked.

"Ah, who knows! But perhaps it won't be far, perhaps we shall be there tomorrow, the day after. They've got it all planned out, the high-ups."

"Yes yes, it's all planned out!" the others said.

On the second night a boy with a rheumy-eyed, expressionless face (I doubt if he was more than seventeen) gave me the fleece jacket he had been wearing beneath his coat. "To cover up the kid," he muttered; and there must have been few in that truckload who did not pay us some attention—offering any titbits they could find for Conrad, arranging their bundles for my comfort, or at least taking pains to prevent their own necessities from offending me. They were considerate with Julius as well; for although Zukol had left us and got himself a place in a covered wagon, they seemed to have heard that Julius was a prisoner virtually under sentence. ("It's something bad—a serious crime?" one of them asked me.

"The old man has cheated his co-operative, perhaps?"") But to him their courtesies evidently meant no more than the caress of a dog's tongue: he had known so many soldiers, and now the margins of his interest were converging, as those of the really old do, so that he had no room for fresh experience. Even the intense discomfort of this mode of travel seemed hardly to affect him: within that slight body of his there was, I suppose, a peculiar resistance to the cold, or else his power to suffer from it was exhausted from over-use. Sometimes, when the track was bad and we were viciously jolted, the painfulness of that treatment showed in a tightening of his mouth. More often he was faintly smiling; and in those long reaches where time was empty I would find myself absorbed in watching the minute activity of the muscles beneath his eyes, that alternation of stillness and motion in the eyes themselves which is all that betrays the myriad currents flowing in another's mind. So close, these eyes: the man so far away. Yet here was a sentient creature, just so far from the origins of life as I, whose thoughts must be subject to the same laws as mine, who must know in some degree the same emotions. And we suffered in common that ulti-mate captivity from which no mortal ever escapes, the heart's solitude.

"Stefanie! Stefanie, is he all right? I thought he wasn't breathing properly." This was at early morning, when the dull light pene-trating a pall of smoke from the engines showed the quivering truck as a refuse-yard, bodies sprawling on top of each other, faces that looked sub-human, open-mouthed, stuck at queer angles amid the litter of rifles, mess-tools, bundled kits. "Listen: in my brown case—it's underneath that fellow—there's one more tin of milk, I got it at Popelsk. It's for emergency, you understand? You must see that no one else gets hold of it—if I don't last this trip, I mean—you're quite likely to need it for Conrad later on."

"I'll remember, yes. But you don't mean that, about not lasting the trip?"

"One can't be sure," he said. "It makes no difference, anyhow. But Conrad is going to be all right—I'm certain, I know that."

"How? How do you know?"

"Because it's God's will," he answered, as if impatiently. "A merciful God doesn't demand the lives of us all. Victor's gone already. There's got to be someone to fulfil His purposes. I tell you, I know the child is going to live."

Was that just to give me fresh heart? When the subterranean river of his thoughts emerged to flow for a little way above the ground, sometimes a narrow torrent, sometimes a broad and placid stream, I could never tell what course it had followed when out of sight. My own mind was hazed with the remnants of the night's broken and shallow sleep. I said, feeling my way:

"You know there's nothing I won't do for him. I mean—not only for what he is to me——"

And with a sudden eagerness, which greatly moved me, he responded, "Yes, Stefanie—yes, I know that! It's strange—I can't understand God's ways—it's strange to me, but I can't think of anyone else, anyone I've known, who'd show herself a better mother for Victor's child."

A little afterwards (or it may have been on the next morning) he said, "I wish my own father could have lived to see him. He was devoted to children; I used to think the coming of each generation started a new life in him. You knew my father? Yes yes, of course, he used to speak of you, you commanded a great deal of his affection. Perhaps Conrad will be like him—I see a resemblance in the eyes sometimes. (Yes, Conrad, you! Your great-grandfather, it's a pity you won't ever know him.) Is he all right, do you think? Shall I take him for a little now? . . . Yes, in his young days he was a great patriot, my father, they said he was destined to be a leader in the Polish resurgence. That was before his exile. They crushed him, these people, his life was really over before he was twenty-eight. And when a man like that is lost to Catholic Poland it's a loss for all the civilized world. No, one doesn't understand these things, I can never understand the working of God's will."

I said, "I suppose the Count may still be alive."

He shook his head. "No—my mother told me. He died just after she was taken away from him. She's certain of that—I don't know how she found out. . . . And you, petit-fils, you're all that's left of us, you're the only one who can live to make Poland great again."

If physical hardships affected him little, he was, I think, troubled prematurely by a sickness of the mind which commonly afflicts the aged: his brain, for most of fifty years, had been used to working under load; and now that nothing was required of it—no plans, no organization—he had to manufacture fresh outlets for its ceaseless energy.

". . . Listen, Stefanie, there's something I want you to do. If there's a tribunal of any sort, I want you to take notes—mental notes, it'll have to be—so you can make a record afterwards. Who was present—any names you can find out—what the judges said, what I said myself. That's not for my sake—it doesn't matter whether anyone remembers me as a person—it's for the purpose of history. It's important for future generations of Poles to know what sort of charges were brought against us, what really happened. They need to be given chapter and verse."

I recall the business-like voice in which he laid this curious charge on me, and with it comes a quick, confused impression of the place where it was uttered: a tunnel-shaped building lit by acetylene burners and filled from end to end by nondescripts like ourselves, some sleeping where they stood, with a swarm of officials smoking and jabbering against the tables on one side. The train had stopped in the middle of the night. Zukol, arriving in a fluster, had ordered us to climb down, and the friendly soldiers had helped us drag our baggage across a wide area of sidings interspersed with banks of frozen snow. In the reception shed I sat with my back against the wall, a little dazed by the sensation of being indoors, by the light, the pressure of human breath and voices; while Julius, with Conrad in his arms, stood looking down at me with Gallio's patience.

"And then, if possible, I think people ought to know how the business ended. Of course it's a thousand to one against their letting you witness the execution—I shouldn't wish it, in any case, I know that women dislike that sort of thing—but you may find someone who can give you details. I want the record to be as complete as you can make it."

I was longing to fall asleep, but in their moods of earnestness men have to be answered. I said:

"You're jumping to conclusions, surely. I don't believe—after all this time—I don't think anything's going to happen."

"Then why did they send that youth to bring me all this way? And why did they send for you as well?"

This last was a troublesome question for me—it raised a subject which we had avoided until then. He saw, of course, my embarrassment; and he said, after a moment's hesitation:

"Listen, I realize it's going to be a strain for you, this business. But in fact, you know, your side of it will be perfectly plain sailing— I know how justice works in this country, I've been through it all before. They've got your evidence already. All they'll want from you is your assent to the written statement—every comma of it. And you may as well give it without blinking, because the result would be just the same if you didn't."

I said in confusion, "I signed that statement when I didn't really know what I was doing—I didn't understand my own mind——"

That made him look at me with one of Victor's expressions, gravely, as if I had put forward something new and profound.

"Yes," he said reflectively, "and when we act like that, outside our will, I wonder if we're really responding to a will which overrules our own."

Every few minutes Zukol was coming back to us, like a dog reporting on the pleasures of the woods.

"It's all going quite nicely. The transfer document requires one more signature, then my responsibility will be over. Later on I may be given leave to go to Sverdlovsk, I have my sister and my aunt there."

"That would be most agreeable for them," Julius said.

"I think that in spite of the delays the journey has been managed very successfully."

"Yes, indeed, you're much to be congratulated."

Zukol lit up with pleasure. "You think that really, under all the circumstances, it was all quite satisfactory?"

"But of course! I have never travelled with greater economy. You must tell your aunt I said so."

"Oh—oh, that is most kind."

When Zukol had been swallowed again in the crowd at the office tables, Julius turned rather wearily to me. "Yes, they're all the same, he's after a gratuity. If he gets me some milk for Conrad I'll give him something—not unless."

"Shall I take Conrad now?"

"No, you must rest."

"But you——?"

"I'm tired," he agreed, without moving, "I'm very tired." (And I doubt if he had ever spoken those words before.)

"Can't you sit down? These people could move a bit."

"There isn't any rest," he said abstractedly, "not for me, not yet. Not till this is over. But it's got so much nearer—that's what I find so heartening. I agree with that jackanapes, the journey's been most satisfactory."

He was shifting so as to get Conrad, who had begun to whimper, into a new position; but that was a mechanical action—he had become expert in this handling—and I saw that he was still oblivious of everything but his own thoughts: the hubbub and laughter from the reception tables, an old woman moaning and gesticulating at his feet, these were not even stirring his senses.

"Of course, it's like one's profession—you get the commands you don't ask for, they find the dullest theatres for you to serve in, the whole shape of a battle's different from the one you planned.

You know, I was ready to live for Poland, and when I saw that Poland was going under I thought I should have the happiness of dying for her. And you see how it's worked out—I'm going to die for a senseless crime, a crime against one of my own people, which I didn't even commit. The only thing you can tell Conrad—if you ever tell him about me—the only thing you can say is that in the end I accepted the will of God, that I accepted it gladly. . . . I don't know if one is really at rest, in the end. They don't seem able to tell one with any certainty. But one must be released from one's own failures, from trying to find one's way back, we can surely count on that. Yes, it's good to have got so near deliverance, after all this time." He bent to examine Conrad's forehead, as if there might be something he could read there. "I'm sorry I shall never have a chance to talk to him. But you'll do it for me, some time? You —you have shown me a great deal of loyalty. I've been grateful to you very often."

Yes, he was tired, encased in weariness; how else, knowing our masters as he did, could he have supposed that they would hurry themselves to do one Polish prisoner the favour of ending his life.

'*So near deliverance.*' We were in that building all next day. At nightfall we were bundled into lorries and driven some eighty kilometres to a wired enclosure where we had leave to make our own arrangements: here, when morning came, the rising mist revealed some features which seemed familiar—the latticed girders of a bridge, an ancient omnibus lying on its side—and I realized by degrees that we were back at Czennik. The impetus of our destiny seemed to have petered out; and when some weeks had passed I almost came to believe that I should spend the rest of my life in that accursed place.

vi

But why should I abuse so innocent a township as Czennik! It was not like Mikirka, no one forced you to any kind of labour, the cold was not unbearable: when we had been there a week (a month? —I can't remember) all the snow had gone. It was hard to find any food there, but we had been short before. Across the river the townsfolk went their own way—happily, as far as one could see— and no one troubled us at all.

The population of the enclosure had changed, there were few women or other civilians now. At a guess I should say there were three thousand soldiers, most of them Poles. In addition to the buildings which had housed us before—boat-sheds, crumbling warehouses, a derelict asbestos factory—there was now a wood-and-iron shelter where two or three hundred could sleep. The flooding of the river bank reduced the space we had to walk in, but according to someone's calculation the area of our liberty was never smaller than three acres; and the flood actually improved our situation by carrying away some part of the fetid rubbish which was carpeting the ground in surprising depth.

Some of the soldiers believed they were awaiting trial for sundry offences; no one exactly knew what the rest were here for. (The place was variously styled a rehabilitation centre and a labour reserve.) Many had been in the mines or with farming co-operatives, others had spent their captivity making extensive journeys which brought them to no useful destination—there were several who, leaving Czennik a year before, had made a circuit larger than ours, only to find themselves back where they had started. The sick were numerous. Those unable to get about—the frostbite cases, men suffering from deficiency diseases—were mostly in the old count-ing-house, where a Russian and a Polish doctor did what was possible for them, as long as they lived, with any drugs that arrived; the rest, though cadaverous of face, appeared to have nothing wrong with them except a disinclination to use their faculties—to move their limbs, to get themselves clean, to look directly at any object or to speak. Behaviour generally was good. Men sometimes begged for things to barter with the traders who set their stalls along the ice or who, later, brought their boats across to the wire, but I never heard of any thieving. Not once was I molested or treated discourteously, though some of the feebler prisoners were always gathering to stare at me as children of the street do. These, when I spoke to them, seemed not to hear me, and if I raised my voice they often burst into tears.

Perhaps I was fortunate in my sex, since women are conditioned, as a rule, to resist the effects of boredom better than men. Even so, I should have come nearer to the state of those soldiers had I not had Conrad to look after—to forage for, to protect both from the weather and from the many sources of contagion which surrounded him. With Conrad to embrace and talk to, with all his future years to safeguard from day to day, my own life was far from purposeless. And so, until the middle of June, I could pity and sometimes encourage those strange-eyed soldiers, the childish ones. Till then, my case was so much happier than theirs.

15

i

IT must have been towards the end of May that there were rumours of a judicial commission having arrived in the town. One heard of men being taken out of the enclosure for examination. I did not happen to know any of them.

Then Julius was sent for. This, I know by calculation, was on the 20th of June—the 20th June 1941. They sent for him in the early morning. It was a day which became very hot, with intense sunshine.

Later in the day I was sent for too. That must have been about noon. I was in the ration queue when I heard my name being shouted all over the enclosure. I went to the Commandant's office, and there was a truck waiting for me there. The Commandant's clerk could not tell me what it was all about or how long I was likely to be away.

There was a woman in the office, a Polish woman, who was waiting to see the Commandant. She said that she would look after Conrad while I was away. But I said no, I should take him with me.

I do not think that this was a foolish decision. I did not know how long I was to be away—it was not even certain that I should return to the enclosure at all.

It was a very fine day, very hot. I had put a piece of cloth over Conrad's face, I was afraid the dust which rose in a great cloud round the little open truck would get in his eyes or throat. I remember the strangeness of finding myself in the busy street that I had seen for so long at a distance across the river, and I remember the sight of a young, pretty woman pushing her baby in a home-made perambulator, with a laced canopy like those you saw in the Ujadowski park in the old days. We passed a shop with pretty hats in the window.

There was a wide courtyard at the back of the police building, hot as an oven at that hour. I was glad when we got into the shadow on the far side, because Conrad could not have stood such fierce sunshine for very long. We were in the charge of a woman officer then; her uniform was much like that of the soldiers, and she had, I believe, a corporal's markings. In reality I think she was just a peasant woman, with a primitive and stupid face. I had no chance to examine it with any care.

The building she took me to was new, a concrete affair which looked rather like a shippen. You went in at one corner and along a windowless passage with a row of doors on one side. The corporal opened one of these and put me into a room about eight feet by five. I asked if I might have some water and she readily brought this in an old meat tin. When she went away she double-locked the door and drew long bolts which made the noise of a safe being shut.

The walls dividing this room from those on either side were sturdily built of wood, I suppose about half an inch thick. Someone may have tried to break through one of these partition walls, and special precautions had been taken to prevent this happening again: they were thickly sown with the protruding points of nails driven through from the other side, a heavy lattice wire of small mesh had been fastened to the whole area of wall, and outside was a further netting made of barbed wire. It was a job in which the tradesman must have taken some pride.

But of course I did not notice such details when I was first in the room. All my attention was taken up by Conrad. I had to hold him all the time, because there was no furniture in the room except a deal form, and I could not put him on the concrete floor.

He was crying a good deal. I thought he must be thirsty, but he did not seem able to swallow more than a drop or two of the water which I poured between his lips from my cupped hand. His breathing was quick and shallow, rather like that of dogs when they are overheated, and it evidently gave him some pain. That, of course, may have been caused solely by the great heat of the room, which had practically no ventilation, but I think there may also have been some obstruction in his respiratory system. It is difficult, now, to remember exactly what his condition had been in the days immediately preceding this one: he had never, of course, had the appearance or capacities of a normally healthy child.

From time to time I shouted and banged on the door, hoping that I might get someone to bring me a little milk for him. I thought that if I could get him to swallow just a spoonful of milk it would do something to offset the strain which this difficult breathing was imposing on his lungs. I remember that I talked to him, telling him that someone would come soon; and that, for answer, he looked at me distantly, as if I was wrong to trouble him with details of that kind. He kept shutting his mouth tightly, and then there were movements in his throat which were painful for me to see.

After some time they came to fetch me again. It was a man who came. He took me across the courtyard to the main building, which smelt of the excrement of dogs. From the way the shadows had moved I judge that I had been in the cell for five or six hours. I asked this man if I was going to be given some food for my child. He said, "Later on."

I did not have to wait about anywhere in the main building; I was taken straight to the door of the room where I was to be questioned. But in the corridor, just before I went in, a man in uniform stopped me and told me I could not take my baby in with me. That was not allowed, he said, at an interrogation.

I said that my baby was ill and could not leave me. I said that I would not answer any questions unless they allowed me to have him there.

The man told me that my baby would be looked after. He called, and the woman corporal came. This woman said that she would look after Conrad, and the man said the questioning would only take a short time. There was not much light in this corridor, and I could not see the woman's face very well, but, as I have said, it seemed to be a homely face.

I asked her if she would find some milk for Conrad, and give it to him very carefully. She promised to do so. I explained to her that he was ill and could only be fed with great patience. She said that she understood. I also told her that he ought to lie on something soft in some cool place, but that he must not be left by himself. This, too, she seemed to understand.

The man was now in a state of angry impatience. In the end I gave Conrad to the woman and allowed myself to be taken into the commissioners' room. Conrad did not cry when he was transferred from my arms to this woman's. In the poor light I did not see his face at that moment. I did not try to see it.

I have said already that I had no chance to examine the woman's face. Her breath had a sour smell, which is what you expect in people of that kind. There was no other smell that I detected. I have told myself a thousand times that if I had been resolute they might have let me take Conrad into the room. To that there is one answer: I did not believe so at the time. I thought they would use physical force if I did not obey them. You cannot struggle to any purpose when you are holding a young child in your arms.

ii

I have no detailed memory of that interrogation. It was shapeless and quite unreal. They asked me as much about myself as about Julius—Had I taken steps to report my identity immediately upon my arrival at Mikirka? How long had I been a widow? What had been my husband's political affiliations?—until I came to feel that the rôle assigned to me was that of defendant rather than witness. That aspect, however, was of no interest to me at all. No doubt the affair was protracted by my own stupidity: my thoughts were with Conrad all the time, I only half-heard the questions, and I kept saying things like, "Well, have it your own way! . . . Does it matter? . . . All right, I'll give you any answer you like!" which, to men who had their own kind of conscientiousness, must have been highly unsatisfactory. Yes, I suppose they showed great patience with me—patience of the sort you associate with brainless wives—and once, when I fainted, they sent for water and allowed me several minutes' rest. There were four of them, I think; chain-smokers; small, indoor men. One, who wore an enormous amethyst ring, spent the whole of the four or five hours making careful drawings on his writing-pad of very fat naked women.

Afterwards, when I was being led back to the building I had come from, I passed a small group of men talking in the courtyard. I asked them where the woman corporal was who was looking after my child. One of them answered that she had gone off duty. Another, when I questioned him (no doubt rather hysterically), told me that the woman, before leaving, had put the child in the cell I had come from. The child was quite all right, this man said.

It was, of course, dark now. It was some time after midnight, I think. I ran across the courtyard, with my escort following. He was laughing a good deal; I think he had been drinking, and it must have amused him to see me running. It took him some time to get the door of the prison building open.

He had a rather feeble electric torch. I saw the number of the cell at which he stopped, it was Number 11. I do not know if this was the cell I had been in before.

I asked him as he was unfastening the door, "Is this where my child is?"

He said, "Yes."

Directly the door was open I pushed past him and ran inside. This, I think, was a natural thing to do. The light from the torch was just enough to show me a bundle on the floor at the far end of the cell. The thought in my mind was, 'She must have wrapped Conrad in a blanket'.

Although I moved quickly, the light had gone before I reached the bundle and knelt beside it.

When I felt the bundle it stirred, and to my great astonishment I heard Julius's voice, asking sleepily, "Who's that? What do you want?" It took me a moment to recover from the surprise of finding him there; then I said, "It's Stefanie." I think it was just as I said those words that I heard the noise of the door being bolted. I know that what Julius said to me was, "Stefanie? What's happened to Conrad, what have you done with him?"

In the total darkness I threw myself at the door, shouting out, "Wait, come back, you've put me in the wrong cell! Come back! Let me out!"

He heard me. Yes, he heard me all right. He came back—at least, I think he came back, I think he was some way down the passage when I started shouting. He called out:

"What's the matter? There's nothing wrong with that cell."

I shouted, "My baby isn't here! I've got to be with my baby!"

"The baby's all right!" he said.

I said, "My baby's ill, he can't be left alone!"

He must have heard that too—I was shouting at the top of my voice—and I do not see how he can have failed to understand what I was saying: my Russian, though never polished, was perfectly comprehensible at that time. Of course I do not know how drunk he was. He did not sound very drunk. It is possible that he was a man whose speech was not much affected by intoxication.

Julius shouted, "*Open this door, do you hear!*"

The man, answering me, said, "It'll all be seen to in the morning."

iii

The cell where the woman had put Conrad was the one next door. I discovered this shortly after the man had gone away, because, when I paused from shouting and banging the door, I heard Conrad whimpering. He was, in fact, only a few feet away from me. The noise he made was very small, but enough to reach my ear.

I called through the wall that I was coming. I ought not to have done that. Of course the words themselves meant nothing to him, but he must have heard my voice—in the tone I used for him only —and he must have expected me to come.

If Julius had not been there I should have gone on through the rest of the night—or as long as my strength lasted—calling out and thumping the door, and then tearing my hands as I tried to break the wire on the partition wall. Julius, however, did not allow that; after a time he persuaded me to bring myself under control. Even then I was not very sensible, I remember that I kept on saying, "He'll die, I know he'll die!" to which he answered patiently "No, he's not going to die. We'll get to him through the wall, but it's going to take some time. No, I'm not going to let him die."

All this time he was hard at work; not tearing recklessly at the wire, as I kept doing, but attacking it in a man's way, using science as well as force; and I realized from the sound of his breathing that the effort was costing all his strength. (I suppose he had not been given anything to eat since leaving the camp.) He had no tool of any kind. I could not, of course, see what he was doing, but I know from what I remember hearing that he started by breaking up the deal form, to use the pieces for prising away a portion of the barbed wire: this alone must have been a formidable task, as the wood kept snapping. The heavy netting next the wall must have been harder still to deal with, but perhaps the greatest task of all was to force the wall itself, which, protected by the nails, would not yield to kicks or blows: he had, as I learnt afterwards, to construct a tool by twisting up the wire, and with this to make an incision between the boards, so that one of them could at last be levered outwards. All this I realize now. At the time it seemed to me that he kept losing the sense of urgency, that for long periods he was doing practically nothing.

Whenever Julius paused in the work I listened with my ear close to the partition. I cannot tell, at this distance, whether I continued to hear Conrad crying, or whether the sound came only from my imagination. The sound that I seemed to hear was very small.

I do not think that Julius spoke at all while he worked. I heard his strained breathing all the time.

It does not seem possible that I slept during that night. But I must have passed into a state akin to sleep, because I was surprised when I found that there was some light in the cell, as if it had reached us suddenly. It came, this light, from a window in the roof. The time, I suppose, was about four o'clock in the morning. It was possible to see, then, the state that Julius was in, his clothes savagely torn and drenched with the blood that streamed from his hands. But at the time I did not pay attention to that. He had already succeeded in breaking one of the boards, and while we worked to enlarge the gap I was trying to see through into the next cell.

It was some time before I saw Conrad. That was because he had been put down close to the wall at the far end of that cell—farther along than the place where we were enlarging the hole. When I did catch sight of him I saw that he was not moving at all. I don't remember if I called to him.

Even when the hole in the wall itself was big enough for me to squeeze through I could not do so, because there was still the netting and the barbed wire on the other side. It would have taken at least an hour, I think, to break this away, because neither Julius nor I was fit for a severe task at that stage. But in fact we did not have to do this work, because a man came presently and was quite willing to let me go into the next cell. Or a woman, it may have been. The light had improved by then. I have an idea that that day, like the one before it, became hot and fine.

i

WE were not punished in any way for breaking the partition wall. At least, I don't think so.

We were taken back to the enclosure that morning. No, it was the next morning. I believe I spent the intervening night in a room in the main police building. There was another woman in there with me, some kind of wardress, I imagine. Someone told me that when I was back in the enclosure Conrad would be sent to me there, and that the Commandant's staff would make what arrangements I wished. But this did not happen. I do not know where he lies.

I heard, when I returned to the enclosure, that a soldier there had been looking for me. But I felt no duty or inclination to find out about that.

ii

It was not quite so hot that day, I think there was a slight breeze coming off the river. I sat with a number of soldiers on the edge of the concrete ramp running down into the water which had formerly been used for launching boats. Here, when the sun was not too strong, it was pleasant to feel it on your skin, and you had a good view of the river traffic. I could see right along the street through which I had been driven to the police building, but the familiar scene did not connect itself with that experience—I saw it only as the animated model of a street. My eyes were in a curious state at this time, and my judgment of distance was confused; when I tried to walk I stumbled over objects which had appeared to be several feet away.

Yes, my clearest recollection is of the sun's gentle warmth that day, and of the pleasure my senses got from total idleness. For a long time I had regarded my body just as a troublesome necessity, like an artificial limb: much subject to sickness, it had, in my work of looking after Conrad, been mainly a hindrance to me. Now, when that occupation was over, and there was no more happiness, this body seemed to reassert its claims, its latent powers of comfort. Strangely, I was hungry, and in the way that explorers do I found myself making pictures of meals I had enjoyed long before in luxurious hotels. I thought, too, of beautiful things that a woman could wear, of houses where there were deep carpets in handsome rooms; and it seemed to me—as I sat on the ramp looking at the sheds and the triple fence along the river bank—that the small chance of contentment which might offer to human beings lay solely in things like those. But fancy was all that I fed on. The body which craved for exquisite dishes would not be stirred to join the line at the issue shed, fifty yards away. When Julius brought me a plate of borscht I left it untouched.

He sat beside me most of the time, and I was once more grateful for his presence. He did not offer me compassion, as another might have done. In him, grief took the shape of bitter rage—against the gaolers, against all the Russians, perhaps against God—but the fact that it came from the same source as mine provided all the sympathy I could do with then. Between long intervals of silence he talked rather to himself than to me; of how his life's purpose had been frustrated piece by piece, of the hopes he had cherished for his sons, of Henryk's futility, Casimir's defection; and I do not think he was hurt—or even aware—that I made no pretence of listening. Only once, as far as I remember, did he speak to me directly, when he said with a sudden intensity, "You mustn't think that everything's over—you're not too old to bear another child." Those words I heard without understanding; and I found no meaning in the sentences he repeated several times with almost frightening vehemence, "No, it's not all over! I tell you, we have not been beaten yet—Poland will not exist without me, without my breed." There were others—a Lettish woman I was acquainted with, one or two of the soldiers—who came and spoke to me, trying to show me kindness; but I could not respond to them: really I did not want to have anything to do with humans. Julius I accepted, because he had travelled so much with me, because it seemed as natural to have him beside me as to possess my own body. He was a creature who required no responses. Sitting like a statue, grey, emaciated, with his hideously scarred hands on his knees, he belonged to a separate order; he was my last connection with meaningful existence, and as men find comfort in God's permanence, I found it, during those petrified hours, in his.

We were still sitting there, he and I, after all the others had moved away. But when the light had almost gone, and the wind was chilled, I found my way to the place where I was used to sleeping on nights that were not too cold, a space beneath one of the boat sheds, where the ground was soft and where you were not too much crowded by other prisoners. Here, as I lay with my arms empty, in the darkness which made me quite alone, grief came in the fullness and violence of its power, as physical pain comes to those who wake from anæsthesia; and in this desolation I saw the created world as absolute evil, the power to feel, to know, as a curse laid cynically on all mankind. That anguish might have been relieved by tears, but I had lost the faculty of weeping; its heat was like that of a dry and scorching wind, in which tears could not form.

iii

The kind of sleep which at last came to relieve me was not unconsciousness: I continued to feel the pain in my forehead, the unevenness of the ground beneath my shoulders. Only, reality was dulled, and as if I had been withdrawn a little way from my own sensations, I could look upon my grief with something like detachment: there was an 'I' who suffered, an 'I' who witnessed this suffering almost with incredulity. Now, indeed, I wept without restraint, but silently; and feeling the warmth of tears which seemed to flow from a distant source, I watched this weakness of my other self with a compassion like that of parenthood.

In this state of drowsiness I could not remember what distress it was that afflicted me; confused, I supposed it came from the ache and tiredness of my body, which would not yield to the investment of sleep. So, I was dimly grateful when my head was moved from the rough ground to lie more softly on someone's shoulder, when I felt the warmth of a coat pulled over me and the easy weight of a man's arm resting on my side. The sense of comfort increased with the realization that it was Julius who had come to lie beside me, for he was someone I was used to; the feel of his searching hands was like the feel of Victor's, and I had learnt to think of him as of one whose ways were kind.

For a while I was troubled, half-conscious that only Victor himself should be so close to me as this, that some other loyalty was being infringed; then I remembered that I was free from the sanctions of earlier days, for when life had proved to be totally evil the distinction of right and wrong had lost its validity. Reassured, I could accept the solace offered to my body, the restfulness which came from the strength of these enfolding arms, a contentment I had almost forgotten in the feel of a hard skin pressed against mine. No effort was required of me; my spirit was not engaged in this, and the passion of old experience did not return: there was only a vast refreshment, an intoxication, as when one's body is surrendered to the sun's warmth, to the warmth of an Italian sea.

Afterwards I drifted into a deeper sleep, where the trammels of pain were all cast off and where no dream came.

iv

A rumour was blowing through the camp next morning that back in Europe the Germans had turned to march eastward, grasping at that part of Poland which did not already belong to them; and by late afternoon it seemed to be known that the report was true. This brought a flutter of excitement and evidently of pleasure among the Polish soldiers; for prisoners imagine that any change in the outside world must somehow be for their good, and these, I suppose, found artless satisfaction in the idea that it was the Russians' turn to suffer hurt and loss. Strangely, this optimistic spirit caught hold of the staff as well. "It's all we want," one of them proclaimed in my hearing, "a chance to scoop up those Prussian droppings!" And after drinking in the town all morning a very odious officer, whose normal function was to round up parties for fatigues, was actually dancing round the enclosure, shouting that all of us were brothers now and embracing everyone who came in his way. Yes, it seemed curious that they should so rejoice in hearing the war had overleapt its former boundaries. But in these matters men are like children, the noise of drums excites them and experience teaches them no lessons.

"It will make a difference," Julius said judiciously (but not without a flicker of elation) when he came to bring me food. "We shall have a bargaining counter now, something to argue with."

And it seemed to me that he had recovered in the course of hours, that day, some part of his former personality—his old self-confidence, his dedication. These eyes were the ones I had known in the granary billet at Setory.

"Yes," he said, absorbed in his own thoughts, scarcely looking at me, "the picture won't be clear for a few weeks yet. But I think they'll need us now, these muzhiki. And I think we may get our price."

It meant almost nothing to me, this talk of bargains and of partnerships; it did not seem to matter how a world where Conrad had been left to die might be divided under flags. I lay throughout the day on a bed of rubbish beside the hulk of a fishing boat, so empty in mind that sorrow itself was only a shapeless load, a winter that darkened all emotion. As yesterday, my body found contentment in idleness, in the sun's temperate warmth; and now, beneath the wavering vertigo, the lethargy of illness, it reposed in the drowsy comfort which succeeds fulfilment. The shapes that passed, the fluttering voices, were but a frieze drawn hazily on the surface of my understanding.

I could scarcely stir myself when a man was brought to see me, a heavily moustached and whiskered Sergeant of Artillery, veteran of Pilsudski's First Brigade. He had tried to find me two days earlier, he said. His physical state was infinitely worse than mine—he was to live for only a few more hours—but he would not sit down, he stood at attention all the time he spoke, with his two friends (themselves sick men) holding him up on either side. From where I lay on the ground he looked immensely tall, this skeleton of a man with his tattered greatcoat hanging loosely on his shrunken shoulders, and the pale eyes looking down at me from such a distance were unreal and disturbing. I only longed for him to go away.

Was my name really Kolbeck, he wanted to know (as all the inquisitors did), was I actually the wife of Colonel Victor Kolbeck? And when I had assured him of this:

"I have been with him," he said.

A former sense of duty struggled against my lassitude: it had been Victor's wish that I should never fail in courtesy to soldiers, that I should know their names, regarding them as members of a large family. I roused myself, then, so far as to ask him:

"You served with my husband? That was before the War, perhaps?"

"I have been with him," he repeated. "At Karmishkent."

"At Karmishkent?"

He nodded slowly. "I've come from there. From the mines. Colonel Kolbeck was sleeping in the same barrack as me."

There was a childlike eagerness which, as he spoke, showed

through his deference, through the weariness of a mortally sick man. I found it hard to disappoint him, but there was no use in prolonging an interview for which neither of us had strength to spare. I told him:

"You've made a mistake, I'm afraid. My husband is dead, he was killed at the beginning of the War."

Against my will my eyes had fallen shut; but they opened again, and I saw that the Sergeant was still there, still watching me with patience, now confused and unhappy.

"The Colonel was wounded, yes," he said awkwardly. "He was shot from his horse, a wheel went over him, they told me. Yes, when they found him they thought he must be dead. But—gracious pardon—he didn't die."

For a moment or two I went on watching this odd trio, the exhausted and embarrassed veteran still standing at attention, the glum, dutiful soldiers who supported him; then I asked them to leave me. I believe I made that request politely, thanking them for the pains this visit had cost them, and promising to see the Sergeant in the counting-house when I myself was well enough to move about. But as soon as they had gone I fell back into my former lethargy, and a little afterwards I concluded that the episode had been hallucination, a form of waking dream; for if it had been reality, the information the Sergeant had given me could only be true: that would mean there was a possibility of my seeing Victor again, alive; and since the power of evil governed all existence, it was not credible, I thought, that so complete a revolution of my state, goodness of such magnitude, should ever be within my reach. When Julius asked me next day, with a curious air of discretion, if an old Sergeant of Artillery had been to see me, I found myself unaccountably in tears. All I could say was:

"I think that someone came. I think it was yesterday. He had an extraordinary story."

i

IT was not happiness that I looked for when I was making my way by stages towards Karmishkent; not, at least, the happiness which youth imagines, the achievement and the sunshine—for in the long, slow summer of 1941 I was far from young. I did not suppose that when I reached my destination I should find a harboured tenderness, the comfort of intimate understanding; only that I should escape from the desert of my loneliness. I know, now, that a spirit can stay alive when no other is growing near enough to give it warmth or shade; but the mastery of solitude is not learnt quickly by one who has twice been taken away from its misery. To see the loved face, to let the heart's long silence break in words which would need no order or restraint, that was the prize of this difficult excursion, and I could not contemplate a blessedness more absolute than that. Nor was I doubtful of success. While others were searching for their friends with only the slenderest clues to their whereabouts (in a country larger than North America) or even their survival, I was at least informed where Victor had been in recent months. Hope and faith do not stay far apart. To know that he was alive was the same, for me, as knowing that I should find him.

This faith was needed. It was not till August that I got a permit to travel, with a temporary certificate of Polish nationality. (That was two or three weeks after a high official had come to make a speech, telling us of the London agreement and announcing formally that our countries were now 'in comradely alliance'.) I left Czennik in the first week of September. By the end of October I had got no farther than Zuvelsk.

It is a common paradox, I suppose, that among the images which the mind carries, the least distinct are those of people we love. The single photograph I had of Victor was useless—he had always been sulky and obstinate with photographers—and though I could think of him in a thousand situations, remember countless things he had said, his face continually eluded me. In a word, I could recall the whole of him except his personality. Love survives on very little food, it does not need exactness. But in the days when I lived entirely within myself (because there was no Conrad to live with), and when this inward life was absorbed in the prospect of reunion, the desire for a clearer image grew like physical hunger. In the Tseskevoi district, where, needing food and money, I joined for a time in the harvesting, I was working mostly with men, a number of them Poles; and I constantly peered into their faces, hoping that some look of a man whose head was shaped like Victor's, some gesture from one of similar build, would give my picture a fresh substantiality. But no one bore any likeness to him. They were all a little unreal, the men plodding beside me in the fields, the people with bloodless faces and empty eyes who were crammed against me in the slow, swarming eastbound trains. I could not talk to them, because I had not yet recovered the faculty of speech except for simple phrases—What is the fare? Is a train likely this week? When are my papers likely to come?—and sometimes I thought they were hostile to me, for they seemed to eye me covertly and to exchange looks among themselves as if they knew about some crime of which I was guilty. I imagined (in a way that seems strange to me now) that they were blaming me for Conrad's death or that they despised me for being unable to live by myself. When I get to Karmïshkent, I said, the coldness and contempt of all these others will mean nothing to me. Meanwhile, I needed their company, however unfriendly, because I was always in danger of losing my belief in physical progress. As the scenes I came to were repeated and repeated, the bare and squalid stations, the naked immensity of land surrounding them, I was haunted by a sense of illusion, by the recurring apprehension that between me and my destination stood a barrier of infinite space.

I went through a period of depression, when my waking thoughts of Victor took their colour from melancholy dreams. This was in the louse-ridden prison at Yusernoe, where I served a sentence of two or three weeks for illegal use of the railway, sharing a cell with a dozen native delinquents (who treated me with peculiar kindness). Here the old doubts returned. The memories of Victor which I should have chosen for my mind to wander in—his acts of sudden generosity in our childhood, the humility and passion of his secret courtship, the tenderness he had shown me when, for the second time, I had failed to bear him a living child—these had become remote, elusive, like snatches of music heard in a busy street, while the other recollections grew large and vivid in their place. How often had I vexed him with my frivolities, how wilfully disregarded the solemn views men have on fatherland, on the obligations of caste and profession! And he, how careless he had been of my sensibilities, how often ungracious even in public—'You must forgive my wife's conversation, she was brought up mostly in Switzerland' —how unreasonably his rages had been protracted into days of sullen inattention, of meals taken in sepulchral silence . . . The darkness of this mood came partly from physical causes. I was again pregnant; and though I had discovered this with hardly any emotion except a weariness of spirit, it must have affected me more powerfully than I realized at the time. (I remember how, when I was beaten for some offence and thought the shock would have destroyed the embryo's life, I cried with relief.) The cell itself was small, and the courtyard where we exercised for an hour each day was scarcely ever reached by the sun. With eyes affected by amœbic dysentery, I saw the yellow-grey and dirty walls, the refuse that had lain for generations about the yard, as an epigraph of hopelessness, and there were hours when I thought once more that all the goodness of life had for ever escaped me: if Victor had cared for me only in pity, perhaps from a sense of obligation, how could I start so late as this to found the edifice of love!

And yet the flame of confidence was never quite extinguished. When I see his face, I said, and the night of loneliness is finished, my own hoarded power of loving must waken some response in him.

Some soldiers who were friendly took me in their lorry to a place called Eesk, where I had to stay for a time through illness. I was in the cabin of a Sart family who, I think, were horse-breeders, and who gave me food.

ii

I cannot find that place in the atlas my friend has lent me. Probably it was less than a hundred miles from Karmishkent. It seems ridiculous that I took two months or more to accomplish that final stage.

It was winter, but there was no snow here, only a persistent rain which hid the hills; on days when it slacked a yellow fog seemed to lie along the road, confusing distance and perspective, but I think this obscurity may have belonged to my eyes, which were still working lamely. It was a country of few villages, and these became more sparse as the cultivated land gave out. You went for two or three days through wide, coarse pasture without seeing any habitation. There were no trees.

For a part of the way I was walking with some other Poles, a man and (I think) his two sisters, elderly people who also had hopes of finding lost friends at Karmishkent; but when one of the women died, and the brother and sister were discouraged, I was glad to go on alone, since my pace was better than theirs. Once a farrier took me in his cart for something like twenty versts, but there were many others trying to get lifts along that road and few vehicles to take them.

When the road took an upward slope, and went on climbing for several days, I felt the increased weight of my womb, and that meant going more slowly. (The problem was always to make the food I carried last out till I reached some place where I could beg for more.) I was not despondent, however, for having come so far I could not doubt that I should reach my goal. In mind I was always far ahead of the place my body had got to, and I often suffered the kind of vexation you feel when you are late for some engagement, and a child, too big to be picked up and carried, is dragging you back. Yet there is comfort of a sort in physical weariness, and there were times when the heart's music sounded so triumphantly that all fatigue and pain were lost in it. The road wound narrowly between grey bastions of rock, here smooth as a child's skin, here wrinkled like an old woman's, and I thought these quiet spectators were in friendship with my purpose. The cold, upland wind bore the clean smell of rock and fern; the rain was hardly sensible by a body so long used to its attrition, and the dullness it gave to the light, its monotonous whisper on the gravelled road, wrought in the scene a uniformity which strangely contented me. For now, when there was nothing to tell me of progress in space, I had the sense of being borne through time in a vessel of safety. Here solitude itself was grateful, since any companion would have divided me from the imagined companionship. He is alive, I repeated, he is alive, and time, however slowly, will bring him to me in the end.

Some men who found me sleeping near their roadside camp told me I had not far to go. A labour camp it must have been—I do not think these men were soldiers. When I had been with them for a day or two—a week, perhaps—sewing and washing to earn the food I needed, my legs were at my command once more.

Rather, they worked in obedience to a will that I hardly recognized as mine; for in those last miles I forgot where I was going.

I must have set out in daylight, but my memory is of walking in darkness, where all that showed was the shape of the road for a few yards ahead. I was troubled, because I imagined this walk had started at Setory, I could not think why I came to no familiar landmarks, or why—as my heaviness told me—I should have to go through the pain of bearing Conrad all over again. Were there others with me at that stage? There were voices, I think, not far behind, but the people who seemed to walk beside me cannot have been there, for Victor was among them, and Annette. Another day may have intervened, I do not remember now: I know that my anxieties were hushed at last beneath the tide of pain and sleepiness, leaving only the realization that I must keep going on. The road was descending. The cliffs had fallen back, the only boundaries were those that moved with me, a tent of darkness woven with rain in which the whimper of my breathing, the scrape of my feet on the loosened gravel, continuing more slowly and more slowly, seemed to measure the faltering of time.

In the first slackening of darkness I thought the rocks were gathering towards the road again; but these, presently, took the shape of box-like houses, a dome and minaret. Here were voices in the shadow, a dog that barked, a man who carried a pail across the road. I asked a woman drowsing in a doorway, "Is this a place, some place where people live?" and at last, when I had turned the question into Russian, she answered me, "But this is Karmishkent."

iii

It was not so difficult as I had feared. Here were many Poles, humble people but with native intelligence, who seemed to understand the trouble I had in keeping my thoughts collected and turning them into speech. These told me that a great number of our men who had worked in the mines now occupied a camp some ten kilometres on the other side of the town, awaiting transfer to the Polish corps which was forming near Tashkent. My husband might well be found among those, they said.

I had to wait for several days before I could make that trifling journey because my feet, which had hitherto behaved so well, now refused to obey me. It was not their painfulness that mattered; it was that when I tried to stand up the muscles controlling them would not respond. Indeed, my body was then so little the servant of my will that it seemed rather to be the master, as if a performing animal after long ill-usage had turned upon its trainer. I lay, with some others, in a half-ruined house near the mosque, where the walls gave us some shelter. The Poles brought us food when they could, and a Turcoman woman bandaged my feet and legs.

It was a Turcoman, in the end, who took me out to the camp. He had a little springless cart and an undersized donkey to haul it. He did me this service out of kindness alone.

iv

The camp had features in common with those of the enclosure at Czennik; it was really a vast system of bivouacs—there were bodies everywhere which looked to be uninhabited, and smells that I recognized. You could see, though, that some attempt had been made at organization; and in the shed I was taken to, labelled 'Central Adminstration', I found Polish soldiers working at tables with the sober industry of bank clerks. What was my business, please? Ah yes—and my husband's name? Yes yes, they had a list of everyone in the camp.

It was, in fact, right in front of the Corporal who was speaking, a sheaf of papers—envelopes, fly-leaves of books, margins of newspapers—on which the names had been pencilled in a neat, clerical hand; but before he would start to go through it he passed it to the man beside him. "This morning's corrections, please." This man took the list and turned the pages over quickly, glancing at a slip he held in his hand. On every page or two he put his pencil through one of the names.

The Corporal, I think, was short-sighted; probably he wore spectacles in ordinary life and had lost them: he began to finger his way through the list as if it was a cuneiform inscription, and I should have seized it myself had not an attack of weakness prevented my hands from moving. I sat quite still, then, watching his little, puckered face, which seemed to grow immense, coarse and stupid, like the effigies in a carnival. The stillness was oppressive, even the sounds inside the shed were muted and remote.

After a long time he looked up and spoke to me in a colourless voice, as if he was selling me a ticket at a railway station:

"Section 9."

This, of course, meant nothing to me.

"Section 9!" he repeated, with a touch of impatience.

I became aware, just then, that others had followed me into the shed and were awaiting their turn for the Corporal's attention. But I still did not move or speak.

"You understand?" he said. "Colonel Kolbeck is in Section 9."

"You mean—my husband?"

"You said he was."

"You mean he is here—in this camp?"

"Good God!" the Corporal said.

"You say he—you mean he's alive?"

Tiring of this business, the Corporal beckoned a man who was sitting by the window. "Albrecht! You'd better conduct this lady to Section 9. And on your way, get some water for her to drink."

But I did not need the water. My body behaved faultlessly now, it followed the guide with perfect docility. Probably my walk was lame, but my feet gave me no pain at all, and I remember thinking, as one does in dreams—How simple, how marvellously easy! There was some distance to go, perhaps half a mile.

I found myself sitting on a wooden box in what must formerly have been a farm building, with adobe walls and a reed-thatch roof. Here the smell was faintly that of a hospital. A man washing vessels in a bucket told me several times that the doctor would be here before long.

"You have come to see Colonel Kolbeck?" he asked me shyly, when we had been together for some time.

I nodded.

"You know him well?" he asked. "You knew him, perhaps, in the old days?"

I did not reply, for my mind was again working in retard: words came, and after an interval their meaning—or a part of it—followed.

"Of course," he said awkwardly, "you understand that the Colonel is—he is different. You realize that, of course."

Different? I was looking straight across the narrow room, which must have been the one the doctor used as surgery; against the wall was a packing-case with a canvas bucket standing on it, a piece of soap, and above, something I had not seen for a long time, a small looking-glass.

"This is the doctor now!" the man said.

But this arrival did not at once take my attention from the face in the glass. I had realized, of course, that my looks had long deserted me, and—given a moment to reflect—I should have expected to find my features those of at least an ageing woman. I had forgotten, however (because the inconvenience was comparatively so trivial), that my cheeks were still blotched and suppurating from a skin infection I had picked up at Yusernoe. When you are concerned simply with the business of living, of keeping a child alive, you do not even remember that appearance is a part of life. I remembered now.

". . . very useful to me in a number of ways. Useful to all of us, in fact. And of course we like him very much."

The doctor was talking to me, picking his words as a stage foreigner does. He was Russian, a city man by his appearance, scrimp and bald, as if he had grown old without growing up; a dead cigarette hung from his yellow lip.

"I just wanted to be sure," he said, "that you understood how things are."

I looked away from him, and my eyes, sedulously avoiding the glass, rested on the soap: a great slab, it was, perhaps 200 grammes. It was ridiculous, I thought, that a few people in the world should have such wealth as this.

"You see," the doctor was saying patiently, "it is remarkable to recover at all from an injury like that. It was very fortunate that he should have been taken to the Sverdlovska Hospital—there were many prisoners, many wounded, only a few of them could be given specialized treatment."

"It belongs to you," I asked him, "the soap?"

"Yes. . . . So I thought I'd better tell you. And now I won't keep you any more. You would rather go by yourself, I expect—it's only a few yards, I can show you from the doorway here."

It was plainly necessary for me to say something; so I asked again:

"You say the soap belongs to you?"

"Why, yes. You are ready to go now?"

"To go?"

"To see your husband?"

"He is here, my husband?"

"But I've been telling you——"

"No," I said, "no, I don't want to, I don't think I want to go."

The doctor acted in a way which now seems to me remarkable. He came behind me and stood there for perhaps half a minute, with his hands resting heavily on my shoulders. "You must weep," he said, "it is very important that you should weep." Then he went outside, leaving me quite alone.

I had not felt like crying at all: I had been faint and tremulous, but not tearful; yet such was the suggestive force of this insignificant-looking man that I began almost at once to cry, and for several minutes I allowed my tears to flow in senseless luxury. After a time the doctor returned.

"You are ready now? Yes, I think so, I think so!"

With his arm round my waist, he took me to the door.

"You see over there—beyond all that rubbish—you see the two shelters in a line? It's the second one, you'll find him there."

And now, as I did not move, he turned to face me squarely, holding my hands. He asked, rather sharply, "You have come a long way to get here?"

I told him, "Yes."

He nodded. "Possibly," he said, "there is one thing that you and I understand equally well. In your language I think it is called 'courage'. You have to use that now."

With that he smiled; and the reason why I remember so clearly his sallow, insipid face is that it produced, all of a sudden, the astonishing sweetness of that smile. Then, as one does with a lazy child, he turned me to the direction I had to follow and gave a little push to send me on my way.

Courage? It seemed to me that all I needed was to prevent myself from getting confused again, to keep my hold upon reality, and this was easy, because nothing here was unfamiliar in kind—the dull sky, the angry pain of my feet, the shelters themselves were all exactly what I might have expected. 'All that is happening is very ordinary,' I told myself, 'it is simply that I am going to see my husband, from whom I have been parted for a considerable time.' In the first shelter, as I passed it, the men lying on the straw looked up and some smiled at me. That, too, was a repetition of old experience. In the second shelter it would be the same, except that one of the men there . . .

Yes, this second shelter was much the same, the rather dirty straw, the men wrapped untidily in their blankets, a dozen or twenty of them: one, with a huge foot stuck out, was laughing and cursing while a bearded fellow stooped to bandage it, using his mouth and his left hand. With my body still in strict control, I walked on slowly, glancing at each face in turn.

There was none that bore the smallest resemblance to the one I looked for.

I said to myself, 'It is all right, everything is quite all right, there has only been a small mistake, there cannot be two men with his name and rank or I should have heard so long ago: the man who held my hands must have been confused about the shelters, he can't have been deceiving me, he can't have been entirely mistaken'. I went back, looking at each face more carefully.

I was not sure whether my voice could be made to sound, and I was nervous about trying; but when I had almost completed that second inspection my tongue worked loose. I was facing the man whose foot was being dressed.

"Please—Colonel Kolbeck—here?"

He looked at me as if I had used some language he did not know, and then at the man who was bandaging him. He too—the bearded man—was silent, but he slowly unbent until his body was almost erect. (I had had the impression of a small man, but it now appeared that if he straightened his shoulders and held up his head he would be above the normal height.) He made a small gesture, inviting me to follow him, and set off very lamely, round to the back of the shelter, where he stopped and waited for me to catch him up.

I did not want to walk too close to him. An instinct of nervousness towards deformed people which had afflicted me from childhood had come into play, and I was also faintly scared because I could not see where he was leading me—we appeared to be at the edge of the camp, and I saw no habitation beyond the fallow which lay ahead; but since he neither moved nor turned his head I had no option but to go up beside him. I came to his right side. I saw, then, that he had a deformity more forbidding than what I had already observed—his forehead was all one scar, and the hair which covered most of his face only partially concealed the fact that half of it, the half I looked at now, had neither life nor any shape at all. I turned my eyes away and stared at the rubbish which lay about my feet, a litter of tins and broken earthenware, the remains of a leather trunk in which grass and thorn were growing in great luxuriance; but presently I was compelled to look at the man again. He had turned towards me: he was crying, and though (at Mikirka) I had often seen men cry like children, I remember a moment when this seemed a curious spectacle—a man weeping who had only one eye for the tears to flow from. He did not move, he waited, looking at me with the shame and desperation of a disgraced child.

I knew him then.

I think some moments must have elapsed before the paralysis which had returned to my body was broken. I first took one of his hands—his right, the crushed and almost useless hand. We fell on the ground together, with my face against his, and lay like that, gasping. After some time I heard him speaking, but I had not then learned to understand the altered, whispering voice he had, I caught only the words 'God is so good, so good'. Men came and looked and spoke to us, it started raining and darkness came.

[333]

18

i

I GOT him to Tushlusk. There, on the floor of the Polish Information Office, he lay very patiently (as Conrad would have done), only making signs from time to time that he would like some water to drink.

Tushlusk: I believe it is a large place, with shaded avenues on the Russian side; a friend has told me there are mosques of peculiar interest there. To me the name brings nothing but a building like a warehouse flanked by railway-sidings, the press of rancid clothes in a perpetual dusk, a voice that says over and over again, "No record. No, no trace. . . . I can only tell you that the application must be put on file. . . . A week, perhaps—it's impossible to tell." The tired voice belongs to an elderly man, not too well shaved, in clothes just recognizable as the uniform of a Polish Captain. The men lounging beside him, younger and a little smarter, are numb with boredom; these have no function, they are just observers for the N.K.V.D. The grey tide that flows eternally towards the counter is composed chiefly of Poles, but among them are White Ruthenians, a number of Russian Jews, peasant farmers from Ukraine.

"Kolbeck? No, no trace. Wait! Kolbeck, did you say? You don't mean General Kolbeck, some connection of his? His family? Yes yes, everyone wants to rejoin their friends, that's one of the little difficulties we have to cope with. No, I'm sorry, I've no information about the family. I did hear that the General himself had reached the Headquarters Area—that may have been only a rumour. No, no one can enter the Headquarters Area without special papers, that may take a week or a fortnight, possibly more. No, that's one of the things I can't tell you—everyone asks me how they're to live while they're waiting, it's a topic of general interest here. To tell the truth, I'm not sure how I live myself. . . . And you, Madam? . . . No, no record, I'm afraid."

But others were more helpful. A man standing beside me in some queue—an artilleryman, I think he was—had come from the No. 2 Polish Formation Area at Vilchak, some twenty miles away. There, he told me, a great number of Polish civilians were living round about the camp, and I had probably a better chance of finding my friends among those than anywhere else.

"Yes, there are people of your quality there—they say it's the best of the civilian settlements. Not much, of course, in the way of food or anything of that sort—but it's better to die among people you know, hn? Permission?" He looked at me quizzically and spread his hands; it was a gesture of the Warsaw alleys which I had almost forgotten. "You can apply at Headquarters, I suppose—if you ever get there. Three or four years, I should think it would take you. Or you might just go."

This was a sensible and—as it proved—a fortunate suggestion.

ii

My need for the support of friends seemed urgent now, since I was doubtful if I should have the strength much longer to care for Victor by myself as his condition required; I could not go on for ever begging lifts from place to place, waiting for applications to be answered. Moreover, I longed intensely to see Annette. And yet when I got to Vilchak I waited for two or three days before I attempted even to find out if the Kolbecks were there. This was not from laziness. I had come to a peculiar state of mind, where I could not bear to share with others the treasure I myself had hardly learnt to possess.

So great was the force of this senseless jealousy that for several days after I had found them I could not bring myself to let them know that Victor was alive: I told them I had found a place of my own to live in, and that was all. In retrospect, that behaviour appears to me ridiculous as well as ignoble. How could I deny such news to people who had so little to live for, so much less power than the rest of humanity to do any harm!

iii

At least I experienced some of the sensations of homecoming: the surprise you feel at finding people smaller, more ordinary, than those you have been picturing, together with the impression that while you have grown far older nothing has altered them. In fact, I believe that in appearance the Kolbecks were not much changed since I had last seen them. It took me a little time to appreciate the distance they had travelled during our separation; to read their silences.

"You would really have done better to go to some other place. Here there are so many people, everyone seems to come here, they think the Army can provide for them."

There was no unkindness in those words of Sandra's, uttered during my third or fourth visit to the penthouse where they were living; she was only thinking her worries aloud, as she had often done in the nursery when I was a child. She was watching Paul as she spoke—her eyes were seldom far from him—and I remember how she suddenly looked up at me, with her old shyness, and put on for an instant her social smile.

"But it's nice of you to come and see us, we haven't so many friends here, you lose touch with people—it's because of the War, you know." She glanced at my face again, as if begging me to understand some problem of her own. Her grave, confiding voice was a little weaker than of old. "You have had a good holiday? I can't quite remember—it's difficult to remember everything, we've been moving a great deal—I think you went away when we were at Mikirka? I shall remember everything much better when we settle down again. Mikirka—the weather was always so bad there. Your father—no, you know who I mean—Casimir's father—your father left us there. He has been away for a long time, of course there's always a great deal of business for him to attend to. You haven't seen him lately, by any chance? I know you've been about a great deal."

I told her—as I had told her several times already—that when I had last seen him some months before he had been in passable health. And I added that I had heard talk of his being at the Polish Headquarters. But that seemed to confuse her.

"No," she said, "no, you're making a mistake, dear; you're mixing him up with someone else. The General has enemies, they wouldn't let him be at Headquarters." She beckoned me closer, she had become slightly tearful. "You wouldn't understand that—I don't think you've ever understood what kind of man Julius was, how good he was. But we won't talk about that—I don't want you to turn against me, we have so few friends now."

Wanda, sitting in the doorway where she could get light for

sewing, said prosaically, "I think you've done enough talking, Mother. I think it's time Stefanie went back."

"But she must have something to eat before she goes," Sandra said firmly. "There was some bread that Henryk got yesterday, there must be some of that. Where's Stefanie? Annette, I mean— where's Annette? It's time that Casimir—it's time that Paul was put to sleep. I don't think she understands, I don't think she's old enough to manage him."

Wanda said without moving, "Henryk will be back soon. He'll put him to bed. . . ."

No, there was no unkindness, but they did not need me. The place I had occupied in their corporate existence had been a narrow one; it was closed now, as the earth where you take a plant away is overgrown before the season is finished. In a sense their life was settled. At the entrance to the camp—within sight of where they were squatting—the Polish flag was flying. That much they had won by staying alive. Perhaps, dimly, they still dreamed of a freedom which meant more than this. But when they were still so near starvation they lacked, I think, the force of mind which is necessary for such dreaming. To find a little food each day, to work upon an ancient undergarment so that it would give a month's more use, these tasks were enough for their ambition as well as their remaining powers. Their movements and their regard were slow, they talked little, and in subdued, slack voices. The picture that comes to me, as I recall that time, is of soldiers who have lost a long-fought battle; who continue to march in line, to carry their arms as they have been taught to do, when their minds have long since fallen asleep.

To Wanda I was wholly a stranger. She asked me no questions —not even what had happened to Conrad or what I knew of her father. More than once, overcoming my own weariness, I tried to say something which would recall the days of our friendship, and I would search with a smile of my own for one of hers. She could not respond. She was patient with me, as with an old servant of failing wits, but in the eyes that encountered mine there was no faint afterglow of the old affection. This coldness was not, I believe, deliberate or even hostile; she scarcely showed more warmth to Annette, whom I know she never ceased to love. In all the time that she had been chiefly responsible for the lives of the family, emotion would have been a luxury too expensive for her moral reserves. So (as I see it now) she had forgotten the use of tenderness; and perhaps her heart itself, once stricken almost mortally in the Lublin hos-

[337]

pital, was now scarcely alive. There was, in this haggard face, a mysterious residue of the beauty which had once flamed there; but of all the richness of her voice nothing was left but a listless monotone:

". . . Yes, Henryk is not a bad nursemaid. But of course it's very unlikely the child will grow up. No, I don't see what else Annette could have done. She gets a daily ration issue from the Women's Corps—it all goes to Paul. That means her being in the camp all day, they'd strike her off, if she wasn't there. They don't do anything, of course. They stand in a line and fill up forms."

I asked her what had happened to Rosalia.

"Rosalia? Oh, Rosalia got killed. At Mikirka. She argued with the guards, she got to lecturing them. They got tired of that, in the end one of them knocked her down. Then they took her out and finished her off."

And when I expressed my anger she answered dispassionately, "Yes, Rosalia never had much of a life. She was a tiresome woman, but I don't think she deserved to end like that."

But she seldom gave her reflections so much freedom; she kept her use of speech to essentials, to controlling her mother's more trivial anxieties, keeping Henryk at heel. In a life so scant as this, where the nearer past was something to be forgotten and the future chimerical, there was not much use for conversation; even the common courtesies had been reduced to a threadbare pattern, for where there were no formal meals, no definition in the start and finish of a day, the occasions for politeness were scarce. It was kinder, as I realized soon, not to ask anyone how she was feeling; to keep one's eyes away from many small actions which could find no other privacy. And you ceased to expect that people would look up and smile when you came in.

They belonged, after all, to the settlement, where a common climate of feeling possessed us all. The physical barriers were thin. In the yard where the penthouse stood a dozen families had made their homes, plots walled with kerosene tins, awnings of hurdles crudely thatched; the yard was open to the street, and along this ragged thoroughfare, to the point where the houses petered out and a line of posts marked the boundary of the camp, you saw at any hour perhaps a thousand people standing silently or sitting in the mud. Viewed casually, this shabby concourse appeared to be waiting for some spectacle, for royalty or a ceremonial parade; but when you looked closely at the hollow faces, when you spoke to the children, you knew that they expected nothing. Broadly, they had arrived already at their promised land: for here no one obliged them to hew or dig, they could come and go as they pleased; and if this was deliverance, what should they look for next?

It was not possible that a group of people living within this legion should escape its infection; I saw in the penthouse the same dullness of the eyes, the lag in simple movements, which confronted me everywhere outside. But always there was Wanda's voice, which, weary and almost lifeless, could still echo faintly the authority of her father's: "Mother, I've got some water here, it's time for Grandmother to be washed. . . . Henryk, you go outside. . . . Yes, I know, but it's got to be done. She's one of us, and we can't live like cattle. We, we are Poles."

iv

My life had its centre a quarter of a mile away, where, in a derelict workshop which he and I shared with two families, Victor was lying in great weakness; and so little did my visits mean to the Kolbecks that I should have kept away from them till I myself was nearer health in body and mind if I had not needed to see Annette. Strangely, the happiness which had come to me made me realize more acutely that her existence was an essential part of my own.

To all appearance, my return had counted for no more with her than with the others; she had welcomed me with nothing but a look of faint surprise, and almost at once had turned her back on me to attend to Paul. That was not mere shyness, of the kind which in earlier periods had sometimes hung like a screen between her and me: I know now that it was more deeply caused. On my departure from Mikirka she had supposed (with reason) that she would never see me again, and since then her life had grown into a shape where I was superfluous: she belonged to the Kolbecks absolutely. The ordeal of Mikirka had lasted longer for her than for me, and its imprint upon her was no less deep than upon the others. In the slightness of her body, in her undeveloped carriage and in her forehead, I could still see something of the child she should have been at sixteen years; but in her eyes and mouth there was, beside the listlessness and hunger of Vilchak, the maturity of one who has traversed the scale of experience. She had learnt instinctively to close herself against any depth of feeling, as eyes which have once been harmed will close when they are turned towards the light.

And I, loving her as never before, could not submit to this estrangement.

She had an hour off from her duties at the camp in the middle of every day, and I would arrange my programme so as to be at the penthouse when she arrived. I remember clearly how she looked on those occasions. She was one of the few who had been given a uniform, which consisted of the blouse and trousers that are worn by British soldiers; hers had been made for an unusually small man, but of course it was still too large at every point for her wasted form, and it made me think of urchins I had once seen in Montmartre bravely supporting their fathers' clothes. Her hair was loose, her face generally dirty, she was white and tired. She would go at once to Paul, who lay on the ground in a kind of nest she had made for him with turves and sacking, and if Henryk was there she would order him unceremoniously to fetch her water; then, without a word, and rather with the air of a factory girl on piece-rates, she would start the baby's daily cleaning.

My grandson, nearly a year old, was pathetically small; he had hardly tried to crawl yet, and when he was put to sit up his head, absurdly large in proportion to his thin trunk and tiny legs, leant over to one side in a way that was rather frightening to see. It was, however, a head to excite admiration, with very thick black hair, the modelling of nose and mouth so sharp and firm that—in spite of its lack of flesh—it might almost have belonged to a boy twice his age. The eyes, red and watery as they were, already suggested to me a being who would have intelligence, and these I think may have come from his mother's side. For the rest, the face must have been like his father's; he had in embryo the aquiline features I have seen in Kazaks of the Don—nothing of the Kolbeck distinction. The puny body was not easy to handle, and though he had not much strength he used it with determination to resist his mother's attentions. I wondered at her skill—it was only physical weakness which occasionally made her heavy-handed. But what surprised me more was the lack of sentiment she showed. She had none of the little-language which to a normal mother seems almost a part of her duty; she did not even smile at him. You would not have guessed that the baby was her own.

At first all that I could do was to sit with my back against the wall and watch; but soon she allowed me to hold things and hand them to her as she wanted them—the treasured fragment of soap, torn-up pieces of a nightgown which did for napkins, the two priceless safety-pins. Then I got to holding Paul himself while she did his hair. And although our eyes hardly met, I talked to her, trying to ignore the embarrassment of having the other women all round me.

"I think he's very good—of course it's good for him to cry now and then. I think when the summer comes he'll do more crawling, perhaps he'll be walking before long. I remember how you started walking all of a sudden when your legs looked much too feeble. . . . Darling, did they make you work again after I'd gone? At Mikirka?"

"Yes."

"I sent a letter to you when I was at Czennik, but I don't suppose it ever got to you."

"No."

"Do you know if they've got any medical supplies at the camp? I was wondering if you could get some boracic to do these eyes; I think it might be a good thing."

"I suppose so."

"Did you think you'd ever see me again?"

"I don't know."

"Darling, aren't you finding it too exhausting, what you do at the camp? Wouldn't you like me to go and see the Commandant?"

"No. No, it's all right."

"You know, I think perhaps he's got your father's hands. Your father had long fingers just like these. I think they're lovely little hands."

"Oh."

"Perhaps he'll be a pianist when he grows up."

Yes, I remember making that idle remark; and I remember how, for the first time, she raised her head to look at me. She said impatiently:

"Of course not!"

"But why?" I asked her gently. "Why shouldn't he have your father's marvellous gift?"

She answered impatiently, "He won't grow up. Everyone says he won't."

I was startled by that touch of vehemence. I said, "But darling, you surely don't believe people when they talk like that! Look how well you've done with him already, look——"

"It doesn't matter!" she said.

"Doesn't matter?"

She was silent for a moment, and then she spoke in a voice that was adult and entirely bloodless. "I thought of killing him. At Mikirka. Only I hadn't quite the nerve."

[341]

From the other side of the shed Wanda, who had shown no signs of listening, said tersely, "Annette, there's no need to go through all that again!" For myself, I could not speak coherently. I said, "Annette—you mustn't—you're not thinking what you're saying! You love him, don't you? Of course you love him!"

"I don't want to," she said. "I don't see any point in his growing up. Him or anyone."

There was a way in which I might have answered her, but the slackness of my faculties—or perhaps some rudimentary wisdom—prevented me. It was not till the next day, or perhaps the one after, that my feeling of powerlessness was lifted for a space.

We happened to be alone then; or rather, only the Countess was with us, and her monolithic presence constrained me no more than the child's. The washing was finished, and Annette, tired, sat back against the wall with Paul wriggling and whimpering a little on her knees. I was moved suddenly to take him from her. I held him against my breast, kissing his head, while she watched me with a distant curiosity. I said to her soberly:

"You realize he's very precious to me! You know I'll always love him as if he were mine—as if he were Conrad."

She looked away from me. She said, with more breath than sound, "Conrad—he died?"

I told her, "At Czennik. In the prison there."

Then, as if under compulsion, she leant towards me and laid her forehead against my arm. She did not cry, because (I think) the act of crying needs some nervous force which often deserts you when you have had no proper food for a long time. But the movement which I could feel in her body was that of someone in bitter grief, and this enabled me to put my arm about her, so that I held her and her son together. It did not last very long, that embrace, since I myself had not the strength for it. Yet in those few moments I saw that her love for me, which I had so little earned, was still alive; I knew even then that the fresh, warm stream which flowed from my surging gratitude would not be staunched again by the heat of circumstance, by any mood of hers or mine.

What passes for reality, the accidents which crowd upon the physical senses, closed over the interval of vision. Henryk returned, well pleased with his morning's scavenging. He went to stroke his grandmother's cheek, as his habit was, and then stood over Annette and me, laughing in his beard, stooping to administer to Paul a boisterous kiss. (He must have suffered no less than we from physical privation, but it was his peculiar fortune that a mind so

[342]

rudimental as his could be little wounded by experience.) Soon
Sandra came, with Wanda supporting her, and as Annette was
drawn into their common talk I could almost have doubted if our
moment of sympathy had occurred at all.

"Annette, did you see that man who talked about fish?"

"He wants fifteen cigarettes for half a kilo. It's Ural salmon, he
says."

"A woman said she'd give me ten cigarettes for my underskirt."

"That's not enough."

"Do you mean the one who's got no legs? She's dead."

"I didn't know."

"Yesterday—her daughter told me."

"Then the daughter's got the cigarettes?"

"I don't see why we can't be sent home. I don't understand what's
happening. If your father was here he would know. Men always
know what's going on."

v

Lying still in the darkness of early morning, before my will had
taken command, I would sometimes hear the smothered voice
which I had learnt to know as Victor's, now quick and anxious,
now pleading with a desperate patience. 'There, to the right, man,
to the right—you can stop them there. Where is that fellow, where's
he got to, what in hell has happened to the guns? . . . Wait! Not
yet, I'm not unconscious yet! . . . I can't, I tell you I can't stand
any more! Please, please—for God's sake—you've got a rifle!'
But from this palingenesis of fear and pain he must have passed
into a safer depth of sleep, for when the light came the living part
of his face reposed as tranquilly as that of a healthy child. The
people who slept next to us—a baker from Bialystok and his
daughter—were always abroad early, hoping at that hour to pick
up scraps about the camp, but the fuss of their departure did not
disturb him; and though I was sometimes in discomfort, when the
weight of his shoulder was on my arm, I kept quite still to let him
sleep as long as he could. These were minutes of immeasurable
value. When the eye was closed there was little in the ravaged face
with its mask of hair that I could recognize, little that the senses
alone could love. But this that remained, the sickly flesh that was
yet alive and in the human shape, this was a possession more dear to
me than the memory of his young, unblemished face, because it was
more ultimately mine. In this calm hour I saw no ugliness in the

[343]

mutilated body, in the shapeless hand, the clot of blackened tissue where his ear had been; it was enough that in the broken frame the heart still beat, that I could feel against my cheek the faint, warm current of his breathing. And as, listening to familiar music, you wait for a phrase which peculiarly stirs you, so with a patience that was itself delight I waited for his eye to open; to see the obscurity give way to wonder and to joy, to hear the whisper of my name. "Stefanie! Oh, Stefanie!"

Awake, all that he gave of himself he gave to me. And in those days his dependence on me was almost as complete as Conrad's had been.

The journey from Karmishkent, which would have taxed a robust man, had greatly weakened him: he could stand up only with my help, and could scarcely walk as far as the road. I do not know how much he was still suffering: when I asked him, he denied that he suffered at all. There were small movements of his crooked mouth, sometimes a heaviness of breathing, which made me think that the pain was often severe; but he seemed to have found in absolute stillness either a refuge from it or a disguise. These stillnesses were of the body; not, I think, of the brain. His open eye, staring at the wall, showed me nothing of where his thoughts might be; but a mind of such virility could never have stood empty, and I fancy that the place to which his spirit escaped, discovered in long loneliness, was one of such refreshment as a swimmer gets from warm and lively seas. If I spoke or touched him in those periods of abstraction, there was no immediate response. And yet I was never jealous of the thoughts which held him. I waited patiently, as one does for a baby's smile, knowing that in time he would return to me.

Yes, it was like having a young child under my care, but one whose faculties advanced almost from hour to hour. At first I could be sure that when I got back from foraging he would be lying almost exactly as I had left him; but on the second or third day I found him sitting up and looking curiously about him. I had thought that people would be repelled by his deformities. It was not so; and his old capacity for winning friends had not deserted him. The baker's daughter, a motherly woman, soon charged herself with caring for him when I was absent, and a dour old man who had spent his early life as a soldier became his constant companion. From these he must have learnt more of what was going on than I should have troubled him with so early as this; and though as yet he showed no restlessness, he was soon asking me questions.

"This camp. This camp they talk about. A Polish camp? . . .

But—but the Russians. They—don't interfere? They—don't worry?"

His power of speech was improving, and for me he was not hard to understand. But the whispered words came slowly and irregularly, as if, needing to fetch each phrase from some dim cabinet, he sometimes forgot his purpose on the way.

"A Polish Corps? To fight? To fight for the Russians? Then there will be work. Work for me. A job for me."

Cautiously, as with a boy, I tried to make him see that he would never again be fit for military employment. And with that he seemed to agree. He said, cocking up one side of his mouth in what I had come to recognize as a smile, "Yes. Yes, I suppose. A mess. Nothing—nothing but a mess—me. No use. No use at all." But he returned to the subject again. "Perhaps—perhaps I can write. This hand. I can learn to write. Write a letter. A letter to the Commandant. You—you would take a letter? A letter to the Commandant —from me?"

"But Victor, you can't feel that you want to do any more fighting! Even if you were fit and strong."

He considered that for a long time.

"There are—jobs," he said. "Men who can't fight. They make use of them." And much later, when I hoped that the question had passed from his mind, he said suddenly, "Records. Welfare. Jobs —jobs like that."

"One day," I suggested, "when you're strong again, when we're back in Poland, there'll be useful work for you. Some sort of civilian job. There'll be plenty that wants doing in Poland."

He nodded gravely, as if he almost agreed. But presently he was back in his old position.

"I think—I think I—I think I've got to be with them. With soldiers. Soldiers—they need people. They need—people who— understand them. They—they don't get much. People who like them. They need—people like me."

I was faintly troubled by this turn of his mind. It was not that I had any fear of his being taken from me, for although not one in twenty of the men in the camp was in even moderate health, I did not think it possible that a body so shattered as his would ever again be put to military use. Rather, I was anxious because this wakened interest marked an increase in his powers of observation and reason for which I was not yet ready.

Till now he had seemed to be content with my existence, with my love, as I with his: we had not needed to explore the stretch of life

[345]

which we had spent apart. So simple a relationship was grateful at a time when my own brain functioned cumbrously, and when I had yet to find my way into a mind which was partly strange; I had felt (deferring, as one does, the hardest task) that when our fresh discovery of each other had grown into total understanding, I should be able to tell him more easily of what had happened to Conrad and to me. But now it seemed that the moratorium I had counted on was not to be granted. His weakness and quiescence belonged to the body which kept him prisoner; within, I began to see looks I recognized, his old intelligence, the impulsive curiosity. "You have—you have been through—a great deal, Stefanie. You—you have had a—had a hard time!" I took that only as sympathy, but it might well have been an invitation. He appeared, with that one eye of his, and with his head permanently bent forward, to notice small things: I could see that he was interested and even amused by the way in which the baker's daughter, dressed in rags as we all were, still fussed over her hair. How long would it take him to notice the signs of my pregnancy? Since Conrad, my body had had little shape, and it was shapelessly clad. The Kolbeck women had evidently noticed nothing. How long would it take a man to observe what they had missed? How long would it take a husband?

But in truth this was not a large anxiety: we had come some distance from the ordered world, and in Vilchak we were less concerned with European virtues and conventions than with finding something to eat. It was only at night, in those sombre stretches where hunger kept me awake, that I found myself concocting speeches of excuse and argument, rehearsing the scene in which I should break the truth to him.

And how little use are those fashioned scenes for the casual theatre of reality!

Thinking that he needed a change of view, I took him one morning, with the help of our friends, out to the street; there we sat for a while, I with my back against the wall of a house, he leaning against me, with an old potato sack to cover us both. He seemed to be absorbed in the sight of some children who were sprawling on the other side of the road—he was actually making friendly signals to them—and I was taken completely by surprise when, resting his good hand on my belly, he whispered gravely:

"You—you are—you are large. You are large here."

I mumbled something about having no figure any more, and the usual space of silence followed. Then, still looking at the children, but now with a tired perplexity, he said:

"But—I thought. I thought I remembered. I thought. I thought you—I thought we——"

I said abruptly, "Yes. Yes, that's right." The voice that came from my mouth was toneless and almost casual, as if I was anxious to be done with a small boy's troublesome questions. "Yes, I was going to—I did have a child. He died. At Czennik, that was."

I should have stumbled on, explaining, unloading myself of everything I had longed to tell him about Conrad; but he did not seem to be greatly interested. Without looking at me he was nodding in a thoughtful way, reminding me for an instant of Julius in his moods of formality. He asked suddenly:

"Those—those children there. Do they—do they belong to somebody?"

"I expect so," I answered vaguely. "There must be someone who's responsible for them."

For a time he seemed to be puzzling out this matter, and I supposed that the other subject was closed. I was at once relieved and frustrated, as if an operation to cure some chronic complaint had been pronounced unfeasible. Then he startled me again.

"But now," he said, groping, "but now—but this. But this—will be—another child?"

I went through a long moment not so much of panic as of grey distress. The question was not to be answered by a simple 'Yes'; and because there was so much that could not be conveyed from my tired brain to his, I felt with misery that all my claim on his understanding must be lost by default. Even my voice refused to help me: it sounded, when my answer came, with a note of recalcitrance which had no relation to my feelings.

"It just happened. It happened to a lot of us. I'd been told that you were dead."

There was no look or movement to show that he had even heard me. He was staring at the children again, beckoning to one of them; and for another ten minutes or so we sat in silence with the life of the shabby street flowing torpidly past us, the scrawny, vulpine women with their empty bags, skeletons of boys who poked their way from one heap of dirt to the next. Then he said, as if to himself, "Too cold. Too cold here," and I went to fetch the old man and we took him back to the workshop.

All that day he had nothing to say to me; I kept returning to him between my expeditions in search of food, but he hardly seemed to realize I was there. In those hours the light and meaning of my life were extinguished.

In the night I waked to hear him groaning; it was such a sound as a child makes in fever. I asked him sleepily, "Victor, is something wrong?" and I heard him whisper, "I can't bear that. I can't bear that."

"What is it?" I asked. "Is it some pain?"

He said, "That you—that you should have been through that." And again, a little afterwards, with a grief and gentleness I had not imagined to be in any man, "Yourself. All by yourself. You going through that!"

There was nothing to restrain me then. No feebleness or confusion of speech need have kept me from pouring out what I had longed for him to know, of the darkness I had lived in when I believed him dead, of what Conrad's life had counted for in mine. But now there was no necessity. What sympathy could he have given me that would not have been feeble beside the flooding music of his compassion! I cried for a while, holding his hand against my cheek, and in the warmth of these unhindered tears I sank into a calmer sleep than I had known before. In the morning he was again withdrawn, wearing that look which prisoners have who have made their solitude a temple of safety. But while I was washing him he started trying to talk and when it was time for me to go he held me back, pulling me down beside him again, so that he could put his head against my body. He had got ready something like a speech, which he was able to deliver almost consecutively:

"This—this will be—a new son for me. Another—another Conrad for you and me. I shall be—fond of him. Always. I shall—always love. Always love him."

In that there was more for me than the joy of relief. It was not that it opened up a golden prospect, a life where, with some place to live in and with food to eat, we should care for my child as if he were Victor's as well as mine: I had ceased to feed my courage with such dreams as those. It was rather that I realized now, though still but feebly, what kind of man had been restored to my possession. That day, in company with some other women, I trudged with a small barrow I had made to a place three or four miles away where we had heard that rotting swedes were to be had for nothing. The track was difficult, rain fell incessantly; and I remember how one of my friends turned on me in anger, demanding why I should be smiling. I had not been conscious of the smile. And how could I explain to her that all the goodness in life had suddenly been shown to me!

You pay for the follies of selfishness and procrastination. I no longer wanted to hide from Victor the fact that his family were near us; but now I could not see how I was to break this news either to him or to them. To the Kolbecks I had not only to explain my disingenuousness; it seemed important to warn them (suffering as they were from those maladies of the mind which come from prolonged hunger) of what kind of being, physically, they were going to see.

But again events provided a quick, callous solution to the problem I had lacked the courage to solve. It came on an afternoon when my visit to the penthouse was extended beyond the usual time: Paul had been very sick, and as Wanda was much occupied with her mother, who was also lying ill that day, I had promised Annette to stay with him until he was asleep. I had got him to a state of drowsiness, and I think we were all half-sleeping, when Henryk came in from one of his expeditions. He seemed to be pleased with himself, he stood in the entrance scratching his head and giggling with childish ebullience. I begged him to be quiet.

"Did you get anything?" Wanda asked him casually.

He went on laughing for a time, and then, stopping suddenly, he said with naïve importance, "I saw a man. In the street, the street where I got the cigarettes. I saw a funny man."

"What do you mean—'funny'?" Wanda asked.

"He was funny," Henryk repeated, serious and rather worried now. "No face. He hadn't got a face."

'The street where I got the cigarettes.' I didn't know what he meant by that; but I remembered that I had asked the baker to take Victor out to the road for an airing if the weather cleared up enough. I said urgently:

"Henryk, I'm trying to get Paul to sleep. I wish you'd keep as quiet as you can."

He was not to be silenced, however. Knowing as children do when he had won attention he rejoiced in the achievement, and his climax was just ahead. He frowned at me and turned to Wanda.

"Wanda, I can talk, can't I? I saw him looking at me, this man, like this. One eye—see? He'd only got one eye."

Wanda said, "Yes yes, there are lots of people like that."

"He talked to me. In a whisper, like this—'Henryk! Henryk!' He said he knew me. He said he was Victor. Yes, that's what he said."

All this might have led to nothing, since no one ever took much notice of Henryk's excitements, but Wanda happened to be looking my way and I could see that my face betrayed me. I had to be truthful then.

"Yes, Victor is here," I said, as if the fact was of no great importance. "I wanted to get him better before you saw him—he's still in a bad state."

Henryk started to laugh again. "I told you so! It's right, old Teffy says so! I told you it was Victor I saw!"

"Be quiet, Henryk!" Wanda snapped. She turned to me. "I suppose it's something in your nature," she said. "I suppose you never will be honest with us!"

I was saved from trying to answer. A sound made us both turn, and we saw that Sandra was struggling to her feet.

"Mother, you can't get up!" Wanda commanded.

But Sandra did not seem to hear her. She said, "My shawl— where is it?—I know I had a shawl. I must have something, I can't let Victor see me looking like this."

It did not seem to matter that her skirt was one which a peasant woman would have thrown away, that her shoes were falling to pieces; and it was useless for Wanda to try to persuade her that she was not fit to be out of bed. "But of course," she said with dignity, "of course I must see my son! You will have to show me the way, Stefanie. Wanda, you must stay and look after your grandmother. Henryk, come here, I think I may need your arm!"

I tried, as we went painfully along the road, to give her some idea of what she would find. But she hardly listened. She said, between her gasps for breath, "I have had a great deal of experience with illness. I am used to dealing with soldiers—my husband, you know, my husband has always been a military man. You must understand me, please, Stefanie, you must understand that I insist on being with my son."

i

I SHOULD like to believe that Victor owed his rehabilitation entirely to such care as I was able to give him from the day when I found him at Karmishkent. The facts speak otherwise. I can see in retrospect that his progress became more rapid as soon as he was restored to his family: his strength so increased that before long he was able to walk a hundred yards or more with only a little support from Henryk (who found a pleasure of his own in this tutorship); he learnt, with an effort which evidently cost him pain, to get his head very nearly upright, and though his voice remained a whisper his power of speech advanced from day to day. I admit that my jealousy was nursed a little by this development. And yet it worked wholly for my good. I had been like a mother so demanding of her only son's devotion that she tries to keep him away from other children; not realizing that he, and she in her turn, must be impoverished by such seclusion.

Fortunately—since there was typhus at Vilchak—we were moved before long to the civilian settlement attached to 'F' Camp. We had always been lucky—the places where the Russians sent us had never been the really bad ones—but in this move under Polish Army authority there was, I am afraid, an element of favouritism: the name Kolbeck was one which had some meaning to senior officers, and it is not unlikely that Julius himself, having learnt at Headquarters of our whereabouts, exerted his influence. Certainly this settlement was privileged. We had two small tents to ourselves, one of which Victor and I shared with Annette and Paul. From army stores a blanket of sorts was found for every two women, and there was a small issue of foodstuffs on alternate days.

Ironically, I responded to this access of comfort by falling sick. The illness may have been a delayed result of the Vilchak shortages, which pregnancy had made me less able than the others to withstand; or perhaps it was largely an affair of nerves, since the main symptom was a weakness more of the will than of the body. For a fortnight or more I found it an effort to get up from the ground, and a major undertaking to drag myself as far as the latrine. All day I lay quite still, so much detached from what was happening about me that when Paul was crying, and Annette nowhere about, it sometimes took me several minutes to summon the energy I needed to attend to him.

Our parts were then reversed, Victor's and mine. Although Annette did all she could for me, and Wanda kept an eye on me in the way that a Ward Sister does, it was Victor who most constantly attended to my needs; who, when I betrayed some pain or discomfort, would presently be kneeling beside me to shift a little the bundles which supported my neck and shoulders, to moisten my wrists, whispering a word or two of encouragement, "You must rest, kochanie, you must rest, rest!"

ii

The tent was of brown canvas, and in its constant, yellow twilight I once more lived passively, removed a little way from the tangible world, like a child who stares at the street's traffic from a basement window. The waves of sound which rolled continuously against the walls differed hardly at all from what I had known at other stages of our journey: it was the closely woven noise of the market-place in little Polish towns, stilled and flattened as if by summer heat, punctuated by a distant hammering of wood on wood; the unexpectant voices of idle labourers, incessant, peevish cries of children mechanically answered by women's tired voices, a murmur which had no climax and no music: and with this there came like a flavour of the sound itself the faintly nauseous odours of anxious living, of staled, infected earth. Yet that time is as far removed in memory from all that precedes it as if it were filled by the sensations of a single visit to a strange country.

It was the nearer voices, those at my side and those which came through from the other tent, which seemed to be changed; to be warmer, to have taken a little colour, like the skin of sick people when they are brought into country air.

Was it that one man could so alter the feel of life in a company which had been almost entirely of women? For me the mere knowledge of Victor's presence was enough to fill the emptiness left by the loss of every other possession. Could he, in such quiescence, with so little to give in gesture or speech, do as much for them? "That is for Victor to say, Victor will decide for us when he feels well again. . . . Now that Victor's with us we shall be all right." This voice was Sandra's, and it was natural, I suppose, that she should look to her son for all she was deprived of by Julius's absence; she may even have fancied in her wishful mind that the finding of one lost piece had restored the pattern which she needed, the only one she understood, the pattern of Setory, where the part of women was to fill in the background of men's designs. But it surprised me that Annette, escaping from her long reserve, should accept him with a gentleness that she might have given to her father; that without shyness, almost with gaiety, she should hold out Paul for him to kiss, murmuring, "Yes, Paul, yes, it's Uncle Vic! Vic won't hurt you, gosling, he's nice, he's dear and nice!"

And now another voice was reaching me through the flimsy walls, one which, in my sleepy state, I could not at first identify. It was a long time since I had heard as much as one intelligible word from the Countess; but I realized soon that it was she who spoke, deeply and huskily, and yet with a semblance of the cutting edge which had once so easily brought us all to subservience:

"That man. That man who came in. Who was it? Tell me! Tell me! Who was it?"

"That was Victor. I say, that was Victor. He was wounded. Your grandson. Julius's eldest son."

"Victor? Of course it was. I know that. I know my grandson. Wounded?"

"Yes, he was very badly wounded."

"Of course he was!"

"We must be thankful to God that he's still alive."

"What rubbish you talk, Sandra, you're a brainless girl—you Lithuanians, none of you has any brains! Victor? Do you say it's Victor? Victor's a good child, he's like his father. You will send him to see me. Not now. When I'm well. There's something wrong with my stomach now. Yes, Victor, I should like to see him. Victor's a good boy. Not Henryk, I'm tired of that creature. I want Victor to come and see me. I'm getting old now—I'm tired of it, the way you move me about—I'm a very old woman, I don't get anything now, I want someone to look after me."

It is hard to guess how much she perceived or understood. Lodged in a body that merely stayed alive, her brain may have ceased to be anything but a mechanism which responded to

[353]

familiar impulses as plants respond to daylight and dusk; but I think that Victor's presence or his name alone may have waked in her, as in the others, a sense of having recovered some portion of the ravished past. I wondered then how far he would ever fulfil the part they had assigned him. The nervous force of his early manhood, the self-will that had shown itself even in his generosities—these surely were integral in the man who had once been a portion of their substance, whom they looked for now: and of these, were any roots still left to grow again? For each of them he had some kindness—I could hear, when he visited the other tent, how patiently he answered Sandra's questions, with what forbearance he treated his grandmother, and I came to see how much he gave in small, laborious services to Annette and her child. But was this enough, when they so needed his virility, the reassurance which comes from a man's strength and resolution? Sometimes he seemed more ghost than living creature; he said so little of his own accord, he kept so still. I felt increasingly that his inclination was to live in the world of private safety which he had discovered in loneliness; that although he struggled to share in other lives he could not realize the longings in which they were centred—their hunger for old certainties, for food to which they would have an absolute claim, some morsel of dignity, a freedom which meant more than the absence of police.

On the day when Annette brought us definite news that Julius had been appointed to General Anders's staff there was a chatter in the other tent, continuing for hours, which might have amused me if I had been in better health. The Countess, when Sandra had made her understand what the talk was about, would not admit that the appointment was news to her: Julius had kept her informed, she said, of all his movements, he had always consulted her before accepting any post that was offered him.

"Anders? General Anders? Yes, of course, I know him very well, I told him he would be a fool if he didn't have Julius while he could get him. That was weeks ago, I arranged it all with Josef Pilsudski, I told him there was going to be trouble from that cheapjack Austrian."

While Sandra herself, unable to cope with so great a demand on her emotions, fell into a melancholy fuss about her clothes—Julius would want her to meet his colleagues, he would expect her to be dressed in accordance with his position, it was unthinkable that she should disgrace him. Only Wanda maintained her equanimity; and even in her tired voice I could detect a current of excitement when she came, that evening, to sit beside Victor in the darkness and talk to him in whispers.

". . . You see what I mean—I didn't really believe in this business before, this new army, I thought it might be nothing but a stunt of the Russians. But Father wouldn't have anything to do with it if it wasn't a reality, if it wasn't truly Polish . . . Is Teffy awake? Teffy, are you awake?"

I could not stir myself to speak. Presently Victor answered, as if he himself were all but asleep:

"No, I suppose he wouldn't. . . . You think, you think he's all right? He must be old now. I can't remember—he must be sixty now."

"He won't ever be old," she said, "while Poland has to be fought for."

"No. No, I suppose you're right."

"Only for the time he's got to work in a Russian framework. That's what worries me. I mean, to some extent he'll still be taking orders from them—passing on orders that they give him. I don't quite know how he's going to bring himself to that."

He did not answer.

"I suppose," she said, "they've had to make a kind of bargain. We help the Russians fight their war, and in return they give us back our country when it's over."

"Yes, perhaps that's it."

"I think Father must hate that. I mean, the idea of taking anything from them as if it was a favour. That's what they'll make it feel like."

"I don't know," he said, "I don't really know."

"I know one thing. In the end they've got to pay for it all. If we can't make them, our sons will. They've got to pay for what they've done to us."

Annette, turning over, murmured sleepily, "What did you say? Who's got to pay?"

"It's all right!" Wanda answered. "Everything's all right."

Presently Victor said, groping from word to word, "I suppose he'll like it, having some work to do, being a soldier again. I want to see him—it seems so long. I wish I could know he was happy."

I heard Wanda sigh as an exhausted teacher does. She said, "Happy? Do you think he even wants to be? With Poland like it is! *I* don't want to. Not till we're back in Poland. Not till I've seen them getting what they've given us—all those others—not till I've seen them suffer."

I do not know if Sandra had been listening all the time. I heard her voice just then, sounding forlornly through the canvas, "Wanda, what are you doing, what are you talking about? Have you heard something about going back to Poland?"

"No, Mother. I only said I can't be happy till I'm back."

"Yes, oh yes—we shall all be happy when we're back!"

Like a slow walker who only catches up when the others stop to rest, Victor said, "To Poland? Back to Poland? But I—I don't think it depends on things like that. Our being happy. I don't think it's to do with things that happen to us."

"Victor's tired," Sandra called weakly, "you must let him go to sleep."

Wanda said lifelessly, "Happiness is something children believe in. You don't when you've lived. It's not a reality."

Again Victor seemed to have been left behind. "But I . . ." he said at last, struggling as if with physical pain ". . . but to me it has been—it's a reality for me."

iii

Almost every kind of news has some value for exiles, but the report that the new army was to be shunted to the other side of the Caspian, camp-followers and all, was received by the settlement at large without intemperate optimism. Such a move would not bring us manifestly nearer Poland, and outside Poland it did not seem to make much difference where they moved you: Iran was said to consist of deserts and high mountains, it appeared unlikely that we should find any food there.

But a few were hopeful. They had heard that the Russians did not own Iran, and that was everything. We Poles, they said, we have always made much out of very little: give us a few hectares without a Russian in sight, and we will make a Poland for ourselves.

By degrees it appeared that some kind of deal had been arranged: the Russians, according to some, had got as much out of us as they could, and now the British were to have their turn. What sort of people were those, when you came to deal with them? (The question was often referred to me. It had got about that I understood English—though in fact my knowledge of that grammarless and unpronounceable tongue had never been more than fragmentary —and from this it was argued that I must know the people who spoke it.) The common opinion was that if the British had bought us from our present owners they would squeeze the last drop out of their purchase, for they were known to be a commercial race, a kind of Scandinavians with the admixture of a German taste for settling arguments by force of arms. Was it true, I was asked, that British children were taken from their parents and sent to military schools almost as soon as they were born?

"All I want from the British," an old man said significantly, "is a rifle and cartridges. They needn't tell me who to shoot."

iv

Our own interest—the Kolbecks' and mine—was shortly turned to a more immediate object. A notice appeared in camp orders—where Annette saw it—that Julius would arrive to make an administrative inspection next day.

The effect of this news on Sandra was strange and distressing. I believe that in her depths she may have experienced a joy not far in kind from that which Victor's return had given to me, but again her nervous reserves were unequal to the strain. Perhaps none of us realized at the time the extent of her physical deterioration: so many of her looks and gestures, her turns of speech, were ones we had known all our lives, and in a society where nobody is in normal health you do not remark the uncertainty of one person's movement, the pallor and poverty of her flesh. That day she was like a singer who has lost her voice for many years and who suddenly receives a royal command to perform. Again and again she called for Annette to ask if she was certain she had read the notice rightly —could there not have been a mistake about the inspecting officer's name? She cried a great deal, once more she rummaged feebly among the bits and pieces she still possessed in the vain hope of finding something to disguise her shabbiness; and now, believing that Julius would come to see her where she was, she became distraught about the appearance of the tent and started trying to clear the mess which always surrounded the Countess's bed, constantly falling faint but refusing to let anyone help her. We spent that day, and much of the night, as actors in a wretched farce for which we had no parts.

As I had expected, Julius did not come to the tent at all. He sent a message—which struck me as faintly oriental—that he wished to see his family at the Camp Adjutant's office, and that transport would be sent for them. A small truck which served as staff-car came early in the afternoon. There was some debate about who was to go, but the question was at last settled—not without tact—by Wanda: Henryk and I were to stay behind, to look after the Countess and Paul.

Thus I missed seeing the reunion; without regret.

I had somehow presumed that my father-in-law would not want to see me at all. In the past two years we had been much together, we had enjoyed a kind of friendship, an hour of physical love. That was over, at least for him; and I had, I think, no false conception of my importance to a man whose life had been scaled by great affairs. My assumption was wrong, however. When the truck brought the others back there was a message for me, delivered rather stiffly by Wanda: her father required to see me on some special matter, the truck would take me to him straight away.

On reaching the camp I was led at once to the Adjutant's tent, where Julius, seated at a table with two other officers, perfunctorily motioned me to sit down and then appeared to forget I was there. A wizened man with a broken mouth was recounting his official troubles in a voice of subacid resignation: ". . . The Russians have two answers, sir. One week they say we don't need any transport and the next they haven't any to give us . . .": and while Julius dealt out his terse comments, "I'll see to that. . . . I'll report that. . . . No use—you must do the best you can", I was able without embarrassment to study his face. I had not, of course, expected him to look as I had last seen him, and yet his appearance startled me: shaved, clean, in a new uniform of British serge to which the Polish badges had been sewn, he had so far recovered his former personality that for a moment I had the sense of waking from a dream—it was as if the person I had worked and travelled with had been not only distinct from this one but actually unreal, a figment of my own imagination. This feeling changed. Watching him closely, I saw that the eyes fixed so attentively on the Commandant's face were clouded, straining to keep open, that the muscles of his jaw were fluttering as if he were having a thorn pulled from under a finger-nail; and the thought came—'This, the face of suzerainty, is the mask, worn easily from old usage. The other was reality'. These were impressions only: one fact was plain. This body, which had seemed to withstand privation more stiffly than any other, was not an instrument of unlimited resistance. He sat up straight, not even resting a hand against the table. But I think I realized even then that he was dangerously ill.

"That's all, then? Well, I'll do what I can for you. . . . One thing one has to remember, Colonel—a great many of these problems are going to solve themselves when we get to the other end of the move. The British are extremely odd people, I'm not suggesting they'll be easy to handle, but at least they don't actively dislike us, as far as we know. Yes—yes, there's one thing I'm quite certain of: in the end the new Polish Army is going to be a genuine force, whatever things look like now. . . . Look, I want to talk to my daughter-in-law for just two minutes—I'll follow you."

There was a cursory fuss, introductions and compliments, offers of substitute-tea. The Commandant went off, and the other officer would have followed, but Julius rather irritably stopped him. "No no, I'm not turning you out of your office. Sit down and get on with whatever you were doing." He came, then, and sat on the bench beside me, but his thoughts must still have been engaged with the interview which had just closed—for several seconds he looked at me in silence as if he were trying to remember who I was. He said at last:

"Oh yes, Stefanie, I wanted to see you about Victor. He's told you? No—well, I think I can get him employed. Nothing magnificent—virtually a Staff Captain's job. He's not of course fit for anything active, but there's going to be a lot of paper work to be looked after and a one-handed man can do that as well as anyone— it means freeing someone in a higher medical category. What were you going to say?"

"Only that I should have thought he'd done his share. The army's had—well, most of him. I thought that what was left might belong to me."

He shut his eyes. He said, with a strained patience:

"There's Poland to be thought of—well, I won't talk about that. But there's also Victor himself. I don't suppose you've really thought of it from his point of view. A man who gets badly damaged, there's one thing he needs more than anything else—it's to get back his confidence. The worst thing for him is to feel that he's useless—finished. There's only one way of proving to him that he's not, and that's giving him a job of work. I believe in the end you'll see that. Incidentally, the casualty rate among base staff officers is generally thought to be indecently small."

The Adjutant was shouting into a field telephone, men came and went and stood about with papers in their hands. It was like being asked one's views of art and philosophy in the middle of an auction.

"I suppose it is," I said.

"Well, I thought I'd better have a word with you." Julius had opened his eyes, but again I wondered if he really saw me. He said abruptly, like a guest forced into conversation with a stranger, "Well, you did get to Karmishkent. It can't have been easy. Really, I thought it was a crazy undertaking."

I told him, "Yes, there were troublesome stages."

"And I thought it most improbable that you would find Victor at the end of it. We have to be very thankful."

"Yes."

"Well, I expect I may see you again—probably after the move. At the moment I don't seem to have a great deal of time on my hands."

"No, of course not."

I saw how things were with him: a man who needs to make his physical resources balance with his responsibilities, hour by hour, has nothing to spare for private intercourse. It was slightly humiliating to be so casually dismissed, but the end was appropriate to a meeting which had felt like a visit to a bank. I thanked him for having seen me.

Outside the tent I was at a loss. The truck was nowhere in sight, and the walk of half a mile to the civilian camp was far beyond my strength. But when I had moved a little way along the central avenue I heard my name called and saw Julius coming after me. He said rather vexedly:

"I forgot, you'll need transport. Look, I'll take you to the Provost tent, you can sit and wait there. I'll get the truck sent to you."

It would have helped me to take his arm, but that was clearly impossible: as it was, he evidently found it awkward to match his pace with mine. I could see there was something he wanted to say; and when we had walked some fifty yards, very slowly, with a foot of daylight between us, he spoke again, looking straight along the road and hardly parting his lips:

"It's unfortunate that this should have happened. Your condition, I mean—I suppose I'm right about that? Yes, I was afraid so. And Victor knows, I suppose?"

"He knows the child's coming. That's all."

"Very well. Then it's my business to tell him the facts. I shall do that. Whether anyone else is to know is a separate question. It's one where I'm very much in your hands."

There was much that I could have answered—at another time,

finding him in a different temper—but I was actually thankful to be saved from doing so now. I simply told him (in a voice as prosaic as his) that Victor had accepted the situation with peculiar charity, and that since he had shown no curiosity about the fathering of the child I saw no purpose in approaching the subject gratuitously. If at any time he put the question to me, I was myself the best person to give and explain the truth to him.

He walked a few yards in silence.

"Very well," he said, "we'll leave it like that for the time being."

I thought that would be all, but presently he said, "I confess I'm relieved. Or partly relieved. It's not only a question of my private interest."

I said, "I see what you mean."

"You may like to know," he continued, labouring, "—though I suppose it concerns me and no one else—that I've received Absolution. No, I suppose that can hardly mean anything to you. It means a great deal to me."

I said, "Yes, I know."

We had reached the Provost tent and we went inside. It was empty.

"As to the child's maintenance," he said, "I shall naturally give all the help I can. And that of course will not be subject to any conditions. I told you—I remember—how I wanted you to bring up Victor's child. I shan't—I'm not in a position to lay down anything about my own. I have certain hopes, but that's all. It's a matter for you and Victor to settle."

I said, "I understand."

I saw no reason why he should stay any longer: he had said, in his own way, what was needed, he had made his position clear. But still he had not finished; and as he stood facing me, haggard, engrossed, I realized afresh the helplessness of one whose inward life was enthralled by a styptic masculinity. When he brought himself to speak his voice was such as I have heard consumptives use in their bad hours—slow, exact, each breathload conveying physical pain.

"Stefanie, I think you ought to know—if I hadn't to think of other people, my wife especially, I shouldn't hesitate to acknowledge the child. You may not understand me—or possibly there's nothing for a clever woman to understand. Only I wanted you to know that. Of course I don't express myself very well, not on these things. I want you to realize I have a sense of gratitude. You're doing something valuable for me, bearing me a child. Even if it's not to be mine in any other sense. I mean that in a particular way. I mean, you and I have been together a great deal—I think you know of my affection for you. It's wrong, I suppose. But I don't feel it so. I shall feel—a kind of satisfaction—something more than that. I shall have a kind of happiness, knowing there's a person who comes from me and also from you."

I said, when I had found my voice, "I'm glad. That makes me glad."

This, which I cannot explain, was sincerity.

A man came in. After staring at him for a moment Julius faced me again.

"I must go now—the Commandant will be wondering what's happened to me. I'll have the truck sent here."

He bent suddenly and kissed my cheek. It was what one would expect from a father-in-law; but he had never done so before, and that kiss was one that I remember vividly. Then he turned to the soldier.

"Why was there no one in this tent? Have you read the Standing Orders? Where's the Provost Sergeant? . . . I don't care about that —the Provost Sergeant is to report to me personally at the Commandant's tent. Yes, immediately. Wait! Some of you men imagine that because you've been prisoners of war you can lead a go-as-you-please life from now on. You can't. Poland is going to be won back by an army—not by a rabble. Do you understand!"

v

A dozen times we heard that the move was cancelled, a dozen times that it was to start in the early summer—next week—next day. One day it was rumoured that the Russians were collecting the necessary transport at Kyzyl Orda, the next that no transport was to be allotted—we were to march to the Caspian coast. Three times we had orders originating from Polish Headquarters to get our baggage on to the road and stand beside it till the lorries arrived.

On the third occasion there was trouble with Jadwiga. We were supposed to be on the road at nine o'clock, and as soon as it grew light we were getting our things together, slowly and in great confusion because of our feebleness. This activity the Countess regarded with an attentive eye—she reminded me just then of an old fowl watching the preparations for her capture—and when the time came for carrying her out she rebelled. She seemed to have her wits about her now, they were concentrated on a simple issue, and she needed only a few short sentences, reiterated with astonishing vehemence, to make her wishes plain: she had journeyed far enough, nothing was to be gained by moving from one place to another, she only wanted to be left where she was.

"But we are all going!" Sandra pleaded. "The tents are going to be pulled down."

"I don't mind about that."

"But you'd be all alone, you'd die!"

"What difference would that make to me!"

It was arranged in the end that we should leave her quite alone, except that Henryk should be posted near the tent; later, when she had been given time to realize her situation, Wanda and Annette were to go back for her. It seemed likely that she would resist even then, and we were prepared for a painful scene.

But I had an inspiration. As soon as our party was established in the crowd which formed a thickset hedge on either side of the road, I slipped away and went back. In her tent I found the Countess exactly as we had left her, sitting up on her palliasse with her eyes open, looking rather bored than distressed. I knelt beside her, and without raising my voice (for I believed that her hearing was good enough whenever she wished) I said:

"I have come to say good-bye."

"Why?" she asked.

"I'm going away. Everyone's going."

"That's nothing to do with me," she said. "Who are you? I don't know you."

"I'm Stefanie."

"I don't know you."

"Your husband was a friend of mine. I had a great affection for him."

"My husband? He's dead. The Russians thought they would have him again, but they didn't.t. I saw to that. He's dead."

"But I haven't forgotten him."

I talked then of the Count and his goodness, his kindness to me, speaking slowly and simply as one does to young children; I told her how often his conversation had been of her, praising her courage and constancy. There was nothing in her face to show that she was listening, but her very stillness seemed to tell me that this gateway to her mind was open; and when I said, "He would be sad now!" she broke her silence:

"What? What are you saying?"

[363]

"He would be sad," I said, "to know you were staying here—here on Russian ground. He'd be grieved that you had given up—now, when the others are starting to make their way back to Poland."

That was dishonest, I suppose. I believe it was justified.

I had never been able to imagine her feelings about her husband; she had appeared to me a creature whose sensibilities were too rugged ever to be responsive to his, and yet I had realized that the gravitation of her life was her devotion to him. So, as I watched her now, I could not even try to penetrate her thoughts; only, I saw that in this shrivelled head the mind was awake, and I believe she was glad to have heard his name spoken, to know that another person still thought of him. It was some time before she spoke:

"My husband—you knew my husband?"

"I used to read to him. At Setory. He liked to be read to in the evenings."

She nodded then. She said, "I know quite well who you are, you're the peasant child that Betka used to look after—Sofia."

"Stefanie."

"You took some tea to my husband, the day those Russians came."

"That's right."

"And now they're going back to Poland—Sandra, all those?"

"They're starting," I told her. "It will take a long time, it's a long way round."

"Then why has nobody come to take me?"

"But Henryk is waiting to take you now," I said.

So it was that I, who had been closest to her in the departure from Setory, was with her at the start of this new journey, the one which she may have thought would bring her to Setory again; and if, in that, I did her doubtful service, at least I had the sense of fulfilling a duty to one whose memory had not ceased to mean much to me. We did not carry her, Henryk and I. When he had got her upright, with a strength and gentleness which both surprised me, she firmly told us that she would walk by herself; and though nearly all her weight was on Henryk's arm, while my arm too was round her, her legs did move very much as if she were actually walking. A strange spectacle we must have made, two graceless, labouring figures with a dreadfully fashioned marionette between them. But this was not a time or place where oddities were remarked on; and when I bent to glance at Jadwiga's face I saw in the stoicism of her contracted mouth, in the sunk, disdainful eyes, something I thought not far from dignity. Once we stopped to rest, and then I heard her say in a perfectly even voice, "It's not to please Sandra or anyone else. I shall go with the others because it's my husband's wish."

Luckily the trucks did come this time, manned by hearty Turcoman soldiers who made easy work of the loading: one of them picked up the Countess as if she had been a child's toy, Annette and Paul were lifted as one piece, and while I was trying to get Victor aboard the truck a grinning giant leaned over the side to grasp him by the collar of his coat and tumble him in with the rest. It was done in twenty minutes. In less than an hour the long convoy, piled high with baggage and three thousand Poles, was jerking along the stony track which was to wind all day through the cold mists, the rock-strewn desolation of Urzyl Kum.

i

"YOU must be patient, kochanie—please, you must be patient with me. You see how it is, I get dreaming, I forget things. You understand, you see how it is with me? I was so long by myself I didn't hear what people said, it was like being quite alone. Even the soldiers, my own people, I couldn't see their faces, I forgot who they were. Nothing I could do, no responsibility. You forget how to live, you forget what people think about—where they are, who's with them—you forget those things have a meaning to people who move about, people who are well. Yes, it's much too easy, living alone, too peaceful. Sometimes it's hard for me—you see?—to get back again. To see the meaning of things, their importance to other people, things which aren't important any more to me."

I cannot remember why Victor asked for my patience. (Had he neglected some small thing that I had wanted him to do for Annette and Paul?) The words return to me with the smell of oil fumes and of sickness, the eternal creak and shudder of bogie-wheels: they must belong to an early stage of that migration, to the train which at last dragged us into Krasnovodsk.

In its outward shape this move was a mere extension of old experience—delays and promiscuous confusion, the stress of communal entombment in machinery which gnawed at infinite distance. And yet those days as they return to me have the calm of evening. Was I so far acclimatized to the sores and constriction of that kind of living, to the monotony of sleeted wind and leaden sky, that it came to me no more harshly than the weather of arctic lands to animals that live there? Was it that I felt my own day to be closing, since my time was near and the chance of surviving that fresh ordeal was a small one? "This time," I heard an old man say, "this time we travel into freedom." But for me it was not an imagined future casting a glow upon this march which distinguished it from those I had made before. I believe that it came to me, this tranquil light, from living so much in Victor's life that I drew from the depth of his resources rather than my own. He was never far away. I slept, as a rule, with my head upon his thighs. Waking, in the vast litter of bodies at the roadside, in the packed train, I would find him watching me with grave attention, and presently the corner of his mouth would lift in the awkward way that the broken muscle prescribed, and his eye would light in a smile of peculiar serenity. When movement was possible he would leave me for a time, to speak to his mother and the rest, to limp about exchanging a word or two with other damaged soldiers; but soon, when his strength was spent, he would return to sit beside me, to feel my hands; the smile came back as if he had made some fresh discovery, and in the quietness of his presence I found a contentment which made me insensible of our squalidness and hunger. In a way it was gain to me that his whole appearance had been so savagely changed. If his face had been unaltered I should have searched in him—how fruitlessly—for every trait which had once delighted me: here, instead, was a travesty which forced me to explore him as one does a stranger. And yet this was not an adventure into trackless country: you cannot spend so much of life with another being and catch no glimpse of what is immutable in him. I do not say I understood him now—that would be a facile claim. But it seemed to me that in the months of helplessness he had lost not only the power but the desire of masterhood; that here was no new creature, only one who walked in freedom since the encrustment of anxieties had been stripped away. And if I had loved him once for his outward virility, responding to his arrogance with a pride of my own, now when I was old and ill I found my love for this emasculated soldier burning with a clearer and steadier flame.

"Stefanie! Are you there, are you all right, kochanie? How long now, how long do you think it'll be till the child comes? I think we shall be there by then, somewhere you can be warm and quiet. It's hard for you, all this, this being shaken about, it's hard for you. For me? No, I don't feel things now, I've got used to this old carcass—they did so much to it, it was such a plague to me, I learnt to pretend it wasn't mine. . . . Iran—I don't know what it's like, I don't know what they'll have for us there. I'd like to see my mother in a little house, perhaps they'll find some place for her, there must be people who have some thought for an old lady. And Annette, they'll surely do something for her. The little boy, little Paul, it's a marvel how she cares for him. Yes, if I had a body I could use, a body with some guts in it, I'd do something for the children."

But at Krasnovodsk, where I think those words were spoken, the children presented too large a problem for anyone to handle with success: they appeared to outnumber the older travellers, and it seemed as if their preponderance increased as each fresh train spilt out its contents to swell the crowd along the quay. Many were un-attached. Some, limp and impervious, stayed where they were put, sprawling in pools of excrement, but those who had some use of their limbs would cluster whimpering about us, they would press their filthy faces between Paul's and Annette's, snatching at any morsel of food she had got for him: like animals, they stole what-ever they could find, attacked each other with a savagery which only the weakness of their sickly bodies held in check. This was a situation that exhausted travellers could hardly deal with, and officials hurrying through the rain towards the harbour-master's office had evidently no time. A kind of optimism served to increase inertia: this is the last of Russia, people said, things will arrange themselves as soon as the mud of this place is off our feet. A ship lying out in the harbour was understood to be the transport allotted to the first flight. A day and a night passed, she showed no movement. But we are used to waiting, they said, and to our older people dying while we wait.

There were those who wearied of this delay. I was summoned one afternoon to the tiny shelter that Wanda and Henryk had rigged for their grandmother by the wall of a timber-shed: the Countess wanted to speak to me, Wanda said. For several minutes I sat beside the old woman while she mumbled unintelligibly, then she motioned me to raise her head and shoulders, and with this change of posture her throat became relatively clear.

"I am tired of all this," she told me. "These Russians, they mismanage things all the time. I've told that child—Wanda—I've told her I've had enough."

I answered by speaking as well as I could of the need for a little more patience—we should soon be in other and better hands. But she took no notice of that.

"I told the child," she said, "that you are to come to me. I have to thank you for a kindness—you took some trouble in amusing my husband—that was some time ago."

I started trying to tell her once more how great a refreshment my visits to the Count had been for me. Again she cut me short.

"Why?" she demanded.

I said, faltering, "He was always kind to me. I've never known anyone the same. He was a man of very great goodness."

That made her nod, as if I were a pupil who had answered with the accuracy she demanded. Startlingly, she caught hold of one of my fingers; her shrivelled lips parted and I thought (though an emotion of my own may have tricked me) that I saw a momentary gentleness in her staring eyes.

"You," she said, "you, after all, have intelligence. Sandra—those others—no one else has said that to me."

I did not see her again. Wanda, going to attend to her that evening, found the shelter empty. A crippled man lying not far off thought he had seen her at dusk crawling by inches towards the edge of the quay, some thirty feet away.

I think that later on we all experienced a sense of loss: she had existed as something more than a burden, she had been the strongest ligature between us and Setory, and in a small society framed by impermanence the value of a single life is not measured by its utility alone. For many days some part of my mind was always wondering where she had got to, whether anything could be done for her. At the time of her disappearance, however, I was under-sensitive to the distinction between life and death. People were quiet here. The greater part, put down from the trains, walked only far enough to find a space on the ground for their baggage and themselves; there they sat or lay, waiting for what should happen to them next, and many were so still, their gaze so vacuous, that you could not tell if they were living or already dead.

And we, after all, were of this company, which caught from its surroundings an air of phantasm. The level, salted wind which filled our lungs with the stench of rotting fish and oil could never clear the sash of smoke which hung in the twisting rain; through this unsteady screen a locomotive ploughing back and forth beyond the sheds, a squad of oil-tanks crouching over the chaos of roofs and spars, showed flat and lifeless as a novice's photograph; and in such a frame you came to see your fellow-travellers not as the people who had talked and laughed in Polish villages, not as parents, lovers, vehicles of memory and hope, but as a mere agglomeration of shapes cast vaguely in the human form. My own body, its weight and hunger, became unreal. And so it is that I have no visual memory of Victor as he sat or lay beside me through the long vigil, though I know that the peacefulness which illumined those desolate hours accrued from him. I remember only the stillness of his presence there, the calm of his inveterate fortitude; how his whispering voice seemed to come rather from some distant spirit than from the mouth of a shattered man.

"If only I can get you to some sheltered place! For me, yes, for me it's been the best of all my journeys, it wouldn't matter how long it takes for me. I thought you had to be in your own country, I used to think that happiness was incomplete except in places you knew. It's altered, for me it doesn't matter now. You're so patient with me, kochanie. You know, I had a great deal of pain, it was dark for a long time. If I could only show you the light you see where it's darkest of all!"

ii

"Yes, Mother, yes, it's Victor, yes, I'm here! Annette, is Paul all right? Wait, I'll come in nearer. I can keep some of the wind off. Not long to go—they say they've seen some lights, I think we'll be in by morning. Are you there, Mother? It won't be long now—not long to go."

All night there were other voices sounding fitfully along the deck, the mumbling of a scared old woman, '. . . *in hora mortis nostrae . . . et benedictus fructus ventris . . .*', a girl's monotonous complaint, '. . . a trick they've played, I tell you it's a trick to make us want to be back!' But these were no more than threads in the screen of sound—the wind's noise and the scraping of loose gear, the whimpering of children; it was Victor's tranquil voice, returning and returning like a lighthouse beam, which kept me within the field of sanity through the cold, sleepless hours when the tanker swayed and floundered in the swell: "There's no real danger, they build these boats for rougher seas than this. I think the wind's dropping, you can see it's lighter now. . . . Look, let me hold him for a bit—yes, he's wet, poor mite, but he won't come to any harm."

At some time in that night (unless it was the one before) I found that Sandra's head was close to mine, and through the drowsiness which had to do for sleep I heard her talking in a tone that was strangely free from the agitation of the neighbouring women's voices:

"You don't think I've been unkind to you, Stefanie? I've been forgetful at times; it's difficult to manage things when I've always been used to having my husband's guidance. But you know, Stefanie, you know you're very dear to us—I shouldn't like Victor to think anything but that. I imagine Julius must have gone on an earlier boat. Naturally he couldn't arrange for me to be with him, no doubt the Russians made all the arrangements—one hopes they had a more suitable boat for him than this. You thought he looked quite well when you saw him? I was not quite sure, I couldn't feel certain he was well. It worries me, you see—I keep wondering if I shall be able to look after him properly when I'm with him again. You understand, I've looked forward to that so much—to doing my duty again. Only now I get so tired, it worries me when I'm awake at night."

Presently Victor's voice, "You mustn't be worried, Mother. It'll all feel different when you're on land again."

"But Victor, you must remember I've always tried to keep up to certain standards. It's only right, when you think what your father's position is. I couldn't bear him to be ashamed of me, a man such as he is, so loving and so good. . . ."

With the first light there came what appeared to be a mirage. Beside the lifeboat which had given us a little shelter I saw through drifting snowflakes the faint semblance of a Swiss lakeside resort, shallow white houses and ornamental trees, something shaped like a bandstand, a balconied hotel. A woman lying near me—a doctor's wife, possibly feeble-witted, or merely old and half asleep—called, "Europe! We've got to Europe—it's Zoppot, I think!" But one of the sailors put her right: this was Bandar Pahlevi, he told us, a piece of Iranian nonsense: if we wanted to see a real port, he said, we should travel to Baku.

For ourselves we did not mind what sort of place Pahlevi was, it would satisfy us by being level and still. In the stifling quarters and along the open deck there were living more than a thousand souls (with a total of three toilets for their use): given leave to spread ourselves on the firm ground, we should not have complained if the pleasures of Pahlevi proved tamer than Warsaw's or Lausanne's.

A mirage it remained. The harbour was too shallow, the sailors said, for a vessel of our draught, we should have to be taken ashore in smaller craft: that was a matter for the harbour authority, which would signal its intentions when these had been worked out. (If tenders were not available, they added sagely, the tanker might be ordered to return to Krasnovodsk.) So, less than a mile from streets where we could see horse carriages and motor-cars, we lay at anchor, now gently heaving, now rolling so steeply that the seas breaking against the side of the ship were sousing us with spray.

[371]

All day an electric bell kept sounding somewhere below, and there were sanguine passengers who supposed each time that this was the signal we awaited. But nothing we could see, looking hungrily towards the miniature town which dipped and rose beside us, suggested that our presence had been noticed there.

Some way along the deck a one-armed priest and some others were making tea with a samovar they had coaxed from the sailors, and giving it to anyone who had strength to get there. This was beyond my power, and both Wanda and Henryk were still incapably sick; but Sandra, to my surprise, succeeded in making the journey half a dozen times, always returning with a drink for one of us in the little meat-jar she kept among her odds and ends. My memory of that wearisome day has narrowed so that only this episode remains distinct: not so much for the mouthful of tea (which greatly refreshed me, though it was hardly anything but lukewarm water faintly stained) as for the spectacle of my mother-in-law returning again and again from her arduous pilgrimage. She had always been an ungainly walker, and even in her robuster days I should not have thought it possible for her to balance herself along some thirty metres of tilting deck; yet now, as she steered her fat, stiff legs through the jumble of baggage and prostrate bodies, as she slipped and staggered on a carpet of slime, she never once fell over or lost control of the precious jar in her hand. All the time she was vaguely smiling: on her travel-worn face it looked peculiar but not contemptible, that foolish, social smile.

We could not endure another twelve hours of such vertigo and exposure—or so I should have said. But endurance is happily a business one can learn as one goes along. Darkness came, there was still no signal from the shore, or none that the cargo heard of; we realized by degrees that the unimaginable night was to be lived through again. After some hours I slept; more exactly, I came to the familiar state where the body seems to be tightly pinioned and discomfort serves as its own narcotic; so that the straining of the ship, its disparate voices, appeared to reach me from another room.

". . . changed their minds, those British—perhaps they don't require us any more." ". . . be trouble before long, I tell you, there'll be trouble from these bloody Poles." "What—trouble from these!" "They say it's a fair exchange—they say they get one aeroplane for twenty-five of us." "Did it myself, I did it with my scarf at Kolpashevo. I couldn't stand it any longer, seeing him like that."

"I tell you, someone's going to pay!"

"It isn't all like this, Pauliska, it isn't all like this!"

And now the wind felt not so cold, and the lights appeared to rise and fall more soothingly, the sea's phosphorescence and the points of light along the shore.

"Not just for Poland, Poland for itself, that isn't large enough—but there are things I'd fight for if I could. It must be wrong to have such peacefulness when others aren't at peace. . . . Come closer—there, like that, now I can get my arm round—no, don't wake, kochanie, you mustn't wake up! I think the wind's quietening. Are you warmer now, is it better like that? No, for me there isn't any pain, not when you're so close. . . . These people, yes, they've lost so much. But losing things—in the end—I've found it's the way you escape. You know, kochanie, I feel it can't be something only happening to me, such joy as this."

iii

"We didn't know, you see, we didn't know you'd be here so soon." He spoke to the crowd at large in a bastard French with a Polish word or two thrown in, the tired youth who seemed to be an English officer. "They wouldn't let us come, our Russki friends, not till today—we've had no time to get things planned."

Already the swelling mass had overflowed the jetty and spread for some distance along the beach. I would not let myself be pushed that way. Parted from the others in the confusion of transhipment, I had come ashore in one of the earliest boats, and in fear of not finding them again I edged my way to a space where I could sit and watch the stage. Comparatively it was warm here, with a cluster of bitumen casks between me and the wind.

"You must give us time, we'll get you under cover in time. . . . Yes, sir, fourteen hundred, they seem to think, this first batch—fourteen hundred at least. They say there's another transport on the way, two more perhaps, the signal wasn't clear. Well, with any luck we'll get a clear day in between. No, no one's seen the Polish Staff, they say they're holding a conference in one of the hotels, it'll probably go on all day. Yes, sir, Wilson says he's bought up every loaf in the town, but I've sent him round again."

The tenders came in at intervals of half an hour—the landing-stage was never clear—and as they bobbed below me the pier I stood on seemed to rise and fall. Drowsy and sick, I constantly forgot what was happening. Where did it come from, this endless stream, were these the people I had lived with, or hollow images that moved along the wall of a tired mind? Mounting so slowly, with such empty eyes, were they themselves asleep? A group of sepoys on the steps were helping where they could, some of the oldest people were carried bodily, babies passed up from hand to hand. But among the men in uniform were some who climbed—however slowly—by themselves, upright, hands to their sides; even civilians made a show of independence, supporting each other or clutching the iron rail, while some, refusing all assistance, were clambering from step to step on hands and knees, dragging beside them the last of their belongings, clothes tied in filthy shawls, valises held together with knotted string, a starving dog, a sewing-machine. For some the effort was too severe; a few, close to the top, fell back on to those behind, and some who reached the upper stage could make no further ground; under the eyes of curious and dumb Iranians they crumpled and lay down in the soiled snow. But the greater part trudged on like driven cattle, following the ones ahead, and there were even some who tried to march in ranks, swinging their arms as soldiers should. A various legion: beneath the wasting and fatigue you saw what kind of faces these had been, you could tell farm labourers from townsmen, you guessed that this was a schoolma'am's, this a lawyer's face. And yet what fastened on my mind as these travellers dragged past me was their family likeness, the uniformity of faces that had ceased to record experience, eyes which in the place of hope or purpose showed only a naked resolution.

"Yes, keep them moving, those who can, we're getting jammed round here. Tell them there's soup coming—find Mr Wilson if you can, tell him he'll have to raise another lot of tea."

"Excuse me, please!" And I vaguely recognized the solemn face of the child who stared at me with colourless, demented eyes. "I have come to do my shopping, I should like you to show me an evening gown."

"I'm very sorry, I've nothing in today."

"If you please, Madame"—the English soldier was beside me again—"if you could move a little way, we're getting a bit too crowded here."

"But I'm waiting for my friends."

"Your friends? Yes yes, I'll tell them you've just gone ahead."

But then I caught sight of Henryk, who was crying a little as Annette and one of the Indians pulled him up the steps. Sandra came just after them, walking unsteadily but with a certain importance, and turning her head to right and left as if the crowd of on-lookers were there to give her a distinguished welcome. I smiled as she drew close, and she nodded graciously, but I do not think she realized who I was. Some way behind, Wanda and Victor came together, she supporting him with one arm round his back, while with the other she held Paul on her shoulder—I should have said from the way she walked that she had wholly recovered, and in that contingent I saw no one else who appeared so much at his own command. I do not pretend that I observed those five impartially: you cannot look with a scientist's eyes on those who have been the close companions of a march through arduous country. I merely record that as I watched them mount the steps, slowly but scarcely faltering, they seemed to wear in common the dignity of a peculiar fortitude; and I was glad, just then, that these were the ones to whom I specially belonged.

Presently Wanda was beside me.

"Stefanie, you must try to keep close—it's hopeless if we get scattered. The important thing is to get Mother and Paul under cover—he's pretty bad. I'm going to find Colonel Wojciewicz if I can, he's responsible for civilians at this end, I'm not taking any orders from these Englishmen. Look, you must carry Paul for half a minute, then I'll have him again."

I took him from her just in time, for she fell flat a moment after-wards. But she was on her feet again almost at once, and we started to move all together the way the rest were going, helping each other along.

iv

And now it was Sandra who gave trouble. She had got it into her head that Julius was travelling in a ship which had followed ours and would shortly be landing. It would look very strange, she thought, and would lead to gossip among the foreigners, if she were not on the pier to greet him.

"You go on, all of you!" she said. "You must get a conveyance and go to one of the hotels for the time being. Your father will make fresh arrangements when he comes."

Then, catching sight of me, she took me aside to speak in my ear.

"Listen, Stefanie; there's something I want you to do for me. Wanda's tired, poor child, I don't think she quite understands. I want the General to find his room exactly as it always used to be, he'll be so pleased with that, he is a very orderly man. Those men, those soldiers—they were Russians, I think—they made his room in a dreadful state. I can't do everything myself, I find a sea voyage very fatiguing. You will—won't you, Stefanie—you will see that everything's put straight? You must get hold of Anusia, you must tell her to dust the General's desk very carefully, and to go behind the picture-frames as well."

It was apparent to me that, like Jadwiga, she had grown tired of being moved about; and even Wanda saw that it was useless to argue. All we could do for the time being was to make her tolerably comfortable with a coat round her shoulders, her back supported by a pile of baggage, and to leave her there. She was utterly composed—indeed, I cannot remember that I ever saw her look so free from anxiety: sitting rather rigidly, with her eyes fixed on the end of the pier, she wore the expression of mingled aloofness and affability which she had once acquired as part of her social uniform; and within that shield I thought I saw the contentment of one engrossed in work which she has brought to perfection.

There were others lying nearby, and these the British were collecting by degrees on stretchers; I supposed that before long they would take her as well. But an hour later, when I managed to return with a cup of soup which a soldier had given me, I found her still there. She was lying down now, with the coat over her face. That one had died, the harassed officer informed me; and he went on to explain, laboriously, that the cases which were still alive had to be dealt with first.

When I got back to the others it was growing dark. By then a number of our people had wandered into the town: these were simple folk, who had lived without comforts for a long time, and it was natural they should want to exercise their freedom hoping to barter any trinkets they still possessed—or the bits of clothing which had been given them—for some small celebration. But the British were vexed by this truancy—they thought it wrong to have people like us, who carried more dirt and lice than they were used to, getting mixed with the Iranians—and they set themselves to keep the rest of us corralled on the beach. It was not done harshly. There were young soldiers who went about trying in their own fashion to make us cheerful—they were sorry about all this, they said, but things were going to be *all right*, they had sent for a quantity of blankets and tents, soon there would be another issue of tea. Meanwhile it was enough for me (although I was in some pain) that Victor was alive and near, that Annette was tucked against my side, already sleeping, with Paul cuddled in her breast. And the rest of that large company, making as little complaint as we, and falling soon into the mode they had learnt in many comfortless places, were settling themselves to get what warmth they could from each other's bodies, to lie still, to hope for sleep.

In that familiarity—grouped figures showing like huge wormcasts on the fainter darkness of the sand, the murmur of uneasy sleepers, a cold and restless wind—we might have fancied we were back in some earlier epoch of the journey; only that we had enclosing us, in place of the steppe's tremendous silence, the scrape and thunder of waves. It may have been this element of strangeness, more than the cold, which kept some of us awake; and perhaps it was a need for reassurance which made an old labouring man who lay not far from me begin to sing. He sang a marching ditty which they call *The Krakow Guard*, one that was heard in the old days at every village festival and was dear to soldiers; and because they were so far from home, on this waste ground between the sea and the alien houses, it wrought with curious force on my fellow-travellers' emotions—there were aged women near me who burst into tears, and some of the sobbing I heard must have come from younger people as well. It passed, this wave of melancholy. Now, as if recalled to some discipline of childhood, the sleepers all about us came stiffly to their feet, a second voice took up the song, a dozen more, till it swept along the beach as fire is borne by wind and like fire rekindled from a smouldering heath it blazed against the desolation of the place and hour:

> *By all the blood of Poland's slain*
> *Our Polish earth is sanctified:*
> *Poland shall rise, shall rise again!*

It was crudely sung: these were tired performers, and the memories it stirred may have worked in them as a clamp upon the lungs. I knew what Victor meant when I heard him whisper, "They had so little—these. They've lost so much." But there was in this discordant singing a vehemence, a strain of exultation, by which it transcended actuality as greater music does: so that when the simple tune returns to me—now, through the traffic of this distant street, from the radio by an open window—the scene it brings is always the dark crowd standing motionless on a windy shore, a surge of stumbling voices against the sea's insistent voice.

i

IN the end they did get us—or most of us—under cover that night. I myself was taken by stretcher and truck to a cinema, where, by good fortune, Annette and Paul were sent as well. In this primitive building, where the electricity had failed and the only light came from oil-lamps set beside the doors, two or three hundred of us settled gratefully on the floor. The youthful officer who had been on the pier went round with an electric torch, carefully stepping over the sleeping figures and apologizing to anyone who seemed capable of listening: the place was *affreusement mal nettoyé*, he said; in the morning he would get *une partie des Wogs* to clean it up.

There, a little before daybreak, with Annette to help me, I bore Julius's son—the third son who was born to me, the second to be born alive. His body, much smaller than that of my other babies, appeared to be perfectly formed, and his hands were of exquisite beauty. When I saw his face, in the pale light from the door, I thought I saw a look of Conrad there. He lived for two hours.

ii

The solemn little Indian doctor who was brought to see me had me moved to an Iranian hospital, where the beds had been pushed close together and many patients—including me—had to lie on rugs along the floor. In this busy place we were treated with unremitting kindness, and the only trouble I suffered was the separation from my own people.

Owing to physical weakness my brain was again working poorly, and I could not understand why neither Victor nor Annette had got in touch with me. By this time, surely, the reception staff would have made a register, there must be some office to tell people where their friends had been sent! The picture in my mind—I realize now —was that of No. 5 Camp on the Russian side, where there had been perhaps two thousand civilians. We in the first flight of the evacuation had numbered some fourteen hundred, and that—in the phrase I heard from a British soldier—had been 'roughly a manageable crowd'. The real picture was different now.

I got some glimpse of it from the little Hindu, who continued to visit me every day and whose English was so clear that I could follow almost every sentence. He was always in a hurry, but once or twice he gave way to weariness and squatted beside me to take a few puffs at a cigarette.

"Another lot this morning—just after midnight. Three thousand this time. It's hopeless, there's nowhere to put them, we've got nearly twenty thousand now." He smiled, showing all his gold teeth—that was his way of expressing sadness. "Well, the Colonel will find a solution. That Colonel Ross, he's not like other men, he can live without food or sleep, he's like a hundred men all put together. . . . No, we don't think much about keeping people with their friends, only about keeping them alive. That—you understand?—that is work enough."

It was easier for me to grasp the situation when, to make room indoors for more serious cases, I was moved to a tented hospital which was being erected in what they called the Clean Camp. Here the tent in which I lay with fifty or a hundred other patients had as yet no wall on the landward side, and I was able to watch the parties arriving from the bath-houses after being stripped and scrubbed with kerosene emulsion from head to foot. They were now in the uniform of British soldiers, men and women alike, their feet in great black boots. At the entrance to the camp were soldiers, mostly Indian, whose duty was to shepherd them to the several points where food was being distributed from rudimentary field kitchens. This was a slow business. Dazed by their latest experience, the new arrivals were incapable of following anyone's directions. Children dragged, the old constantly sat down, and there were many who strayed towards the stalls which local traders had improvised along the boundary wire. Among the bewildered Poles a small army of Iranians were moving in every direction: contractors arriving with supplies and stores, voluble gangs erecting tents, boys wandering slowly through the crowd with a plank or a box of nails, carpenters who without apparent method were knocking together the framework of huts and latrines; and beside all these there were men who had come on their own account to sell tobacco or dubious oranges, or merely to stand and stare. On a strip of sand perhaps two hundred metres wide the turmoil stretched as far as I could see; I began to realize what the doctor had meant—'We do not think very much about keeping people with their friends'.

Of the British, whom one supposed to be the owners of this cosmorama, there were still very few to be seen, and these had nothing proprietorial in their appearance. They were mostly on the small side, youngish men, dingily uniformed, who picked their way through the maze without anxiety or palpable haste, as if they were hardly aware of the manifold confusion. If they gave any orders it was by a means unknown to me: I did not hear them shout—indeed, they scarcely spoke at all except to call out as they passed us, with little shamefaced smiles, "All better soon—soon *all right!*" I never saw where their authority came from—how it was that things appeared to fall into some kind of shape wherever one of these unpretentious beings came on the scene.

On the fourth day of my sojourn in that 'hospital' the transports were still arriving. An orderly told me that by then some thirty thousand people had come ashore alive.

iii

But that great confluence of exiles returns to me as a spectacle seen through glass, not as an experience in which I had any part. In those days the people near me were strangers, a bearded soldier on one side, a child of perhaps three years on the other, who could not speak at all; and since there was no one to connect me with the human tide which lapped my feet I saw it as a pageant almost without meaning. Close to thousands, I was in solitude—but not in wretchedness. My life—as I now interpret memory—was in abeyance.

I was roused a little way when a face appeared above me which—though I knew it well—I could not identify. It belonged to a man who lacked both an arm and a leg, a Pole who began by asking me all the standard questions as he surveyed me with an overworked doctor's eyes. After a minute or two he stopped and said, "But you are one of the Kolbecks—you are Stefanie!"

A name came to me then. I said, "I remember—yes, I know who you are. You are Sofietka's husband."

At this he turned his eyes away, as if I had accused him of some shameful action.

"I am Ludwig Radznowski."

"But you were married to Sofietka. Sofietka—she was with me in the train."

"You have an excellent memory!"

"But surely——"

"Yes," he said, "I might have known I should find you here! There's always someone. Always someone who wants to burble at me about the person you mentioned."

I said, "I'm sorry. But naturally——"

"Yes, it's natural, I know it's natural! Well now, what do you want me to do for you? I can tell you what you need. You need a light, progressive diet, and also an oxytocic of some kind. You need to be on a special mattress in a carefully ventilated room. You have got to have sunshine, lots of it, ten hours a day. So I'll tell the sergeant fellow to bring you those things this afternoon."

"Tell me about yourself," I said.

"Myself? I'm pretending to be a ward-trotter—is that the word? —never having been in general practice in my life. It passes the time. And it does no harm—no one dies any quicker because of me looking at them."

"But isn't it too much for you?"

"You mean—will it kill me? No, it won't. That's God's little joke. Everyone else can die—even ignorant and stupid people— they do it without the slightest trouble. Me—I can't get the knack of it. . . . Look, I'll tell these Asiatic bodies you've got to be looked after properly. How, I don't know. And that's about all I can do. I suppose Wanda's been to see you?"

"I don't know where she is."

"Wanda? She's in the army lines—what's left of her—I saw her this morning. They've given her some job, something to do with nursing. I'll get hold of her, shall I? Tell her to come and see you."

"Well, I'd like you to tell her where I am."

He nodded, and then he said, "I shall be round again myself, I'll probably see you. After all, that's what I'm paid for—if they do pay me. I can't leave one case out just because it's someone I used to know."

I shut my eyes, hoping he would go away: I was myself in no mental condition to deal with a man in his. But he seemed to lack the will-power needed to get him moving. When I looked up again he still stood over me, bent on his crutch, intensely watching my face; and now, with a struggle, he got down on a hand and knee so that he could bring his mouth close to my ear.

"Listen," he said, "you've got to tell me something. I've got to know exactly how it was in the end. What was the last thing she said? Was she conscious up to the end? Did she go in a fit of coughing? Tell me—did she cry out, was she in terrible pain? . . ."

He kept his promise about Wanda, and she came to see me next day.

Although her appearance cannot have altered fundamentally in the few days since I had last seen her, her face shocked me. Perhaps the interval had been long enough for older pictures to return, replacing actuality; or perhaps it was just that the filth of travel had previously disguised the impairment of her features. The woman I saw now, clean, compact in her mannish uniform, was middle-aged. I should have recognized this face even if I had not seen it since the days when she had been my pupil, gay and mischievous, because the trenchant Kolbeck structure could never be altered or mistaken; but its loveliness had gone; so withered at the roots, I thought, that it would not flourish again. Grey and tired, she stood watching me rather as Ludwig had done—as if I were some problem extraneous to the work in hand.

"Ludwig Radznowski said you wanted to see me. I'm afraid I can't stay very long, I've got a good deal on my hands. I suppose these people here—these Indians and people—I suppose they're looking after you as well as they can? I'm afraid you can't expect first-class treatment, not as things are at the moment, the reception staff's still hopelessly inadequate. I can't see really that there's anything I can do."

"No," I answered. "No, there's nothing I need, really, I'm being looked after perfectly well." It happened that I was in considerable pain that day, my head was clouded and the question I wanted to ask her would not come. "But you see," I said, "I didn't know where any of you had got to."

"Any of us? Oh, Annette's over in the children's lines—what they call the 'Barnardo'—she's nursing there, she wanted to be where she could keep an eye on Paul."

"Is she all right?"

"Annette? Oh, I think so. Of course she's upset over Paul."

"What—is there something wrong with him?"

"Wrong with him? With Paul? I thought you knew." For a moment she shut her eyes. "I've forgotten—I'm rather tired—I've forgotten when you left us. You know that Mother's dead?"

"But I was the one who found her."

"Yes. Yes, I remember. That's why I've got myself this job, you see. I had to do something, now that Mother hasn't got to be looked after any more."

"But Paul—what's wrong with Paul?"

"Well, nothing new. It's his legs, you know, they never seemed to be right. Only a doctor's seen them now, one of the British doctors. Apparently he'll never walk, the bones aren't properly formed." She paused, frowning. "Was there anything else you wanted to ask me about?"

I could not answer at once; but presently I said, "You'll be seeing Annette?"

"When I can. I don't get a lot of time. Things get in a mess every time I leave those stupid girls for half an hour."

"Look, Wanda, please—I want you to send a message to her. You can do that, can't you? I want her to know that I'll be with her as soon as I can. I think I'll be able to get about in a day or two——"

"But Ludwig said you won't even be starting to walk for another fortnight——"

"That doesn't matter. Tell her I'm coming very soon. Tell her —wait, do you think you can possibly get me some paper? I could write a message——"

She said firmly, "I really haven't a lot of time. I'll send her a message myself."

"It would be better if you saw her."

But now she was upset. She said, "You know I don't really want to see people. Not in that way. Not people I know. I avoid it as much as I can. Of course you won't understand—you don't feel about things as I do. I mean, I haven't got much to spare—much strength, I mean—I've got my work to do, I can't get through it if I let myself get involved in emotions."

I asked her—gently, I think—"But is there anything left in life if you stop seeing your friends? If you stop loving them?"

"Stefanie," she said, "please don't try to argue with me! I'm tired, I really don't feel like arguing. I tell you, I don't want to love people. I've got to see people suffering all the time, millions of them. I've got to see them losing their children—being ill—dying. I can stand that as long as I don't care about them. The stupid thing is to care about people."

"But what else is there to care for?"

"There's Poland." She was quiet and serious now. "No, Stefanie, I'm not a fool. I don't believe in this Polish Corps they think they can make out of all these crocks. It's a gesture and that's all. No, we shan't see Poland freed, not we ourselves. But it will be free. Because of us."

I remember the undertone of passion which sounded in those last words; and I remember acutely the feeling they roused in me, which was not for what she said but for herself. In the days when I had been her governess and some lesson had defeated her, she had often given way to bursts of rage; but after she had attacked me with bitter insults her fury had always changed to fondness, and our gentlest hours together had followed some of those storms. Now, instinctively, I waited for her gentleness to reappear; and if I could have made some trivial gesture, if I had merely caught and held her hand, I believe she might have yielded to our old affection. That was not to be. Ludwig had been right about my condition: I could not even raise my shoulders a few inches from the straw.

My head was aching, and in this state of feebleness I was afraid of giving way to senseless tears. I said wearily, "Well—look—don't bother about the message to Annette. I'd rather you didn't bother. I'll write something and get one of the orderlies to take it."

She answered, "Well, just as you like!"

"And, Wanda—look—there is just one thing. If you should—if you possibly can make inquiries about what's happened to Victor——"

"Victor? But don't you know about him?"

That, too, was a moment I shall not forget. I was certain that she was going to tell me—just as casually as she had mentioned Paul's disablement—that Victor was dead.

"I thought you'd know," she said abstractedly. "Father's got him at Headquarters; they're in the town at present in some hotel —he's supposed to be some sort of Staff Captain. I don't suppose he's really doing much; I don't imagine he could concentrate, even if——"

"You've seen him?"

"What? Yes. Yes, I saw him. When? Yesterday—no, the day before. I was over there."

"Did he—did he talk about me?"

"What? Oh—yes. Yes, of course. Yes, he was in rather a state, he was trying to find out where you'd got to. People will not realize how——"

"But how is he—how did he look? Is he getting food, is he walking about?"

She frowned. I suppose she was dealing all day long with people who asked stupid questions. "But of course!" she said, still looking past me. "Surely you know I'd have done something if there was anything to be done. Do you think he means more to you than he does to me!"

I did not reply: it is better to leave unanswered the interjections of people who are overstrained.

"Yes, he's all right," she said impatiently. "I mean, he's no different—you wouldn't expect him to be any different. Well, you know what he's been like all this time. He may be slightly worse—his mind, I mean. I don't understand that any more than you can. He's very much the same, he's dreamy all the time. I don't think he really knows what's going on."

iv

Her visit left me with a new unhappiness; it was hard to think of Annette's grief and to be prevented from going to her side. But I was still enjoying the protection of my own physical state—that weakness which places a film between oneself and reality. The world of outward perception continued to be remote and strange; I did not start to live again in any positive sense until the hour when Victor came.

He was brought by an English officer—a diffident, well-meaning little man whom I was to know better—in a miniature truck which came twisting and bouncing through the rubbish that now littered the camp: it stopped a few yards from where I lay, and the Englishman helped him to my side. "There!" the Englishman said in nursery-Polish, "now me go forward camp put out stores, me back hour, not so much. *All right? All all right? Tout va bien? All right!*"

Victor got himself down beside me and held my hand. For some time—it may have been a minute or two, it may have been much longer—we did not speak at all. He went on stroking my fingers, 'reading' them as a blind man would, while he intently scanned my face, nodding seriously and then smiling as if he were constantly assuring himself that my presence was real. I believe I should have been content if we had spent the hour in nothing but that.

He said at length, "Tell me! Tell me, kochanie!"

I could not immediately find my voice; but when he had come closer (cautiously, as if he were afraid to damage me) and had let his head sink down to lie in the old way between my breasts, my tongue started to work by itself. I did not talk in a sensible fashion:

[385]

that was not in my power then, nor was it needed. Between those who have learnt each other perfectly there is a kind of speech, not the least in value, which is like a restful breathing of the mind; and even had I been able to talk coherently of all that had filled my thoughts in this last separation, I do not think we should have put our time to better use. There was much that he cannot have understood. When I spoke confusedly of how I had lost my child, he said with a depth of gentleness, "Yes, kochanie, yes, you told me. In the street—what was that place?—we were in the street and you told me. Kochanie, I have been so sad for you. . . ." But I did not need that he should know so soon as this the very shape of what I had suffered. To let grief flow without restraint, to repose in his limitless patience, was all I needed.

I came near to behaving senselessly when the truck returned: like an over-mothered child I was suddenly alarmed and desolated by the thought of his leaving me even for a short time. But then his firmness saved me from the disgrace of tears. "You see," he said, standing and speaking with a slow kindness, "you see, I've got to make myself some use. I've got to be with soldiers." He was faintly smiling, as if I were bound to understand a foolish weakness of his. "There's nothing I know how to do, except with soldier fellows. And you see, they were so good—those months when I was helpless—my soldiers were so good to me."

His eye had turned away from me, he was looking across the camp and out to sea. Against that emptiness he watched, perhaps, the faces of the soldiers he spoke of, returning to the stretch of life where he had been with men alone. But I do not believe so. I saw in his face neither sentiment nor pain, but rather the calm of a private certainty; and I believe the experience he had returned to was farther from this hour than any which I could place in space or time. Just then he was more remote from me than he had ever been. But I know it was not through any want of goodness or of love that he had once more gone where I could not follow. Within his understanding was a region unencompassed by my own. I had possessed the whole of him. I should have been wrong to grieve that within the whole was a part which was only his possession.

He said, before the truck took him away, "We are always together." His eye was towards my face again, though he seemed to watch me from a great distance. "We are always together now."

"I don't believe in this Polish Corps. . . ." It is curious to remember that Wanda said those words, for it was she who afterwards saw the Polish Army in the East in the days of its greatest glory: with her detachment of nurses she followed it through North Africa to Italy, and she had reached a place not far south of the Volturno before the disease which she must have got at Mikirka completed its slow advance and killed her. I have wished that I had been able to go with them as well, for that would have been an experience to dwell on in the months to come, when a darkness like that of winter settled upon our patriot hopefulness; but at least I was present at that army's birth—or so I think of the day when General Anders came to Pahlevi to review his men.

It had rained for a whole week, putting us in great wretchedness, for the tents were sodden and even the huts could not withstand that deluge: in all the four camps by which the original Clean Camp had been supplemented there cannot have been a dry blanket or one inhabitant dryly clad. But early that morning the sky cleared, and soon, along the four or five miles of beach we occupied, the tents were steaming in a strong sun. A space half a mile in length had been left between the third and the fourth camps: here, when High Mass was celebrated by Cardinal Kraszewski at a great altar erected under the Polish flag, a crowd of twenty-five thousand bedraggled people knelt on the wet sand; here, soon afterwards, the band of the Carpathian Brigade took its position at the water's edge, and a little after noon the parade began.

In other days, on the Kosciuszko drill-ground, such a display as this would have looked like a savage burlesque; but these hastily renovated soldiers had their excuse: the sand was not easy to march on; among them were short-paced men, and men with one stiff leg, who had to scramble to stay in line, and as they wheeled by companies, fifteen men abreast, into the broad avenue between us onlookers and the saluting-base I wondered that they kept the ranks as straight as they did. They had a mile or more to go; that was enough, for some of those who marched had been carried from the boats on stretchers less than a month before, and some had only been on their feet for a matter of hours; yet if it had been doubled in length I doubt if any would have shirked the course. As rank after rank went by I saw bodies which seemed to work by themselves while the owners were engrossed in pain, their eyes halfclosed, their faces blanched and drawn; I saw once and again a man gasping for breath, and one who stumbled and swayed—but I did not see a man fall out, or one who failed to swing his arms and to keep his head erect. A thousand of them passed, a thousand more, then there were women marching, solemn and zealous in their uniform, and when I saw Wanda at the head of her detachment I thought there was not a man who marched more soldierly than she. They were followed by a company of veterans, men who had marched and fought in Pilsudski's First Brigade; and now came a group of officers and men who could not march at all but who had claimed a right as soldiers to go with the rest—some on stretchers or in chairs wheeled by their friends, while some with the help of sticks or crutches made their way alone. I knew that Victor had meant to walk with these, and I was prepared for moments of distress, for I could not believe he had strength for such an effort. But when he came in sight he appeared to feel no strain: he was supported on one side by Henryk, who, grinning self-consciously, was shambling forward at his own eccentric gait; his crumpled body moved like a marionette's, his head lay almost on one shoulder, and yet as he painfully brought his arm to the salute I caught a glimpse of the soldier he had been in earlier years, assured, aloof, performing a duty he perfectly understood. Behind these invalids a space had been left, and I thought at first that the column ended with them. But now fresh heads appeared, another thousand came, five thousand more, and when nearly an hour had passed there were still fresh ranks emerging from behind the civilian lines which wheeled at the marking-point, which closed and shortened step to trim their alignment, and then came steadily towards us in the sunshine, stiffening their shoulders, swinging their shrunken arms, company after company turning their heads in a fierce salute. Among these many thousand faces it was strange to catch sight now and again of one I knew. In the women's ranks I saw the 'Star' Janina, marching with an insolent gaiety; I had one glimpse of Sulkiewicz as he plodded along with the rank and file, and in a little man who marched not far from him I recognized the Piotrkow mechanic who had been in the wagon with him and me. There were others I could not identify except with places where I had known them—here was a man I had seen (I fancied) going up with the early shift at Mikirka, here a narrow, scholar's face which recalled for an instant the crumbling sheds of Czennik, men's bodies wasting amid the rubbish along the river bank—and these I may have recognized only in imagination, for my vision was often clouding, and as the endless skein was unwound the uniformity of shade and motion worked like a drug upon the eyes. There was, besides, a uniformity in the faces themselves—these grey, emaciated faces which had once belonged to labourers and herdsmen, to keepers of small shops in one-horse towns: you saw in their riveted mouths, their seared eyes, the insignia of a common heritage, the genius of infinite endurance. In a sense they were ordinary people. But they were what I am not and what I would give my last possession to be, they were Poles, and these are not of ordinary clay. There are nations of more evident importance, there are other valorous peoples; but in their spiritual stature these—as I saw them march that day and as I see them now—these are alone.

From where I sat on the ground I could seldom see General Anders himself, only his hand going tirelessly to the salute. About him stood others whom I saw intermittently between the advancing lines; there were British officers in whose punctilious faces I read a latent sympathy with the curious legion they had fathered; there was Kireyeff, most chivalrous of Russian soldiers, and beside him members of the Polish General Staff. On Anders's right, a little way behind, my father-in-law stood separate from the rest—it was probably an illusion of my own that made him seem much taller than they—and I wished I had been near enough to watch his face closely, for among the spectators at that parade there must have been few to whom it meant as much as it did to him. As it was, I could see that he looked pallid and ill—and yet there was nothing of the sick man in the way he stood to attention. He had, of course, the lifelong habit of a soldier to help him; but I think it worth recording that throughout the hour or more which the column took to pass I did not once see the smallest movement of his body or head.

Only when the last rank was clear did he relax that ruthless self-control: having made his own salute, he turned about rather clumsily, started to walk off, and suddenly sat down on the sand. Men crowded round, a truck came very quickly; I saw him lifted on to it, and before I could get any nearer he was driven away.

vi

If he had died ten years earlier he would most likely have been given a state funeral; Pilsudski himself would probably have followed the coffin, and the body might even have been laid in the

Wawel. That thought occurred to me as I heard the strange thin notes of a requiem call sounded by an English bugler, and as I saw the party of six Polish veterans rather shakily raising their borrowed rifles to fire the salute. Here the business was managed with dignity; but when the standing order was for funerals to take place at the same time every second day, the performance must needs have a certain flavour of routine.

There were, I think, eleven coffins that day. All except Julius's came on two lorries; his was brought separately on a little truck, with a British flag as well as our own. That was the only distinction. But there was, I remember, a wreath which bore the name of a British commander, and one which had been sent on Sikorski's behalf.

That burial-ground was the first of a chain which was to extend from the Caspian to the Mediterranean coast, and which will serve to mark the later stages of our journey until the sand which blows in great volume about those countries has silted up against the graves and buried them as well. When I saw it it was nothing but a strip of sandy soil, a little way inland from the camps, but already our people had made it tidy, and beyond the rows of wooden crosses there were trees like Polish aspens, delicate and lovely against the moist Iranian sky. A southerly breeze was blowing that day, and the scents it carried reminded me faintly of a Polish spring. The burial party had been digging since early morning, and now these soldiers, having cleaned themselves as well as they could, had to get the coffins off the trucks and carry them for fifty yards or more to the graves—not an easy thing for tired men to do with solemnity. I remember how the sun shone on the trees and on these men's homely, anxious faces; how Ludwig, who had come with us to ease his loneliness, stood by himself and watched the ritual with intense, expressionless eyes; and I remember the sight of Henryk sitting contentedly on a mound with his back to us all, while Paul, engrossed with a wooden horse that a British soldier had made for him, sprawled happily on his knees. When I saw the grave a few days afterwards, the cross had already been placed above it, with the words 'Julius Stanislas Kolbeck, Polish Soldier'. That, I believe, had been Wanda's direction. I think he himself would have been satisfied.

I have wondered since whether Henryk had any idea at all of what was happening that morning. He did not appear to do so. And yet as we were being driven back to camp in the truck he began to cry, and when Annette tried to comfort him we found it was Sandra he was missing—he could not think what had happened to her.

Neither am I sure that Victor really grasped the meaning of that makeshift and rather unreal ceremony, though he conducted himself as the occasion demanded, and was at pains to shake the hands of the men who had taken part. The mood of abstraction which came to him so often in those days seemed to have increased its hold that morning, and he was more than usually silent. With me his behaviour was as gentle as ever, he smiled his gratitude at every point where I helped him, but his eye never lingered on my face; this was a stranger's gentleness, and I felt as if he himself had kept away from the proceedings, sending a lifelike image in his place. I should have guessed, with another man, that he was overcome by grief at the loss of his father; he had never been lacking in the feeling you expect in a son; but the affection of the Kolbecks for one another seldom took the shape of overt emotion, and in his still, reflective eye I could not see any sadness. We were not unused to people dying. He may have felt even then, as I have done, that death is too large a happening to be dramatized in such observances as those. But I believe rather that he had come before this to an understanding of life where death had dwindled in significance. Was it imagination, once again, which made me think that others were staring at him not as at a curiosity—a creature that still lived and moved about when so much of his body had been crushed away—but because he had travelled farther, and was greater in presence, than themselves?

"I'm glad that's over. I'm glad he's at rest."

It was Annette who said that. She had been rather tearful, and our silence on the drive back had been intolerable to her, as silence is to the young. We were sitting on the sand now where the little truck had put us down; tired and disinclined to go back to our routine.

"At rest—yes, I suppose so!" Ludwig said, rather to himself than to her. "We say that, anyway. As if the object of life, really, was to get to the end of it. Well, I suppose it is, I've not discovered any other object."

Wanda said, "At least he was in uniform when he died."

"Does that—somehow—make it better?" There was no sarcasm in Ludwig's voice, only a great weariness. "Better for him?"

She answered listlessly, "You won't understand—Father was never understood. He had one aim in life, he wanted to give himself to Poland—the whole of himself. All his life he was being frustrated by people who were too small themselves to believe that."

I said—as I should not have done if I had paused to reflect, "I don't think it's quite so simple as that. He wasn't a simple person."

"You, Stefanie," she answered, without raising her voice and without looking at me, "you never knew him at all."

"But Wanda, does it make sense?" Ludwig asked, still quietly. "We are Poles, we give ourselves to Poland. The Germans give themselves to Germany, the Russians to Russia. What's the answer? You, you've seen the results—some of them. You've got your own patients over there to remind you, if need be."

"To remind me, yes!" she said. "Yes, I've got all I need to remind me who we're going to fight against in the end!"

"But what for?" he demanded. "To achieve what?"

Victor was sitting with his back leant against my side. I had supposed that his thoughts were very far from this chatter, and I was surprised when his hesitant, sleepy voice sounded at my shoulder.

"We don't know," he said, "I don't think we ever know our real objective—the final one. We can only fight towards limited objectives. Possibly that's all we need."

Ludwig turned to look at him with curiosity.

"But how do you know they're worth anything—your 'limited objectives'? How can you know, if you don't see anything beyond?"

"How? We merely know. We know that certain things have value. People. Children. We know that if children are being put into darkness we've got to stop that happening."

Annette said sorrowfully, "People? If people have 'value', why have we got to be always trying to destroy them?"

Because I saw no answer to that impetuous question, I wanted to save Victor from trying to answer it. I knew that even the lightest talk soon exhausted him, and his voice was already tired. "Look, Annette," I said, "some time you and I——" But his voice broke over mine:

"Annette, I'm sorry—I talk so badly. I mean, the value in people, it's not in their being alive. At least, I don't think so. I mean, physical life's so fragile, you can't think of value—not final value—in a thing that's destroyed as easily as that. It must be in what lies behind the things people do and feel, the part of them that's indestructible."

Then Wanda's voice came again like a small, cold wind. "Value? We get rid of rats and snakes. They're no value to anyone. Nor are the humans we've got to get rid of."

She reminded me just then of Jadwiga. I thought it would be best to get Victor away, but when I tried to put him on his feet he would not respond. He was looking at Wanda as if some slip in her speech had confused him. I felt once more that he was remote from us, and had constantly to exert himself to attend to what anyone was saying. "But Wanda, every human being has infinite value. Surely we know that! Surely we can't ever doubt it!"

She jerked her head towards the shore. "Those over there, those as well? The guards at Mikirka? The people who let Conrad die?"

Again he seemed, for a moment, not to understand her. Then he smiled, and I recognized in that private smile one that I had seen long before. He too was looking towards the sea. He said, as one who exercises infinite patience with the slow mind of a child, "But there is a Christ in them. That must be so. In them as in ourselves—waiting for release."

A Staff-Sergeant had come across from the Headquarter lines and was standing to attention before him. He was sorry to have interrupted, but there were orders waiting to be signed; they had to be out by three o'clock, and Captain Albrecht had gone over to No. 2 Camp; also a number of men were waiting for personal interview; perhaps, if the Colonel was free now . . .

Victor said briskly, "Yes, Josef, I am a very lazy fellow! Here, give me a hand!" and before anyone could help him he was nearly on his feet. All the weariness seemed to have fallen away from him. He set off at the Staff-Sergeant's side, moving, in his lopsided fashion, almost as fast as a whole man would. I heard him say, "These people who want to see me, are they professional grousers or is there something I can really do?"

vii

Two or three mornings later I was on my way to the tent he worked in (where I was sometimes able to give him clerical help) when a Corporal from the British Liaison Office stopped me. Was I the Countess Kolbeck? Then could I please spare a few minutes, Major Ushensen would like to see me. I followed him rather nervously—I had not got out of the habit of thinking that any interview meant some sort of unpleasantness—and presently found myself seated opposite the Englishman who had brought Victor to see me in the hospital tent. He was sorry, he said, to trouble me, but he wanted to fill in a few particulars on a record he had to keep. Perhaps I would be good enough to answer a few questions.

So—it was the same everywhere! The world was largely popu-
lated by little men in uniform whose only business was to get your
particulars in their grubby little books. I found the words 'I have
never had any political affiliations' coming to my lips.

"Your name I've got already," the Major said. (He spoke in
what he imagined to be French, interspersed with a few Polish
words of which he was evidently very proud. He was a shy, grey
creature, who gave the impression that he only just had time to get
everything tidy before the end of the world.) "Yes, and some of the
other details—I'll get you to check all this in a minute. Your age
I'm afraid I've got to put down—very silly, all this—it's just a bit
of red tape they go in for."

I told him "Thirty-three—no, thirty-four."

He gave me a quick, tactful glance. I saw, just before he covered
the entry with his blotting-paper, that he had pencilled '55'.

"And you were deported—or rather you left Poland—early in
1940? And you then had one child? . . . And she was also—I mean,
she left Poland with you? . . . Look, I'm terribly sorry, you haven't
had any tea. *Abdul!* Where is that fellow! Abdul—*chai*—two cups,
very quick. . . . Yes, you people must have had a shocking time; I'd
like to hear something about it some time, it interests me, if you
know what I mean. And then you came over here in the first transport from Krasnovodsk? . . ."

He came at last to the end of his questions, and sat back with the
air of one who has done a hard day's work with ability and success.
Then, "Look," he said, "you know your husband's a friend of
mine—I admire him very much—his influence with all your people
seems to be quite extraordinary. Well, you see, being a friend of his
I was wondering rather about your future." He paused, staring at
me anxiously; he had, so to say, several layers of pomposity which
he kept putting on and off like a man distrustful of the climate. "I
can't really commit myself—I mean, there's going to be a terrible
lot of your people looking for employment. Only up at G.H.Q.
and elsewhere they are at the moment rather hard up for inter-
preters, it's just possible you might get fitted in. Possibly later on
in my own office. You say you're fairly fluent in Russian? . . .
Could you translate letters into that language? Your English, you
say, is fairly rusty? Well, I suppose my French isn't quite all it
might be either. I did take a vacation course at the Sorbonne once,
that was rather a long time ago. . . ."

All this came with a ludicrous mixture of embarrassment and
affability. (As he confessed to me much later, he had seldom had

any dealings with foreign women, whom he had been brought up to regard as subtle and dangerous characters.) His intentions were kind; and he must have been a good deal hurt at finding me so unresponsive.

The curious truth is that I had hardly thought about my future. As a prisoner you are close to your horizon; the future, in effect, means the next day, the next meal. I had lost the habit of thinking that one should work and plan to get food tomorrow, a year hence: food was something that you stole or queued for, or which there was no chance of getting at all. In short, I had become mentally lazy. But there was cowardice in my mental behaviour as well.

I must have known well enough that the Polish Corps was not going to be moved into a theatre of war with its womenfolk and children clinging to its coat-tails; so I cannot have failed to realize that sooner or later I should find myself once more alone, having to make independent plans. But to this logic I had simply shut my mind. I had persuaded myself that a man in Victor's condition could on no account be posted forward of the Base, which I thought of as an invulnerable area; and although my application for employment in the women's auxiliary force had been refused on medical grounds, I had still vaguely supposed that in such an area I should find some means to stay near him. No doubt my inmost intelligence had warned me that this was self-deception, but you have no peace if you are for ever listening to such inward voices. Perhaps, after all, the intelligence, like the body, needs constantly to be refreshed with the gift of sleep.

But now this moral evasion had to end. I told Victor about my interview with the English Major, and after an interval of silence (which he always needed to withdraw his thoughts from some problem the day's work had brought him) he said:

"Yes—yes, I was talking to him. I told him you were a linguist. It was his idea, though, the idea of getting you employed as an interpreter." He was coming to the point circuitously, as men will do; pretending to me—and perhaps to himself—that what we had to discuss was just a business affair. "He's quite a decent creature—not very intelligent. I think anything he fixed up would be all right. And of course, if you can get on to a British Army establishment they've got to look after you, they've got to see you're in reasonable quarters and so on."

I said, "I'd rather be looked after by you."

"Yes," he said, "yes, I'd rather too."

"But——?"

"They're starting a depot at a place called Khanaqin—it's a place over on the western border—they're starting a Polish refitment and training centre. That's where we've all got to go."

" 'We'?" I asked. " 'We've got to go'?"

"I mean the Polish Corps."

"But no civilians?"

"No. The women auxiliaries are going with us, but no one else. But of course I shall get plenty of leave. And if you were in Baghdad, that would only be about a hundred miles away."

"And when do you go?"

"Well, strictly, no one knows. They keep a security tab on that sort of thing. But the second Headquarter party probably moves today week. It seems fairly likely I shall go with them. . . ."

I had then to practise a business in which I had previous experience. When a parting is in sight you have to live your ordinary life (or whatever counts as such), you must be level-headed, make sensible arrangements. It is necessary to tell yourself that something may occur to alter the plan—the move may be cancelled, the war may end—since without that sedative medicine you would find your emotions out of control; but at the same time you must not preserve any illusion so far as to neglect to say things which, in the empty days, you will torture yourself for not having said. In this trial the woman's part is, I believe, the harder one. She must make plain to him the truth that her life will be maimed so long as he is away. But the duty of pretending that this ordeal is not, after all, very serious—that time goes quickly, that her suffering will not be intense—this duty falls chiefly on her as well. I was, as I say, not inexperienced. I should have been able to perform my part perfectly; but it is one for which, I think, you need to be in sound physical health, and mine was not yet very good: I had a great deal of pain in my back, and was unable to take much food.

I became frightened, as a woman does, lest the actual moment of parting would find me behaving with cowardice, and thus putting an intolerable burden upon him. But the fear was needless. Like some other moments I have dreaded, it did not come.

The second Headquarter party did move on the day which Victor had mentioned to me, but he did not go with it. Ludwig Radznowski had come the previous day to tell me that he had been pronounced medically unfit to travel. Had he, Ludwig, had anything to do with this, I asked him. Well, he had recommended a fresh medical examination.

"But of course," I said, "it only means a postponement."

He said, "I suppose so."

"For how long, do you think?"

He gave me no reply.

So, we were to have at least a few more days. Victor went on with his work. Now that many of the other staff officers had gone there seemed to be more than ever for him to do—he was in the office tent for nine or ten hours a day. I think he could only work very slowly; he may sometimes have been a trial to his clerks, but they continued to serve him with great devotion, and he himself showed no new signs of tiredness. He was a man who (as Julius had reminded me) was most content when fully occupied.

Then, on a sunny and very warm morning when I was helping with some children's washing, a man came to say that I was wanted quickly in the Headquarter lines. This slightly alarmed me, and I went off without getting the stick I usually had to help me in walking; but I made the journey (of three or four hundred metres) quite successfully. Victor was not in his office. I was greeted there by the 'Tiger', an elderly soldier of Kazak extraction whom I had known many years before. He seemed to be in a nervous state and had some difficulty in speaking. The Colonel, he told me, had been taken by a fit of giddiness and had gone outside to rest. "I don't like it!" he said; and to my great confusion I found that the old man was weeping.

But when I reached Victor himself there did not seem to be anything wrong with him. He was lying in the tent's shade, where he had a small breeze from the sea to keep him cool: someone had put a rolled blanket under his head and another over his legs. His eye was closed, but as soon as I went near him it opened, and when he saw who I was he smiled and spoke to me. Yes, he had felt rather faint; there were so many letters, so many of people's personal problems that he had to deal with, he had found himself getting confused and stupid. But how nice that I had chosen this moment to visit him—just when he felt he ought to rest but was getting bored with it! "That old idiot—Tiger—he bullies me. I only just stopped him sending for an ambulance!" And he went on to talk in a gentle, discursive way of whatever came to his mind. He had been thinking of Paul, he said. Annette ought not to give up hope, whatever the army doctors had told her—he had been talking to Ludwig. Ludwig had told him that every year brought huge advances in surgery and medicine. "I shall take him to America when I can. Apparently the Americans are more advanced in orthopædy than anyone else. As soon as I can get some leave. I'm afraid my memory's not awfully good, I can't remember when I last had any leave.... " No doubt it was foolish of me to let him go on talking. But then it was impossible to remain anxious when his voice ran so easily.

I can recall the particular music of that hour, when unbroken sunlight held the farther tents in stillness, when the camp's stench and its many bustling voices seemed to be quieted by the smell of the sea wind, the distant noise of waves falling slackly on the beach. We were not entirely alone. As the scene forms again before my mind, I see faintly the 'Tiger's' troubled eyes, and other anxious faces, appearing in the dark entrance to the tent a few feet away. But I could not be disturbed by presences so quiet as those. His voice was pitched so that only I could hear it, and I remember that conversation as if it had taken place in absolute privacy.

After a time I told him that I thought he had talked enough, and he said, "Yes yes, I'm a terrible windbag!" But when he had kept quiet for a few moments, playing with my hand, he started again. He said, laughing, "You are so marvellous, kochanie! You are so clever, to get everything settled like this!" I was not sure what he meant. Did he imagine it was I who had privately arranged for his move to be postponed? He saw that I was puzzled, and presently he made an effort to explain. He said soberly, "It makes such a difference, knowing you'll stay with me—I didn't think it was possible to have you with me all the time. You see, I'm a gutless fellow, I get frightened when I'm by myself. It got so dark before, when I was travelling—you need to have someone with you when it gets like that, someone of your own kind. I didn't realize any human being could come as far as that, not even you. I didn't realize you would be with me all the time."

Even then his meaning was not clear to me: it needed time—it needed the solitary days that have come between then and now— for sentences shaped so haphazardly to reach in my own under-standing the level from which they came in his. When he was speaking I was again in some anxiety. His hand felt cold. I begged him again to rest, and he said, "Yes, kochanie, I think I'll have a sleep now." He went to sleep almost at once, as babies do; and did not wake again.

I am using a word advisedly when I say that this parting seemed less serious than the other would have been. In the misery of separations the cruellest part for each lover often lies, I think, in the thought of what the other may be suffering. I was spared that agony now. It is true that for a great part of our earlier separation I had believed him dead, and according to reason I should have had at least the same comfort then. It was not so. The difference may have been a little in myself; but I believe it came rather from the shape into which my love had grown (and love is no possession of your own, it is something by which you are possessed). Because I had loved him more perfectly in those last weeks—when we had lacked so much of what lovers need for their gentleness—it was easier to lose him. For, in a sense, I could not lose him again. There was sorrow, and emptiness. There were no uncertainties.

No doubt the colour of that grief is softened by the screen of time through which I see it now. You remember pain's concomitants, you do not remember pain. But I recall that a few days after he had died, when I was sitting at the roadside near Kazvin, and Paul, lying on my knees, was laughing, Annette said to me suddenly, "Oh, you are happy! Oh, at last you look happy!" That cannot have been happiness as the word is ordinarily understood; and yet I remember that as the long, slow convoy bore a thousand of us civilians south and westward, up towards the snow, my sorrow was already dulled by a new tranquillity. Then (as now) I was in some physical pain, and though we were shown much kindness we did not travel in luxury. The comfort I experienced may have come partly from feeling myself so much at one with the patient, shabby company in which I journeyed; for I had come a long way with people of their sort. But if Victor had not been restored to me for the last weeks of his life I do not think I should have realized fully what those fellow-travellers seemed to make plain to me: that the human claim to a portion of divinity rests safely on the capacity of men to suffer, on the genius by which they transcend their suffering. I know, at least, that during the cramped, interminable hours when our convoy was labouring to the summit of Aveh, when we crawled in a plume of dust across the seemingly boundless plateau of Hamadan, I felt glad to have been born with human faculties, to have seen a little of what is possible in creatures of my kind; that it stayed to warm my spirit, this reflection of a measureless grandeur, as we continued our protracted journey, climbing again into the coloured mountains which guard the pass of Asadabad, descending by Darius's highway through the breakneck windings of the Pai-Tak gorge, down to the hot sand of the Mesopotamian plain.

Baghdad, 1945
Crondall, 1948–51

FICTION

CRIME/ADVENTURE/SUSPENSE

☐ Masterstroke	Marilyn Sharp	£1.75
☐ Air Glow Red	Ian Slater	£1.75
☐ Sledgehammer	Jasper Smith	£1.25
☐ Deadline in Jakarta	Ian Stewart	£1.25
☐ The Seizing of Singapore	Ian Stewart	£1.00
☐ The Earhart Betrayal	James Stewart Thayer	£1.50
☐ Jenny's War	Jack Stoneley	£1.25
☐ Bloodwealth	Blair Stuart	£1.50

HORROR/OCCULT/NASTY

☐ Death Walkers	Gary Brandner	£1.00
☐ Hellborn	Gary Brandner	£1.25
☐ The Howling	Gary Brandner	£1.25
☐ Return of the Howling	Gary Brandner	£1.25
☐ The Sanctuary	Glenn Chandler	£1.00
☐ The Tribe	Glenn Chandler	£1.10
☐ Croak	Robin Evans	£1.10
☐ Transplant	Daniel Farson	£1.00
☐ The Quick and the Dead	Judy Gardiner	£1.00
☐ The Unbegotten	Bill Garnett	£1.25
☐ Rattlers	Joseph L. Gilmore	£1.00
☐ The Nestling	Charles L. Grant	£1.75
☐ Slither	John Halkin	£1.25
☐ The Unholy	John Halkin	£1.25
☐ The Wicker Man	Robin Hardy and Antony Shaffer	£1.50
☐ The Skull	Shaun Hutson	£1.25
☐ The Beast Within	Edward Levy	£1.25
☐ Night Killers	Richard Lewis	£1.25
☐ Parasite	Richard Lewis	£1.25
☐ Spiders	Richard Lewis	£1.25
☐ Parasite	Richard Lewis	£1.25
☐ Spiders	Richard Lewis	£1.00
☐ The Web	Richard Lewis	£1.10
☐ Gate of Fear	Lewis Mallory	£1.00
☐ The Nursery	Lewis Mallory	£1.10
☐ The Book of Shadows	Marc Olden	£1.25
☐ The Spirit	Thomas Page	£1.25
☐ The Summoning	John Pintoro	95p
☐ Bloodthirst	Mark Ronson	£1.00
☐ Ghoul	Mark Ronson	95p
☐ Ogre	Mark Ronson	95p
☐ Plague Pit	Mark Ronson	£1.00
☐ The Scourge	Nick Sharman	£1.00
☐ Deathbell	Guy N. Smith	£1.00

NAME ....

ADDRESS ....

....